A fourth-generation grazier, Nicole Alexander returned to her family's property in the early 1990s. She is currently the business manager there. Nicole has a Master of Letters in creative writing and her novels, poetry, travel and genealogy articles have been published in Australia, Germany, America and Singapore.

She is the author of six previous novels: *The Bark Cutters*, *A Changing Land*, *Absolution Creek*, *Sunset Ridge*, *The Great Plains* and *Wild Lands*.

Also by Nicole Alexander

The Bark Cutters
A Changing Land
Absolution Creek
Sunset Ridge
The Great Plains
Wild Lands

Divertissements: Love, War, Society – Selected Poems

River Run

NICOLE ALEXANDER

BANTAM
SYDNEY AUCKLAND TORONTO NEW YORK LONDON

A Bantam book
Published by Penguin Random House Australia Pty Ltd
Level 3, 100 Pacific Highway, North Sydney NSW 2060
www.penguin.com.au

First published by Bantam in 2016
This edition published in 2017

National Library of Australia
Cataloguing-in-Publication entry

Alexander, Nicole L., author
River Run/Nicole Alexander

ISBN 978 0 85798 946 8 (paperback)

Families – Fiction
Country life – New South Wales – Fiction
Farm life – New South Wales – Fiction
Nineteen fifties – Fiction

Cover photo of woman © Trevillion Images; landscape © Getty Images
Cover design by Blacksheep
Internal design and typesetting by Midland Typesetters, Australia
Printed in Australia by Griffin Press, an accredited ISO AS/NZS 14001:2004 Environmental Management System printer

Penguin Random House Australia uses papers that are natural, renewable and recyclable products and made from wood grown in sustainable forests. The logging and manufacturing processes are expected to conform to the environmental regulations of the country of origin.

An opal-hearted country
A wilful, lavish land –
All you who have not loved her
You will not understand

'My Country', Dorothea Mackellar

January 1951

Friday

Readying for Invasion

≪ Chapter One ≫

Lifting the corner flap of flyscreen, Robbie pushed against the stained-glass window of the schoolroom. The timber frames creaked ominously, revealing the steely bark of trees, scattered branches and a glimpse of bush beyond. Breath held, he waited for the footsteps of the governess on the veranda. When no board squeaked, Robbie tiptoed across the polished wooden floor to peek out the door. Sure enough, the woman was already sitting at the opposite end of the porch. He studied the pinched-face yard of pump water known as Miss Hastings, although Robbie called her Duck Face on account of her beady eyes and beaky nose. He watched and waited, knuckles still stinging from the harsh rap of the ruler. He wondered why it was so vital to be able to name each of the red-shaded countries on the large map on the wall. Everyone knew those lands belonged to England and, as he never intended leaving River Run, Robbie figured that he'd never need any more information than that.

The governess turned the pages of a book disinterestedly and then, leaning back in the cane chair, gazed out across the expanse of dirt to the green oasis of the homestead garden. Ponds and shrubberies were bordered by a white timber fence that stretched like a weathered spine past the house and thorny rose bushes, to where massive bougainvilleas proclaimed the entrance to the grounds. Somewhere within the house surrounds was a well dug by the first Rivers to have settled this land. It was filled in now, the water having been found brackish. Robbie's mother explained that a tree was planted on the very spot. Rex, the gardener, said it was one of the bigger trees, on account of a stockman having been dropped down the deep hole. Excellent fertiliser, Rex explained. Robbie was yet to discover if the story was true or not, but it sure riled Duck Face.

The governess's eyelids grew drowsy, her wrist slipping from the arm of the chair to hang languidly in the afternoon heat. Robbie retreated back inside the schoolroom, closed the study guide sitting on his desk and scrawled on the blackboard: *finished*. He studied the copper-plate handwriting with some satisfaction, before his attention was drawn to the teacher's satchel. There was never much inside it. A lined exercise book, writing paper and envelopes, a long pencil box with a sliding lid and an outline of the day's study.

From inside his flip-top desk, Robbie retrieved a glass jar with a screw-top lid and held the contents up to the light. The slimy tadpoles were tiny frogs now, although some retained stumpy tails. It didn't take much to fish the little critters out, and they seemed pretty happy in Miss Hastings' pencil box, their new home. With the slippery transfer complete, he replaced the box in the satchel and returned the jar to the desk.

At the window, Robbie wormed his slight body through the hole, angling down the side of the building until hard ground braced his palms. The toes of his boots caught on the sill, halting the escape, however, he twisted one way and then the other, and then slid himself to freedom.

⋘ Chapter Two ⋙

River Run village appeared deserted for a Friday afternoon. Eleanor Webber left her suitcase at the station master's office, crossed the street and turned into the main thoroughfare. At the intersection, she tugged a beige hat over red hair and straightened her grey skirt and pink blouse. Old weatherboard houses, some dilapidated, others inhabited, intermingled with newer dwellings, vacant lots and public buildings, the line of randomly placed structures crowned by the two-storey Royal Hotel and the peaked roof of the Catholic church.

Two men leaning on the hitching post outside the Royal Hotel eyed Eleanor with interest as a willy-willy of red dust careered down the street, before turning a corner, caught by the changeable wind. Eleanor clutched at her flapping skirt as someone whistled appreciatively from the upstairs balcony. A row of men leant on the railings, a yellow dog among them. Feeling conspicuous, Eleanor lingered on the kerb as a truck with a load of hay came by, throwing up a cloud of dirt. The vehicle continued down the street, passing the church and the Memorial Hall to stop outside the garage. A few seconds later the mechanic, Sweeny Hall, appeared. He talked briefly to the driver and then, lying on the road, pulled himself under the vehicle.

Cutting diagonally across the street, Eleanor headed to the Post Office-cum-telephone exchange.

Pattie Hicks stuck her head out the door of the building, a cigarette hanging from her mouth. 'Thought I heard a pair of heels a-clacking.' She stepped down onto the cement footpath. 'You home for a visit then, Eleanor?'

'I am. How are you, Pattie?'

'Me?' The woman took a puff of the cigarette. 'Nothing that a trip to Sydney wouldn't fix. You must find it right boring when you come back here.'

Boring wasn't the word that came to mind. 'Actually, I like the peace and quiet. It's a nice change,' Eleanor conceded, the sun biting at her skin through her blouse.

'Well, I guess you have to have a change to know the difference.' Pattie took a long drag then ground the cigarette out with a ruby-red sandal. 'Missed the festivities, you did. We had a march and everything down the main street for the jubilee celebrations. Imagine, fifty years since federation, two wars, the blasted depression and now those slanty-eyed Koreans are picking a fight. Well, you chose your week, coming during this hot spell. Fry an egg on the pavement you could these past couple of days, and no sign of it ending soon.' She stepped from the kerb onto the road, grimacing at the dirt. 'Those Greeks down the road reckon I should be rubbing fat into my face to stop my skin from cracking up.' She looked unconvinced. 'Might as well sit a woman out in the middle of the road and cook her, I say. And what about the stink? Mutton lard on my face in this weather?'

'I think they probably meant olive oil,' suggested Eleanor politely.

'I know I ain't the prettiest in the west,' Pattie lifted a foot, brushing dust from her toes, 'but do I look like a flaming tossed salad?'

This time Eleanor didn't risk an answer. Only a few years prior, the telephonist had stabbed a woman in the back of the hand with a blunt fork for making eyes at her beloved husband.

'So then, what's the news from the big smoke?' She looked at Eleanor's ring finger. 'Nothing, eh? Well, maybe you're the smart one.'

Not that smart, Eleanor thought. Dante had stolen her novella and published the work under his name. The man she'd fallen in love with, had given herself to, had betrayed her.

'It's not what everyone says it is, this marriage caper, and I should know. Had two of them I have. One dead and the other not far off.'

'Oh, Pattie, I'm sorry. Is Bill sick?'

'Sick? He will be once he feels the rolling pin on the back of his head. Good piece of wood like that, well, I mean, you can't just be using something like that for making scones.'

'I guess not.' Eleanor did her best not to laugh. The glint in Pattie's eyes suggested she was serious. 'Could you call River Run for me and let them know I'm here?'

'No need. Rex is in town picking up some trellis from Stavros. That's if you're happy to ride with the help,' Pattie challenged.

Sure enough Eleanor could now see her father's old blue truck parked at the far end of the street outside the General Store. 'Of course I am. Thanks, Pattie.'

'Unexpected visit, eh?' the operator pried. And when no answer was forthcoming, she gave an off-hand wave. 'Be seeing you, Eleanor.'

Rex March and Stavros Pappas, the owner of the General Store, were sliding the length of trellis into the tray of the truck as Eleanor approached. They were complete opposites, with one dark-haired and thick-set and the other wiry with skin burnt red from a life lived outdoors. Chuckling quietly, they only noticed her when she was a couple of feet away.

'Miss Eleanor?' Rex had droopy spaniel eyes and a craggy neck but his gap-toothed smile was one of the happiest she'd seen in quite a while. 'It's a treat for an old man to see you again.'

'Hello, Rex, hello, Mr Pappas.'

Both men tipped their hats in greeting.

'Miss Eleanor,' Stavros Pappas said loudly, 'welcome home. It is good to see you. You come when the sun is very hot, yes?'

'Yes,' she agreed.

'You're a sight then, Miss Eleanor,' the gardener said, 'appearing out of the blue.'

'I thought I'd surprise Mother.'

'That you'll do. But she'll be real pleased to see you.' Rex unwound a length of rope and began to loop it through the trellis. 'You'd be needing a lift,' he surmised, securing the lattice-work to the truck.

'That would be great. My suitcase is at the station.'

'Well, I'll just finish up with the River Run order,' Mr Pappas said amiably, stepping onto the pavement and walking back inside the shop.

Rex tested the knot on the rope. 'Stavros's family has arrived from Greece since your last visit. Got here a good six months ago. Fitted in real well they have. One of the boys has taken up an apprenticeship with Sweeny Hall while the eldest girl is real fine with a needle. A new frock or a fresh wound, you name it, either way she's a boon to the district.'

'She's a nurse?' Eleanor noted the shiny new rabbit traps piled in the tray.

'Served she has. Sad story there,' Rex replied cryptically.

'Mr Pappas must be happy to have them all out here with him at last. I know he's wanted them to emigrate for a long time.'

Rex weighed her reply. 'Yes and no. Neither of the grandmothers came. Couldn't shift them with a barge pole, Stavros told me. They lost boys over there. Killed in the war. And those old ladies won't leave them behind. But as I said to him, that's their choosing and I can't blame a person for not wanting to be buried in foreign soil. Of course it's real hard on him and the others, leaving those two old girls behind in Athens, knowing they'll never see them again.'

The wind blew down the main street, bringing with it the

sounds of another vehicle. A battered taxi drew up outside the hotel to the interest of the shearers on the balcony above. One man got out, popped the boot, dropping a swag in the dirt.

'Hey, Don Donaldson,' a young man in a red and yellow flannel shirt yelled from above, 'in the wrong district, aren't you?'

The heavy-boned man with bunched muscles for arms looked up briefly but said nothing. Hefting the swag over a shoulder, he walked inside the building.

'For a young pup you've got a mug on you,' one of the men on the balcony accused the flannel wearer. 'That man you're chiacking with, well, he can throw a punch that would send your teeth to your feet, he can.' The voice grew reverent. 'Donaldson. Gun shearer from the Riverina, but he ain't never come to River Run before.'

The inhabitants of the balcony, eight men and the mangy dog, craned their necks over the railing. The taxi lurched forward as if struggling to gain momentum before continuing down the street and out of town.

Rex resumed their conversation. 'I should tell you too, Miss Eleanor, your mother's having one of her weekends, so be prepared. Mrs Howell has been making a din in the kitchen since Wednesday.'

'Oh, I didn't time that very well.' That was the last thing Eleanor needed. Her return home after a year's absence was a last-minute decision. She needed to escape. To forget the Italian she'd so adored, so trusted.

'And there's shearing about to start. It's a busy month ahead.' Rex rubbed a lined cheek, his attention diverted by raucous laughter. There was a scuffle occurring on the hotel balcony. A thin, short man, the one who'd backchatted the gun shearer, was being edged over the wrought iron balustrade by Donaldson and dangled above the street by his ankles.

Eleanor's eyes grew large. 'Rex? What are they doing?'

The laughter from the men on the balcony grew loud and encouraging.

A dog barked. Someone yelled out *you bloody mongrel* and the man was dragged back to safety.

Rex gave a snort of laughter. 'That's some of the team. Started arriving in dribs and drabs a couple of days back. I reckon a man would be right entertained just by pulling up a chair here on this very street and watching the village come alive at shearing time. Come every-which-way this year they have, girl. Came early to get their fill before heading out to River Run come Sunday.' Noticing Eleanor's confusion, he elaborated, 'Dry camp. Some of them don't drink, mind, and there are others happy to take a few weeks off the beer and rum to dry out, although they gripe about it. But there's them that can't exist without it. They can get real cranky.' He rested cracked brown arms on the edge of the truck. 'Ah, shearers. We were kings once, Eleanor. Kings. Forty-six degrees in the waterbag and each man's tally two hundred and twenty ewes a day and rising. It was an honour to be in a good team with fast men. The rouse-abouts back then were terribly religious. We kept them that busy that they'd drop to their knees at the end of the day and pray, pray for rain, so they could have a break. And the musterers and penner-ups, why, they could barely keep the sheep up to us. I shore in places where the boards were that long you could run a Stawell Gift.'

'Dad always said you were a gun shearer,' Eleanor replied with admiration. Rex stored so many stories that she'd never heard the same twice.

Rex frowned. 'I weren't no gun,' he said seriously, 'but I was good, real good.'

Mr Pappas reappeared carrying three large brown paper bags, his black hair falling across a ridged brow. Rex opened the passenger door and the shopkeeper slid the groceries along the bench seat. 'That be all then, Rex?'

'Yes, that's it, mate.'

'Here you go.' Mr Pappas handed Eleanor a white paper bag. 'Boiled lollies for young Robbie.'

'Thanks, Mr Pappas.'

'Keep them hidden if I was you, Miss Eleanor,' Rex advised. 'Your mother's not in a real good mood on account of young Robbie destroying two of her rose bushes, and the new governess is on the warpath again.'

'Another one, Rex?' queried Eleanor.

The older man scratched furiously behind an ear. 'Number eight by my reckoning. Yup, eight governesses in three years. Impressive by any standard.'

When had Robbie not been in trouble? 'I'm glad to hear your family has joined you, Mr Pappas.' Eleanor opened the packet and took one of the lollies for herself. The sweet was chewy, a sugary jube.

'It's wonderful. Very wonderful. I am a lucky man. Now don't forget, my Athena she would make you a beautiful frock. You come and see Athena.'

'I will,' Eleanor promised, climbing into the truck.

'And I see you, Rex, for the shearing order. Sunday?'

'Sounds good. Sunday it is,' he confirmed, before shifting the gearstick on the column of the steering wheel. 'First stop the station master's office,' he said to Eleanor, as the truck crawled down the road, 'then River Run.'

'We're starting shearing later than usual, aren't we?'

'It's the overseer. Talked your mother into shearing now.' Rex tapped the side of his nose. 'Got a plan, he has. Wants the ewes joined earlier this year to bring the lambing forward. I've seen him, you know, in the yards. Hour after hour he'll go through a mob. Looking, always a-looking. Writes everything in his notebook. Brings the same mob back in a couple of months later and, blow-me-down, does the exact same thing again. Last November he brought in a new classer, Nevin. Took him to the yards to go through a mob. Didn't ask. Didn't tell no-one about it. But the Boss, well, she lets him have the run of the place.'

They were soon outside the railway station and Rex was quick to open the door. A few minutes later the suitcase landed with a thud in the tray of the truck.

'Hugh wants to split the flock up a bit more,' continued Rex as he put his foot on the accelerator. A spray of gravel spun up as they turned left and then right, heading swiftly out of the village. 'Divvy up the stud ewes. That means more fences and more paddocks. Course the only reason the Boss has given him the okay is because he's gone back to your grandfather's ways. The wethers and rams have been out on the western edge of the run since the middle of last year, hardening up on Old Man saltbush. Toughen them up. Grow them out, he says. And your mother agrees. Well, if it was good enough for your grandfather . . . He's all about improving the flock.' The road quickly altered from the packed, relatively smooth dirt of the street to a potholed single lane.

'That's a good thing, isn't it?' replied Eleanor.

'In the bush a man does well not to have delusions of grandeur. I don't see a shingle hanging above Hugh's door saying Stud Master.' Rex blew his nose on a piece of rag.

'If Mr Goward's ideas are good,' Eleanor reasoned, 'why not?'

'We're doing fine. And with wool worth a pound a pound, I can't see the point. If it ain't broke, you don't fix it.'

'I thought you were friends?'

'I'm not saying we aren't.'

Eleanor decided not to pursue the topic. Instead she shuffled across the cracked leather upholstery until she found a more comfortable spot. The wireless soon replaced the need for conversation and Eleanor settled back contentedly, turning her face into the harsh, hot wind.

≪ Chapter Three ≫

Robbie shadowed the sheep trail leading from the woolshed to the river. Large blowflies followed his progress, swarming and settling on the carcass strapped to the horse's back. The insects hovered and buzzed, and were soon joined by hundreds of small black flies, so that one hand was fully employed swooshing them from his eyes and mouth. The earth was well-trodden along the route and Garnet, an ancient horse who'd seen finer days, bobbed his head continuously, one minute snuffling the grass, the next eyeing their destination. The cattle-pup, blue and squat, kept its distance. Twice he'd been yelled at for nipping at the horse's heels and on each occasion he'd growled and yapped in response like a sulky child. Robbie glanced at the stubborn dog, barely six months of age. He should have tied the animal up before leaving the stables. Even in this heat the pig-headed heeler followed. Occasionally horse and rider veered from their path to halt under spreading trees. It was then that the dog approached warily to sit close by, one eye on his master, the other on the horse, his nose snuffling at the stench of the rotten meat.

Under cover of a half-dead tree, which held the stick-fused home of an eagle's nest, Robbie turned Garnet to survey the direction they'd come. He squinted against the glare. The country looked deserted. There were no iron roofs between treetops, no screech of the governess and no prowling staff. Satisfied they were alone, Robbie urged the horse into a trot. The gelding reluctantly obeyed, swishing his tail and letting out a neigh that sounded like a sigh. Behind, the dog kept pace, short legs powering through the dirt, pink tongue hanging. The land rose and fell in gentle waves, the sweep of brittle grass bending in the hot wind. With each rise the line of dense trees marking the river grew closer, as did the scent of sheep carried on a lifting wind.

A box-like structure was visible in the distance. Diverting from the trodden path, Robbie stopped at the timber framework with its wire-netting sides and roof. The door to the trap was open. Bleached bones and feathers lay on the ground. Pocketknife in hand, he cut the twine binding the stinking meat to the horse as the flies rose in protest. The sheep's hind-quarter fell in the dirt and the horse jolted at the thud. The cattle-pup was into it immediately, teeth tearing and paws plying the decaying flesh.

'Get out of it, Bluey!' yelled Robbie, lifting the sheep's remains and tossing it into the wire pen. The flies followed. Then Robbie himself. Above him a central round opening was edged by long pieces of dangling wire. The bastards could get in, he thought, but they won't get out. Crows, how he hated them. Robbie shut the door, wiring it securely, and then resumed the journey.

'Not long now, mate,' he said softly as the haphazard line of timber grew more distinct. Robbie patted the bulging saddlebag, briefly resting his hand on the contents as the land began to slope down towards the river. He looked back at the dog, gave an encouraging whistle and then horse and rider picked their way cautiously across the rough ground. The afternoon sunlight was flickering through branches as the woody plants thickened, the closer they drew to the waterway.

Next to the river, in a clearing ringed by timber, Robbie dismounted. Leaving Garnet to graze, he slung the saddlebag over

14

a shoulder and walked to the base of a wide-girthed tree, rifle in hand. Once free of the horse, the dog came running to sniff at his moleskin trousers and whine for attention. Giving the animal an absent pat, Robbie craned his neck. The towering canopy obliterated the sky.

'Go for a swim, Bluey,' he suggested to the panting animal, tying a rope to the rifle and knotting it at his waist. The bark was slippery beneath his boots, but gnarly enough to provide some grip, and with a concentrated effort he grasped the limb closest to the ground and hoisted himself upwards. The rifle swung in the air, bashing against the tree as he clambered, goanna-like, through the boughs, finally reaching the makeshift platform, two planks of wood wedged among concealing branches. He pulled the rifle up and dropped the saddlebag on the boards.

There was a hollow in the trunk and the partially rotted timber provided an excellent hidey-hole. Robbie checked the contents of the crevice and unpacked the saddlebag. It had taken a bit of sneaking about to get to the pantry this time. He was sure that Mrs Howell was on to him and the housekeeper was right fidgety about her tinned goods. His mother said it was on account of the last war when the tin shortage had led to Heinz stopping supplies to Australian shoppers. The cook had a thing for Heinz spaghetti and soups and Robbie's father often remarked that he wished he had shares in the company. Aggie Howell might eat more tinned food than all of the household put together, but she also had enough of the stuff stored away to last a year.

Robbie removed the four tins from the saddlebag, secreting the food in the hollowed portion of the trunk. Lastly he took a tin-opener from his pocket, wedging it inside the tree as well. He now had eleven tins of food and a waterbag. He reckoned on the supply lasting him a week based on the fact that if there was fighting to be done, on those days he'd be hungrier. The problem, of course, was if he had to feed more than himself. Robbie peered through the leaves, snapping some smaller branches that were obstructing the view of the homestead. Part of the second storey was just visible through the trees, its location marked by a curl of smoke hanging above the kitchen chimney.

He swivelled in the opposite direction. This new angle took in the rich river flats and the sprawling plains that angled away into the distance like a shimmering inland sea. Below, steep-sided banks lined a river stretching deep and wide, its surface busy with long-legged waders and numerous ducks. White, beige, black and blue contrasted with brown water as birds dived and fluttered and splashed. Lifting the rifle, Robbie aimed at a black duck. They were good eating, but better target practice. He took a breath, noticing how calmly this particular bird floated on the water. He placed a finger lightly on the trigger.

A great commotion of squawking fowls and flapping wings arose as the cattle-pup barrelled into the water, barking with delight. Within seconds the river was empty, save for the dog swimming happily in circles. The animal bobbed and lapped at the cool liquid and Robbie grinned as he lowered the rifle. Bluey swam back to the bank, shook himself and then rolled in the sand.

Across the waterway, tufts of white crossed Robbie's field of vision as sheep fed into the wind. If the communists came from this direction, Robbie knew he'd have them in his sights long before they reached the river. And it made sense that they would approach from this direction. Boats would bring them to the north of Australia and then they'd march south following the quickest route. Hell, he'd just thought of something. The communists might even join up with those Islamic Indonesians that his father said were fighting for their own state. An attack on two fronts. Jiminy Cricket. He needed more supplies.

Robbie rubbed at his chin, sure he could feel a stubby hair. It didn't matter how many of the enemy there were. When the moment came he'd be ready. As sentry, his warning shots would give the family time to prepare for the attack. Best of all, the reds wouldn't be able to see him up here. Although he really needed another lookout. One of his sisters, Eleanor, drew pictures and wrote stories. Robbie knew from the time he'd spent in the tree that a man could get easily bored waiting to be attacked, but as Elly was in Sydney and his dad was a crack shot and had already been to war, the decision was easy.

Slinging the empty saddlebag over his shoulder, Robbie lowered the rifle and climbed slowly down the tree. The dog was wriggling in the dirt, four legs pointed to the sky. He called to the horse and the animal stared back. Robbie called again and gave a low whistle. The gelding didn't budge.

'I should send you to a cannery.' Robbie ruffled Garnet's mane affectionately, before sliding the rifle in its holster. Further along the river he had a couple of cray-bob traps which he'd laced with rabbit meat and it was in this direction he now headed. He led Garnet along the sandy riverbank, Bluey padding by his side as the edge of the waterway gradually flattened and smoothed. During a flood this was one of the safer places to cross. A wire was permanently strung taut across the waterway and tied between two stout trees. The life-line glistened in the afternoon light as Robbie imagined men swimming their horses across the river in flood, stringing a rope over the wire and tying it to the saddle so neither horse nor rider would get washed away.

Beneath overhanging trees the submerged traps were still tied securely to sticks wedged in the dirt, but as he grew closer Robbie could see that one of the traps had been dragged from the water and cut open.

'Crikey.' Whoever had stolen his crays had busted the wire to get at the catch. There were footprints in the sand but they extended only to the trap and then headed back towards the river. Robbie tipped his wide-brimmed hat to the back of his head. The thief who had taken his crays came from across the water. He scanned the opposite bank, frowning in concentration. The trees threw shadowy shapes on the surface, but nothing moved on the other side. At the water's edge, the pup growled.

'You see something out there, dog?'

The animal took a step closer to the river. Robbie kicked at the empty trap and then fished out the remaining one. Seven cray-bobs tumbled around inside and one by one he grabbed their slimy bodies, carefully avoiding their nippers, and dropped them into the saddlebag. Overhead the wedge of sky between the trees was white with summer light. Garnet shook his head, long mane swishing. The cattle-pup barked. 'I know, I know,' Robbie said unenthusiastically, 'time to head back.'

The grassy plain spread out wide and flat. The sun was getting lower. Robbie scowled at the lingering heat ruining the last few hours of daylight, noticing a spiral of darkness in the distance. It sat far out on the horizon. A dirty tinge silhouetted by a tawny sky before it slowly faded from sight.

≪ Chapter Four ≫

River Run. A spread of acreage stretching from the soft undula-
tions and distant promontories of the east to the flat grassy
plains of the west. It was a land of far horizons. Of patchy, fragile
dirt made green with rain. Of great tracks of open grass country
dissected by floodplains, red earth, belts of timber and clumps of
saltbush far to the west. Here the soil was fertile, but poor rainfall
and high temperatures made it a battle to realise pastoral poten-
tial. But they were still here, Eleanor mused. Eighty years on. The
world was altered, especially since the end of the Second World
War, but some things would never change. The bush was one of
those things. You could leave it, but the land would never leave
you. Leaning against the seat, Eleanor's head vibrated in time with
the rickety progress of the truck. She closed her eyes, tiredness
and emotion clouding her thoughts.

Everyone had warned her to stay away from Dante. She'd met the
Italian immigrant, ten years her senior, at the Artists and Models
Ball at Sydney's Trocadero Club. He'd been to all the places she'd
dreamt about: Paris, Rome, Milan, London, and he was an artist,
a very attractive artist. As a woman raised in a prosperous landed

family, Eleanor was confident in her judgement of people. And here was this sophisticated intellectual with his enquiring eyes and gentlemanly ways, rendered homeless and penniless by war. Of course, were she not instantly smitten, Eleanor may have eventually noted the inconsistencies: the lack of detail offered regarding his background, the interest shown in her scribblings, a quickness to anger when she was not forthcoming in discussing her work and the man's insistence that their weekly trysts be accompanied by wine. Wine she invariably purchased. Never, not once, did she listen to her friends when they warned, *he can't be trusted*. Why would she listen to them? Eleanor had been deeply in love. The very concept of taking advantage of another, in order to survive, was not a world she understood.

Her cheeks grew hot at the thought of the last night she and Dante had shared. It was a month to the day and the images of his swarthy skin entwined in crisp sheets continued to haunt her. Forget him, she scolded, *forget him*.

A leather folio lay across Eleanor's lap. Inside were glossy cover sketches and partially finished manuscripts. She wondered why she'd ever attempted to write a novella set in inner Sydney, but then she was a keen observer of life, a quality instilled in her by a bush childhood. And the challenge of making the asphalt come alive intrigued Eleanor. In hindsight, however, she would have been better off sticking to the comic book stories that sold steadily at newsagents and train stations. She'd written the novel on spec, hoping and praying that one of the Sydney publishers would buy the manuscript. And they had, from Dante.

'Problems?' asked Rex.

'I guess turning up unannounced makes it pretty obvious,' Eleanor answered.

'Nothing's ever as bad as it seems, so my mother told me.'

Then why did she feel so miserable? 'Do you believe that, Rex?'

The gardener gave a chuckle. 'Nup. But you're home now.'

He was right, and the sense of home was tangible. Every tree, every ramp, every dirt track, every paddock carried with it a memory, of horses and motor-bikes, of scraped knees and motherless lambs, of shooting pigs and trapping crows. However, homecomings were bittersweet for it was here on her family's land that she felt closest to her dad and here that his loss hit the hardest.

The rushing air was a blur of browns and beige and grey. Trees thinned and thickened. The land opened and closed about them revealing stubby bushes with birds made listless by heat, sheep gathering along the bore drains to drink, and kangaroos lying in the shade of trees. Then the wildlife disappeared as the sides of the track grew dense with timber, the only thing visible the red shimmer of the unfurling road. They rattled over a stock-ramp. Behind them a cloud of dust filled the rear-view mirror. It felt longer than the year it had been since her last trip home.

'Twenty miles to go,' Rex said cheerfully. He'd spent most of the trip humming along to country and western tunes on the wireless. 'You'd notice the country's looking a bit barren. The rabbits have been real bad. Got us some new traps from Newcastle that will keep Robbie busy, but he'll have to be quick.'

'Why quick?'

'Myxomatosis. The disease is spreading fast since it was introduced last year. Wiping the buggers out it is. And none too soon for the grassland. Rabbits nearly had this country eaten out. 'Course it's the end of a living for some. In my day I could earn a pretty penny from the skins. Something on your mind, love? Is it the old problem?'

Rex was perceptive, and having been employed on the property for nearly forty years, he knew the intricacies of Eleanor's extended family.

'Humour an old man, Miss Eleanor. Every time you come home you get that look about you and it has been a while now. Time to move on, eh?'

The scenery sped past. Rex was right, but it didn't make things any less uncomfortable. 'It's just difficult sometimes.'

'Aha.'

No-one ever talked about her mother's second marriage eleven years ago. Even for Eleanor and her more avant-garde Sydney friends, it was still just a bit too tacky. Eleanor had been fourteen at the time and still reeling over her father's death, but she was not immune to the innuendo that circulated. Her mother walked down the aisle for the second time within a year of her father's death.

'Now there's a sight for sore eyes,' Rex said brightly, as they rounded a bend in the road and the vehicle climbed a slight rise.

Ahead the iron roof of the homestead appeared above the treetops only to disappear again as the car descended to a one-lane wooden bridge.

Ten minutes later the homestead reappeared, ringed by an oasis of trees and bounded by ancient bougainvillea bushes which had been planted when the house was built. The stark two-storey building with its sandstone base and the timber upper floor girded by a wrought-iron balustrade was softened by the surrounding garden. The grounds encompassed a series of interconnecting ponds, shrubberies, paved entertaining areas and an expanse of lawn. Such an area required the digging of a large dam, ensuring a plentiful supply of water whether from the heavens above or the river from which it could be pumped. Her great-grandfather Frederick Barnaby River and his brother, Montague, had been intent on creating a semblance of the great Irish estates, a seat worthy of two self-made gentlemen determined to build a pastoral empire. It was a powerful heritage to have been born into but Eleanor would have been far more comfortable with less.

'The bougainvilleas are beautiful, Rex.' A profusion of reds and pinks, the plants were clearly enjoying the weather.

'We've been lucky. There were some hot winds last month that would have ruined these flowers, but we weren't so lucky with the roses.'

The River Run rose garden, planted in the late autumn of 1914, was a brave attempt to introduce a centrepiece for the circular gravel drive, while creating an everlasting gift of love for an adored wife. Over the years the area was replanted with many different varieties. It was Eleanor's father who'd initiated the project. At age twenty-six, two years before he volunteered for the Great War, he began experimenting with some of the most beautiful flowers available, intrigued with the idea of selecting ornamentals originating from all over the world centuries prior. And so River Run enjoyed the fleeting life of China roses from East Asia, Bourbon roses from off the coast of Madagascar in the Indian Ocean, and a sub-class of the Noisette, the first of which was raised as a hybrid seedling by a South Carolina rice planter in the early 1800s. These striking specimens lived and died among sturdier types, such as tea roses, small insignificant wild roses and the rambling type. Eleanor imagined her father choosing these plants based on the exotic countries of origin, waiting with anticipation for the arrival of each seedling, each one of which was documented in a notebook. Most lasted a season or two before succumbing to the cold of winter or the harshness of summer.

The sixty rose bushes were mostly bare, except for the late summer flowering species that trailed over a central wall displaying the remnants of sun-withered heads. Carefully tendered to by Rex, the wild roses were still a leafy green, the mass planting intersected by a low hedge and made formal by a central water fountain. The fountain in question was covered with bird poop and held a handful of peewees and topknot pigeons, all trying to cool off in the heat.

'Rode straight through the middle, the little bugger did,' Rex explained, referring to Robbie, the youngest of the Webber clan. 'Clipped three or four bushes and damaged the hedge and then took off smart as you like.'

'I didn't think Garnet had that much lift left in him,' Eleanor replied as the vehicle stopped outside the house. She peeled her body uncomfortably from the sweaty car seat as Rex carried her suitcase to the veranda.

'Where Robbie wants to go, that old gelding follows. He'll get a shock the young fellow will when they bundle him off to boarding school in a year or so.'

'By his age I was already there.' But then Eleanor hadn't been the only child of a second marriage and it was pretty obvious neither parent was willing to let him go too soon.

'I hope you stay for a while, Miss Eleanor.' Rex smiled his hang-dog smile. 'It's been right quiet here this past year. And young Robbie,' he scratched his neck, 'well, he's a loner he is. Sometimes I think the lad's the only one with any spirit.'

'Thanks, Rex.'

As the blue truck drove around the side of the homestead to the kitchen entrance, Eleanor put her hat back on and retrieved a balled-up pair of gloves from a near-empty handbag. Holding the gloves for propriety's sake, she plucked at the material of her blouse where it stuck to her skin, lifting her hand to knock on the front door.

⋘ Chapter Five ⋙

'It was only Rex returning from the village.' The sitting-room curtains were drawn against the day's heat, however her mother's voice carried quite clearly to where Eleanor dallied outside. 'Did you hear me, Colin?'

Slow, drawn-out footsteps preceded a response. 'Yes. With shearing about to commence, I have other things on my mind.'

'We have a station overseer to handle the logistics of mustering and dipping and a shed overseer for everything else.' Georgia Webber sounded impatient. 'It's always best to leave the men in charge of their respective areas and just check on proceedings on a daily basis. Really, I don't know why you get uptight at shearing. I can only assume it's a control thing. Alan rarely got so worked up.'

Eleanor was about to enter the house unannounced when her father's name was mentioned.

'Yes, well that worked for you, my dear,' Colin retaliated. 'It gave you a free rein to run the property your way and my brother, may he rest in peace, appeared happy with that. I, on the other hand, intend to keep being hands-on, even if my managerial input remains curtailed. Don't worry, I'll be at my best over the weekend' – the sarcasm in Colin's tone was evident – 'but don't come complaining to me about Margaret Winslow.'

Eleanor's mouth gaped. Margaret Winslow was coming? The woman had danced bra-less in a sheer blouse at a party following the Sydney Royal Easter Show last year. Every adult child of every couple who'd attended the Eastern suburbs bash eventually learnt of the scandal. Her mother was especially outraged by the episode. Margaret was married to Georgia's oldest friend, Keith, owner of the famed Ambrose Park merino stud, the two families' association going back to the 1870s. While such behaviour was quickly forgotten by some, such a blatant breach of propriety had shocked many within the upper echelons of the wool industry. Eleanor could only be grateful that their polo-playing son Henry was ensconced down south with his brothers. Henry made it his mission in life to know everybody's business, including hers, and he'd been most outspoken when it came to his opinion of Eleanor and Dante's relationship.

'Anyway, Keith is your friend,' Colin stated, 'and there's business to discuss. But he will be surprised at the change in direction after all these years. We can only hope Goward knows what he's doing.'

'Hugh has some excellent ideas, Colin. Ideas that have been thoroughly researched,' his wife replied.

'God's gift to the wool industry, eh? And him the offspring of white trash from the Territory.'

'You really do have a problem with staff that have ability, don't you?'

Eleanor inched closer to the front door, knowing that she should knock and announce herself immediately, and yet . . . She waited for a retort from her stepfather, which wasn't forthcoming.

'I know Keith will be surprised and disappointed.' Georgia's tone was smooth. 'And I have no doubt that the conversation will be quite awkward after all the years we've been purchasing from Ambrose stud, but I do agree with Hugh, it won't hurt to introduce some new blood into the flock. I'll tell Keith over the weekend that we'll only be purchasing five rams and that the rest will be coming from a competitor.'

'*Who* will be telling Keith, Georgia? I may not have hold of River Run's reins, but we agreed that for appearance's sake –'

Eleanor knocked on the front door, entering the long flagstone hallway. The sheer size of the homestead with its eighteen-foot ceilings and airy rooms brought a smile to her face. The dimensions of her family home made her Paddington terrace look like a shoebox. 'Hello, anyone home?' Placing her suitcase on the carpet runner, she waited expectantly. The house smelt earthy, the air thick with heat. On one of the hall tables sat a large bowl of bell-shaped Agapanthus in varying shades of purple, blue and white.

The sitting-room door opened and her mother appeared, a startled expression on her round face. Behind her came the distinct tap of wood.

'Eleanor. We weren't expecting you, dear!'

Lifting the leather satchel from a shoulder, Eleanor gave her mother a kiss on the cheek. 'Sorry about that. It was a spur of the moment thing.' Georgia looked exceedingly well. There was barely a line on her face although her appearance came at the expense of her figure. She'd put on quite a few pounds.

Georgia lifted a finely plucked eyebrow. 'Look at you all windblown. I hope you didn't get off the train looking like that.'

Eleanor's hand went automatically to her hair. 'Rex had the window down. It's boiling out here.'

'Warmish. Yes. Well, you're lucky Rex was in the village when you arrived, and it's good to see you although you look like a suburban postman with that thing over your shoulder.' Her mother felt the weight of the satchel. 'Whatever have you got in here?'

'Nothing.' For a moment both women held onto the bag. Finally her mother released it.

'Eleanor. How are you, my girl?' Her stepfather was leaning heavily on a walking stick. 'Well, then, we have a full house this weekend. The Winslows are coming later this afternoon.'

'Rex said you were expecting guests,' Eleanor replied politely, placing the strap of the bag over a shoulder. Colin looked drawn and the beginnings of a paunch was at odds with his slight figure. She guessed that the injury to his leg was taking its toll.

'So what brings you back to the family farm?' Colin asked as he walked into the hallway, the tap-tap of the stick muffled by carpet.

Eleanor noted the line that briefly furrowed her mother's brow. Georgia hated River Run being called a farm, as did she. It was far more than that.

He continued, 'Your mother and I thought we'd lost you forever to the secretarial business.'

Sensing the beginning of a cross-examination, Eleanor replied quickly, 'It's a bit smoggy in Sydney. I came down with a cough so I thought I'd take some leave.'

'Summer in Sydney can be delightful but if the winds drop . . .' Her mother gave a disapproving shake of her head. 'I was disappointed you didn't come home for Christmas, Eleanor. Next year you tell that employer of yours that you're entitled to Christmas with your family.'

'I will and I'm sorry, Mum. But I did spend the day with Jillian and her mother at the Queen's Club, and I went sailing with Henrietta on Boxing Day.'

Her mother nodded approvingly. 'I know, you did tell me, Eleanor. My one consolation is that your oldest schoolfriends are now your flatmates, and they're lovely girls.'

The subject was changed to the weather and the imminent arrival of the house guests. Eleanor pleaded a headache and, to her amazement, Georgia agreed she could forego dinner in the dining room and have a tray in her room instead.

'You do look a bit peaky,' Georgia turned to her husband, 'doesn't she, Colin?'

Eleanor thought of the sleepless nights she'd endured since her break-up with Dante.

'I'm not surprised after spending a good part of the day cooped up indoors,' Colin stated. 'Everyone raves about the class of travel our trains are offering these days, but I've rarely got off one feeling rested. Anyway, they'll soon be taking second place to automobiles. I recently read that car sales have increased.'

Eleanor lifted her suitcase. 'I think I'll go and unpack.'

'Then I want to hear all your news,' Georgia told her youngest daughter. 'And your brother's been up to his antics again. Robbie quite ruined my day by riding through the rose garden so a bit of city news will be just the thing to perk me up.'

Making her excuses, Eleanor carried her suitcase upstairs. At the landing she looked left and right. The dark antique furniture that lined the walls of the long hallway shone with polish, the smell of the cleaning fluid thick in the air. The housemaid Alice had clearly been busy over the last few days. Apart from the scrupulous cleaning of the entire house, one of the many guestrooms would have been dusted, aired and the bed made for the Winslows. Eleanor didn't have to open the door to know that even in this heat her mother would have managed to scavenge flowers from the garden to grace the dressing table.

At the far end of the hall, before an arched window, was a round table holding a series of horse-racing trophies belonging to Colin. At the opposite end a similar table held a tall ceramic vase displaying orange-headed bird-of-paradise flowers. It was a long, wide hallway that was just perfect for footraces. The wing-back chairs and marble-topped tables lining the space proved nasty at times when it came to injuries, but the worst of their childhood hurts always happened when she and her older sister Lesley slid down the stairs on large serving trays, ending up in a tangled heap at the bottom.

In the buttercup yellow bedroom, Eleanor flung her hat onto a corner chair and opened the French doors leading out to the balcony. She lingered in the doorway, reluctant to go beyond. There was no breeze and the air hung thickly. To the west the sun breasted the curve of the earth, its rays casting the surrounding plains in a haze of harsh light. Already the thought of a sleepless night taunted. Perspiration dribbled down her neck, between her thighs, patched her blouse and with it came a tugging lethargy. For a moment Eleanor wished she'd not come home.

She thought of Jillian and Henrietta. Her best friends would be rushing home from work, their Friday night already planned. A long bath and then a great deal of fussing in front of the mirror, particularly over hairstyles and lipstick, invariably preceded a night at the flicks. Eleanor hoped they wouldn't think her a terrible coward for not explaining her absence in person. She'd left a note detailing her break-up with Dante and her need to come home for a few days. It just wasn't in her to endure the well-intentioned commiserations, peppered with the lovingly given *we-told-you-so* recriminations. Neither Jillian nor Henrietta had time for the 'new arrivals', as they termed immigrants. And they'd been rather askance at Eleanor's relationship.

Indoors the room was clean but dusty. A light film covered the furniture and Eleanor sneezed as she fell backwards on the bed, sinking into the thick mattress. The contents of the room hadn't altered over the years. A dark hardwood dresser, the dressing table with its flounced skirt, attached oval mirror and stool, two chairs upholstered in a chintz print and the cavernous wardrobe. Only the paintings suggested that a young girl had once slept here: a doe-eyed child holding a white furry cat and a still-life of a basket of flowers. Eleanor didn't recall when they'd been given to her, only that her father had been the giver.

The white plaster ceiling was spotted with a half dozen water-marks created over the years from errant rain, while a long crack inched its way down the wall to one of the skirting boards. In her childhood Eleanor listened to the contractions and expansions of the great homestead, imagining them to be the groans of a giant. Even now the house seemed more of a living thing than the grass castle her mother's family forged through sheer determination.

'I've made a bit of a mess of things, Dad.' Her father stared at her from within the gilt-edged frame on the bedside table. She'd thought Dante was the one, the man she was meant to spend her life with, although she knew their relationship, once out in the open, would have been more than difficult. It was hard recalling his kind words, the way he'd believed in her, the way he'd made her feel, for those wonderful moments were now tempered by a distasteful reality. Dante had used her. He'd stolen her work, yes. But ultimately he'd stolen away her dream of love. And it had been her fault. She'd trusted him.

Eleanor took a breath, refusing to cry anymore, refusing to berate herself. She was blessed to have somewhere else to come to. A home. The land. Although running away from her life in Sydney was only going to provide a brief respite. Eventually Eleanor had to go back. She would have to swallow her pride and admit that her girlfriends had been right. That wouldn't be so bad once she'd come to terms with things a little better. But the achingly boring secretarial job and a writing career over before it had begun were a totally different matter.

Leaving the photo on the bed, Eleanor opened the suitcase, digging down to the bottom. The diaphragm was in its pink container and she wrapped a scarf around it, secreting it in a drawer of the hardwood dresser. At some stage she would find a way to dispose of it. Above the chest of drawers hung a large wooden crucifix. Eleanor crossed herself automatically. Unknown to her mother, she was no longer practising. The waving of incense and the sprinkling of holy water may well provide comfort to some but as far as Eleanor was concerned, if there was a God he never would have taken her father. Or allowed her sister's fiancé Marcus to do the unspeakable.

The croak of a frog drew Eleanor outside to the balcony. In the garden below sprinklers were being turned on. One after another the fine sprays of water began to form circular patches on the brittle lawn surrounding the interconnecting series of ponds. Rex entered her view. Hands on hips, he checked the position of each sprinkler before circumnavigating an outer pond to where he began installing the new piece of trellis.

Somewhere dogs barked and a horse neighed. Her stepfather could be heard calling to the gardener, asking Rex to join him in the rose garden. His abrupt request was answered with a hearty *right-e-o*. Beyond the manicured vegetation and the iron-roofed outbuildings, an irregular tree line marked where the river flowed through the property. And still their land stretched on. Into distant paddocks she'd never been to. Across a country marked by fire and drought, rootless drovers and torrential rain, war-made swagmen and blacks on walkabout. This was a big land. As a child Eleanor wondered what else was out there, what lived in all that emptiness? Sometimes, she decided, it was better not to know.

'Mr March? Mr March?'

The governess was walking across the lawn, doing her best to avoid the recently watered grass.

Rex, having left the installation of the lattice, was heading towards the front garden. Miss Hastings was gesturing towards the schoolroom. Rex was shaking his head. Although Eleanor couldn't hear the conversation, she knew immediately who they were talking about. Her half-brother, Robbie.

❧ Chapter Six ❧

'And then there's the roses. Have you seen the damage to them?'
Robbie lifted a finger to his lips and Garnet gave a soft
nicker in response. He'd been leading the gelding behind the tennis
court, intent on taking the long way back to the stables, which were
a good mile from the house. His mother's voice stopped him in his
tracks. Through the wire netting surrounding the court his parents
were talking to Rex, his mother commenting to both men that the
damage was worse than she thought. The gardener began pruning
the damaged bushes and after a few seconds his mother walked
towards the house. Robbie tugged on the lead and together he,
Bluey and the horse hid behind a flowering bougainvillea. Garnet
immediately began to nibble on the bush oblivious to the spiky
branches. Robbie shook his head. 'Don't I feed you enough?' he
whispered. The gelding bared his teeth, revealing papery petals.
Lifting a prickly red-flowered branch, Robbie peered out cautiously.

Rex and his father exchanged glances and then with a shrug of
shoulders his father also headed towards the house.

'I don't know what the matter is with that boy. The girls never
behaved like this.'

His mother's voice had that high-pitched squeaky sound that usually meant trouble.

'No, we've got other problems when it comes to them,' responded his father, irritably.

'Tit for tat, eh, Colin? I think it's time Lesley came home for a visit regardless of her inclination. We know she's much improved and with Eleanor here, well, those two used to be so close.'

'Lesley?'

'Why not? We've been talking about the possibility for months. I'd hoped Lesley would have made the decision herself but as she has not, and the convent seems loath to give her a gentle push, we'll have to take the initiative.'

'Do you really think that's wise, Georgia? I mean the girl did have a nervous breakdown and there were –'

'Difficulties?' Georgia interrupted. 'I'm well aware of what happened after Marcus died. I was the one who found her in the bathroom, remember?' His mother's voice wavered. 'But that was five years ago. And based on the convent reports Lesley appears to be leading quite a normal life now. I don't want my daughter hiding from the world anymore. And now Eleanor is home.'

'We don't even know how long Eleanor's staying for, or why she's here,' replied his father. 'Let's face it, Georgia, no telephone call. No telegram. Nothing. For the past year you haven't been able to budge the girl out of Sydney. And suddenly she comes home unannounced in the middle of a heatwave just before shearing, and you want to drag Lesley back too and play happy families? I suggest you sit the girl down and find out what's going on.'

'This is her home. Eleanor grew up here. It's not that she doesn't like the country anymore, if that's what you're insinuating. She has a life in Sydney.'

His father lifted his hands in mock defence. 'Forget it, Georgia. We both know why she doesn't come home much.'

'The Winslows are late.' Georgia changed the subject. 'Just as well.'

Robbie tugged on the reins and reluctantly Garnet followed. 'Eleanor's back,' he muttered. Keeping close to the thorny bougainvilleas he broke into a run, the horse trotting behind. He was pleased there were visitors coming to stay. With luck he'd only be locked in his room overnight. After that his mother would be too busy with her friends to worry about what he was up to. It was the perfect time to tell Eleanor about the communists and the coming attack.

At the schoolhouse he slowed. The building was quiet, as was the adjoining governess's cottage. Miss Hastings always helped in the house when there were people visiting but that didn't mean she wouldn't be lurking about trying to find him. He sent Bluey on ahead, waiting as the animal snuffled around the old buildings, returning without a show of teeth or hackles raised. Reluctant to take any chances, Robbie stayed at the rear of the buildings, moving quickly from the sheltering walls of the meat-house, the disused smoke-house and past the skeletal remains of three old cottages. Ahead, the large structure of the woolshed was visible. Robbie expected all the men to be out, either readying the woolshed and adjoining yards or mustering sheep. To his dismay, two of the younger jackeroos were outside the stables as he approached.

'What cha doing then?' the younger of the jackeroos asked.

Robbie gritted his teeth. 'Nothing.'

The hairs rose along the length of Bluey's spine.

Archie the albino was standing beneath the speckle-barked tree that shaded the hitching post outside the stables. His companion, Murph, a few years older, was busy shoeing a young colt.

'Nothing?' Archie repeated. 'A person can't do nothing, not on this here run. But we forgot, didn't we, Murph? The boss's son is too young to do anything but learn his reading, writing and arithmetic.'

'Am not.'

'Leave the kid alone, Archie.' Checking his handiwork, Murph lowered the colt's hind leg. The animal was upset. The horse backed up and snorted and gave a half-hearted pig-root.

35

'Call that cattle dog away, will you, Robbie?' asked Murph.

Robbie whistled Bluey to his side.

'Whoever heard of a cattle dog on a sheep station,' Archie commented.

'He was a present,' Robbie countered.

'Well, you better keep the mutt chained during shearing or Mr Goward will have your guts for garters. And the dog . . .' Archie made a slicing motion across his throat. 'What cha being edumacated on today then? How to count your mother's money?'

'Archie,' Murph warned.

'It's a fair question, ain't it? Robbie being the heir to it all, well he's gotta be able to count all that dough, don't he? I mean if it was good enough for his acre-chasing father and uncle to learn how to count the Missus's money, then it goes to reason it won't be no hardship for the son and heir to do the same, eh?'

If he'd been bigger, Robbie would have punched Archie in the nose.

'What's it like then? Having sisters that are also your cousins. Hey, I just thought of something.' Archie turned to Murph. 'Maybe this place won't be the kid's. Maybe it'll go to one of the girls. If it's good enough for the mother to wear the pants, well then –'

Dropping the reins, Robbie charged, head down. He heard Bluey snarl as his skull met Archie's soft belly and the impact pushed the older boy to the ground. Robbie landed on top.

'Get that dog offa me!'

'That's enough,' Murph said quietly but firmly, grabbing Robbie by the collar and yanking him to his feet. As soon as they were parted Bluey loosened his grip on Archie's ankle. The jackeroo sat up, glowering.

'Don't mind him, Robbie. His girl dumped him last weekend and he's been in a filthy mood ever since.'

'Bugger off.' Archie moved to slouch against the stable's timber walls. 'That Bluey should be shot. He'll give someone a real bad bite one of these days.'

'Come on, Archie,' Murph continued, 'your turn. This colt isn't going to wait all day.'

Robbie watched as Archie dragged his boots through the dirt. He only had to say one word to his dad, one word, and Archie would be fired. But he hadn't been raised to be a tittle-tat. That was something girls did. Mr Goward said Archie was a fish out of water because he came from the coast and knew nothing about big stations, or sheep for that matter. But Robbie reckoned it was because he was pale-skinned with freckles. Ugly, Robbie decided, just plain jug-head ugly. But then Murph said Archie had a girl-friend. Robbie had never had one of those. Not that he wanted one, mind. No, he had enough problems what with the communists coming any day and now someone stealing his cray-bobs.

Archie lifted the colt's other hind leg as Murph placed a shoe over the hoof to check the correct fit. 'Watch what you're doing when you're filing, Archie,' Murph warned. 'The idea is to smooth the sharp edges of the nail where I've cut them.' He walked into the stables to the familiar noise of a horse shoe being belted into shape.

Archie glared at Robbie. 'Think you're pretty good, don't you?'

Robbie couldn't think of a reply. When Murph reappeared, he walked to the far end of the stables where he unsaddled Garnet, sitting the gear in the closest stall as the gelding trotted through the open gate into the horse paddock. Rifle and saddlebags in hand, Robbie was about to leave when he saw that Archie's backside was pointed towards him as he bent forward, concentrating on the colt's hoof. Murph was walking back inside the stables. The jackeroo's shirt was untucked and his trousers had slipped showing the pale moon of his bottom.

Quick as a flash, Robbie grabbed a cray-bob from the bags and, shaking the creature to antagonise it, crept slowly towards the jackeroo, the waving pincers directed at Archie's backside. Robbie tentatively poked the cray-bob at the target, before pushing the thrashing creature at white skin. The cray-bob latched on. Archie let out a wild yelp. Robbie ran. Bluey gave chase.

Archie chased after him at a cracking pace. Robbie's breath soon caught in his throat as he began to worry that the older boy would catch him. Above the beat of his heart he could hear Murph yelling and a quick glance over a shoulder confirmed that Archie was indeed gaining on him. Robbie dropped the saddlebag on the dirt road, his fingers still gripping the rifle. If he let go of the .22 calibre he might damage it, so he held onto it and gritted his teeth. His legs were growing tired, his breath raspy.

'Stop!'

Robbie nearly collided with the station overseer as Bluey charged into his leg. He stumbled forward, briefly unbalanced, as the man stood in the middle of the road and, pushing Robbie to one side, unfurled a stockwhip and cracked it once, twice.

Robbie, bent over and gasping for breath, clutched at his side where a stitch pained.

Archie halted in a spray of dirt, his riding boots slipping on the gravel. Behind him Murph was still running.

'What's the matter with you lot? Aren't you hot enough already without busting yourselves running around in this weather? It's Friday,' Mr Goward said tersely. 'You should be in the quarters washing up for dinner, Archie Gough. Tomorrow the plunge dip has to be filled and the patch on the tank didn't hold so there's that to repair as well. Come Sunday I expect you to be up at sparrow's ready for the muster. Are you hearing me?'

'But he put a bloody cray-bob on my backside, Mr Goward,' Archie said indignantly.

Robbie stole a glance at the overseer. The expression hadn't changed on his face, but then the man was wonky-eyed, with one green and one blue. The blue one had a habit of drifting inwards when he was angry, so that a person never could tell who Mr Goward was looking at or, for that matter, what he was thinking. Robbie figured this could go either way. The silence grew. Very slowly, the overseer commenced curling the stockwhip. Archie shoved his hands in his pockets.

'Well?' asked the older man.

'Yes, sir, Mr Goward,' Archie replied, as Murph finally reached them, breathless and red-faced.

'Do you have a problem keeping your men under control?' the overseer asked the senior jackeroo. 'Because if you do, Murph, the both of you boys can pack your bags.'

The older boy grew instantly flustered, his first few words a stutter. 'It was just a bit of misunderstanding, Mr Goward.'

'Go,' the overseer directed.

Archie and Murph walked away quickly. When they reached the saddlebags, the younger jackeroo gathered up the cray-bobs that had crawled free and then lifted the bag in the air, waving it antagonistically.

Robbie turned to the overseer. 'They're mine. I trapped them.'

'Well then, you should have hung onto them. My advice is to never pick a fight with someone who's bigger than you. If you do it will surely turn bad. Sod's Law.'

'What's Sod's Law?' asked Robbie, trailing the overseer back to where the man's horse was tied outside his cottage.

'It means things won't just go bad, they'll go real bad.'

'Oh.' Robbie digested this. 'Like the communists invading.'

The older man gave a slow nod. 'Well, if they did invade, it would be bad.'

'So do you think it could happen, Mr Goward?'

A thoughtful expression replaced the overseer's usual stony stare. 'No-one thought that the Japanese would bomb Darwin. No-one thought there would be another war, but here we are and our boys are over in Korea getting shot at all over again. So I guess I'd never say no to the possibility of anything happening. And Menzies doesn't strike me as a fool. If he reckons we should be on our guard from the commos, well then we should probably take his advice.'

At the sloping veranda of the three-bedroom cottage, Mr Goward halted. 'You wouldn't happen to be in trouble with your folks, Robbie?'

'No, why?' he asked, chewing his lip.

'Because you've got a habit of turning up on my doorstep when things aren't going so well.' He looked at the cattle dog who'd taken up position at the end of the veranda. Close enough to keep an eye on the boy, far enough away to escape the toe of a boot. 'Nothing to say, hey? Well, you better come in and wash your face and hands before you head home. You look like you've been rolling around in the dirt.'

Robbie looked at his pants and shirt. His clothes appeared pretty clean to him.

The cottage consisted of an open veranda at the back and the front and a kitchen that was big enough to hold a sofa and two armchairs. There was a bottle of rum on the sink and, as Robbie washed up, the overseer poured a nip into a glass, skolling the drink straight. He then sat at the kitchen table where two note-books were open, displaying numerous entries. Next to them was a stack of *Hoofs and Horns* magazines.

'Shearing supplies,' the overseer indicated with a dirt-rimmed nail. 'And this book is for the team. The shed overseer, Mr Lomax, will be here tomorrow, and the wool classer on Sunday.'

'They bunking in with you, Mr Goward?'

'Always do, son. It's important to maintain the hierarchy. Besides which, the men like their space.'

'Can I help during shearing?'

'I thought you had that nice Miss Hastings schooling you?'

Robbie ran his fingers across the pages of the notebook. 'Duck Face?' He looked warily at Mr Goward, waiting for a reprimand that came in the form of a crinkled brow. 'Well, yeah,' he said deflated, seeing his chance of wagging school disappearing. 'But Dad always lets me help out in the shed.'

The overseer leant back in the chair. His blue eye pointed to the right, the other straight ahead. 'Okay,' Mr Goward finally replied, 'what can you do?'

Robbie's brain was blank for a moment. 'I can push the sheep into the pens,' he began. 'I can run the tar to the board, I can skirt the fleeces and sweep up –'

'And eat a lot of cake at smoko if I remember from last year.'

Robbie shrugged. 'It was good cake,' he admitted.

'Well, you're in luck. The same fitter and turner is coming back to cook. Fit it into a pot and turn it into food, that's Fitzy.' Mr Goward moved to the sink and poured another nip of rum. He was known to drink only on Fridays. Glass in hand, he turned to Robbie. 'I'd offer you a drink, kid, but I run a dry shed and I don't want to be giving you a taste for the demon grog before shearing begins. That's if you're going to be helping out.'

Robbie's chest swelled up with pride. 'No, sir, Mr Goward. I mean, gee whiz, thanks, Mr Goward.'

'But don't forget, at day's end it's up to the shed overseer, Mr Lomax, whether he'll have you or not.'

'But you'll put in a word for me?'

The older man considered the question, dragging out the process until Robbie was perched on the very edge of his seat. 'I'll put a word in, but,' he lifted a finger, 'don't you get me into trouble with that governess of yours, or your mother for that matter. And that cattle-pup has to be chained up. I don't want him anywhere near the sheep.'

Robbie jumped to his feet. 'No, sir, he won't, promise. Thanks, Mr Goward.' He opened the cottage door and was about to leave when the overseer called him back.

'And Robbie, unless you want to find yourself in the dirt with Archie on top of you, don't go stirring up trouble. No more cray-bob attacks.'

Robbie put on his serious face. 'Yes, sir.' But he was pretty sure that the older man was chuckling as he walked outside, nearly colliding with . . . 'Dad.'

His father was leaning on his walking stick on the veranda, his hat tilted back slightly so that Robbie could see his bald patch. He didn't look cranky, so Robbie gave his best grin and thought he saw the slight creasing at the corners of his father's mouth that sometimes became a smile.

'Robbie. I hope you're not annoying Mr Goward?'

Robbie rolled his lips together. He knew from previous occasions that if he said no, no-one ever believed him.

'He just came over for a talk, Mr Webber,' the overseer explained, standing in the cottage doorway. 'We were having a chat about shearing. I said we could use him in the shed after he's finished his lessons, of course, if Mr Lomax's agreeable.'

Colin ruffled his son's hair and Robbie squirmed uncomfortably. 'Well, if you can convince the Chinaman, Hugh,' he gave his son a pointed look, 'and he doesn't cause any problems –'

'I won't, Dad, I promise,' interrupted Robbie. He jumped from the veranda and began twisting the heels of his boots in the dirt. 'One day I'm going to be just like Jackie Howe and shear hundreds and hundreds of sheep in one day.'

'It took sixty years for a machine shearer to equal Jack's blade-shearing record,' Mr Goward reminded him, 'so you better build yourself up a bit if you've a mind to be the next Bradman of the Board.'

Robbie beamed as his father and Mr Goward began to discuss the team. Some of the men they mentioned, Robbie recalled from last year. There was Fitzy the cook, and Dawson the butcher, and Mr Lomax the Chinaman, and the classer Spec Wilson. But most of the shearers, apart from Billy Wright, he couldn't remember at all. Mr Goward went back inside the cottage, reappearing with the notebook from the kitchen table.

'The Grazco's man, Rickard, suggested Johnny Smithers,' the overseer explained, 'but I said we refused to have the drunk back. The man smuggled in grog last year and stirred up everyone.'

'I remember,' his father answered. 'A dry shed is a dry shed. No excuses.'

'Just what I told Rickard. Of course if you complain about a man invariably you'll get someone worse. The bastards. Sorry, Robbie.' He cleared his throat.

His father ruffled his hair again. 'He'll hear worse next week.'

'Anyway, the new bloke is from out Riverina way. Don Donaldson. So we can only wait and see. Had cancer of the throat, but they say he can shear a bit. Might give Billy Wright a run for his money and break the highest tally record he's held here for twenty years.'

'As long as we've a full team, Hugh, that's the main thing. We just have to hope that they all sign their agreements. We don't need a replay of '49.'

'Anyone would think we owed them a living. Beats me. We need the sheep shorn and they get paid to do it. And I don't see many other sheds putting on beef and mutton in the mess. You know we could do it ourselves,' Mr Goward suggested. 'Do the hiring and the firing without the Graziers' Co-operative organising things on our behalf, without the union.'

'Scabs? No. No, I'll not take that path. Some of these shearers have been coming here for years. And there have been few problems.'

'And some are a bit long in the tooth,' the overseer countered. 'I'm not saying they weren't good in their time.'

'As long as they keep pace with the average count per run. There's been a massive growth in flock size and wool output over the last five years and the bush is suffering from a lack of labour.'

'And the shearers and shed-hands know it,' Mr Goward cut in.

Robbie watched as his father chewed the fleshy inside of his cheek. He never did take to being interrupted, and the overseer, as everyone knew, wasn't too keen on being given orders. 'Keep them happy, Hugh. That's all that's required. We have to get the wool off the sheep's back and onto the auction floor with the minimum of fuss. And at the moment with the price of wool, we can pay what they want to a certain extent. Don't forget, large profits make it difficult to justify any opposition to wage increases.'

'But what happens when the price falls?' the overseer queried. 'They'll still want their pot of gold and we won't be able to deliver. It won't be economically feasible.'

'Let me worry about what's economically sound for River Run.' Colin's tone never varied. 'We've a good team. And as long as they think they're receiving a fair go, which they are,' he confirmed, 'we'll be right.'

'The wethers have a lot of wool on them this year and there's the odd ewe blown. They'll complain. Argue for an increased rate for the trouble.'

'Just get them to sign the agreements.' His father was beginning to get impatient. 'At least then they can't bargain for conditions above what's in the contract. The last thing any woolgrower needs is to pick a fight with their employees.'

Standing between the two men, Robbie was starting to get a crooked neck from looking up. He wondered why his father didn't tell Mr Goward that he'd talked about this with his mother and that she'd already made a decision about such things. His mum and dad talked about everything and argued about everything, including the shearing team, and then they argued about arguing. No-one was meant to know that it was Robbie's mother who really ran the property, but he reckoned that some people guessed the truth. After all it was his mother who spent time liaising with the Australian Workers Union, assisting them like other leading graziers to keep control over their members. And most days she was either studying the ledgers in the station office or driving around the run in an old beat-up truck, checking fences and their mobs of sheep, a colourful scarf tied under her chin to keep the dust from her hair and a battered hat on her head. Nope, Robbie figured every man on the station knew who really ran River Run. Rex said it didn't have anything to do with Robbie's father. Things had been done this way with his mother's first husband as well. They'd married into the River family after all. They'd married a wife and landed a sheep station.

'If the weather holds we'll be finished in a month,' Colin continued. 'This heatwave will keep everyone's heads down.'

The overseer didn't look convinced, his mouth briefly puckering. 'This hot, well, I'd be surprised if something didn't blow up from the west. Settle the dust. It wouldn't hurt none. Weather like this, it's hard on man and beast.'

His father dipped his chin in agreement.

Robbie knew Mr Goward fought with one of the shearers last year. Rex reminded him recently when they'd been out fishing. The shearer had been thrown off the place, dumped on the main road with his swag and a busted nose. The union rep went off his block. Wrote a letter of complaint and everything, not that anyone took notice of that. No-one messed with Mr Goward's fist.

'Well, we'll be yarding and drafting the first mob on Sunday and you can expect the men to start arriving from tomorrow on,' Mr Goward explained. 'Rex is collecting the food for the mess Sunday as well. I bet old Stavros is rubbing his hands together.'

'He usually is at this time of the year,' Colin granted. 'You know Mrs Webber and I have talked about your ideas for the flock, Hugh, and although I'm not convinced I'll tell Winslow when he's here over the weekend.'

'I appreciate you giving me a chance, Mr Webber.'

Colin grunted in reply.

With their business discussed, Robbie found himself keeping pace with his father. He wanted to run on ahead but instead he was forced to slow, as the cane made drag marks in the dirt.

'Can I really work in the shed, Dad?' asked Robbie, reaching down to give Bluey a scratch between the ears.

'If you behave yourself.' He gave his son a quick glance. 'Your mother is going to have a say about the mess you made to her roses.'

Robbie had hoped that had been forgotten. 'I didn't mean to,' he answered, dropping his bottom lip.

'How about trying not to upset her?' At the back gate his father stopped. 'You know what she's like when it comes to those flowers of hers. Women like to keep things neat and nice, especially your mother. Alright?'

'Okay,' Robbie mumbled, stuffing his hands in his pockets.

'And that pup of yours.' His father nodded at the cattle dog. 'You'll keep him tied up, won't you, over shearing. If he attacks any of the sheep I'll have to put him down, Robbie. Damn stupid idea,' he muttered as if Robbie weren't present, 'being given a cattle-pup when you live on a sheep run.'

'Mr Pappas thought I'd like him,' argued Robbie defensively.

'Mr Pappas doesn't know much about the bush or sheep. You know you really can't keep him, son. Not here on a sheep stud.'

'But –'

'We'll talk about it later.'

'But –' Robbie looked from the pup to his father and back again. He couldn't bear to lose Bluey. The dog was his friend. He'd talk to his mother. Yes, that's what he'd do. Usually when one of them said no, the other said yes. Mrs Howell once told Robbie it was because his parents were contrary. Robbie didn't know what that meant, but the process usually worked. 'Dad, you know the war in Korea?'

His father lifted the latch, closing the gate behind them. 'Yes.'

'Does Menzies –'

'Mr Menzies,' he corrected. 'He's our Prime Minister, you know.'

'Well, does Mr Menzies think the communists will invade Australia?'

They walked across the lawn, avoiding the wet spots where the sprinklers had soaked the earth. 'There's no doubt that the communists have been a problem here in Australia for a while. You wouldn't remember, but a couple of years ago we had to call in the army to break up a coal-mine strike. The Communist Party was to blame for that.'

'The army?' Robbie blanched. 'Did they shoot the reds then, Dad?'

'No.' His father gave a chuckle. 'At least, not that I know of. But men were jailed. It was quite a big thing at the time.' They reached the first of the linked ponds and, with their path barred by Rex's irrigation system, they detoured past a rockery, white trellis and a trailing vine. 'You see, the communists don't like capitalism and that's people and businesses like us. They want to see businesses and governments run by the people. Shared. You understand, don't you, son? They'd want to take over River Run.'

'Live in the house and everything?'

'Probably,' his father responded vaguely.

Robbie couldn't believe it. Communists living in his home. 'So, if they invaded . . . You know if the communists did come here . . .' But his father wasn't listening, he was talking about class conflict and the working class struggle. Stuff that didn't interest Robbie at all. A frog plopped into the brown-green water of the pond. When his father paused, Robbie spoke up. 'Tell me again, Dad, about when that bloody German shot you in the leg.'

'Seriously, Robbie, I've told you a hundred times,' he chortled. 'He got me here, here and here.' He pointed to a number of places on his thigh.

Robbie couldn't imagine being shot. His father was the bravest man he knew. 'What was it really like at the war, Dad? What's it like to kill a man?'

The cane made a scratching noise on the paving stones. His father's face grew dark. Robbie was sorry he asked. 'We don't talk about it, remember?'

'But, Dad —'

'Go see your sister. Eleanor is home.'

Robbie knew when it was best to do what his father said. His skin was turning the funny grey colour that usually meant he'd soon go all quiet and sad. His mother said it was because of the war but as his father never wanted to talk about it, ever, Robbie guessed he'd never really know.

'Off you go, Robbie. I'll be in soon.' His father sat heavily on a garden bench, his breaths long and leaden, the blue of his shirt darkened by sweat.

Robbie lingered for just a second and then ran towards the house. If the communists did come, he'd be ready.

≈ Chapter Seven ≈

Eleanor was sitting on the bed sketching the front of the home-stead from memory when the bedroom door opened with such force that it slammed into the wall. Hurriedly gathering the contents of the satchel scattered across the chenille cover, she hid the papers beneath a pillow. Her young brother grinned at her, while a half-grown blue cattle dog padded into the room to sit by his feet.

'Hello, Robbie. And this is?'

The dog tilted its head, eyeing her suspiciously.

'Bluey.'

Eleanor smiled. 'Very appropriate.'

'I didn't know you were coming home,' Robbie commented.

He had the stocky build of his mother and the dark hair of his father. The eleven-year-old had grown. 'It was a last-minute thing.' Eleanor tucked a curly red tendril of hair behind her ear and sat on the edge of the bed. 'So when did Mum start letting working dogs in the house? And a *cattle-pup?*' She was surprised.

'You won't tell her, will you, Eleanor? He's harmless and anyway he's only a pup. Mr Pappas gave him to me last year. Dad said

I couldn't keep him. He said he'd chase after the sheep and kill them but,' he shrugged, 'I want to keep him, and Mum hasn't said anything about him yet.'

Eleanor was surprised her mother hadn't instantly got rid of the dog. She wondered if there was more of a battle of wills going on between her mother and stepfather than what she'd overheard earlier. 'I won't breathe a word, but you better keep him hidden.' She curled her legs up on the bed. 'What have you been up to?'

'Not much.' He went directly to the door leading out onto the balcony. In the distance the curve of the river was marked by a band of trees.

'Hmm, that's not what Rex told me.'

Robbie scuffed his foot on the carpet. 'Well, I don't like Archie.'

'I was talking about Mum's rose bushes.'

'Oh. It was Garnet, sis. He made me do it.'

'Really.' Eleanor laughed. 'Obviously Garnet doesn't like flowers.'

'Well, we have got an awful lot of them and they're right in front of the hedge.' Robbie shrugged. 'I didn't mean it.'

'You're not in trouble with me.' Eleanor received a grin in reply.

'It's been pretty boring here.' Robbie turned from the balcony to sit in a flowery barrel-backed chair, flinging a leg over one of the arms. The wood gave an alarming creak, which he didn't seem to notice. 'I don't like Miss Hastings much and Mr Goward has been busy because of shearing.'

'Rex tells me we start Monday.'

Robbie's face brightened. 'I'll still have to do my lessons and everything but Dad always lets me finish early even if Mum gets annoyed and Mr Goward said I could be part of the team and help.'

Eleanor's eyebrow lifted. 'Really? Well, you will be busy.'

The boy touched the dog lightly with the toe of his boot and the pup rolled onto his back, wriggling happily on the carpet. 'The men finished walking the first mob of sheep into the one-tree paddock this morning. There's good feed there, but Mr Goward's worried about the grass cutting out too soon when there's another twenty thousand head that's gotta come the same route. I wanted to muster with them yesterday but of course the old bag wouldn't let me.'

'And who is the old bag?'

'The governess,' Robbie explained. 'Duck Face.'

Eleanor burst out laughing. 'Duck Face?'

Robbie picked at the arm of the chair, not seeing the humour. Fact was fact, after all. 'Is it hotter here than Sydney?'

'Absolutely. It's positively boiling. Anyway, what else has been happening?'

'Well, Mum and Dad have been arguing. About shearing, about Mr Goward, about buying rams, about their friends coming to stay and about a new car. Dad wants to buy a Holden but I heard Mum say that they're like arseholes, everyone has one.'

'Robbie!' Eleanor was shocked. 'You shouldn't say things like that.'

'Like what?' he asked innocently. 'Anyway, Mum said 1949 and '50 was the time to buy a new car, but she doesn't want one of those anymore.'

'Really? Why on earth not?'

Robbie's smile grew so wide that nearly every tooth in his mouth became visible. 'Because she wants to buy an aeroplane!' He rubbed his hands together. 'There's money in wool,' he announced, clearly imitating his parents. 'And Mum says we could see where all the sheep are lots easier from the air, and we could check watering points. And planes could even help out at mustering time.'

'A plane for mustering sheep, now I have heard it all.' Eleanor was agog at such an idea. 'What's the matter?' she asked at the young boy's changed expression. 'Is something wrong?'

His face grew grave. 'It's the war.'

'What war?'

Robbie swivelled in the chair, repositioning a leg. Crusty bits of mud fell from the hem of his trousers onto the carpet. In the stuffy room Eleanor began to decipher a mixture of scents, one minute something that resembled rotten meat, the next the familiar tang of horse hair and saddle-grease.

'You know, sis, in Korea.'

Eleanor stifled a yawn. It had been a long day. 'Oh, that war. Quite frankly I don't think we should even be involved in it.'

'It's on the wireless and everything,' Robbie went on passionately, 'and Dad says that with the Russians involved that it could be another big war.' His words tumbled over each other. 'We only just stopped the Chinese, you know.'

'Robbie, relax. It's miles away from us. The other side of the world, really.' Eleanor didn't mean to sound dismissive, but the last thing she wanted to discuss was yet another war. It only seemed like yesterday since the last one ended.

'But they're shooting our men,' he argued.

'I know. I have read about it.' She'd been pretty self-absorbed over the past few weeks but Eleanor was sure that the United Nations and the countries fighting under that banner would soon have the battle between north and south under control.

'You can't trust the communists.' Robbie said the word slowly, for emphasis. 'You know one lot of Koreans invaded the other lot,' he told her knowingly. 'And Dad says that Mr Menzies –'

'Bloody old Menzies,' Eleanor scoffed. 'He's got half the country scared witless about the threat from communist regimes and the other half complaining about all the immigrants he's allowing into the country. The Italians are more threat to us than the reds.'

Robbie's eyes widened. 'Even Mr Pappas who owns the store?' He hadn't counted on the Italians attacking as well.

'No, not old Stavros. He's Greek.' An unwelcome image of Dante came to her. 'By the way, he gave me these to give to you.' Eleanor handed him the bag of lollies.

'You didn't eat any, did you?' He began sucking on one of the sweets.

Eleanor crossed her heart. 'Of course not.' From beneath the pillow she selected a couple of American western comic books, handing them over. 'Don't show anyone those, will you?'

'Wow, thanks.' He examined the covers. One of them was called *The Outsider*, and depicted a big-hatted man on horseback carrying a rifle. In the distance was a figure crouched behind rocks, watching his approach. 'I bet that's a Winchester,' Robbie said. 'It sure looks like one. Dad took me to the flicks last year in Sydney and we saw Jimmy Stewart in *Winchester '73*. That's the rifle that won the West. Did you know that?'

'No, I can't say that I did,' Eleanor said.

'Well that figures, you being a girl and all. Did you know that the only comics Mum lets me read is *Ginger Meggs* when Dad's finished with the paper and they make me listen to *The Argonauts* on the wireless?' He rolled his eyes theatrically. 'But I've kept all the comics you've given me, Eleanor. I keep them hidden. Have you had more stories made into comics?'

Eleanor was desperate to share what Dante had done. 'A couple. And I did write something, a book actually,' she paused for just a moment, 'but a friend stole it and printed it under his name. I'll never forgive him for doing that.'

'But that's just wrong.' Robbie's face turned indignant.

'Yes it is, but there's nothing I can do about it.' Eleanor plucked at the bedcover. 'Don't tell anyone, will you, Robbie. Promise me? I don't want to make a fuss about it and you know that Mum and Uncle Colin hate my writing. They don't know I still do it,' she confided. 'I only told you because, well, I just wanted to.'

'Don't you worry, I won't tell anyone. Cross my heart.' Robbie spat on his palm, extending a hand to his sister. 'Come on. You have to do the same thing. Then we have a pact. I won't tell on you if you don't tell on me.'

How disgusting, she thought, but reluctantly Eleanor spat on her palm and they shook hands.

He slipped the comics down his shirt. 'Anyway, you could write something else. A bush story. How about me and Garnet?' he asked hopefully. 'Or Bluey.'

The canine lifted its head.

'Maybe I could,' Eleanor replied thoughtfully. 'We'll see.'

'You know I don't think Mum and Dad really hate your writing.'

'Sure they do. We're a conservative bush family. It's bad enough I'm still single and have decided to work in Sydney, but the descendant of Frederick Barnaby River writing comics and short novels . . . I'd never hear the end of it. It's better if everyone thinks it was just a stage I was going through.'

'Right,' Robbie agreed, although he didn't, not really. 'You don't like my dad much, do you?'

Eleanor answered carefully. 'He's your dad and you love him, but he's not my dad. You understand, don't you?'

Robbie knew his half-sister missed her father. He could see it in Eleanor's face. When she talked about him her eyes grew large and watery. But that wasn't the only thing he knew. He'd figured out a lot of things. He wasn't a kid. But some of the stuff he knew, Robbie didn't like. He got angry when he heard people talking about his family like it was their business. Like they knew stuff. His dad was Eleanor's father's brother and most people, even Rex, thought that the marriage had been a bad idea. Sweeny Hall, who owned the village garage, once said that Robbie's father was a money-grabber. Although Mrs Howell said not to believe anything the man said on account of him looking at life through the bottom of an empty beer bottle. Then there were the jackeroos like Archie, but he wouldn't think about him, at least not right now. 'Well, I think your writing is neat.'

The loud crunch of gravel coincided with a car's engine. Sister and brother exchanged looks.

'Mum's friends are here,' Robbie announced. He rushed out into the hallway, shutting the door in Bluey's face. Eleanor listened to the pad of his feet, to the opening and closing of a door and then he was back in her room, panting.

'It's the Winslows. In a big flash car. And the woman,' Robbie took a gulp of air, 'Mrs Winslow, well she's got a dead dog wrapped around her shoulders.'

'She has a what?'

'A dead dog, sis.' Robbie's eyes were bright. 'You can see its head and everything.'

Eleanor felt like a kid again. Intrigued, she followed Robbie into the hall, tiptoeing along the passageway to the staircase. At the landing they dropped to their knees and peered down the stairs, to where the Winslows were being greeted by their mother and Colin. Eleanor caught a glimpse of the angular woman, a narrow fur draped nonchalantly around her shoulders, the head of the unfortunate creature trailing over a shoulder and down her back. The Winslows were ushered into the sitting room amidst an enthusiastic greeting. Behind them, Rex stared at the luggage, two medium-sized trunks and a travelling bag and, lifting the first trunk, trudged towards the staircase. Eleanor felt warm puffs of air on her arm. The cattle-pup was crouched beside them.

'Told you,' Robbie whispered.

'It's a fox fur,' Eleanor explained, 'not a dog, Robbie.' Although she wondered at the need to make such an entrance, especially in this heat.

'Do I look like a bellboy?' Rex muttered, dropping the trunk on the floor at the bottom of the stairs. 'If a man's employed as a gardener, then he should be a goddamn gardener, I'm saying, I'm just saying.' He walked back to the remaining baggage.

The unmistakable signature on the Louis Vuitton trunk attracted Eleanor immediately. Tapping Robbie on the shoulder, they backed out of sight, returning to the bedroom as Rex plodded up the staircase. They listened while their mother gave the gardener instructions as to which room the Winslows were to be sleeping in.

His shoulders against the wood of the door, Robbie whispered, 'If Mum finds me, she'll tan my backside because of the roses and probably lock me in my bedroom.'

That wasn't to be the worst of it. The cattle-pup lifted his leg and peed on the carved chair leg as he spoke.

'Good heavens.' Eleanor didn't know whether to laugh or cry as the pup sniffed his mark, and sat back on the carpet.

Robbie wasn't taking any chances. He was out on the balcony in seconds, Eleanor following. 'Hang on, Robbie, I'm sure –'

A knock sounded on the door.

'Eleanor, are you in there?'

'Coming, Mum. Go,' she mouthed to her brother.

Robbie ran the length of the building, the cattle-pup on his heels. At the corner of the house, the limbs of a tall tree angled across the balcony. Balancing on the balustrade he reached out and grabbed one of the thicker branches. Eleanor winced at the thought of the drop to the ground as Robbie swung forward to grasp another branch. He was partially concealed by the leafy boughs when he whistled. The pup squeezed through the wrought iron and jumped into the tree. Leaves shook violently. Eleanor turned to find her mother standing in the middle of the room.

'What on earth are you looking at?'

'Just getting some fresh air.'

'I'm sorry we didn't have a chance to chat more, Eleanor, before everyone arrived. I've told Mrs Howell to make up a tray for your dinner.' Georgia checked her reflection in the dresser mirror. The coral silk calf-length dress with its full skirt and cinched waist gave shape to her otherwise portly figure. 'I should have purchased something new. I forgot how fashionable Margaret can be.'

'You mean infamous,' Eleanor clarified.

'Come now, Elly, Mrs Winslow is a guest under our roof.

Are you going to tell me why you've arrived home unannounced? Has something happened?'

'No. I just wanted a break, that's all.'

'Well, if you're sure nothing's wrong. You make sure you get a good night's sleep. I can't have you poorly with the Winslows here. And if you see that brother of yours, tell him I expect him to stay in his bedroom tonight, seen and not heard.'

'Oh, has he done something wrong?' asked Eleanor innocently.

'This is Robbie we're talking about.' Her mother's eyebrows squirrelled together to form a thin unbroken line. 'And he's just at that age. This afternoon it was my rose bushes, this morning it was tadpoles in the governess's satchel. A week ago, frogs in the poor woman's bed. And there are tinned goods missing from the pantry. That's all we need, for Mrs Howell to go on the warpath. You may well laugh, Eleanor, but when you finally marry and have children of your own, you'll realise that they can be somewhat of a chore at times.' Her attention was drawn to the wet spot on the carpet at the base of the chair. 'What is that?'

Eleanor winced as her mother bent down, touching the dampness. 'I have no idea.'

Georgia sniffed her fingers, her nose wrinkling. 'That smells like –'

'Oh,' Eleanor said dismissively, 'it couldn't possibly be.'

Her mother looked at her suspiciously. 'Couldn't possibly be what?' Georgia's glance moved from the discoloured carpet to the balcony. 'I'd ask you what happened but I don't think you'd tell me, would you?'

Eleanor gave an enigmatic smile.

'I'll see you in the morning.'

'Have a nice evening.' Once her mother had left, Eleanor looked out over the rear of the garden. Robbie was nowhere to be seen.

❧ Chapter Eight ❧

The pocketknife sliced cleanly through the inner tube. Robbie tested the spring of the rubber from the old tyre and then, tongue stuck out between his lips in concentration, tied it to one of the forked branches and then the leather pouch of the shanghai. Standing, he placed a small stone in the pouch, aimed the shanghai at a magpie perched in a tree a few yards from the machinery shed, pulled the rubber back and fired. The stone hit the bird in the chest, dropping it to the ground. Garnet, tethered to the same tree, backed up in fright as the cattle-pup meandered over to sniff the dead bird. Satisfied with his handiwork, Robbie tucked the shanghai in his back pocket, picked up a coil of rope, slinging it over his shoulder, and walked past the row of rabbit traps hanging from a peg on the wall.

'Stay,' he ordered the dog. With a whimper, Bluey lay down in the cool of the building.

At the rear of the shed there was a clear view of the jackeroos' quarters. The oblong building sat unevenly on stumps that over time had begun to sink into the ground. This gradual movement was altering the structure of the house so that the boards at the bottom twisted in places while the fascia holding the gutters on the roof were beginning to droop. The building was to have repair work done on it during the winter, but until that happened only four bunk-rooms at the end of the building were usable, the doors on the remaining three either impossible to open or difficult to close.

Through the line of washing strung untidily between two leaning poles, Archie and another jackeroo, Stew, were sitting at a table on the veranda playing cards, while Murph was working on a rawhide stockwhip. The senior jackeroo was cutting strands of kangaroo hide from a skin, stopping between each length to sharpen the knife on a whetstone. There was another jackeroo, a pie-faced boy from way out west who looked perpetually hungry, but he wasn't about. The men called him Wormy, as if the nickname might account for his skinny frame. Three other jackeroos had the weekend off. It was some time since the rooms were filled with twelve young men. War and the after-effects had taken its toll, which, for the most part, Robbie didn't mind. He liked it best when there weren't a lot of young blokes working on the property, treating him like a kid and laughing at him when they felt inclined. They always arrived quiet and polite, but most of the time it didn't take them very long to get all puffed up with self-importance and knowledge that Rex said took a lifetime to learn.

'They're smart,' announced Archie, peering over the top of the cards he held. 'Blokes like us, well, we're at the bottom of the rung.'

'Of course they are,' Murph answered from his seat on the veranda. 'If they weren't smart they wouldn't own a big spread like this.'

Archie selected a card from the deck on the table. 'My dad says the bush was made by the squatters placing their boots on the back of the little man's neck.'

'Well,' Murph examined a length of leather cut from the hide, 'if he thinks that, why'd he send you out here? And why'd you agree to come? Exactly,' he continued answering the question on Archie's behalf. 'So you'd learn something from them.'

Archie slammed the card down on the table.

Stew, a rough looking, scruffily shaved individual, steadied the surface with his hand. 'Go easy, mate.'

Murph spat on the sharpening stone, placed the blade on the spittle-wet rock and began to rotate the flat of the blade. 'Getting ahead in life is about being smart, not being a smartarse.'

Archie didn't reply.

'Look at the shearers, making a fortune they are with the current boom,' Murph explained. 'There's smarts on both sides if you ask me. In '47 they complained at every turn. They demanded specific terms and more pay, thinking that Mrs Webber would agree simply because labour was short after the war and she needed to get the shearing done. They were taking advantage and they won. The Boss did agree.'

'So the shearers were smarter?' Archie asked with interest.

Murph ignored him. 'Trouble is, it happened all over the country. So the growers realised they had to protect themselves and their income by making sure workers weren't overpaid. A wool allowance was introduced that attracted more labour to the industry. That reduced the bargaining power of the established shed-hands and shearers and such-like.'

Archie sighed. 'And? What's that to me?'

'Well, your father sent you here to learn something, didn't he? You just did,' he answered with a grin. 'The moral of the story, Archie, is don't be a smartarse, don't take advantage of people and never ask for more than the job's worth, or what you're capable of.'

'You're just full of knowledge, aren't you?' replied Archie gruffly.

'Are you playing cards or what?' Stew asked. 'It'll be dark in half an hour.'

'A word of advice, Archie. Leave Robbie alone,' Murph stated. 'If there's a choice between you and him when it comes to getting marching orders, it won't be Robbie Webber that goes.'

'Don't bet on it. The little bugger will be off to boarding school soon. After all, they all get sent to Sydney for their education.'

Murph gave an irritated sigh. 'Keep your mouth shut and yourself busy, Archie, and if we're lucky we might all get a bonus when the clip's sold.'

'Fat chance,' Archie replied.

Keeping an eye on the jackeroos, Robbie made a quick dash across open ground to the ablutions block. Twenty yards away were the outhouses, two narrow buildings made of corrugated iron. One door was propped open, the other closed. A pile of clothes sat in the dirt outside. Robbie squashed his body flat against the wall of the building as the whitewashed door of the other long-drop swung open and Wormy appeared. Hitching his trousers up, the youngest of the jackeroos scraped a boot on the ground, removing a square of paper stuck to the heel. The jackeroo watched the piece of paper as the breeze lifted it and the fragment of toilet paper began to top and tail over the bare ground in the wind. Wormy gathered the pile of washing and walked into the ablutions block. A tap was turned on and water ran loudly into one of the deep tubs.

'Argh! Bloody cray-bobs!' Wormy said loudly from inside the building.

Robbie guessed Archie must have left the cray in one of the tubs until he was ready to cook them. Creeping around the building to where the rainwater tank stood on stumps, he paused a moment and then continued on to a straggly tree suffering from die-back. The tree provided a clear view of anyone heading towards the showers or outhouses. More importantly, it also gave a person a head start if they had to make a run for it.

The tree was easy enough to climb. With half the branches near dead and bare of leaves, Robbie made quick work of it. Shifting his bottom across a long limb, he tied the rope to the branch. In his pocket was a small handful of dried sheep manure. The pellets made excellent ammunition and he loaded a couple in the pouch of the shanghai and waited.

'What's the go keeping them bloody things in the wash-tub, eh?' asked Wormy when he met Archie at the door to the showers and laundry. He held a wooden washboard and Sunlight soap.

'Don't get your knickers twisted, Wormy.' Archie moved the towel he carried from one shoulder to another. 'I'll have a wash and then cook them up. Everyone likes a bit of cray. It'll go down real well with a piece of fresh bread before we tuck into some chops for tea.'

Wormy retreated back inside the building, returning with a basket of washing under one arm. 'I don't eat those filthy things, you know that. They're bottom-dwellers. Sifting through mud. Living off carcasses and stuff. You can have the lot of them.'

'Suit yourself.' Archie clutched a pair of shorts in his hand. He walked inside the block to have a shower while Wormy hung his work clothes on the line.

'Don't use all the bloody hot water,' Stew yelled. Struggling with his boots, he sat them on the floor and then, rounding the corner of the veranda, he disappeared from sight.

The water was running. Robbie wiggled back and forth on the branch. A tap squeaked. A pipe gave a groan. The jackeroo was whistling a tune. Then he started to sing.

Oh, give me land, lots of land, under starry skies above
Don't fence me in
Let me ride through that wide open country that I love
Don't fence me in

Geez, Robbie thought, as Archie's tuneless voice rang through the air, he's terrible. At the veranda there was no sign of anyone now. Robbie lifted the shanghai just as Archie reappeared in the doorway with a towel over his shoulder, shirtless, wearing shorts. He was still singing as he dumped dirty work clothes on the floor of the ablutions block and walked towards the outhouse.

This is for what you said, and for nicking my cray-bobs. Tongue poised between his lips in concentration, Robbie aimed the shanghai and fired, quickly reloaded and fired again. The sheep pellets were flung through the air with force. They landed on Archie's chest, the tiny missiles biting into his skin with stinging accuracy.

The boy let out a whoop of pain.

Jamming the shanghai in his pocket, Robbie uncurled the rope and dropped from the tree to the ground, landing like a cat on all fours.

'You little bastard!' Archie yelled.

Robbie ran like the wind. He ran past the kitchen, circled around the quarters and then continued onwards down the track to the machinery shed. Nearly out of breath, he reached Garnet ten feet in front of the jackeroo, flung his slight body up into the saddle and, digging the heels of his boots into the animal's flanks, yelled out: 'Go, boy, go!'

Archie's hand reached for him just as the horse bolted. Garnet headed straight up the road, past the stables towards the overseer's cottage, and still Archie kept running, the cattle-pup close behind. Shoeless and shirtless, Archie kept coming. Robbie grinned and gave the horse his head as Bluey overtook the youth and sped after his master. The last he saw of the jackeroo was Archie standing on one foot, picking burrs out of the other.

❧ Chapter Nine ❧

The buzz of the generator powering the electricity to the house flickered slightly, waking Eleanor from a sweaty evening nap. She lay on the bed wondering if her decision to come home to River Run had been the right one. Eleanor wished she was more like her mother, strong and decisive. It was one thing to be let down by a man, quite another to run away from her job and her friends because she was having problems coping with the situation.

Outside the coloured markings on the horizon shifted from pink to crimson until the lack of light eventually forced her to rise. She'd dreamt of a dog barking, of someone calling out, shouting, but now the only noises were of jazz music wafting through the house and spurts of laughter. Beyond the bedroom the ground floor was ablaze with lights. Convinced that everyone would be ensconced in the sitting room, Eleanor changed from her travelling clothes and tiptoed barefoot downstairs. At the bottom of the staircase she turned a sharp right, intent on escaping the public areas of the homestead. Ahead was the door that led into the servants' area and kitchen, a sanctuary of sorts.

'And who do we have here? Staff or wayward daughter?'

Eleanor stopped and turned slowly. She hadn't seen the woman lounging in one of the hall's wing-back chairs. Expensively dressed in gold silk, the underskirt layered with tulle, the woman tapped a cigarette on the edge of a silver case and lit it with a matching lighter. A massive ruby and diamond ring shone on her hand.

'Hello, Eleanor,' the older woman slowly exhaled a long trail of smoke through scarlet lips. 'My son Henry and I had quite a discussion about you. My, I forgot what a flame-haired girl you are. You remind me of one of those Renaissance Masters hanging in the Louvre.' She tilted her head as if inspecting something of interest. 'I can see why that Italian was so taken with you.' She didn't wait for Eleanor to reply. 'Are they natural, those curls?' The woman examined Eleanor critically. 'They're not in style, you know, however, you are interesting enough in your looks to carry them.'

'Mrs Winslow, I . . .'

The woman took a brief puff of the cigarette and, stubbing it out in the ashtray on a hall table, walked towards her. 'Affairs can be good and bad, but if you're going to have one, go where the money is, darling. God knows a woman receives few perks in return, after all.'

Eleanor was desperate to escape the woman's calculating stare but she was transfixed to the spot. The dress was undoubtedly of French design with a waspy waist, soft shoulders and yards of fabric. It was such a beautifully decadent gown to behold after years of wartime rationing. And it was reminiscent of couture house Dior's much lauded New Look. Up close Mrs Winslow had a slightly receding hairline and too fine a nose for her overly long face, which could only be described as horsey. But as a whole there was something rather handsome about her, handsome and formidable. All Eleanor could think about was that Henry Winslow had actually told his mother about her and Dante. She really wanted to ask Mrs Winslow not to say a word to her mother or Uncle Colin, however, the woman's lips were twitching in amusement, adding to Eleanor's discomfort.

'I gather your mother doesn't know about your liaison?' Mrs Winslow waved a hand when Eleanor was slow to respond. 'She does wear the pants around here, doesn't she?' Removing a gold compact from her purse, Mrs Winslow touched up her lipstick. 'Well, it's to be expected. If a father has no sons and he wants his dynasty to survive, he has little choice but to cede succession to an only daughter.' She picked briefly at a cuticle on a fingernail. 'Such responsibility has to change a woman.'

Eleanor had never felt quite so uncomfortable in someone's presence.

'But of course then there is the dilemma of choosing a suitable husband. Which begs the question of how your handsome father managed to do so well for himself. And now we have the younger son ensconced on River Run, name but no money.' Mrs Winslow tapped her chin thoughtfully. 'Did your mother acquiesce to your grandfather's original choice or was it the other way around, do you think?'

The woman was actually waiting for an answer. 'Perhaps it was mutual,' Eleanor replied sharply, wondering how this woman dare be so outspoken. But then she was Margaret Winslow, wife of the owner of one of the most famous sheep studs in Australia.

'Actually,' the house guest went on amiably, as if their conversation was quite tasteful and not one of the most inappropriate discussions Eleanor had been party to, 'the whisper is that what your parents shared was pure love, which rather makes a second marriage second-best, don't you think?' The questioning tone was timed to perfection. 'But I'm sure I don't have to tell you that, do I? She has done well, your mother.' Mrs Winslow nodded approval, her eyes flitting over the tastefully decorated entrance hall. 'Very well. Of course it's not like she started from scratch. Georgia had the bones of this place to mould. She's nearly matched Winslow standards,' she said thoughtfully. 'Nearly.'

Eleanor wanted to feel offended, but the remark was made in such a way that it seemed quite without malice and was, in fact, simply an observation. She tried to excuse herself. 'If you don't mind, Mrs Winslow –'

'Oh, yes, yes. We oldies are so boring to you bright young things.' The woman stood, revealing a shapely figure that looked as if it had been poured into the dress. 'Dior,' she offered, observing Eleanor's fascination. 'I only wear Dior. Although we're always a season behind Europe. Before you disappear, Eleanor, do tell me, how is that sister of yours? I know she's still in Sydney but she hasn't done something else unmentionable, has she?'

Eleanor stiffened.

'Your mother is quite monosyllabic when I ask after her.'

'Lesley is quite well, thank you,' Eleanor replied politely.

'She's quite different to you, isn't she?' Mrs Winslow said thoughtfully. 'You know, I can still recall your father's funeral. Lesley was inconsolable that day. Anyone would have thought that you were the stoic older sister. And then, of course, after her young man's death we heard that she'd tried to take her own life. A shocking thing. Was it five years ago? It seems much longer.'

'Yes, it was five years. I'd really rather not talk about it if you don't mind, Mrs Winslow.'

'Of course. They do say time heals, my dear. Remember that. But can I ask one more thing? Has Lesley returned to nursing? I'm told that keeping occupied can help greatly. Takes the mind off things.'

'Yes, she's nursing at the hospice attached to the convent.'

'Good. Well that's all I needed to know.' Mrs Winslow gave the slightest of smiles.

Eleanor was beginning to remember why she'd never really liked Mrs Winslow. She was the type of woman who, while a guest in someone's home, would search for the maker's mark on a piece of fine china to check the quality.

'Let's hope she can get on with her life instead of wasting it.'

The woman made it sound as if Lesley's life was over.

'Now you best scat, otherwise your mother will discover you dawdling about down here and we can't have that, not when she gave such a pretty speech about her youngest daughter being poorly.' She gave Eleanor a knowing look. 'They've been talking about Menzies and immigrants,' she gestured towards the sitting room with a bored air, 'and some muscled-up gun shearer from the Riverina. Gawd,' she intoned theatrically, 'in this heat. And I thought we were having a party.' With a wink she walked away.

Eleanor watched the sashaying stride of the woman and then, entering the poorly lit corridor, she closed the door and leant against the wood panelling. Eleanor would never forgive Henry Winslow. Ever. It was bad enough that Henry, who was more acquaintance than friend, chose to discuss her personal life so blatantly, but to tell his mother, knowing how intricately the Winslow and Webber families were linked. It was too much.

And as for his mother . . .

≪ Chapter Ten ≫

The stone passageway was slightly cooler than the rest of the house. This area had been the domain of the servants in the last century and into the present, but now the disused rooms were either empty or used for storage, apart from the housekeeper's accommodation. Only the kitchen at the opposite end of the hall remained abuzz with activity. Eleanor walked in that direction, the sound of voices growing.

'Of course it would have to happen right now. Didn't I tell you to change it over before tonight? You mark my words, if this dinner is ruined, Rex, I'll not take the blame for it. In all the years I've been cook here, this has never happened. Running out of gas halfway through cooking a meal! I *told* him the flame was going yellow. Told him this morning again, but no, he had to drive seventy miles to pick up a piece of trellis for the garden. The *garden*. They can't eat roses, although you'd think they could with the amount of time and money that goes in to the growing of them.'

Eleanor could hear Mrs Howell clearly. Luckily the kitchen was positioned at the rear of the house, and the building large enough to ensure that the staff's voices didn't carry to where her mother and uncle entertained their guests.

The kitchen door was partially open and the housemaid Alice sat cross-legged outside cradling a tray. It was obvious the girl was waiting for Mrs Howell to calm a little before entering. She started on seeing Eleanor, got to her feet and gave a surprised but welcoming smile.

'Hello, Miss Eleanor. We heard you were here. You come for your dinner then?'

'Call me Eleanor, Alice, please.'

The girl smiled, but they both knew she'd never address her as an equal.

'It sounds like Mrs Howell's on the warpath.'

'Rex forgot to change the gas bottle,' Alice explained, 'and the fire in the stove died when Mrs Howell was taking her afternoon rest. The wood ran out. I've been waiting here on account of Mrs Howell getting angry. The chicken Marengo is still cooking.'

'Disaster.' On more than one front, Eleanor thought, thinking of Margaret Winslow.

'And once she starts talking to herself, then you know that things have really gone bad.' Alice's tray held a single pineapple. A scattering of toothpicks with cellophane tips suggested the dinner guests were hungry.

Eleanor did her best to sound cheerful. 'How's the party going?'

Alice opened her mouth to speak but then, thinking better of it, bit her lip.

'I'll go first, shall I?' offered Eleanor.

Every surface in the kitchen was covered with platters and pots, some clean, others dirty. Tomato and onion skins filled the scrap bucket while a massive bunch of parsley from the herb garden sat next to a stack of sliced bread with the crust removed. Mrs Howell was at the gas stove stirring a large pot, seemingly oblivious to the insects flying in through the open back door to mass around the overhead light. Outside, Rex staggered under the weight of a gas bottle as he manoeuvred it to the rear wall. There was a clang of metal and then a loud expletive. The room was boiling. A single electric fan barely stirred the air.

'Dreadful man,' Mrs Howell commented, sitting the saucepan on the adjoining Aga stove that she refused to part with. 'Plenty of wood for the shearers' mess, but the homestead . . . I never should have agreed to that new-fangled oven. You just don't change what works, ever.'

Alice cleared a space on the long table by shoving the tray against a stack of crockery. Tin and porcelain came together in a crash, attracting Mrs Howell who turned instantly.

'Eleanor!' she exclaimed, ignoring Alice. 'Heavens, girl, you scared the daylights out of me. If you want your dinner you've come at a bad time. The soup's going lumpy, the chicken's not cooked and dessert . . . Well, I haven't even got to that.' She frowned at the housemaid. 'I was relying on Miss Hastings to help instead of poor Alice but of course she's late and then the gas ran out and Alice is so terribly slow, aren't you, Alice? Mrs Webber was very adamant that everything had to be perfect this weekend. Dear me.'

'It's not like we're entertaining the King.' Eleanor tried to ease the older woman's concerns.

The housekeeper wiped her hands on a tea towel. 'And just as well. God bless His Majesty.'

'God bless,' Alice muttered as she stabbed cubes of cheese, cocktail onions and pineapple onto toothpicks.

'Well, how are things going out there, Alice?'

'The ladies are on their second martini, Mrs Howell, and the men have had at least three western wobblers. I don't think they'll notice what they're eating by the time dinner's ready.' She began to insert the laden toothpicks into the pineapple.

Mrs Howell looked unimpressed. 'Of course they'll notice, you silly girl.'

'Can I help with anything?' Eleanor offered, swatting at a moth. Alice was beginning to sniff.

'Heavens, no.' The cook strained the soup through a colander and began to bash the lumps with a wooden spoon. 'But you will have to give me a moment to get these hot savouries ready for the oven before I get your dinner.'

'I'll get my own, Mrs Howell, but thank you.'

'You modern girls,' the cook commented. 'Well, suit yourself, I know *you'll* be able to find what you need.'

Mrs Howell had almost resigned when her mother remarried but, convinced the household would fall into ruin if she left, the housekeeper remained. Everyone was grateful. Georgia barely knew her way around a kitchen, such had been her upbringing, and her love of the outdoors had stymied any tendencies towards domesticity. Eleanor cut two slices of bread and added wedges of cheese and tomato. She would have loved a glass of sherry after her recent altercation with Mrs Winslow but she didn't dare raid the sideboard in the dining room in case she was seen. Barefoot with ankle-length pants and a shirt tied at the waist didn't constitute clothing in her mother's eyes. Neither, it appeared, did her outfit meet with Mrs Howell's approval. She was now studying Eleanor's shoe-less feet with a frown.

'Done.' Rex stood at the back door, a flashlight in one hand and a spanner in the other.

Mrs Howell lit a match and, turning the gas knob, took a good two steps back and held the flame gingerly to the cook top. The gas flared. Mrs Howell blew out the match. 'Well, you took two years off my life, you did, Rex. Gallivanting into town instead of tending to your duties here. Not keeping the wood pile topped up. Just because petrol rationing has ended doesn't mean you can just take off when it suits you. I've a busy household to run here and –'

'Nice to see you too, Mrs Howell, on this fine evening.' Rex winked at Eleanor. 'And you're right, of course. We shouldn't be bothered about picking up oils and rabbit-traps or cutting wood for the mess just because men have to be fed during shearing, not when there's entertainments at the Big House to consider. We're only bringing in thousands of sheep from paddocks that could swallow a whole country in an effort to get some of the finest fleeces to market.'

'Impertinent man,' Mrs Howell mumbled with Rex's departure. 'Alice, come here and light this oven. I'm too old to be getting down on my knees.'

Alice obeyed as Mrs Howell began to ready a tray of prunes individually wrapped with bacon. 'Why we have to be serving this up when we could have had some nice toast with a bit of fish paste and parsley atop, I'll never know.'

Eleanor ate as the women worked, a glass of water from the rainwater tap finishing off her meal. Her offer of help was declined politely so she cleared a space on a bench top and sat watching as Mrs Howell made the garnish for the chicken dish. Bread was fried and placed in the warming oven and parsley was finely chopped and set to one side. Alice returned after handing around the cheese and pineapple and promptly left with the cooked prunes and bacon.

Mrs Howell glanced at the kitchen clock on the wall. 'Fifteen minutes and then I'll serve the soup.'

'Timed to perfection as always, Mrs Howell.'

The woman twitched her nose and sat down for a brief rest. It was as close to a smile as one could expect. 'And what brings you back here, Eleanor? It's not like you to up and leave Sydney without letting us know in advance. You certainly gave Rex a surprise, appearing in the village the way you did.'

'I needed a break.' Normally she would be grateful to talk things over with Mrs Howell. In the past they'd shared tea and cake whenever she came home from boarding school for holidays. But her meeting with Mrs Winslow had left Eleanor feeling more than

73

fragile, and there was a definite line that couldn't be crossed when it came to confiding in the older woman.

Mrs Howell folded a damp tea towel. 'Is it this writing of yours?'

'Yes and no.' Having revealed her hobby some years ago, proudly announcing that her work had been published and sold in newsagents and railway station bookstands, Eleanor had found a surprising ally.

'I, for one, would rather see people handing over their money to buy stories written by our own kind, rather than paying for rubbish penned by the Yanks. I remember visiting my aunt in Sydney during the war. Americans everywhere there were. The dance halls were full and our young things were queuing to be seen on the arms of those boys. The stories I heard from my niece of money and choco-lates and fancy hosiery.'

The older woman waited for a response. Eleanor guessed that Mrs Howell knew that she wasn't dabbling in literature but she didn't judge, loyalty keeping her confidence. But things were different this time. 'I don't really want to talk about it,' Eleanor finally stated.

Mrs Howell rose to place the kettle on the stove top.

Eleanor valued the older woman's friendship, however, she couldn't talk about the reason for her unannounced visit home without mentioning Dante and once she started talking about him she knew it would be impossible to stop. She respected Mrs Howell. The two of them had forged a friendship over the years but the housekeeper was strictly old school. Eleanor didn't doubt that the woman would have a conniption if she heard the truth, and the truth was that Eleanor had been unbelievably stupid and naive.

'It's my view that a woman born of the country can never live in the city,' Mrs Howell said matter-of-factly as she began to clear a space on the table for the laying out of the soup bowls. 'You young things rush to the bright lights and, just like a moth, stray too close and get burned.'

Eleanor yearned to disagree but it felt as if the housekeeper had seen straight through her. A respectable young woman would never

74

tarnish her reputation, or that of her family, by sleeping with an Italian immigrant out of wedlock.

'How's that sister of yours?' asked Mrs Howell.

'A lot better. She still gets melancholy at times, but she's making herself useful, tending the convent garden and she's nursing in the hospice when needed,' replied Eleanor, grateful for the change of topic. 'I still wonder how I would have coped had I been Lesley. Finding Marcus the way she did.' She broke off, trying not to think of the day her mother telephoned her in Sydney to say that Marcus had hanged himself on River Run. A week later, Lesley slit her wrists and would have followed her fiancé had Georgia not found her eldest child in time.

'I still think the girl would have been better off in the care of professionals instead of that convent.'

'It was Mum's decision.' Eleanor also wondered whether a private facility would have been more appropriate for her sister. The melancholia engulfing Lesley was beyond severe. She'd literally withdrawn from the world in the first year following Marcus's death and even stopped speaking for six months. Then, of course, she'd been hidden from the world in a place where visitors were restricted.

'That lovely girl closed up within those walls.'

She thought of Mrs Winslow's comment, *such a waste*. 'They say she's improved a lot over the past year.'

'She was never like you, Eleanor. Lesley was always a shy, fragile young thing and she doted on your father. When he died I wondered if your sister would ever be able to stem her grief, to go on as you did, then she met Marcus when she was training to be a nurse. Those two were made for each other and we all know that he became the centre of Lesley's universe.' Mrs Howell coughed and made a fuss of pouring hot water into the soup bowls to warm them. 'Had we known what the future held, it would have been better if those two had never met.'

'But they adored each other,' Eleanor replied.

'In some cases you can love someone too much. That's what happened to your sister. She loved Marcus and lost him and decided that she couldn't live without him. Life's hard enough without over-sentimentalising.' The housekeeper lifted a chastening finger. 'Don't make the same mistake, Eleanor. Still,' she reflected, 'he was a fine young man, that fiancé of hers, but not without faults. What man shares the horrors of war with his fiancée and then kills himself?'

All the family knew that Marcus would be forever altered after his time as a prisoner of war working on the infamous Burma railway. But no-one ever imagined that he would take his own life having survived such a terrible ordeal.

'If your father was still alive, Lesley would be here in this house.'

'If my father was still alive,' Eleanor replied carefully, 'a lot of things would be different.'

Mrs Howell nodded. 'Indeed.'

The kitchen door swung open and Alice appeared. 'Mrs Webber says she wants the soup served directly, and the sherry. They can't find the sherry.'

'Fine, fine,' Mrs Howell replied as Miss Hastings appeared. The housekeeper gave the governess a firm dressing down for her tardiness but Eleanor knew she'd be secretly pleased by her appearance. She wore a neat grey dress and a crisp white apron, stockings and black heels. The governess and Eleanor acknowledged each other with a brief greeting. She had to agree that Robbie's moniker for the woman was rather apt.

'I am sorry, Mrs Howell, but I've had no end of trouble with young Robbie today. He's missed half his lessons, damaged Mrs Webber's garden and placed tadpoles in my satchel.' She gave a sniff. 'I fear he's become quite uncontrollable.'

'A firm hand is what's needed,' the housekeeper answered dismissively as she poured the warming water from each bowl and wiped them dry. 'After you've served, you'll find the sherry decanted on the sideboard. Pass it to Mr Webber.'

'Yes, Mrs Howell.' Opening a drawer, the governess retrieved a clean tea towel. 'It was Mr Goward that held me up. A jackeroo has made a formal complaint against the lad. Apparently Robbie attacked one of the boys late this afternoon. Shot him in the chest with a shanghai.'

The soup Mrs Howell was ladling into one of the bowls splashed onto the table. Eleanor knew she shouldn't laugh, not when Miss Hastings had the look of someone who'd swallowed something sour. The woman frowned as Eleanor stifled a giggle.

'Stop chattering,' Mrs Howell reprimanded, continuing to spoon soup into the bowls. Alice added a dollop of sour cream while Miss Hastings ensured the edges of the dishes were clean of any spillage. The housekeeper gave the servings a final check. 'Right then. Off you go.' When the women left the kitchen, Mrs Howell cleaned up the soup puddle. 'You might have a talk to Robbie while you're home, Eleanor. Miss Hastings is right. The boy's been running wild this past year.'

'He's just having a bit of fun,' she replied, 'and we all know the jackeroos can get a bit peeved at times.'

The housekeeper turned her attention to the stove, fiddling with the temperature control. Clearly, speaking to Robbie was not a suggestion. 'We might be employees, Eleanor, but we are still human beings.'

Was it her imagination or did everyone seem very uptight? 'Yes, Mrs Howell.'

'Well, we don't have to worry about Robbie.' Miss Hastings reappeared in the kitchen with a self-righteous expression. 'Mr Webber's just marched him up to the bedroom and locked him inside.'

'Oh.' Eleanor had a vision of her stepfather thrashing Robbie with his belt. It would not be the first time.

'Best place for him.' The governess met Eleanor's gaze, as if the remark was made to provoke. 'It's ridiculous letting Robbie behave the way he does. My father believed in a firm hand and it certainly never did my brothers any harm.'

She barely knew Miss Hastings, however, Eleanor sensed the woman's dislike for her half-brother. 'Boarding school is the answer, of course, if Robbie's that much trouble.' Now it was Eleanor's turn to await a response. It didn't come. 'Oh dear, but if Robbie goes to boarding school,' she said sweetly, 'you'll be out of a job.'

'Miss Hastings,' Mrs Howell intervened, 'I do hope the soup isn't sitting on the sideboard cooling?'

'No, Alice is in the dining room –'

'Off you go then.' The housekeeper shooed the governess out of the kitchen. '*Eleanor.*'

'What?' Eleanor countered with a wicked smile.

Saturday

Down by the River

❧ Chapter Eleven ❧

Robbie had been awake since first light, pacing around the bedroom desperate to escape. He rattled the doorknob and then crossed the carpet to try the French doors on the balcony again. Anyone would think he'd done something really bad instead of breaking some silly rose bushes and attacking Archie. But at least Alice had brought him dinner last night. Two soft-boiled eggs with toast soldiers and a glass of milk. That seemed like days ago now. His stomach was rumbling and the round bedside clock confirmed it was past mid-morning.

Pressing his nose against the warm glass door, Robbie could see half of the tennis court. He watched as one of the men raced across the ant-bed surface. The ball went high and wide and a woman lunged for it, batting the ball awkwardly as if she were playing cricket. It flew towards the net, lodging in the middle of the mesh. Everyone was dressed in white, making it impossible to tell who was who, not that he cared.

Frustrated, he returned to studying the balcony door. 'Eureka!' he said loudly, before dragging a chair forward, standing on it and sliding the bolt open at the top. With this extra security gone, the old door gave way just a little. On the gravel drive below, Miss Hastings was making her way to the tennis court carrying a tray of glasses and a pitcher of something cool to drink. Robbie licked his lips and then fell on the bed, bashing the pillows. It just wasn't fair. He was nearly twelve and he was sure that no-one else locked nearly twelve-year-old boys in their room. He lay there for some minutes wondering about Garnet and why Eleanor hadn't come looking for him.

On the dresser sat silver-framed photographs of his father and Eleanor's father, Alan. Both men were in uniform. Both men had been wounded in the Great War. His father still had shrapnel in his leg, while his Uncle Alan had survived his war wounds but had then got sick and died from cancer. The two brothers looked almost exactly the same. They had moustaches and wore their AIF hats at an angle and staring at them made Robbie wish that he could go to war as well. His father once told him he'd be a good fighter. And Rex assured him it had to be true, after all it was in his blood and Robbie was a crack shot. Shoot the arse out of a black duck at two hundred yards, that's what Rex said.

Robbie reckoned that was how he knew about the communists coming. A soldier just understood these things. Yikes. He'd missed the morning news on the wireless downstairs and who knew what the communists had done in the meantime. Jiminy Cricket, they could be in their boats already, coming this way. Everyone would be really sorry if the reds attacked and he wasn't on sentry duty to warn them. And what about the stolen cray-bobs? He should be out baiting the traps, fixing the broken one and then stalking the area to see if the robber returned. He stared impatiently at the mobile hanging from the ceiling. Four Spitfire fighter planes stayed motionless in the stuffy room.

Jumping on the bed, Robbie tugged at one of the metal planes in the mobile until the wire suspending it broke. He hesitated for just a moment and then began to wiggle one of the plane's wings up and down until it snapped off. On hands and knees, he wedged the metal beside the balcony lock and began to wiggle the handle. Maybe, just maybe, he could slide the metal between the lock and the door.

Tap, tap.

Robbie fell on his backside in fright. Eleanor was standing on the balcony, knocking on the glass to get his attention and, having caught him trying to break the lock, was now laughing. Robbie frowned and told her to go away.

'I'm sorry, Robbie,' she told him apologetically, 'I didn't realise you were still locked in.'

'Where have you been?' He shoved his hands in his pockets.

'I got up early to go for a long walk before the heat of the day.' She held a lit cigarette in her fingers.

'Mum will kill you,' he called to his sister through the glass door as she took a puff.

'Well, you'd know all about that. Wait a minute, I'll be back.'

Eleanor walked along the balcony until she was out of sight. Robbie's eyes followed her retreat, not expecting her to return, but she did a few minutes later, clutching a small key.

'I'm sure it'll fit,' she told him, glancing towards the tennis court. 'I know it fits Lesley's old room.' The players were grouped around the governess, finishing their drinks. 'I finally asked Mrs Howell where you were.'

'Bloody old Mrs Howell.'

'Robbie,' Eleanor exclaimed, fitting the key in the lock, 'you shouldn't swear like that. You've been hanging around with the men too much.'

The key gave a click as it turned in the lock and the door opened.

'You're the best.' Robbie beamed.

'I know,' Eleanor replied with a look of satisfaction. 'Now what?'

Robbie bustled past her. 'Food. I'm starving! Then I want you to come with me.'

'Come where?'

Lowering his voice, Robbie grew serious. 'We have to make sure that there's no sign of them.'

'Them?' Eleanor repeated. 'Who or what is them?'

'Communists, sis,' Robbie revealed. 'The reds.'

❊ Chapter Twelve ❊

It was after one by the time they'd thieved some leftover sandwiches. Robbie packed a spare one in his saddlebag and checked
the number of bullets in the ammunition belt that belonged to his
father during the war. He could tell by Eleanor's expression that
she didn't see the need for a .22, let alone so many bullets, but he
ignored her querying look, flinging himself up into the saddle as
Garnet gave a complaining whine.

'You could use the stirrup,' Eleanor suggested, attempting to
quiet her mount, an aged mare called Hilda.

'It's faster my way.'

With one foot in the stirrup and the other on the ground, she
hopped awkwardly alongside Hilda as the horse walked forward.
'Faster for what?' Her words were breathy. 'For heaven's sake,
Hilda, will you please stand still?'

Robbie shrugged. He wasn't keen on explaining his rush to get to
the river and the probability of the communists attacking, until the
time was right. Besides, he knew what adults were like. They needed
to see everything before they believed a person. They couldn't just
take your word for it. Which intrigued Robbie, especially when Miss

Hastings said everything that she read out of his lesson books was right and that he shouldn't argue or ask so many questions because fact was fact.

'Where are we going? Not far I hope, it's a bit too hot.'

'To the river,' Robbie explained impatiently, waiting as Eleanor did a couple more leg hops before finally swinging into the saddle. Normally he'd never ride out in the middle of the day during summer, however Robbie wanted to be away from the house and his parents and out in the bush. Most importantly, he wanted to make sure his supplies were safe and that there was no sign of anyone strange. The theft of his crays and the breaking of the trap made him more cautious than usual.

Hilda needed a few swift kicks to her flanks before she started to move. 'Okay, you lead the way.'

Leaving the stables, they cut diagonally across the road, riding clear of the overseer's cottage. Bluey whined, straining on the chain where he was tied under a tree. Robbie wanted to take the pup along but it was darn hot and until Bluey trusted Garnet enough to sit in front of him on horseback, he couldn't take the little fella out in the hottest part of the day. It wasn't fair. The dog was more likely to drop dead from the heat rather than turn back and be left behind.

'I heard you hit one of the jackeroos with your shanghai,' said Eleanor.

'Archie doesn't like me and I don't like him,' Robbie answered. 'He's always trying to pick a fight.' Behind them the roofs of the station outbuildings sat like silver squares among the trees.

'Did your dad give you the strap?'

'Sort of.'

'How many this time?'

Robbie held up three fingers and gave a sneaky smile.

The heat rose up from the ground and spun at them from a too-hot sky. The air was thick, sullen, deadening the countryside so that it seemed as if the grasses wilted and the trees faded before their eyes. The horses plodded. Robbie wiped at the sweat on his face while Eleanor complained of the scorch of sun on skin. He couldn't blame her. It was hotter than yesterday. He told her that she didn't have to come, that she could turn back. That he'd rather she didn't come if she was only going to whinge. Yet Eleanor continued on, noting they were already halfway to the river. So they rode quietly side by side, growing used to the sun's burn, eyes squinting, foreheads creased.

'What's that?' asked Eleanor. The structure sat in the middle of the paddock. A square box of netting, inside which a mass of blackness moved.

'A crow trap,' answered Robbie. 'Remember? Usually we set it up a month or so before lambing, but if I find something dead I bait it myself. Rex says it's a good idea.' He led her across the grass to where half a dozen crows began flinging themselves against the wire, desperate to escape. 'They can get in, but they can't remember how to get out.'

Leaving Garnet to stand in the sun, Robbie searched around for a sturdy branch. With one in hand, he unwired the door and stepped inside. The crows fluttered anxiously about the confined space as Robbie lifted the stick and began to hit them.

'Robbie! Stop that. It's awful!'

Halfway through bashing a crow to death, he looked up. 'Seeing a lamb's eyes pecked out, that's awful,' he retorted, before continuing on with his task. He swung the stick until his arm tired and his shoulder ached. All but one of the crows was dead and it lay in the corner, spindly legs kicking at the dirt. Outside the trap, Robbie rewired the door, leaving the bloodied branch nearby. Eleanor had ridden some yards away.

'You shouldn't be doing that,' was his sister's only comment when he caught up with her.

Robbie hunched his shoulders, not knowing what answer was expected. He was only doing what his father did, what Rex did, what the jackeroos did. They rode on in silence, which suited him just fine.

Finally the tree line marking the river grew closer. It snaked towards the west, twisting and turning as if some mythic creature from another world. Twitching the reins, Robbie took the lead. Now they were heading slightly downhill towards the waterway, he was getting an anxious feeling in his stomach. It was always the same just before the first glimpse of the land beyond the water. And there it was, straight ahead. Wide, flat and seemingly empty. Sensing shade and water, the horses increased their ambling pace as the timber closed in and the land beyond was curtained from view. Robbie touched the holstered rifle, wishing he'd thought of making Eleanor bring a firearm as well. Now wasn't the time not to take every precaution.

'I forgot how far the river was from the house.' Eleanor squinted from beneath her hat and shifted in the saddle.

Robbie took a different path every time he rode to the waterway and this afternoon he led Eleanor over fallen timber and through close-knitted trees. The going was difficult. Twice they could barely squeeze their horses through the trees. Eleanor complained of grazing her knees on knobbly bark and questioned the route they'd taken, her complaints only ending on reaching the water's edge ten minutes later. The bank was steep and dangerous in parts and glimpses of the river showed the liquid glistening like the shards of broken glass.

'We're here,' Robbie announced. Leaving Garnet to graze, he tucked his sandwich down his shirtfront, strung a pair of binoculars about his neck and tied the rifle to his waist with rope.

'What are you doing?'

Robbie looked upward. 'I'm going up there. Are you coming?'

'I'm not climbing that,' Eleanor stated. Dismounting, she bent from side to side, stretching out aching limbs.

He glanced at her cotton trousers, pale shirt and old leather boots. 'Are you scared? You're bigger than me.' He shimmied up the trunk, grasping branches and pulling his body skywards. Once seated on the platform Robbie dragged the rifle up after him. 'It's a great view.' A scatter of sheep moved across the open plain. 'Come on, don't be a sissy. Give it a go.' Robbie tied the rope to a branch and dangled it down through the tree limbs towards his half-sister. 'You only have to pull yourself up a couple of feet and then there's a branch you can reach.' He watched nervously, with one eye shut, grimacing as Eleanor tried unsuccessfully to climb the woody plant. 'Girls are useless,' he said loudly. Maybe his father was a better sentry to have. Even if he did have one bad leg, he could always get a ladder. 'Come on, Eleanor. You just have to try.'

Eleanor grabbed the rope and began climbing, her face contorting with effort. Her hat fell to the ground, her hair came loose, but she succeeded in placing one foot in front of the other and finally, inch by inch, branch by branch, she pulled herself upwards. He shifted a little to make room as she squeezed next to him, pale and shaky looking. One of her nails was ripped and bleeding. But Robbie couldn't help feeling just a bit proud. He offered her half his sandwich. 'It's nice and warm.'

Eleanor screwed up her nose. 'No thanks.' She rubbed at her biceps. 'That was hard work.' She sucked on the injured finger.

They sat silently, surrounded by a cascade of leaves, their skin clammy with the heat, Robbie chewing on his sandwich as they gazed out across the river.

'You're right,' Eleanor finally acknowledged when she'd got her breath back, 'it is a good view.' She wiped at the dots of perspiration on her brow, noticing the hollow in the trunk. 'What have you got in there?'

'It's for when we're attacked.'

'Attacked?' Her voice was disbelieving as she sorted through the stash of tinned food. 'Where did you get all this from? Mrs Howell?

She'll tan your backside if she discovers you've been stealing food from the pantry. Robbie, you don't really think the communists would come here, do you?'

'Have you even listened to the wireless?' he replied crossly. Finishing his sandwich, he folded the paper wrapping, stuffing it into a pocket.

'Of course I have. But, Robbie, really? Out here? We're in the middle of nowhere.'

'We're not. Well, not really.' Robbie drew a map in the air. 'See, here's the north of Australia. That's Indonesia.' A grubby fingernail traced an imaginary path from northern Australia over the New South Wales–Queensland border down to the middle of the western plains. 'Then there's us. River Run is right in the middle.'

'The middle of what?'

Girls were so dumb. 'An invasion, silly.'

Eleanor looked at him as if he were mad.

'Mr Goward says that no-one expected the Japs to bomb Darwin,' Robbie continued, 'but they did, didn't they? And no-one thought there'd be another war either. But there is. This will be the third war that my dad's lived through and he told me about the army and the coalminers and Mr Goward said that anything could happen.'

'You're serious?' Eleanor hung her legs a little further over the edge of the platform.

At last, he had her attention. 'You should listen to the news, Eleanor.'

'I do, but no-one ever talked about Australia being invaded,' she replied. 'The war's in Korea, Robbie. It's miles away.'

Eleanor sounded and looked a little like his mother. One eyebrow was raised and there was a questioning expression that plainly said she didn't believe him. 'So this is my sentry post. What do you think?' he asked. 'If the Russians join up with the Indonesians, they'll come south to invade Sydney. They'd head straight there. They couldn't come at Sydney direct from the east because of the submarine nets. Remember when we caught that Jap sub? Well, anyway. We're right in their path, but it's alright because I've got a good view up here of the north, so I'll see them coming and I'll be able to warn everyone in time.'

'I see,' Eleanor said, her voice flat. 'I think you've been reading too many comics.'

'So what I wanted to know,' Robbie persisted, 'now that you're home, was if you'd help me. Cause we really need two people. I was going to ask Dad, him being a crack shot and all, but I don't think he'd be able to climb the tree with his bad leg. And I figured that you could be a runner. I'd let off three shots and that would be the signal for you to get home as fast as you can and let everyone know they're coming.'

'Wow, you have got it all planned out.' The doubt hadn't left Eleanor's face. 'But I really don't know if the communists would travel this far, Robbie,' she said carefully. 'And I don't want you wasting your time. You know, when you could be doing other, more fun things.'

'But you don't know for sure that they won't come,' Robbie probed.

'Well no, but I really doubt it. Besides, even if they did, they'd travel through other towns first, wouldn't they, and you'd hear about it on the wireless.'

Robbie hadn't thought of that. Eleanor was ruining everything. Pulling his knees up under his chin, they sat in silence. A bird twittered in the branches above. When his half-sister finally asked if she could have a look through the binoculars, he pushed them across the uneven planks towards her.

'I suppose I'm in your bad books now. I'm sorry, Robbie. I don't mean to ruin your fun, but I just think you got a bit carried away, that's all.'

Robbie chewed his bottom lip and stared through the leafy branches at the land below. The afternoon sun was slanting through wispy clouds, throwing shadows across the grassy plains.

The sunlit shapes changed size as they crisscrossed the land, elongating and then shortening.

'There's someone down there.' Eleanor rotated the lens, trying to focus the binoculars. She held them to one side for a moment, attempting to spot the object with the naked eye and then returned to peer through them. 'There, can you see?' She pointed. 'A man on a horse.'

'Jiminy Cricket,' Robbie stammered.

'Another idiot out riding in this heat.' Eleanor moved closer to the edge of the wooden boards as she continued to peer through the field glasses. 'I bet he's one of our men.'

Robbie wasn't listening. 'A scout, for sure,' he decided.

'From this distance it could even be Mr Goward.'

'No it can't. He's supposed to be overseeing the jackeroos fixing the plunge dip and the busted tank. Give me the binoculars.' Snatching the field glasses, Robbie quickly found the man. Horse and rider were heading for the river. Straight towards them. 'He's only about a mile away.' The .22 calibre rifle wouldn't even poke a man's eye out at that range.

'Can you see who it is yet?' asked Eleanor. Sunlight and shadows made visibility difficult.

'No, no I can't. But he doesn't look like anyone we know.'

Eleanor gave a groan. 'Robbie, it probably is just one of our stockmen.'

'Yesterday someone broke one of my cray-bob traps and stole my catch. That's never happened before.' His hands tightened on the field glasses. Someone had needed food. A stranger on their land.

'So I suppose you're going to tell me that's a Russian in disguise or something?' Eleanor gingerly levered herself over the edge of the platform, briefly looking at the ground. 'I should never have climbed up here,' she grumbled, as her boots made contact with one branch and then another.

'Wait, where are you going?' Robbie called anxiously.

'And I thought *I* had an imagination.' She climbed down the tree clumsily, the descent marked by nervous mutterings.

Wiping sweat from his face, Robbie observed the man through the binoculars as Eleanor let out a string of objections as she inched her way to the ground. Sure enough the rider hadn't budged from his direction. In a few minutes he'd be half a mile away.

From the ground, Eleanor called out to him to come down from the tree. 'It'll be dark in a couple of hours,' she reminded him. 'I have to get changed in time for dinner.'

'Fine. Go!' he yelled back down to her.

'Don't get cross, Robbie.'

He wished Eleanor would be quiet. The man might hear them. Setting the eye-glasses down, Robbie lifted the rifle and inserted a bullet into the chamber, then wedged the stock of the gun hard against his shoulder. He looked through the sight on the barrel. The man was still coming. He could see the outsider more clearly by the second.

'What on earth are you doing up there, Robbie? Come on, we have to get home. You don't want to be locked in your room again, do you?'

The rider stopped. Maybe Eleanor was right. Maybe the outsider was one of their men. Robbie scratched his head. But something didn't feel right. He didn't feel right. There was a blackness inside of him itching to be released. He thought of the crows, of bashing them to death. The metal trigger was cold against his finger.

'Robbie!' Eleanor yelled.

The stranger scanned the river before urging his horse forward. He'd heard them. Robbie swallowed, his throat dry and lumpy. This was exactly like the story in *The Outsider* comic. The outlaw had ridden closer and closer, convinced that he hadn't been spotted by the sheriff. Robbie guessed the man to be less than a half-mile away and the distance between them was closing quickly.

'That's it,' Eleanor shouted from the ground, 'I'm leaving without you.'

Robbie reasoned that if it was one of the men who worked on River Run, they would have let out a *coo-ee* by now, or at least given a yell to say who they were. After all, the man clearly heard Eleanor, for that was exactly when the rider began to move in their direction. Robbie's hands grew sweatier; the rifle heavier. Across the waterway the stranger lifted a rifle and pointed it. In Robbie's direction. That definitely wasn't right. He was on their land. Webber land. Robbie repositioned the butt against his shoulder and took aim. He'd fire one shot. A warning shot. That's what his dad would do. But maybe, just maybe, it would be better if he winged the man, then he couldn't give chase.

Robbie gritted his teeth and pulled the trigger.

The gunshot rang out, echoing along the river. Startled birds flew from the trees.

'Robbie?' Eleanor called in annoyance. 'What are you doing?'

His mouth went dry.

'Robbie?'

Hands trembling, he set the rifle down and picked up the binoculars. His heart beat loud and hard and he was vaguely aware of Eleanor yelling at him as he slowly pressed the binoculars to his face.

It took time to focus on the countryside as his hands kept shaking. Finally Robbie took a breath as his father taught him when he'd first learnt to shoot, before panning the binoculars across the paddock. He located the horse some distance away, riderless. The hairs rose on his arms. The stranger lay face down on the ground.

'Robbie?' his sister shouted up at him. 'You get down from that tree this instant.'

'I got him,' he whispered, then more loudly, 'Eleanor, I got him.'

'What did you say?'

Robbie lowered the rifle to the ground and then climbed down, falling the last few yards in haste. He landed on his backside at Eleanor's feet.

'I hit him,' Robbie said breathlessly, standing. 'Winged him.'

His sister's eyes grew to the size of plates. 'What?'

Robbie whistled to Garnet and the horse came immediately. 'We've got to go,' he told her, holstering the rifle and flinging himself up into the saddle. Eleanor had turned white. 'Come on,' he urged.

Not waiting to see if his sister followed, Robbie raced Garnet along the water's edge, hitting the horse's rump with his hat, urging him on. The gelding snorted but obeyed. Soon they arrived at the spot where the cray-bob traps were usually set, and it was here Robbie turned Garnet towards the river. A sand bar straddled the middle of the waterway and knowing it was a reasonably shallow place to cross, Robbie clucked his tongue, tapping the horse's flanks with his heels. 'Come on, Garnet.' The horse walked out begrudgingly. 'Come on.'

The cold water climbed quickly, reaching the girth straps, but it dropped almost instantly as they reached the shallow bar midstream. Garnet wasn't impressed. The horse whinnied in protest and backed up at the sight of the faster current. Digging his boots into the horse's flanks once again, Robbie fought the animal's inclination to turn back.

'You haven't got any choice, Garnet. We're crossing this river and that's an end to it.'

Eventually Garnet relented. He nickered softly, walking from the shallow stretch of sand. Immediately the river swirled about them, quickly inching higher and higher. Robbie felt the wetness creep up his legs to his thighs and then the river bottom fell away, forcing Garnet to swim. Robbie coaxed the horse with gentle words as he held on tightly, but the gelding didn't need any encouragement, he swam straight towards the opposite bank, his hoofs finally striking the bottom. Eventually they reached the sandy flats on the other side.

'Robbie?' Eleanor called from across the expanse of water. He waved at her to follow before turning his concentration back to the thick-rooted trees that lined the steep slope.

'Come on, Garnet.' Robbie kept the reins slack as the animal found purchase in the loose soil, finally making their way to the top of the riverbank. Robbie caught a glimpse of Eleanor as she walked Hilda into the water, following in his wake, and then he was twitching the reins and steering Garnet through the timber. Once clear of the trees, the plain spread out before them, flat and wide. Free of the water, Garnet happily cantered across the paddock.

Robbie found the man still lying face down. Arms by his sides, one leg twisted under the other. He rode around the body slowly, cautiously. When he was convinced that the man was not dangerous, he dismounted and, rifle in hand, walked carefully towards the prone figure, nudging the body with the toe of his boot. The man didn't move. He pushed a little harder. Still no response. There was blood on the back of the man's head. A lot of blood. Robbie paled. Had he done that? He was sure he'd only winged him.

A hat and rifle lay in the grass a few feet away. The horse grazed in the distance. The wispy clouds had been replaced by streaks of red and yellow and a shimmering heat-haze danced across the land. Everything seemed brighter, colourful and far too real. Robbie stared at the figure, lifeless before him, wondering what he should do next. Part of him wanted to ride away, to not look back. To never tell a living soul what he'd done. Instead, he gingerly reached out, touching the man's arm. It was still warm.

Was he dead? Had he really shot a man in the head? What would his father say?

Every soldier carried identification papers or wore dog tags. Robbie tasted vomit as he reached into one pocket and then the other. His fingers touched paper. In one of the man's pockets he found a wad of bills, a few coins, but there was no wallet, no licence, no identification, and there was certainly nothing around the neck.

'Hell, Robbie.' Eleanor arrived at the gallop.

Robbie turned to his sister. She was drenched from head to foot and river-mud splattered her trousers. 'I-I shot him in the head.'

'What?' She didn't move immediately and then Eleanor was on her knees by his side, staring at the body in the grass. 'Shit.'

'We should try to roll him over, shouldn't we?' Robbie asked when his sister's shocked silence grew too much to bear. Eleanor was still looking at the body, her face blank. 'Shouldn't we?'

'I-I guess,' she stammered.

Together they reached out and, with a nod of mutual agreement, pulled the man onto his back. 'You shot him in the shoulder,' Eleanor stated in disbelief and then she was on her hands and knees, being sick. She coughed and spluttered before wiping her nose and mouth on a shirtsleeve.

Robbie peered at the wound and crinkled his nose at the smell of vomit. 'But his head is all bloody.'

Eleanor spat into the grass, wiping her lips with the back of her hand. 'He must have hit it when he fell from his horse.' She took a few steps backwards, staring at the blood seeping into the man's shirt. 'I don't recognise him. Do you?'

'Nope. Is he dead?'

His sister looked like she could be sick again at any moment. 'I don't know. Put your hand over his mouth and see if you can feel air.'

'No way,' Robbie replied. 'I'm not doing that.'

Eleanor put hands on her hips. 'Well, you shot him.'

Robbie shook his head. 'I'm just a kid.'

'Damn you, Robbie.' They both stood there, staring at the man, at each other. Finally Eleanor gave a sigh of frustration and leant over the wounded stranger, her palm wavering across his face. 'I-I don't think he's dead. No, he's breathing. Thank heavens for that.'

Robbie suddenly felt a whole lot better. 'I only winged him then. Thought so.'

'Thought so? *Thought so?*' Eleanor's hands curled into fists.

'You're not going to faint or do something girly like that, are you?' asked Robbie. "Cause that's what happens when girls see blood, they get sick and then they fall over.' Maybe not, he decided, taking a few steps away from his sister, for safety's sake. He'd never seen her looking so mad.

'We have to get your father,' Eleanor decided when she'd calmed.

'No way,' Robbie argued.

'We can't leave him here!'

'But we don't know who he is,' Robbie reasoned. 'I only found money. Nothing else.'

'You've already been through his pockets? Geez.' Eleanor counted the roll of money Robbie placed in her hand. 'There's a lot here. What about a wallet? Did you find anything else?'

'Nothing.'

'Well, one thing's for sure,' Eleanor said accusingly, 'he's not a bloody Russian, is he?'

Robbie wasn't so sure about that. He didn't know what a Russian looked like. But his dad once told him that the Germans looked just like them and he'd seen them up close in the trenches. 'So why doesn't he have a wallet or something that says who he is?'

'He could be from another property in the district,' Eleanor suggested.

'So why is he on River Run, sneaking about on a Saturday afternoon? This isn't my fault, sis, he heard you calling out to me when I was in the tree and I saw him aim the rifle at me.' He kicked at the dirt, feeling inexplicably annoyed that he had to justify what had happened, as if it were his fault. 'It was either him or me. I only meant to warn him off.'

Eleanor gave him a long, hard stare.

'If he isn't a Russian, who is he, Eleanor?'

'How the hell would I know?' Eleanor ran fingers through her hair. 'I'll ride back and tell Mum and Uncle Colin.'

'But I shot him. What will happen?'

'Honestly,' Eleanor replied, 'I have no idea.'

'But by the time you get home it will be getting dark and I didn't mean to shoot him. Eleanor, wait. I don't want to stay out here by myself.'

'You should have thought about that before you fired the rifle.' Unstrapping the swag from Garnet, Eleanor shook out the blanket. 'Here, put that over him.'

'What for? It's not cold.'

'Because of shock and things like that.' She lifted a warning finger. 'And don't you dare move until I get back.'

Robbie looked from the blanket to his sister and then to the man on the ground. He was beginning to get a very bad feeling. Draping the man with the cover, he turned to Eleanor but she was already riding away. There was no way he was sitting beside the stranger in the dark. What if he woke up or, worse, died?

Robbie backed away from the body and it was at that moment that he spied something shining in the grass.

❧ Chapter Thirteen ❧

The stretch of shadows was disconcerting. The mare trotted doggedly onward, weaving through the sparse trees, firm-footed across ground marred by depressions, spiky grass and fallen branches. The horse needed no guiding for the last mile and maintained a steady pace. Eleanor was grateful, for the land at night was a stranger and she was desperate to reach the house before light left the sky. Not even the faint glow of burnished copper that sat low above the tree line provided comfort. Already the familiar nervousness that had accompanied the arrival of darkness since childhood was seeping through her. None too soon, Hilda trotted past the tennis court and rose garden, the trickle of the fountain loud in the air. Eleanor gulped at the scents of habitation. The earthy smell of freshly watered lawn, the aroma of food, the faint whiff of perfume.

Outside the homestead Eleanor slid from the mare, her knees buckling. Her wet clothes were nearly dry. On the second crossing of the river she'd managed to keep her seat on the horse, but even with the earlier drenching it felt as if her body would never cool down. Eleanor clung to the mare, steadying herself, trying to catch a breath that would not come to her.

Breathe, she willed, breathe.

Overhead insects gathered about the veranda light. The thickness of night would soon be upon them and already the familiarity of the garden was being altered into something unknowable as the darkness encroached. They had to get back and find Robbie. Tend to the wounded stranger. And yet Eleanor hesitated, her mind a blur. The gunshot, the wounded man, an eleven-year-old boy bashing crows to death with a stick. The gravel crunched as Eleanor willed her legs to movement. How could she explain to her mother what had occurred? It was all so unbelievable.

Walking into the house, Eleanor was heedless of the dirt that trailed her. At the door to the sitting room she paused in an attempt to gather her thoughts. It was useless. There was no right or wrong way. From within came the sound of laughter and chattering. Turning the doorknob, she walked into the room.

Margaret and Keith Winslow were sitting on one of the large floral sofas. Clearly a humorous tale had been told, for Mr Winslow was wiping away tears of mirth while Uncle Colin stood at the mahogany sideboard mixing their pre-dinner drinks. Her mother, in the midst of passing around savouries on a silver tray, stopped the moment she saw her daughter.

'Eleanor!' she exclaimed, nearly dropping the platter. 'Where have you been all afternoon?' Georgia looked her daughter up and down. 'And what on earth have you been doing?'

'I, that is –' Her throat was raspy and dry. Wetting her lips, Eleanor could only imagine how she appeared. Clothes unkempt with patches of dried mud, her shirt untucked, boots still on. Heaven knows what had become of her hat.

In the shocked silence came the sound of gas bubbling in the soda siphon her uncle held.

Her mother was by her side immediately, trying to lead her to the sofa, asking what had happened, where she'd fallen, if she were further injured. If Robbie was with her. Eleanor met her uncle's questioning gaze from over her mother's shoulder, pleading silently with her eyes. He placed the soda bottle on the sideboard.

Mrs Winslow inhaled deeply. 'Goodness gracious, let the girl speak, Georgia.' Tonight she smoked with a long black telescopic cigarette holder and when she spoke, fumes appeared from both her nose and mouth. 'My dear girl, have you had a tumble? That's a nasty scratch.'

Eleanor probed at the wound to her cheek, oblivious to how she'd received it.

'And where is that young brother of yours?' asked her mother. 'Somehow he managed to get out of his room. I sent Miss Hastings down to Mr Goward's cottage in search of him. Was he with you?'

'Here, take this.' Her uncle covered the short distance between them, pressing a glass of whisky into her palm. 'Stop bombarding her with questions, Georgia,' he chastised. 'Looks like you need to wash up, Eleanor.'

Georgia's lips drew together in a tight line. Eleanor took the drink gratefully, skolling the contents in one gulp. The room fell quiet.

'Is Robbie alright?' asked her mother.

Eleanor nodded.

'Why don't you lot continue on?' Colin suggested. 'I don't think Eleanor looks like she's up to an inquisition, especially with the likes of you polo-playing Winslows passing judgement on her riding skills,' he joked. 'Keith, I'll leave you to attend to the drinks. A gin fizz for your dear wife, a martini for Georgia and a western wobbler for me.'

'Of course, of course. If you're sure you are alright, Eleanor?' Mr Winslow enquired kindly.

Eleanor didn't have a chance to answer. Her uncle was escorting her from the room, closing the door quietly but firmly in her mother's face and leading them into the hallway. Colin placed a hand on an elbow, and Eleanor allowed herself to be steered the length of the long room to the opposite end.

'Is it Robbie?' asked Colin, his features tightening.

The whisky pooled in her stomach, warm and comforting, fortifying. 'He's fine, but –'

The relief showed immediately. 'Then what the hell is going on?' They reached the foot of the staircase. 'I've seen enough men in shock to recognise the symptoms.'

Eleanor took a deep breath. 'Robbie shot a man down near the river. A stranger. He's unconscious.' The words tumbled out. 'I tried to stop him.'

Colin turned a paler shade of his usual grey. He leant on the balustrade for support. 'He shot someone? I don't understand. How, why? What the hell happened and where is Robbie?'

Heavens, he looks so angry, Eleanor thought. 'Robbie was in a tree. He saw this person and yelled down to me and the next thing I heard was rifle fire. Robbie said the man aimed a gun at him.' The story sounded quite unbelievable, but her stepfather listened intently. 'So, afterwards, when we found him lying in the grass, I told Robbie to stay with him. That I'd get help. I didn't think the man should be left out there by himself.'

'Jesus Christ. He actually shot a man?' Colin ran a hand through thinning hair. 'Who is this man? Did you recognise him?'

'No.'

'Well, it's dark outside now.' He thought for a few seconds. 'Alright. As you know where Robbie is, Eleanor, you'll have to go back with the men to give directions.'

'But –'

Colin limped towards the passageway, his cane a steady tap. Once in the hall he headed towards the kitchen, where light outlined the closed door. 'I'll get Alice to run and fetch Rex. He can go out with you and Hugh,' he said, talking over his shoulder.

'But why do I have to go? I can tell Rex where Robbie is.' Eleanor knew she sounded like a coward, however, the last thing she wanted to do was go back out to where the stranger lay, shot, maybe dying, in the grass. And the dark, all that unfathomable space. She increased her pace, not wanting to have a disagreement with her uncle in front of Mrs Howell. 'Uncle Colin, I'll give Rex directions.'

'No, you won't.' He turned briefly towards her. 'It will be pitch black by the time you go the long way round and take the bridge road. And as Rex and Hugh weren't there and you were, you can help guide them to Robbie and this injured man. God, I can't understand you, Eleanor, how the hell did you let this happen?'

She stopped dead in the passageway.

Her stepfather continued on. 'I'll get Mrs Howell to make you up a thermos and some sandwiches.'

'I'm not hungry.'

At the kitchen door he finally turned to her. 'And you're sure Robbie is okay?'

'He's fine,' Eleanor answered sharply.

Colin gave a grunt of acknowledgement. 'Well, that's something at least.'

≼ Chapter Fourteen ≽

They drove home slowly. Too slowly. In an evening when the hot breath of the day was barely diminished by night. From within the safety of the vehicle's cabin, Eleanor kept looking down at the child asleep by her side. Even now it was impossible to comprehend what had happened, how it had occurred, but she'd been there. Pressing herself into the upholstery, bones aching, Eleanor doubted she'd sleep at all tonight, despite the exhaustion. For the last hour she'd kept reworking the afternoon, searching for any clue as to why Robbie had done the unthinkable, and how it had come to pass that she'd unwittingly been party to such a crime.

And the man himself. The innocent victim. Having finally located the stranger, Eleanor's memory of the exact moment that he'd been found was a mixture of torchlight, of the overseer and Rex efficiently checking the man's injuries, of grass patched red by blood and Rex's words: 'This is a messy business we've found ourselves in.'

Then there was Robbie, skulking in the dark, complaining of being left behind when he was only a kid, whinging about being hungry and tired and wanting to go home.

And still the stranger lay there, pale and unconscious.

'Bad night for it, with the moon on the wane and all,' Rex remarked, shifting down a gear to navigate the bumpy road.

He was right. It had taken some time to locate Robbie and the stranger. If not for the campfire her brother had lit, they might still be out there searching in the dark.

The gardener cleared his throat. 'A scant moon, this heat. No good can come of it, ever.'

Eleanor picked irritably at a piece of dried mud in her hair. 'What are you talking about, Rex?'

He cleared his throat and spat out of the open window. 'Nothing, just an old man rambling. Trying to make sense of things.'

'And can you . . .' asked Eleanor, feeling the weight of Robbie's head against her shoulder, 'make sense of things?'

'You were there, Miss Eleanor,' said Rex a little stiffly, 'you tell me.'

There it was again, the voice of accusation. Outside, the sky seemed heavy with stars. Eleanor fixed her gaze on the fading moon. Soon it would be a crescent shape before disappearing altogether. Behind them, Mr Goward was barely visible as he kept vigil by the stranger's side, intermittent torchlight reflecting through the rear window as he checked the patient. It would be a rough ride for both of them, despite the mattress.

Their route was reduced to the two narrow beams of light provided by the headlights of the blue truck. They illuminated the corded bark of trees, foraging rabbits and startled kangaroos who bounded across their path into an impenetrable black. The ground ahead seemed to unravel endlessly and, as Eleanor wearied of ever reaching the rutted track that merged with the bridge road, suddenly their passage smoothed to the jolt and jarring of potholes. Relieved, she leant back into the cracked leather of the bench seat.

'Summer shearing,' said Rex. 'My father used to call it a blood summer when he shore in those big stations up in Queensland. No storage for the meat back then, Miss Eleanor. You either wrapped it in a wet bag and hung it in a tree or used a Coolgardie safe. But it didn't keep long and the men got sick of it salted or brined, so near every second day they were slaughtering sheep to feed the men. Same as here. A blood summer. Winter and spring, that's the time to shear, but every cocky's got his idea about when's best, when lambing should start and, of course, these days a place often has to fit in with the labour.'

'We have fridges now, Rex.'

'If this heatwave keeps up the generator will probably cack itself, girl. Anyway, them old fridges in the shearers' mess with their dodgy batteries ain't real reliable, not when it gets real hot and we ain't got the cool storage for more than a few days. Slaughter and eat the meat fresh. It's the only way to be sure no-one gets crook. Be tough though. If meat doesn't hang for a couple of days it's always tough. They'll be whingers. There are always whingers when it comes to the tucker. Me dad used to hang a carcass for a good week or so. You want it ripe. The blowies buzzing. Cooks up a treat then. Cut it with a fork. Old mate in the back,' Rex gestured over his shoulder, 'he'll be right lucky if he doesn't have a few maggot eggs in that shoulder of his already.'

'Rex, that's disgusting.'

'Just nature, Miss Eleanor, just nature. The bloke was right lucky I reckon that he wasn't laying out there in the paddock when the sun was high. I've seen men dead of the sun. After a time their limbs shrink and stiffen. Saw a cobber I did one time, way out west, and his arms and legs were bent all out of shape and pointing towards the sky. Like one of them ancient mummies.'

'Rex, please.'

'I'm just saying, I'm just saying.' The gardener looked at Robbie. 'Sometimes, it's just in a person, this killing thing.'

'Rex,' Eleanor rebuked. The last thing her young brother needed was to hear remarks like that.

'Sorry, I just thought, well, it helps to talk about things.'

Maybe it did, but not now. Eleanor felt unnerved. In her world, night had never been a friend. Her night-time paranoia didn't lessen with the death of her father and later Lesley's fiancé. Both men had died in the dead of night. Her father through illness and Marcus, suicide. Try as she may, Eleanor could never quite shake the fear that the night had taken both men. Would it also take the stranger her half-brother shot? The boy's head rested on her shoulder. With every bump he gave an involuntary lurch forward in sleep. Robbie had fought for Garnet to be brought home. For his old horse to be tied to the back of the tray. There'd been no choice but to leave him grazing in the paddock. She pinched the bridge of her nose in tiredness. He'd been more concerned about Garnet than the injured man.

'Nearly there,' Rex said encouragingly, increasing their speed a little. A pinprick of light gradually grew in size. The blooming bougainvillea came into view and then the flowerless rose garden. Eleanor's eyes grew moist. The bark of a dog, the splash of the stone fountain, then the front porch lights welcomed them. As they crawled past the house with the headlights dimmed, the lone silhouette of a man appeared in the sitting-room window. Colin. Music drifted on the night air, soft and slow. Gravel crackled under the tyres as the truck drove the length of the homestead, rounded the corner, finally coming to a stop at the rear of the kitchen.

The back door opened almost instantly and Colin limped out to stand on the stone landing. Haloed by a bare light bulb wreathed in flying insects, he leant so heavily on the walking stick that one shoulder was angled much higher than the other. Her stepfather's neck-tie was undone and the look of barely suppressed anger distorting his gaunt features made Eleanor hesitate before opening the car door. Across the bench seat Rex glanced at Robbie sandwiched between them. Switching the gear shift into neutral and turning the engine off, he gave the boy a gentle shake to wake him, followed by an encouraging smile.

Robbie rubbed at his face and then, realising that they were home, drew back like a sea snail retreating inside its shell. He touched her arm. 'Eleanor?' The word sounded like a plea.

'Everything will be fine.' Her reply was brisk, automatic. Eleanor was tired, shaky and although it was still hot, she felt slightly cold. Was she in shock? 'Come on. Let's get out.'

'You found him?' Colin asked of no-one in particular.

'Yep,' answered Rex, slamming the truck's door shut. 'Robbie lit a campfire. Could have been out there driving around all night otherwise.'

'Just as well.' Father nodded to his son. 'You alright, Robbie?'

'Right as rain, Dad.' Robbie's bright answer was met with Colin's sobering stare. 'Dad –'

'Later, Robbie.'

No-one spoke as Rex lowered the tailgate. Mr Goward jumped from the rear of the vehicle. In the lamp light the overseer was tall, his frame solid. For the first time since setting off earlier that evening, Hugh Goward could see Eleanor, and she him, albeit in a shadowy light. They had squeezed into the truck's bench seat on the way to the paddock, discussing the shock of the after-noon as Rex drove, the gardener interrupting them occasionally to check directions. Now they acknowledged each other wordlessly, although Eleanor was aware of his fleeting appraisal. She found herself thinking of Rex's criticisms of the overseer yesterday when he'd driven her from the village. Had she passed inspection, or had Hugh Goward already decided that the younger of the Webber girls should be sold with the rest of the cull ewes? Eleanor had had very little to do with Hugh since his arrival on the property a few years ago. But she remembered his eyes. Green and blue. Anyone would.

The two men began to drag the stranger from the rear of the truck.

'Steady now,' the overseer cautioned.

'Righto.' Rex's response was gruff. 'I've carried my share of wounded men,' he said, referencing his wartime service. 'We'd be better off standing the fella up. We can't carry him proper-like with that shoulder wound.'

Mr Goward agreed. They stood the man upright, supporting him on either side, and then began to walk forward, the unknown man's legs dragging uselessly between them.

Eleanor stood back as the trio passed.

'How is he? Do either of you recognise him?' asked Colin.

The overseer and Rex replied that neither had ever laid eyes on the man before.

'Well, he's not from these parts then. Follow the hallway,' Colin directed, staring at the unconscious stranger as he made way for the men. 'Mrs Howell's prepared a room for him.'

'But surely he should be taken upstairs to one of the bedrooms,' Eleanor complained. 'Those rooms down here haven't been used for years. He'll be surrounded by boxes and dust and . . .'

Rex and the overseer continued holding the man between them, awaiting the outcome of the disagreement. The stranger's head slumped forward on his chest. 'Go on,' Colin told them. The men walked into the house, half carrying the stranger between them.

'But –'

'Stop arguing, Eleanor,' her uncle snapped. 'The sooner he's made comfortable the better, and if he's down here, Mrs Howell can keep an eye on him until we can get a doctor out, as well as the police. But at this hour we won't be seeing anyone until the morning.'

'The police?' said Robbie. 'But, Dad, I didn't mean to shoot him.'

Her uncle looked unconvinced and Eleanor knew why. She'd been angry after her hard ride back to the house to get help and her stepfather had questioned her briefly again while they waited for Rex and the overseer to collect her from the kitchen. Eleanor did nothing but tell the truth of what had happened by the river and the blame lay squarely with Robbie, although she was not without fault. Her mere presence apparently made her partially responsible.

'I want this kept quiet until the morning,' her uncle continued. 'I'll tell your mother after the guests have gone to bed.'

'She doesn't know yet?' Eleanor was stunned. 'That's ridiculous. Mum should be told immediately. I'll go now.'

Colin grabbed her arm as she tried to pass. The scent of alcohol and cigarette smoke was strong. 'What? You're going to barge into the sitting room while they're sipping their after-dinner crème de menthe and tell them that Robbie's just shot someone? I don't bloody well think so, Eleanor.' He loosened his grip.

Eleanor rubbed her arm.

He continued, 'As I said, I'll tell your mother tonight when our guests have gone to bed. Tomorrow morning is soon enough for the others. As it is, they'll all be here when the doctor and the police arrive.' Colin tapped the stick on the stone landing in frustration. 'You wouldn't think it possible that the Winslows could be here with this mess going on. We'll be the gossip of every bush family, every villager, every –' He broke off and stared at Robbie. 'Go to bed, son.'

'But, Dad?'

'Go to bed,' he responded more firmly. 'We'll talk about this in the morning.'

Robbie scuffed at the ground with his boots and reluctantly walked inside, passing Rex and Mr Goward as they reappeared. The overseer ruffled the boy's hair, but Rex's expression was blank.

'Well?' Colin asked the two men roughly.

'The bullet's still in his shoulder. Damn lucky it was only a .22 that the boy got him with, otherwise . . .' Hugh Goward's words trailed as he met Eleanor's eyes.

'Nasty head wound, though,' Rex cut in. 'It looks like he hit the back of it on something when he fell from his horse. A lump of timber I'd reckon. Anyway, he's out cold. Mrs Howell's with him now.'

'Good.' Her uncle seemed satisfied with this news. 'She'll make him comfortable until the doctor can get here. And we really have no idea who he is?'

Rex wiped his hands clean of blood, staining the beige cloth of his trousers. 'Nothing on him, Boss. And I definitely don't recognise him.'

'Robbie found this.' Eleanor held out the roll of notes.

'Nothing else? No wallet?' Colin flicked briefly through the money. 'What about his horse?'

'The saddlebags were empty except for a bit of tea, sugar and flour,' Mr Goward replied. 'We left both horses tied up down by the river.'

Colin swatted aside a buzzing insect. 'I expect the police will want to speak to the both of you as well, and you'll probably have to show them where the accident occurred.'

'And the muster?' the overseer reminded them. 'We were to leave at daybreak.'

'God, that's right. The muster goes ahead as planned,' Colin advised. 'We'll have near thirty men on this place by sundown tomorrow and I'll not have that lot cooling their heels for a day if we're delayed. We'd never hear the end of it.' He turned to Eleanor. 'You're the main witness anyway.'

It sounded like an accusation and in a way it was. Robbie was a child, she the adult.

'I can delay going into the village for the mess supplies,' Rex offered, 'and I can get the two horses later, hitch them to the rear of the truck.'

Colin nodded. 'Good man. Well, that's all we can do tonight. Time we all got to bed.' Rex said goodbye, got into the truck and drove away, the red tail lights marking his progress into the dark. 'You better come inside, Eleanor,' her uncle ordered, walking indoors.

'If there's nothing else I can do?' Mr Goward enquired courteously of Eleanor.

'No, nothing, thank you.' Eleanor listened to the crunch of gravel as Mr Goward left. On previous trips home, the man her mother depended on had kept his distance, observing the on-property hierarchy and remaining respectful of family members. She wondered if, after today's events, that might now change.

✖ Chapter Fifteen ✖

The earlier mess of the kitchen and the aftermath of another dinner party was gone. In its place were clean bench tops and washed plates and platters drying in a rack on the sink. A few moths fluttered about the ceiling light. Mrs Howell's favoured cleaning products, baking soda, vinegar and ammonia, were left on the sink and the lemony scent of her homemade spray pervaded the hot, stuffy room. Colin poured Eleanor a good shot of whisky. She drank it down on his orders before sitting at the table.

'Is there anything else I should know?' Colin screwed the lid on a bottle of disinfectant that had been left on the kitchen table beside the first-aid kit.

Eleanor thought back through the afternoon's events. Now she was home, the whole thing seemed like a bad dream.

Her stepfather joined her at the table, sitting the crystal decanter of whisky between them. 'More?'

'Yes, thanks.' Eleanor had never been a whisky drinker. The odd sherry and glass of wine were the extent of her beverage consumption but the burning sensation in her throat and stomach was helping to ease her anxiety. He poured them both another measure and took a sip.

'I don't know what he was thinking,' her stepfather yawned. 'What was he thinking?'

It wasn't really a question, however, Eleanor was quick to respond. 'The moment I arrived home yesterday, Robbie told me he was bored and he must be for his imagination to have run riot the way it has.'

Her uncle looked at her with the same querying, heavy-lidded eyes that belonged to her father. 'What are you talking about? How can he be bored? He has the run of the place, thousands of acres, as well as a top-class governess. It's not like he's on some hobby farm with a chicken coop and a vegetable patch.'

Electing not to state the obvious, that Robbie was probably lonely, Eleanor moved the tumbler of whisky in small circles across the tabletop. 'He's got tinned food hidden in a tree down by the river. He's expecting communists to invade from the north.'

Colin, his glass midway between the table and his mouth, frowned. 'What?'

If the situation hadn't been so serious she expected that they both would have burst into laughter. 'Exactly,' Eleanor confirmed. 'Robbie thought that poor fellow was a communist.'

'A communist? What? Sorry, I'm repeating myself, I know.'

'You're also slurring your words,' replied Eleanor disapprovingly. Her father would never have allowed himself to get in such a state. In response to her reproach, the man opposite poured another measure of whisky and then made a show of replacing the stopper in the decanter. They sat uncomfortably, only the hum of the fridge and the tick of the kitchen clock disturbing the silence.

'You've never liked me, Eleanor, I know that.'

He was testing her, maybe even hoping for an argument. Eleanor vaguely recalled her father behaving in a similar fashion. Time provided perspective and it seemed obvious to her now that the Webber men were cursed with the need to let off steam, usually at the expense of a family member. Georgia once said that it was the only fault her first husband had. Colin, Eleanor decided, had far more. 'It's lucky the police aren't on their way. It wouldn't look very good for a respected member of the Country Party to be caught sozzled,' she replied.

'Did you assume your mother would stay widowed for the rest of her life?'

How on earth could he dare ask that question and expect a civil answer? Words filled her mind. And he should hear them, Eleanor thought. This upstart accountant nobody who took advantage of her grieving mother and whose only claim to fame came from being blood-related to a decorated war hero. Her father. As if Colin could read her thoughts, they eye-balled each other across the kitchen table, her mouth turning dry, he tapping the base of the empty glass on the timber.

Under the harsh kitchen light it was clear that her uncle was quite drunk, however, he straightened his shoulders and offered her a cigarette. A truce. Eleanor accepted, leaning forward as the lighter flared, inhaling deeply. It was just as well, she thought, that the police and the doctor weren't due until the morning. What a pretty sight they would make, huddled across the table, drinking and smoking. Two adversaries caught beneath the same roof.

'First and foremost we are family.' Her stepfather took a number of puffs, exhaling a line of thin smoke, and dropped the glowing cigarette into the dregs at the bottom of the whisky glass. The embers briefly sizzled and died.

Retrieving an ashtray from a cupboard, Eleanor placed it pointedly on the table. 'How is it possible for Robbie to have got such an idea into his head? This communism thing?' she finally asked when the silence became more than awkward. Eleanor couldn't remember if the two of them had ever been alone like this.

'The news. The wireless. Who knows?' Colin replied, placing the glass on the sink.

'But –'

'In the morning things will be clearer,' he announced. 'Come, we better check on Mrs Howell.'

Eleanor stubbed out the cigarette and together they walked the length of the passageway. A dim light shone from under one of the doors and they entered the room. The smell of antiseptic was strong. The housekeeper was wringing out a cloth in a basin. Folding the material, she rested it gently on the patient's brow before turning to them.

'I've washed the wound as best I could, Mr Webber, but there's nothing much else that can be done for him. At least with my limited experience.'

'I do appreciate you tending to him, Mrs Howell.' All three of them scrutinised the man lying unconscious before them.

'I'm sure it's the lump on the back of his head that keeps him out cold. He must have hit something very hard when he fell.' Lifting the bedcovers, she patted them around the man carefully. 'There's no temperature, but Mr Goward and I agree that the bullet's still in his shoulder. Is it true that it was young Robbie that shot the poor man?'

'A terrible accident, I assure you, Mrs Howell,' Colin answered.

The woman tutted under her breath. 'And no-one knows who he is?'

'Not as yet, but the police and the doctor will be here first thing. I'm going up now to tell Mrs Webber.'

The housekeeper nodded. 'Of course.'

Eleanor and the older woman waited until the door clicked closed and they were alone.

'Why hasn't he told your mother yet?' Mrs Howell whispered agitatedly. 'Rex said that Robbie shot him on purpose. And that' – she looked over her shoulder at the unconscious man – 'that he's a communist. A communist in this very house.' She crossed herself.

'I'm sure it's just Robbie's imagination. We don't know who he is, Mrs Howell.' Eleanor did her best to calm the woman. 'I mean, does he look like a communist to you?'

Mrs Howell lifted her chin and sniffed. 'Well, I don't know what one looks like, do I?'

'It's more likely he's just some poor stockman,' Eleanor told her. 'That's what he looks like to me.'

Both women peered at the man.

'Either way,' the housekeeper considered, 'Robbie could be in a lot of trouble. It's just as well your mother is who she is. She'll make sure young Robbie's protected.'

Eleanor walked closer to the narrow bed. The man appeared to be sleeping peacefully. Dark-haired and brown of skin, a slight stubble covered his face.

'He can't be more than forty years of age,' Mrs Howell decided.

'We should let him rest.' All Eleanor wanted was to fall into bed.

Outside the room the housekeeper produced an ancient brass ring and, selecting a key, locked the door. She met Eleanor's disbelieving stare with pursed lips. 'It's fine for the likes of everyone else. You'll be upstairs, but I have to sleep down the hall from him.'

Although Eleanor doubted the likelihood of the stranger having the strength to get out of bed, let alone attack anyone in the middle of the night, she could understand the housekeeper's concern. 'Until we know who he is and where he's from, it's probably a very good idea.'

'You always were the one with the most common sense around here.' Mrs Howell patted her arm. 'I've saved you some dinner. You must be famished. And don't say no. You'll come to the kitchen and eat something before bed and that's an order.'

Eleanor was beyond arguing. She followed Mrs Howell the length of the long passageway, collapsing in a kitchen chair. Colin's packet of cigarettes remained on the table along with the lighter and she lit one immediately, ignoring the older woman's protestations.

'Just because every movie star has one of those things dangling from their lips, doesn't mean it's attractive,' Mrs Howell scolded.

Eleanor thought of the beaten crows, the slaughter of animals to feed the shearers and the wounded man. At the moment, out here in the middle of nowhere, smoking was the least of her concerns.

Sunday

The Day After

❧ Chapter Sixteen ❧

Margaret Winslow dabbed a napkin to her lips. She wore a floral day-dress and her make-up accentuated large eyes, drawing attention away from her more equine features. 'It must be a wonderful view, looking out at that rose garden during spring. Although it's brave of you to have made a feature of them right where one drives in, Georgia. They're not the prettiest of bushes for most of the year. Still, I do admire your gardener's skills. I'm inclined to make him an offer he can't refuse.'

'You couldn't budge Rex with a forked stick, Margaret,' Colin replied, crossing his legs and leaning back in the wicker chair. 'The man's part of the furniture.'

'And I'm sure he wouldn't be worth his salt without you directing him, Georgia,' said Margaret approvingly. 'I must say, no-one in your family does anything by halves, do they, Colin?'

They were sitting on the front porch finishing an early lunch hastily prepared by Mrs Howell. Margaret Winslow lit a cigarette, inhaled deeply and blew out a smoke ring. Everyone at the table watched the circle as it gradually disintegrated.

Eleanor fiddled with the linen napkin on her lap. Georgia, red around her nostrils and eyes, had done her best to put the events of the morning and previous night aside, at least while they ate, and Mrs Winslow assisted. She was chatty and engaging during the luncheon. She could never, Eleanor decided, be accused of not being full of conversation. She'd overheard Mr Winslow comment to Uncle Colin that Margaret was adept at running diversions, a tactic that had come to the fore over the last hour. The cream of tomato soup and mutton sandwiches, however, were now devoured. And still the doctor had not completed his examination of the injured stranger.

At the end of the table, Georgia sat stiffly in a peacock chair. The high-backed flattened spindles fanning out above her shoulders evoked a bird's tail plumage. Her mother appeared older and there was an emptiness to her usually mobile face. She'd spent the lunch hour dabbing at the perspiration on her face and neck, oblivious to the thick beads of moisture that rolled down her cleavage, almost drowning Jesus on his silver cross.

It was the first time in many years that church was foregone. For as long as Eleanor could remember, mass came first in their household and the services formed the centrepiece of her childhood memories. The white gloves and matching straw hats. The smell of incense, of clothes sticking to wooden pews in the summer and a cold draught in winter, of Lesley pinching her or pulling a plait as their mother took her usual place, reading from the Old Testament. Afterwards there'd been scones with jam and cream, sweet cakes and tea. That was the best part.

'Well, I mean to say,' Mrs Winslow drew long and hard on the cigarette, and took a sip of her gin fizz, 'there's never a dull moment at River Run. That's the worst of marrying into the establishment,' she directed this observation to her husband, 'our boys are positively boring, aren't they, Keith? Although I thank heavens for my youngest, Henry. He's always at the centre of everything and knows exactly what's going on. Doesn't he, Eleanor?' she said pointedly, pausing for effect. 'Heavens, it's hot. I know you warned me, Keith, but I could melt at the moment.'

Mrs Winslow's husband turned the wicker chair slightly away from his wife, subtly engaging Eleanor's mother in conversation. The man had the uncanny ability of acting as if Margaret wasn't present, while simultaneously smoothing the critical innuendos that his wife couldn't help but drop as she prattled on. If Eleanor could have ignored Mrs Winslow without appearing obvious, she would have. There was little chance of doing so, however, having been seated opposite the woman. Instead she gave a forced smile, replying that Henry was the life of every party in Sydney.

'They tell me that the Artists and Models Ball at the Trocadero in George Street was fabulous last year,' Mrs Winslow began. 'My Henry tells me you were a most fetching Cleopatra.'

Eleanor glanced awkwardly to the far end of the table. The expression on her mother's face grew more strained. 'Well, I –'

'Hair piled atop, oodles of bare skin,' Mrs Winslow gave a theatrical pause, 'and a gold beaded, hip-hugging girdle of a belt.'

'You didn't really attend that event, did you, Eleanor? Why, those balls are infamous.' Georgia leant forward, her nostrils widening and narrowing with each breath. 'They're a magnet for bohemians.'

Margaret let out a snort of derision. 'For heaven's sake, Georgia, it's just a party. You were young once too you know.'

'Freethinkers and crossdressers.' Georgia glowered at her guest, before her features rearranged themselves more pleasantly. 'Not the type of people I want my daughter mixing with. She should be finding a suitable man and settling down. Elly is already on the older side of marriageable age.'

The lemonade Eleanor sipped caught in her throat. 'Mum, for heaven's sake, I'm only twenty-six.'

'You should be settled by now, with a child and husband to care for and a house to run.'

'Domestic bliss,' Eleanor muttered.

Margaret gave a chuckle, twirling her glass so that the ice crackled within. 'Ah yes, our Prime Minister would wholeheartedly agree with you, Georgia. Isn't that his line at the moment, that hearth and home are the bedrock of a stable society?'

'Menzies is adept at placing himself above politics and policies at times,' Colin agreed.

Eleanor was grateful when the conversation changed. It had been a difficult morning and everyone was on edge. The police had interviewed all those concerned regarding the shooting and then visited and photographed the wounded man.

'One of the many things to come out of that terrible war,' said Margaret, 'apart from Menzies, indeed most western countries, urging their womenfolk to move out of the workplace and to become homemakers again, is the end of austerity. The return to feminine, flowery fashion.'

'Dior.' Eleanor nodded, having studied their guest's simple Sunday house-dress. She knew that like Mrs Winslow's luggage, all her clothes were quite simply top-drawer.

Georgia poured another glass of homemade lemonade, added a splash of gin from the decanter and took a sip. 'What time are you leaving, Keith?'

'Well, we're not, are we, Keith?' Margaret answered on his behalf. 'I mean, firstly, we couldn't leave you with all this . . .' she waved her hands around, coloured rings sparkling, as if searching for the right word, 'drama.' She said the word slowly and with some relish. 'And besides, if we stay then Keith and Colin can work out the details of the rams that River Run is purchasing.'

Keith patted his coat pockets. 'I have photographs.'

'We are always more than happy with the selection your Stud Master makes on our behalf, you know that, Keith,' said Georgia.

'Mum?' Eleanor quickly interrupted. 'I think that should be left to another time, don't you?'

'Heavens, Colin,' Margaret tittered, 'you do have it all in front of you. Keith would just murder me, wouldn't you, darling, if I tried to run his life, let alone interfere with his business transactions.'

'Of course you must stay,' said Georgia graciously, although her invitation was directed to Mr Winslow. 'But one night. If that suits you, Keith.'

'Probably easier what with shearing commencing,' Colin finally spoke. 'And we're looking at our bloodline, considering making some changes. I was going to bring it up last night, however, the evening just flew. Too many western wobblers I'm afraid, among other things.'

'Well, as long as we're not putting you out, Georgia,' Keith responded, his expression softening. 'I'd rather like to have the car checked at that garage I saw in the village first thing in the morning. It's got a bit of an oil leak and I wouldn't like to get caught somewhere on the road, halfway home.'

'You and that Studebaker,' Margaret interrupted. 'Obsessed with the Yank-mobile he is. We even have two Studebaker trucks for the stud. Forget the war quotas, when it comes to imports, Keith must have his Studebakers, and when I think of those sleek sporty Jaguars. God, if I can't see myself behind the steering wheel in one of my Dior dresses.'

Thankfully, Eleanor thought, the as-new cream vehicle was locked away in the timber garage, safe from both Robbie and the interest of the younger jackeroos.

'Put a man near a new automobile and it's like a child with ice-cream,' Keith agreed with a grin.

'I'll call the mechanic and let him know that you're coming.'

'I'd appreciate that, Colin, but I have to say that you've piqued my interest with regards to River Run's bloodline. I suppose we can have our chat this afternoon when you and Georgia are free.' Keith's voice was flat.

'I'm sure the ladies can amuse themselves while we talk shop.' Colin caught his wife staring at him.

'Our overseer, Goward, has some excellent ideas,' Georgia poured more lemonade, 'with regards to improving frame size and wool quality. He's certainly done his homework and on that basis I've decided to make some changes, but Colin can fill you in on the details later, Keith. For now, though, I want you to know that our stud's relationship will of course continue with Ambrose Park.'

'But in a more limited form?' asked Keith.

'Yes,' replied Georgia, 'I'm afraid we won't be purchasing our usual quantity from Ambrose this year.'

Colin thrust his chair back from the table and crossed his legs. 'Well, there's not much left for you and me to discuss, Keith.'

'So you're still firmly in charge, Georgia?' Margaret's voice, having lost its earlier playfulness, grew serious. 'Of course the industry talk points to you at the helm, although I did wonder if it was just gossip. I would have thought that considering the length of time that you two have been married –'

'That what? I would take a back seat?' Georgia gave a little smile. 'Alan and I were partners. It's the same with Colin.' She glanced at her husband. 'And he quite understands the way things work here at River Run. Besides which, he has made invaluable contributions to the stud,' she said magnanimously. 'No-one can deny that.'

'And it is your property.' Margaret said what everyone thought. 'You acre-chaser, you, Colin,' she teased. The table went quiet.

Eleanor decided that being blunt did have some benefits.

'So here we all are.' Margaret raised a glass, toasting the table. 'We should be celebrating. Wool's fetching a pound a pound.' She took a mouthful and swallowed. 'All that money. Isn't it marvellous?'

Keith lifted his glass. 'And you've always been so good at spending it.'

Margaret gave a satisfied smile. 'New cars, new tractors, fertiliser, holidays and David Jones department store. It makes a girl all tingly with anticipation. So what's on your wish list, Georgia? Car? House? A trip abroad?'

'A plane,' she replied. 'Planes are the future out here. Just imagine how the workload would be cut if you could check paddocks by air?'

'Aerial mustering,' Keith added. 'I spoke to a chap in Sydney about the possibility last year.'

'How marvellous,' Georgia enthused. 'You see, Colin, I said the idea had merit and Keith agrees.'

Colin lit a cigarette. 'Here's to Keith.'

'So, at the risk of raising the elephant in the room,' said Keith slowly, 'what will you do with that young boy of yours, Colin? He's obviously a handful.'

'Not usually,' replied Colin smoothly. 'The police will confirm that the shooting was an accident. I mean, what else can they do? Robbie's not yet twelve.'

'Quite officious, our law enforcers.' Mr Winslow lit a cigarette, took a couple of quick puffs and then tossed it over his shoulder onto the gravel drive.

'What can you expect?' replied Colin. 'You can't tell me that they wouldn't be quietly rubbing their hands together if there was a scandal associated with River Run. The economy is riding high thanks to the wool boom. Why, at the last Sinclair stud sale in the Riverina, politicians and dignitaries from Sydney made up three carloads. There are some out there who'd love to cut one of us down a peg or two.'

'The common people,' declared Georgia, 'understand that there will always be others more successful and wealthier than them. It's the assumption that one considers yourself to be better than another that riles them.'

Colin made a fuss of clearing his throat. 'As you can see, they'd love to see us as front page news.'

Georgia's brow knitted.

'How extraordinary.' Margaret was studying her hosts with renewed interest. 'Usually it's those of us who marry up, myself included, who put the dog on, so to speak.'

Eleanor wondered if anyone would notice if she slipped from the chair, under the table and then crawled away. Georgia's mouth compressed together so tightly her lips almost disappeared.

'Well, I suppose we should all be prepared.' Mr Winslow tapped his fingers slowly on the arm of the chair.

'It is quite a story.' A little of Margaret's gaiety dissipated. 'I hadn't really given much thought to the repercussions, but you're right, of course, Colin. Two well-known rural families, a shooting and the scent of communism in the air.'

'I am sorry,' Georgia said to the table.

'None of us are responsible for what's happened,' Colin placated. 'It's simply a case of a young boy letting his imagination get the better of him.'

'Of course.' Mr Winslow lit another cigarette, studying the glowing tip thoughtfully. Although a large, ungainly man, his warm brown eyes and quiet voice held much appeal.

The question of Robbie's behaviour, of why he'd done what he'd done, was yet to be broached, and yet there was little doubt in Eleanor's mind that her mother and stepfather would have been pondering that very thing into the wee hours and most of the morning. They all hoped for the incident to be put behind them quickly and cleanly. Although everyone involved had been primed by Colin to speak the truth as he saw it, that the incident was a shocking accident, the morning's questioning had turned trouble-some when Robbie admitted to the police that he'd thought the stranger was a communist.

'So you meant to shoot him?' the officer asked.

Robbie replied that he'd only intended to warn the man off their land.

Mrs Winslow flicked the silver lighter repeatedly. 'I blame Menzies for this communism rubbish.' She took a puff of a cig-arette. 'I know that you'll all howl me down, but you can't run Australia as a police state. I mean, really, imagine trying to declare

130

the Communist Party unlawful. When the referendum is held this year Menzies' legislation will fail.'

Colin was of the same opinion. 'I'm a great admirer of Menzies, the coalition with the Country Party remains strong and he has our interests at heart. I do tend to agree with you, though, Margaret. Our Prime Minister has done a poor job of explaining how denying the civil liberties of otherwise law-abiding citizens will protect our basic freedom.'

'He's kowtowing to the bloody Yanks and following their lead, if you ask me,' Keith replied, adding a generous dash of gin to the tonic water in his glass. Georgia passed the ice-bucket and he dropped melting, lemon-flavoured cubes into the drink. 'I know we had no choice other than to send troops to Korea thanks to the United Nations and their one-in-all-in resolution, but the word from cabinet is that Menzies' commitment of Australian troops was to secure a strong relationship with the United States.'

'Well, he's done that.' Georgia began stacking plates at the table. 'The security treaty's signed.'

'In our case, although I bemoan our boys being sent off to yet another war, we can thank Russia and North Korea for helping to send the wool price soaring,' Margaret concluded, grinding her cigarette out in a pretty china ashtray. 'Here's to the River Run clip.'

Everyone raised their glasses, except Eleanor. She felt like a warmonger enjoying the spoils when their growing finances came from market expectation of the increasing need for uniforms.

As the pitfalls of communism continued to be dissected, Mrs Howell arrived, escorting the doctor.

'Mr Webber?' Dr Headley was a tall man with apple cheeks, a jutting chin and a sprinkling of crumbs on his suit-front, evidence that Mrs Howell had ensured he was fed before he embarked on his return journey.

'Yes, Doctor, please do sit down.'

'I won't, thank you,' the doctor responded, his gaze lingering on the bottle of gin sitting on the table. 'I have an expectant mother who may yet need my assistance tonight.'

'So how is the patient?' Georgia enquired, as the housekeeper noisily stacked plates and bowls on a large wooden tray.

'I've removed the bullet. The wound should heal nicely, but I'm afraid he's still unconscious. The constable informed me that you're willing to lodge the man here in the short term.'

'Yes,' Colin answered, the hesitancy obvious in his voice. 'For a very short time, Doctor. Our home is hardly the place for injured strangers of dubious background.'

The doctor scratched his nose. Dried blood rimmed a finger-nail. 'Be that as it may, here he will have to stay.'

'For a few days only, Dr Headley.'

Eleanor was pleased her mother was speaking up. The sooner the stranger was gone, the better.

Georgia continued, 'The door to his room can be locked and –'

'I doubt the need for that, Mrs Webber,' the doctor interrupted. 'The knock to the patient's head has occurred on the same spot to which he sustained a previous injury. A severe gunshot wound, by the looks of it.'

'He's seen service?' Keith asked.

'It's highly likely. He's unconscious but his vital signs are stable and apart from the shoulder wound, there appears to be no other ailments. I couldn't countenance him being moved, at least not until he wakes up, and even then I would be hesitant lest we do more damage transporting him to the hospital. Head injuries can be very tricky things and it's over one hundred and fifty miles to the nearest hospital on roads that, as we all know, leave much to be desired.'

'And how long before he wakes up?'

'Mrs Webber, I have no idea. Such a question is rather like asking me how much twine can be found on a ball of string.'

'But surely we can't be expected to keep him here indefinitely,'

Georgia protested. 'My son may have accidentally injured this man, however, I see no reason why we should be further penalised by having to be nursemaids to a complete stranger. A stranger who may very well be a –'

'A communist,' Mrs Winslow announced. 'Or worse.'

Keith sighed. 'There would be a time-limit to his stay, wouldn't there, Doctor? I mean if there is no immediate improvement then one would have to assume that he'd be better off in a hospital or hospice where he can be properly cared for.'

'That's correct.' The doctor paused. 'But in the meantime, and considering the gravity of the situation, Mr Webber, I took it upon myself after consultation with the police to telephone Miss Athena Pappas. I'm sure you've heard of her. A very accomplished nurse, served in Italy and only recently arrived.'

'Stavros's daughter,' Colin explained to the table. 'Her father owns the general store in the village, a good man.'

'She will have to stay here, of course.' When no-one queried this, the doctor went on, 'She'll move in this afternoon to care for the patient. I do realise this is an imposition, but his needs must come first, regardless of the difficulties. I'll return in a few days to check on him.'

When the doctor had driven away, Georgie turned to her husband. 'I'm not having that woman in my home.'

'Who is she?' Margaret asked with interest.

'She is unmarried, with an illegitimate child. I have no issue with her family, Stavros is a well-meaning, hard-working immigrant and he's a boon to our district, but I'll not have a wanton woman under my roof.'

'Georgia, it is not up to us to pass judgement on the girl,' her husband replied sternly. 'Besides, the child was born in her home country. Who is to say that the father wasn't killed in the war?'

'And, and, and?' Spittle formed in the corners of Georgia's mouth. 'The church is most clear on these things. Besides which, there has never been mention of a husband, dead or alive. It is morally wrong.'

Margaret fiddled with a packet of cigarettes. 'So is abortion, which rather leaves the girl in quite an unenviable situation. You are aware, Georgia, that religious dogma has caused most of the turmoil in the world?'

Georgia began drumming the arms of the peacock chair with her fingers. 'We are not as accommodating in our beliefs as you Press-buttons are.'

'Actually,' Margaret's face was serene, 'I'm an atheist, and a bloody good one. Cheers.' She raised a glass.

'Come on, girls,' Keith Winslow pleaded.

'Europe. The war,' Margaret mused, staring out across the wilting rose bushes where birds perched limply in the fountain, wings outstretched. 'I feel sorry for this Athena Pappas. No doubt it was a tremendous love affair set against a backdrop of pain and suffering. To adore someone and be forever apart . . .'

'Fine. She can come,' Georgia snapped, 'but only until we get someone else who can take her place.'

'Is there anyone else out here capable?' asked Keith.

'Not here, but I know where I can find someone. I'll not have my house overrun with undesirables. If you'll excuse me,' Georgia got up from the table, 'I have to make a telephone call.'

'If you're calling who I think you are, Georgia,' Colin cautioned, 'please give thought to the fact that this may not be the best time.'

'Rubbish.' Georgia strode away, the full skirt she wore swirling as she moved. This time Margaret Winslow refrained from making an aside. Instead, she turned her attention to Eleanor, arching one eyebrow enquiringly.

Keith was suggesting that they contact the Grazier's Co-operative Shearing Company. He argued that their injured guest could well have worked in one of the Grazier's run of sheds and that if they were given a description of the man, they could spread the word.

'It would be easier if we knew his name,' stated Colin. 'I can't understand how a man can be riding out in the bush without any identification whatsoever.'

'Well, he wouldn't be bothered about that if he were working nearby.' Keith took a sip of his drink. 'He could have been out and about searching for stragglers.'

'Damn long way to be chasing stray stock to end up on River Run. But I'll give the neighbours a call.' A slight breeze carried the sound of barking dogs. Colin got to his feet. 'The first mob of sheep are coming in. We might ride out if you're up to it, Keith, and help walk them into the yards. I could use the exercise.'

Keith was quick to agree. 'You and Georgia should have a hit of tennis later on, Margaret,' he suggested as everyone rose, except for his wife.

Margaret lit yet another cigarette. 'In this heat? But I'm forgetting, mad dogs and Englishmen, eh, my darling?' Her husband didn't answer. 'I already feel like I've spent the morning at the sauna. No, I think I'll retire to a dark room with a wet towel on my forehead. There's far too much activity going on here for anyone's good.'

⚒ Chapter Seventeen ⚒

Mrs Howell cornered Eleanor at the bottom of the staircase, a plate in hand. The dish contained biscuits with marshmallow and jam, melted under the grill and sprinkled with coconut. It was a treat Eleanor remembered fondly and one clearly destined for her half-brother. The housekeeper swapped the plate from one hand to the other, immediately expressing concern over dinner now that the Winslows were staying another night. The menu was of prime importance and she wondered if something else should be served other than the usual Sunday roast. The older woman started reeling off a list of possibilities that included lettuce hearts with thousand-island dressing, grilled sirloin and apple crumble for dessert.

'I'd discuss it with your mother, however, she went straight to the station office and shut the door. She's been on the telephone ever since.'

Eleanor wondered if the recipient of that call was the preferred carer for the injured man. 'It's Sunday, Mrs Howell, and considering everything that's going on, let's just have one of your tasty roast dinners.'

'I'm sure you're right, Eleanor,' Mrs Howell replied, crumpling the apron she wore between the fingers of her free hand. 'You know it's a terrible business this thing with Robbie and now having to put up with another total stranger. It's not that I have anything against Mr Pappas's daughter, not at all. In fact I believe she is quite capable. But with everything else going on . . .' The older woman's words hung. 'And this heat. If only Inigo Jones was still forecasting. A person would know what to expect. Oh, I had my doubts initially with all his talk about sunspots affecting the weather, and I wondered about him when he couldn't promise day-to-day predictions, but it was a comfort to know what to expect, long term.'

Eleanor couldn't recall having ever seen the housekeeper so ruffled.

'I've some frozen liver so I could braise that and add the juices to the gravy,' she continued. 'Well, I'm just chattering now. You don't need the details, do you, my dear? No, of course you don't. It was that policeman. Put me on edge he did.' Mrs Howell smoothed the grey helmet of hair that was gathered so tightly at the rear that the skin around her forehead puckered. 'Well, I've never been questioned by the law before and it was quite, quite upsetting. And the constable asked me about Robbie. What mischief the lad gets up to, that sort of thing. Then he questioned me about the Communist Party and whether your stepfather was actively against them, him being a Country Party man and a known supporter of Menzies.' Lowering her voice she concluded, 'He called Mr Webber a capitalist. I don't think he likes this family very much. Of course I said nothing, either way.'

Eleanor didn't respond immediately. Was the constable an aberration within the law enforcement profession to hold such a view, or had she been blind to a disgruntled populace, to the class division within the bush, simply through her own naivety? 'I wouldn't worry, really, Mrs Howell,' Eleanor replied calmly. 'They have to ask all sorts of things, right or wrong. It's their job.'

Her composure certainly didn't reflect her own thoughts. She too was worried about the line of questioning. Eleanor was no legal expert but clearly the police were searching for intent.

'I know, I know.' The older woman absently ate one of the biscuits. 'In the meantime there will be another mouth to feed and I'm supposed to sit with him,' she gestured to the rear of the house, 'until Athena arrives later this afternoon. He's still unconscious.' The housekeeper's voice was hopeful. 'It's just a matter of keeping an eye on him. Your mother was quite emphatic about that.'

Eleanor found herself reluctantly agreeing to take on the task. 'I'll go and sit with the patient for an hour or so while you get the kitchen under control.'

'Bless you, you're a good child. Now I must get this up to Robbie. You know he got the strap this morning.' The housekeeper hurried up the stairs.

Eleanor intended to check on Robbie herself. As far as she knew he'd been locked in his room since last night, but apart from the formidable Spanish Inquisition line of questioning he'd been subjected to from everyone, Eleanor never dreamt he'd be flogged as well. But such things didn't dampen his appetite, he'd already devoured scrambled eggs and toast, a luncheon tray of sandwiches and soup and was now to be treated to a snack, while Eleanor could barely pick at her own meals. The solid clack of the housekeeper's sturdy lace-ups echoed in the hallway above. Perhaps it was best she stay away from Robbie, at least for a day or so. Eleanor's feelings towards him were mixed, a confusion that stemmed from her inability to reconcile the boy she knew and loved with yesterday's actions. What child did what Robbie had done? But then, what child was happy to bash frightened birds to death with a stick?

In the passageway Eleanor stopped at the sickroom. The key hung on a nail nearby. She wondered briefly what Jillian and Henrietta were up to. No doubt reading the Sunday papers and enthusiastically discussing any young man who may have caught their eye. How she wished she were with them. Unlocking the door, she stepped across the threshold. The room was dark and stuffy with heat. A smell of stale air and dust combined with the scent of disinfectant. It took time to adjust to the lack of light but gradually Eleanor was able to decipher the shadowy outlines within the room. A dim square of light marked the curtained window while a narrow closet and washstand stood against the opposite wall, items of furniture that had been used in the 1880s. The bed was positioned against the wall and the shape of a person was recognisable. She hesitated briefly before flicking on the overhead light. The bulb popped noisily, throwing the cramped area into darkness again. Eleanor opened the curtains and lifted the window. Two wide pieces of timber had been attached to the outside of the window, effectively barring escape. These were recent additions. Very recent. It seemed no-one was taking any chances with their guest. She turned to look at the man as light and fresh air circulated through the flyscreen. He didn't stir.

A standard lamp had been positioned next to the patient and a drip hung from it, plastic tubing winding down to a brown arm. A clean bandage dressed the shoulder wound, another bound his head. Clearly the doctor was not exaggerating when he'd advised that it was best not to move him.

Sunlight angled in through the window, highlighting the fine stubble on the man's face. Eleanor sat next to the bed, studying him carefully. The long dark lashes, longish brown hair. The width of his bare chest, emphasised by the pull of taut white sheets. The man looked so different to the bloodied stranger she'd ridden towards yesterday. He appeared younger, harmless, innocent, certainly not some dangerous radical. Memories of Dante came to her, his tapering fingers and olive skin, and she found herself comparing him to the man before her. The stranger's muscular arms were dark from the elbows down and a brown V marked the bite

139

of the sun on his neck. His hands were large and capable and his nails slightly dirty. This man lived his life outdoors.

'Who are you?' she wondered aloud. Now she was here sitting at his bedside, it was impossible not to feel guilty at having wished him removed from their care. Tentatively, she reached out, touching the back of his hand. Her eyes flickered to his. They remained closed, unseeing, a sheen of moisture covering his skin. The room was stifling. A side table held an old-fashioned pedestal fan and Eleanor flicked it on, positioning it so that the weak stream of air was directed at the patient. Then she opened the bedroom door, trying to entice a non-existent draft.

'Can you hear me?' she asked. Somewhere there were parents, perhaps a wife, brothers and sisters, friends, anxiously waiting to hear news of the man who lay before her. 'My name's Eleanor. You're safe at River Run. It's a sheep station.' The anger and shock Eleanor experienced at the time of the shooting returned and she looked up at the ceiling, imagining she could burn a hole through the cracked plaster into her brother's room.

She thought of the stranger out in the paddock. Of the billowing grass and the warm sun as he rode towards the river on a quiet Saturday afternoon. Regardless of what anyone thought or said, or even her initial inclination, the Webber family were responsible for what had happened. 'Don't worry,' Eleanor said softly, 'we'll look after you.'

'So that's the troublemaker.' Her mother stood in the doorway.

'Mum!' Eleanor chastised. 'I can't believe you just said that.'

'Well, he's hardly a welcome guest.' She looked at the patient, taking in the drip and the bandages. 'We have no idea who this man is.'

'He looks like someone who works in the country, if you ask me.'

'Perhaps.' Her mother moved closer. Arms folded across her chest, she leant over the bed. 'He looks foreign to me.'

Brown-haired and tanned, he was rather unremarkable to look

at except for generously full lips and those long lashes. 'Foreign?' Eleanor repeated. 'He looks like one of us.'

'Well, it would be easier, wouldn't it, if he was a communist coming to attack us? At least then there would be an excuse for Robbie's behaviour. He's saved by his age, of course, from having to atone for his crime in any meaningful way but, nonetheless, I worry what effect this may have on us as a family.'

'For heaven's sake,' Eleanor responded, 'didn't you listen to what the police said? We'd hardly want him to be a communist. It seems to me that they're trying to draw a connection between Robbie's actions and our family's political leanings. They could well think that the shooting was done on purpose to support Menzies' views. Dad would –'

'Leave your father out of this,' her mother replied curtly. 'They'd hardly believe that we'd use our own son to make a political point and get a newspaper headline.' Her tone became more civil. 'The police are simply conducting a thorough investigation and, I might say, clutching at straws at a time when everyone's talking about the communists and this damn referendum. Of more concern now is what happens to Robbie.'

'I'm sorry, Mum. You're right. I'm just tired.'

'Of course you are. We all are.' Georgia leant against the wash-stand, absently rubbing dust from her fingers. Her expression softened. 'Colin said you were very brave last night, riding all that way back to the homestead when it was growing dark.'

'Did he say that?' Eleanor shrugged. 'I felt bad leaving Robbie out there alone.'

'Nonsense, you did the right thing.' Dark smudges ringed her mother's eyes. Eleanor guessed if they both looked in a mirror, they would appear equally washed out.

'Colin tells me that a juvenile facility may be suggested for Robbie. I think it unlikely, firstly because of his age and the family connections and secondly, especially if we are the ones who take

141

the necessary steps immediately.' Her eyes grew moist, a most uncommon response for a woman whom Eleanor had not seen shed a tear since the day of her father's funeral. 'It's not what I want, but our only option is boarding school. Robbie must go once shearing finishes.'

'He won't like that.'

'To be honest, neither will I. But he's been running wild on the property for the past year. The governess can't control him. The wooden spoon makes no difference, or the strap for that matter, and he can't spend every second day locked in his bedroom.'

Eleanor wondered if the incident at the crow trap should be mentioned, but decided against it. She didn't know if Robbie was possessed of a violent streak or if environment and an overactive imagination were at the root of his actions. But the glazed anger showing in his eyes as he belted those birds to death, and the palpable excitement that emanated from him as he climbed from the tree with the news that he'd shot the stranger was real cause for concern.

Georgia moved to gaze out the partially boarded-up window. 'Your stepfather believes discipline is key. And I suppose I must agree. If Robbie can't be controlled, if he won't abide by our rules, then he must be put into the care of those who can instil some measure of self-control. Your sister and you certainly benefitted from boarding, although your father and I argued over the necessity of it.'

Eleanor could only imagine how upset Robbie would be. 'When will you tell him?'

'Colin intends to telephone the headmaster at the King's School, Parramatta, tomorrow, to ensure there is a place for him this term.' Her mother moved to stand in the centre of the small room. 'In the meantime we'll leave it until the last moment to tell Robbie. He'll continue with his lessons, but otherwise he'll remain in his room until he departs. He has to.' Georgia gave a little sob. 'I would let him out in a day or so but we can't. Once word gets out about what's happened, everyone will expect Robbie to be punished. It's not right, of course, he's a child, but I have to do it, if only for propriety's sake.'

For her mother and stepfather it was all about perception and decorum, values imposed on the family by the two founding River brothers in the 1870s and stoically carried down through the generations to Georgia, who, as an only child, had married a Webber, two Webbers in fact. Such standards ran in tandem with the family's rise to prominence in pastoral Australia. Eleanor's grandfather had been savvy when it came to land acquisition, with the early death of his brother, Montague, sadly ensuring River Run could be passed down in its entirety. Eleanor didn't have any issues with a family trying to better their standing in the world – indeed she was a firm believer in each generation improving upon the last – but she felt there was something wrong here. It almost seemed as if Georgia was more concerned about public opinion than the shocking behaviour of her son. Were it not for Colin and idle tongues, Eleanor guessed that Robbie would not be sent away, Georgia wouldn't allow it. 'So you think Robbie should be treated leniently, Mum?'

'It was an accident after all, Eleanor.'

'You know I never said that.'

'Outside the walls of this house, that's what people will think.' Georgia's response was curt. 'And they will think that because there is nothing to the contrary to suggest otherwise.'

Eleanor didn't respond.

'What would you have me do? Have your brother thrown into some home for delinquents?'

'Of course not, Mum, but boarding school may only be the first step. He may need more help. I told you what happened and we both know that the shooting of that man was not an unfortunate accident. You yourself said he's been running wild. Well, what if

143

there is something else? What if Robbie shares that same fragility that struck Lesley, except that in his case it's –'

'Stop. Stop right there. I will not have my own daughter drawing such ridiculous parallels. You were with him yesterday, were you not? Why didn't you stop him before this debacle occurred?'

'Why did you let an eleven-year-old roam the bush with a rifle?' Eleanor retaliated.

The fan made a squeak of complaint and then stopped. A burning smell quickly followed.

'The engine's burnt out.' Rising, Eleanor flicked the on-off switch. The fan remained dead.

'Colin . . .' Georgia faltered at the saying of his name. 'Colin gave it to Robbie on his ninth birthday. He and your father shared one at the same age apparently.' She opened the door to leave, hesitating at the threshold. 'I told him not to. I told him Robbie was too young, but Colin said I was just mollycoddling the boy.' She paused, moistened her lips. 'He's an excellent shot, your brother. Everyone says so. Takes after his father, and your father, Eleanor, and they were both snipers during the Great War. Steady and patient. They could stand in a shell-hole filled with water for days on end. And they always got their target. I'm not silly, Eleanor. I know your brother shot that man on purpose.' Georgia swallowed, turned to the man on the bed. The finality of her words, the conviction, was reinforced by the steadfastness in her eyes. She gave the man a dis-interested glance, rolled her lips as if she'd tasted something bitter. 'But don't forget, Eleanor, no matter who this man may be, at the end of the day he was trespassing on our land.' She shut the door.

Monday
Shearing Begins

⫷ Chapter Eighteen ⫸

The sound of barking dogs and the dull hum of an engine carried across the rear of the garden to where Eleanor sat, sketching in the early morning light. A string of jenny wrens preening themselves from their perch on the new trellis caught her attention as they fluttered heavenward. She watched them absently from the bench near the kidney-shaped ponds, before resuming her view of the house. The pale sandstone of irregular-shaped blocks sat squarely on the earth. The expanse of stone on the ground floor was broken up by five narrow windows, a contrast to the rooms above with their white-trimmed doors, windows and decorative louvres. A drooping vine twisted along part of the wall leading to the only door at the rear of the house, the kitchen entrance, while at the corner of the building grew the tree Robbie had scuttled down only a few days prior.

The illustration she'd recently completed captured her half-brother perfectly. He stood with his palms and nose pressed against the glass of the French door leading onto the balcony. Eleanor returned Robbie's half-hearted wave, watching as he disappeared from view, no doubt readying for his lessons. The governess was under instruction to escort Robbie to and from the schoolroom and Miss Hastings had risen to the challenge. Yesterday, although a Sunday, she'd marched her young charge across to the school-house, as if Robbie were a convicted felon and she a prison warden. There he'd spent the entire afternoon. Eleanor guessed that her brother was sorry for what he'd done, for he was miserable, bored and nervous when she'd visited him last night, but he'd not voiced an apology for his actions.

Directly below Robbie's space was the sickroom. The figure of Athena Pappas hovered near the bedroom window, perhaps checking the flow of the drip on its makeshift stand. Eleanor hadn't known what to expect, but the beauty of the willowy, dark-haired woman was almost equalled by the sadness shadowing her almond eyes. Although professionally polite on first meeting, the woman's curiosity regarding her charge was obvious. Athena asked many questions of everybody, curt, intelligent questions, which quickly led Georgia to tell the nurse to mind her own business.

'Morning, Eleanor,' Athena called loudly through the flyscreened window. 'What a fine day it is.'

Closing the sketchbook, Eleanor walked towards the house, agreeing that it was indeed a lovely morning, one that would soon be ruined by the day's expected heat.

The nurse ignored the comment. 'No change, I'm afraid,' Athena continued, as if they were standing face to face and there wasn't twenty yards and a flyscreen between them. 'But it's only been a couple of days. Are you still able to sit with him while I go into the village this afternoon? I need to buy some dressings.'

Eleanor confirmed that she could, politely avoiding further con-versation and the offer of a cuppa out in the sun. It was not that she didn't like Athena, she was still strung out by recent events and idle chitchat was beyond her at the moment. Were the nurse not quite so conscientious, Eleanor would have visited the patient more often, in fact she felt compelled to do so, but she wanted to be alone with him.

Although not to blame for the shooting, despite the allegations of some, an element of guilt remained with Eleanor. Time and again she revisited the events of the afternoon leading up to the incident. She never should have climbed down the tree and left Robbie that afternoon, she should have paid more attention to what he spoke about; noted his obsession with war and communism. In contrast, Eleanor tried to draw comfort from the fact that it would have been impossible for anyone to have known Robbie's thoughts that day, for a childish conviction had overtaken reason. But in the end it was she who'd been with Robbie, no-one else.

This was the bush. Eleanor had been born and raised here. The cosseting she saw in city streets as parents drove their children to class or dropped them off to meet the school bus was far removed from the early independence that came with growing up in rural Australia. But the shooting made her wonder how attentive her mother and stepfather had been to Robbie's needs. How many parents let a boy ride off with a rifle?

Slipping pen and paper into the satchel left sitting on a garden table, Eleanor slung the bag over a shoulder and walked across the lawn and out the gate, joining the dirt track that led down towards the station outbuildings. The blue truck was parked at the meat-house and Rex and the Aboriginal butcher and general kitchen hand, Dawson, were dropping the tail gate. The wiry gardener lifted one of two sheep carcasses from where it rested on the hide on the vehicle's tray and, labouring under the weight of it, carried it inside the meat-house. Dawson helped him hang the sheep from its hocks and then walked outside to lean against the vehicle where he spat on a sharpening stone and began honing a knife. Blood dripped from the remaining sheep hanging from the tray onto the ground.

The blood month, Eleanor thought, waving away flies.

It was some years since she'd been at River Run for shearing. But now she was home again, Eleanor knew that the decision to return had been the right one, marred though it was by the shooting, and shadowed by Dante's duplicity. Her employer had reluctantly granted Eleanor a fortnight's leave. She'd proved more than capable in her secretarial role over the last two years. So much so that Eleanor now handled much of the inventory for the hardware store as well. It was not a glamorous job by any means, but the position suited Eleanor's straightforward, hands-on approach to work. She was pleased now that she'd asked for the extra week. She *had* run away from Sydney, but she was beginning to feel the benefit of being home.

The thought of sketching their sheep, as she'd done as a child, made Eleanor recall mustering on horseback with her dad, his black and white kelpie padding along between them until the dog was called to action. When she smiled at these memories, the absence of happiness over the last few weeks grew pronounced. She'd come home and in the doing, in spite of everything, had found her smile.

The overseer's cottage was quiet, as was the nearby bunk-house where the jackeroos lived. Eleanor didn't expect to see anyone loitering on the first day of shearing, and it was nice for a change to wander around her home without the usual stockmen and young jackeroos eyeing her with interest. Some of the men had been part of the team for years, and Eleanor counted them as friends, but the jackeroos came and went with regularity, with only the very capable having the necessary ability to last the full outback apprenticeship.

The large shearing shed, its iron roof rust-coloured in parts from age, materialised like some primeval dwelling from among the trees. In the late 1800s the shed had grown rather erratically. Old black and white photos showed the gradual addition of skillions with sides made of timber slabs and corrugated iron. Now there were many more providing protection for the engine room and covered holding pens in case of bad weather. The roof cavity held the remnants of saplings used as insulation against the heat of the iron roof, some of the returning shearers still jokingly referring to the shed as the iron lung, remembering bygone days of poor insulation. Still others called the building the old elephant, on account of the weather-beaten timber that resembled an elephant's hide.

Balls of dust rose from the adjoining yards, spiralling into the sky. From this angle it appeared as if the dirt was reaching up to grasp the wispy white cloud above. Captivated, Eleanor sat down in the middle of the road and began to sketch what she saw. She worked quickly, the pencil sliding across the page as the sun left its mark on her skin. As she drew, Eleanor occasionally paused to jot down an anecdote, thought or description. Rex's comments regarding the blood month, Dawson sharpening the butcher's knife, the way the heat shrouded the countryside. So absorbed was Eleanor that when a fat plop of moisture landed on the drawing, she was jolted back to reality.

A large red kelpie was eyeing her quietly, drops of saliva dripping from his tongue onto the drawing. The dog was dirty and wet to the flanks and he wasn't at all interested in moving when Eleanor told him to do so. So she gave him a shove but was more than surprised when he pushed back, showing his teeth. Eleanor moved instead, clambering to her feet and walking away at a brisk pace. The canine was unknown to her, and she to him. The big-boned animal stayed close to her heels as she approached the shed. More than once she checked his progress, a little unnerved by the dog's proximity, but soon the sight unfolding ahead consumed her.

Men and sheep could be seen in the distance, moving in the yards among the dust, while in the paddock beyond, another mob of sheep were being walked towards the sprawling woolshed by men on horseback. Eleanor's artist's mind delighted in the scene. The dust and dirt engulfed both sheep and men, so that the image was discoloured by a veneer of blurry beige. It was a tableau of almost ghostly rendering, which brought to mind all the previous stockmen and shearers and shed-hands who'd toiled on River Run over the decades.

'Eleanor.'

Disturbed from her daydream, she waited as the overseer whistled the red dog. The big animal instantly obeyed, running swiftly forward to halt by horse and rider before springing up into the air to land in front of Mr Goward, his paws resting across the man's thighs. The bay mare whinnied in annoyance. 'How's everything going? How's the patient?' he asked, ignoring the softly growling kelpie and irritable horse.

Eleanor shaded her face against the sun's rays, noticing the worn patches on the knees of Mr Goward's trousers. 'Nothing new to report unfortunately,' she replied. 'The patient is still unconscious and Uncle Colin's gone into town with Mr Winslow.' Eleanor restrained the urge to stare at the blue-green-eyed man. In the dark of Saturday night, the distinctiveness of his appearance had gone unnoticed, but now it captivated her.

'Car problems, I hear?' Mr Goward patted the red dog, who gave a low growl in response.

'Yes, although Constable Graham wanted to ask Uncle Colin some more questions as well.'

The man scratched at a clean-shaven cheek. 'And Robbie?'

'Under lock and key when he isn't doing his lessons. To be honest,' Eleanor acknowledged, 'I'll never understand why he did it. And I know I was there,' she continued quickly, 'but I wasn't in the damn tree.'

The overseer dipped his chin, a nod of sorts. 'Apportioning blame,' he said noncommittally, 'is a pretty common human condition. Can I give you a word of advice, Eleanor? Don't get too upset about what other people think or say, you can't control any of it and one of these days the truth will out. As for young Robbie, he's a tearaway, always was, always will be. I couldn't count the strife he's been in over the past year. On Friday he had an altercation with one of the jackeroos, on two separate occasions. Next week it will be something or someone else. Hopefully not on a par with this most recent incident. But frankly, and I'd only say this to you, I think there's blame on both sides.'

The bay horse shifted the weight on its feet, a pile of dung landing hot and soft on the ground. Mr Goward chewed a bottom lip as if worried about the breaching of his usual reserve.

Eleanor waited. He was referring to her mother and Colin. In any other circumstance such personal commentary would have been totally inappropriate, but then it wasn't every day that an eleven-year-old shot someone.

'Everyone knows that Robbie's fascinated by war,' he carried on. 'He's always asking questions about the Japs and the submarines coming into Sydney, about Mr Webber's shrapnel wound and your own father's service.' Mr Goward stroked the mare between the ears. 'Robbie's surrounded by stories of war, past and present.'

He didn't need to explain further. Lesley wasn't the only one of them to be damaged by war. Perhaps they were all touched in some way. A weak heart brought on by the stresses of combat had left their father little to fight with when he was diagnosed with cancer.

The overseer reached into his pocket, retrieving the makings of a cigarette. 'Some kids just get carried away.'

'I suppose.' Eleanor watched as, with a paper stuck to his lip, he rolled the tobacco in the palm of his hand. The movements were deft, but it was not the lighting of the cigarette that drew her, but rather the taut definition of his bicep and the angular line of his masculine jaw. The horse grew impatient, pawing at the earth. Eleanor could commiserate with the animal. She wouldn't like the red dog sitting on her back either.

Mr Goward folded one hand over the other, the cigarette dangling nonchalantly in his fingers. 'I suggested to your stepfather that the police place a description of the man in *The Worker*.'

Eleanor had heard the Australian Workers Union published this paper. Distributed widely to workers in the pastoral industry, even Dante and his friends talked about some of the content on occasion.

'There'll be someone out there who knows our wounded stranger.' The overseer seemed convinced of this. 'A man just doesn't appear out of the blue. Everyone's got a past and he looked to me like a bloke who'd made his living outdoors. There'll be someone working on a farm, station or in a shearing shed who knows him.'

'That's what I thought too, Mr Goward. He looks like a worker to me.' She didn't want to broach the subject of gossip, her mother and Uncle Colin were worried enough for all of them, but she wasn't particularly comfortable either with the thought of the bush telegraph pulling apart the lives of her family. 'Do the men in the shed know what happened?'

'Not specifically,' he rubbed his chin, 'but they were all told this morning that a stranger had been injured on River Run and they were given a rough description.'

Eleanor could only guess at the talk that was currently circulating. Athena's family would certainly know about the incident and the doctor would have told his wife. The overseer was loyal to the core, as was Rex, however, both men liked a beer at the Royal in the village and it was hardly the type of event that could be kept quiet forever.

'It is best everyone knows.' Mr Goward picked a shred of tobacco from his tongue. 'Stops the talk getting out of hand.'

'I heard Mum say she was concerned about the agreements after what had occurred. Did everyone in the shed sign?'

'Not everyone, not yet. There's always a couple who like to bide their time. Make a show of walking around and having a think. I'm sure the shed overseer, Mr Lomax, will make those that haven't signed do so. The last thing we want is a couple of shearers starting to bargain for conditions over and above what's in the agreement. It stirs up trouble. So far there's been a complaint about the vibration in the overhead gear, another about the burr in the fleeces and one about the thinness of the mattresses in the shearers' quarters, which led to a request for compensatory payments for the accommodation not being up to scratch.' He paused. 'Don't worry, Eleanor, that last one was a joke. They're just taking the mickey. The shed and quarters pass the pastoral industry standards.'

'Anything else?' asked Eleanor.

'The rain water tastes gritty.' They shared a smile. 'Not enough coarse emery paper, a broken rail in the yards, and a complaint in general about old machinery. Well, didn't Mr Lomax get the wind up about that one. The old Chinaman's bookkeeping ability is only equalled by his knowledge of shearing machinery. The shed expert was the next to get toey, he'd gone over the gear with a fine tooth comb.' He stubbed the cigarette out in the palm of his hand, then flicked it to the ground. 'We haven't had any whinges about the sheep yet – apart from the burr – but they'll come.' The overseer doffed his hat. 'Welcome to shearing time at River Run, Miss Webber.'

Although the remark carried a hint of sarcasm, Eleanor found herself blushing inexplicably. 'Thank you,' she replied quickly, 'for Saturday night. We, well, I appreciated you being there.'

The man appeared a little taken aback by the acknowledgement. 'You shouldn't have gone back out there,' he said with concern. 'Anyway, I best be off before these two get even more cantankerous.' He gestured to the horse and the dog and tugged the reins, riding towards the shed. The red dog ducked under the overseer's arm to stare defiantly at Eleanor as they rode away.

⋘ Chapter Nineteen ⋙

At the woolshed, the Lister engine that drove the overhead gear on the board suddenly went quiet. Eleanor's wristwatch read 9.30 exactly: smoko. Halting at the adjoining shed, which provided cover for pressed wool bales, she looked above the double doors to where an etched number immortalised a gun blade-shearer's tally from the previous century. A line of men began to stream from the woolshed across to the ablution block. Shearers first. Tall, short, wide and narrow, most wore Jackie Howe singlets, some had braces to hold up trousers and soft leather moccasin-type shoes. They gradually reappeared with washed faces and hands, some with their hair freshly combed to line up at the long makeshift table, where Fitzy the cook was pouring tea from one of three large enamel teapots. Containers of sandwiches and cake filled the rest of the table, while a beat-up Ford pick-up truck was parked nearby.

The shed-hands arrived next, waiting respectfully in line for the shearers to be served. A black dog ambled out from under the truck to sprawl beneath the trestle table, observing proceedings as the men took what they wanted and drifted off. Some leant on the wooden railings forming the yard boundary, others returned inside the shed to lie flat on the board and rest aching limbs.

Eleanor sat on one of the bales, running her hand across the black stencilling that marked the wool as belonging to them. Having arrived unnoticed, she quietly opened the sketchpad and focused on the interior of the shed. It was a cavernous T-shaped building, some three hundred feet long. The ground section, the T, was for the pressing and loading of wool, the far wall holding a row of timber stalls for each class of fleece. Between these bins, three wide steps led up to the wool tables. Here fleeces were skirted, classed and then thrown into the appropriate bin on the ground level. Beyond this area there were two boards divided by catching pens, which ran down the middle. With twenty stands apiece, the forty stands once used for blade-shearing had been reduced. Now only one board and fourteen stands were used with the current mechanised gear.

The first run of the morning must have been fast, for the wool classer was still examining the last of the skirted fleeces piled on a side table for his scrutiny. Having checked staple length, strength and colour he directed one of the wool rollers working on the table to place the fleece in the correct line bin. With the task finally completed, Spec Wilson and the remaining wool rollers left the shed for smoko.

'G'day, g'day, g'day.'

Three shearers, aged in their twenties, strolled past Eleanor. The tallest, a lanky black-haired boy with blue eyes and a dimpled smile, stopped before her. His right arm was twice the size of his left.

'You got a temper to match that hair?'

'Sometimes,' answered Eleanor, aware the men had made a point of detouring her way.

One of the other youths elbowed the speaker in the ribs. Prompted, the young shearer spoke up quickly. 'I'm Geoff, Geoff Ferguson, pleased to meet you.'

157

'I'm Eleanor, hi.'

'That's the daughter,' one of his mates whispered.

Geoff blushed. 'Maybe see you at the cut-out party, eh?'

Eleanor smiled. 'Maybe.'

The young man grinned and swaggered into the shed with his mates.

Dim rays of light angled through the small louvred windows above each stand, throwing the shearers into relief. Some lay flat on the board, others leant against lanolin-polished timber. Geoff stuck a finger in the little tin sitting on the ledge of the shed, checking his combs and cutters, another was strapping a wrist. Eleanor couldn't see any sheep, blocked as they were by the timber wall between the boards, but the clatter of their hoofs echoed as the penner-uppers walked the ewes up the ramp at the opposite end of the shed and into the series of enclosures and sweating pens, which would eventually lead to the catching pens. Outside, stockmen could be heard calling to dogs, as men talked and laughed. Eleanor breathed in greasy wool, manure and sweat, the hot, dry wind funnelling the dust so that it floated within the shed like confetti.

'You the wordsmith then, girl?'

Eleanor hadn't noticed the sinewy shearer approach but she recognised him immediately. 'Hello, Mr Wright.' River Run's gun shearer was of average height, with the build of an Olympic swimmer, broad shoulders and a tapering waist. Hands the size of dinner plates and ribbons of veins on heavily tattooed, lean, strong arms, suggested he could also fight when required. Only his face betrayed a man ravaged by the demands of his job.

He winked and took a sip of steaming tea from a battered pannikin. 'We both know you should be calling me Billy by now, but,' he shrugged, 'it wouldn't do with this lot.' He indicated to the shed's interior. 'A man's got to keep up appearances.' He patted his sandy-coloured hair. 'So what's this caper involving the boy? Trigger happy?'

'It was an accident.' The last thing Eleanor wanted was to get embroiled in a discussion. 'He didn't meant to shoot the man.'

The shearer bit into a piece of Fitzy's teacake. 'Ah. Word is, the bloke he hit is a red ragger. Did *you* know he was a commo?'

'Mr Wright, no-one has any idea who the stranger is.'

'Ah.' He finished the cake, eating like he shore, clean and fast. 'But you were with the boy.'

'Robbie was up a tree.' Eleanor was feeling extremely uncomfortable. 'I was on the ground waiting for him to come down. It was an accident.'

Billy Wright reflected on this, as if giving consideration to whether what Eleanor was telling him was fact or fiction. 'I heard on the frog and toad a while back that you wrote stories, and drew a bit.' He took another sip of the tea, pointing at the sketchbook with a calloused pinkie. The action resembled that of a genteel woman drinking tea.

'Sometimes,' Eleanor answered softly, wondering who had overheard what at the homestead.

'Ah. Not real popular at the big house, eh? The thing is, girl, I was thinking you'd be needing material, a leading man. Take, for example, myself. Good-looking,' he smiled, revealing a gold tooth, 'athletic in appearance, record-maker and breaker of women's hearts.' Billy Wright nodded enthusiastically. 'And stories. Well, I can tell you a few. Like when I was a young cobber, knocking about in western Queensland. Got me first stand as a learner after two years in the sheds. Started as a tar-boy, then board-boy, watched how they did it. How they shore, how they selected sheep from the catching-pen, the way they dragged them out to the stand to the exact same spot so they were always closest to the gear. Always. So I watched and learnt and then I'd offer to finish off the odd shearer's sheep.' He tossed the remnants of tea on the ground. 'Slept in a sheepskin hammock once, with the legs still attached. Best night's sleep I ever had.'

'I could draw you,' Eleanor offered.

Billy Wright crossed his arms across his chest. 'Done.' His voice grew serious. 'Oh,' he gave a crinkly, bashful smile, 'and my left side, girl.' He touched his cheek. 'My mother always said that was my best.'

'Left side it is,' Eleanor consented. The shearer moved nimbly through the shed, the shearers lolling on the board pulling their legs up so that Billy didn't have to step over them.

Outside, the men began wandering in from the yards while Mr Lomax remained to count out the last of the recently shorn sheep from each shearer's pen. The animals jumped in the air as they passed through each gate, spilling out into a holding yard where they would wait their turn before being subjected to a swim through the plunge dip.

Eleanor studied the golden hues of the polished timber within the shed, noting the indecipherable markings left on the wood by the Chinese builders contracted to erect the shed in the previous century. She lifted her pencil to draw.

'Well, we know their true colours now.' The man was out of sight and barely audible, as if he was losing his voice. 'You seen what they're using for dunny paper? *The Worker*. Torn up in sheets it is and hanging up as clear as day.'

'Someone's just having a go,' she heard his companion reply, a younger voice with a slightly nasal twang.

'Having a go, alright. It's a warning, that's what it is. We've got power we have and they don't like it. So what do they do? Shoot one of us and blame it on the kid. Who's to say it wasn't Webber himself or even Goward what done it, on the Boss's say so.'

'I dunno, mate,' the younger man's tone decreased in volume. 'Seems unlikely. I mean they don't even know who the bloke is.'

'The publican heard that old gardener say to the Greek at the store on Sunday that the boy thought he was a communist.' Tea was tossed in the dirt. The half-choked voice continued, 'Menzies is trying to make everyone hate the commos, and he's using this Korea thing as an excuse. But who else is standing up for the workers, eh? Who else is lending a hand to us battlers? And who's running the unions? Ask yourself that, mate. It used to be that shearers were king. But the squatters have been fighting with us from the very beginning. Wouldn't be no unions in Australia if it wasn't for us shearers. Read up on your history, boy. We started it all. But the squatters, they're always looking for a bit of leverage. Always looking to cut us down to size. So, if they can say that a shady communist was shot on a big run after being found trespassing, don't you think Menzies will rub his hands together, with this referendum thing in the wind? And if the Communist Party is declared illegal, it makes sense that they'll go after those like-minded blokes in the unions. Think about that.'

'I dunno.' The companion was clearly doubtful. 'I mean, it seems to me, it'll be the boy that did the shooting that will get in trouble.'

The faint-voiced man gave a grunt of disbelief. 'Don't kid yourself. Nothing will happen to him. He might be locked in his room now, but he'll be out in a day or so playing merry-hell. They say he's a terror, got it in for one of the jackeroos. I reckon,' the voice grew softer, Eleanor strained to hear, 'I reckon that the toffs know who the poor blighter is. That could be all part of it, you see. Pretend you don't know who he is, when you really do. Picked their target I reckon.'

'Do you know him?' his companion asked.

'Him that's been shot? How would I? It only happened two days ago. I ain't seen no picture of him in the paper yet. Have you? Poor bastard. But they got him, they did. Took him down as sure as if he'd been a kangaroo run over by a truck. Never stood a chance.'

'But –'

'My cousin was one of them that got sent to jail after the strike of '49. His missus, well she did it real tough. Ended up near starving, lost a kid they did.'

161

The chug of the engines reluctantly came to life, gathering in speed and sound until all talking was drowned out by the noise. The men were moving about the interior of the shed. A fizz of sparks shot out from the engine room where the shed expert, Stump Ward, was sharpening combs.

'You want some cake, Eleanor?' Mr Goward yelled across the flat, lifting his voice over the noise. Fitzy, sitting in a canvas camp chair beneath a candy-striped umbrella, held out a round tin. 'A cup of tea? There's a bit left. You'll need some sugar in it though. It's that brewed a spoon would stand up in it by itself.' The cook, a wide, big-stomached man, shot the overseer a look of disgust from beneath the parasol.

Calling out a thank you, but no, Eleanor walked around the side of the rainwater tank. Only the splash of thrown tea on the ground was left to show that anyone had been there. Should she tell Mr Goward what she'd overheard? Strictly speaking, as shed overseer, Mr Lomax should be informed of any problems, however, Eleanor wasn't comfortable speaking to the Chinaman when she'd been eavesdropping and the men were unknown to her, although it was obviously the faint-voiced individual's first shearing at River Run. And he definitely sounded like a troublemaker. Perhaps it would be better if she told her mother instead.

The red dog started to growl at the stubby-tailed dog under the smoko table. Immediately a fight broke out between the two. Eleanor ran towards the unfolding drama, as a blur of black and red rolled about in the dirt, banging into one of the table legs and upsetting the contents. A container of sandwiches fell to the ground, spilling the bread in the dirt. A teapot followed. Mr Goward roared at the dogs to settle down, finally laying in to both of them with his boot.

The cook let out a string of obscenities, pitched the striped umbrella into the air and snatched up his injured animal. 'I told you to keep that half-breed mangy dog of yours away from my little Nettie.'

'Don't mind Fitzy,' Mr Goward advised, beckoning Eleanor as he strode towards the sheep-yards. He told the red dog to sit and wait and the animal obeyed, although he observed every move made by his master.

Eleanor joined the overseer, grimacing at the mess made by the fighting dogs.

'Don't think I'll be making more sandwiches,' the cook called after them, scooping up the bread and filling and half-heartedly shaking the earth from them. 'No, sir, they can eat these ones tomorrow and when they complain, I'll send the buggers to you.' He threw containers and teapots onto the tray of the truck.

Mr Goward winked at Eleanor. 'Who called the cook a bastard, eh? Who called the bastard a cook?'

⧆ Chapter Twenty ⧆

Eleanor tracked the overseer through the maze of timber yards, wondering what he wanted to show her. Some of the fencing dated back to the 1870s and was a mishmash in places of dropped logs, iron mesh, flat and corrugated iron, sawn rails and star pickets. The ground underfoot was soft and powdery and the air hummed with the clamour of the Lister engine, whirring hand-pieces and the click of individual cords as the men either started or finished shearing a sheep. Men yelled from inside the shed and from the maze of yards at the rear where they penned up sheep. Eleanor sneezed. The air was thick with fine, gritty dirt.

From inside the shed came the call of 'Wool away', a shearer yelling loudly from the board, complaining to the frantic picker-ups that fleeces were piling up around his feet.

Freshly shorn ewes slid down the chutes to land on their feet in the counting-out pens, large brown eyes blinking. Dogs barked, sheep called, dust rose in willy-willies about them as the day warmed.

'Another one for you, Mr Lomax,' a shed-hand called out as a dead woolly was pushed out into one of the tally pens. 'Suffocated.'

'Then don't pen them up so tight,' was his reply, as the Chinaman walked along the rows of counting-out pens and, reaching the one holding the dead sheep, hurdled the railing and began to drag it away.

The years faded and Eleanor remembered being a child. She and Lesley were walking side by side, pushing and shoving each other playfully as they trailed their dad. He'd promised to let each of them take a turn drenching the ewes and they were pleased to have escaped the stuffy schoolhouse with its ancient map, hard-backed chairs and musty books.

'Do you agree?'

The overseer broke into Eleanor's memories. 'Yes, yes, of course,' she answered vaguely as Mr Goward pointed to a shutter on the side of the building, which hung lopsided from a broken hinge.

Overhead a wispy cloud of dust signalled that more sheep were being brought in from the paddock to be shorn, funnelled from the large receiving yards through a series of smaller ones.

Gates slowed their progress as the pair continued traversing the yards, securing latches and waiting for sheep to be moved from one enclosure to another. At the long drafting race Eleanor and the overseer paused in the shade of the split timber roof as a mob of shorn ewes were counted out into another yard by Murph.

'Hundred,' the senior jackeroo yelled, his attention never diverting from the stream of animals jumping through the gateway.

'Eighteen,' a young freckled redhead replied loudly, intent on keeping the count. A new recruit, she thought, observing the barely scuffed riding boots and as-new clothes.

Eleanor watched as Murph used his hand, dividing the sheep into groups in mid-air, or took a step forward or back, depending on whether the speed of the passing animals needed to be slowed or quickened.

'Hundred.'

'Nineteen,' the gangly youth responded.

The tail of the mob rushed through the gateway. 'Nineteen hundred and twenty-seven. Good job, Archie.' Murph turned to the overseer, tipping his hat on noticing Eleanor.

'Nineteen hundred and twenty-seven.' Mr Goward pencilled the number in his pocket notebook. 'We'll check it with Mr Lomax's tally tonight, Murph. Murph's getting a bit of counting practice,' he told Eleanor.

'How's he doing?' she asked, as the overseer strode on ahead, beckoning the younger of the two jackeroos, Archie, to join them.

'Improving. It takes some practice to count large numbers.'

The three of them reached a yard where another jackeroo was killing time by throwing stones at a goanna as it ran up a tree. The boy turned on their approach and, as if wary of reprimand, hung back, uncertain. He was a slight lad, almost concave in the middle. Eleanor thought he looked like he needed a few decent meals. A mob of some forty rams huddled in the opposite corner to where the boy loitered. The animals grew still on their approach, lifting their heads with curiosity, the odd one stamping their hoofs in the crumbly dirt.

'Culls,' the overseer told Eleanor. 'Your stepfather wants them all to get their throats cut.'

A truck was parked at the end of a loading ramp and another jackeroo was doing some repairs where a board had come loose from the side of the ramp.

Mr Goward took a step forward, hands on hips. 'The thing is, there are a couple here that, in my mind, should stay.'

Eleanor glanced at the two jackeroos. They were both skinny boys, tall and gawky, yet to grow into their skins. One of them, Archie, scuffed at the dirt with a dusty boot and whispered something to his companion. 'Why are you telling me?' she asked.

'Because you might learn something. Interested?'

Eleanor shrugged. 'Sure.'

'Keep an eye out, rams are pretty unpredictable at times.'

They walked through the mob, spreading apart so that the rams ran back between them, a few eager ones came first and then the rest ran forward. Eleanor kept her back to the rails and her eyes on the rushing bodies. Once the sheep were bunched at the opposite end, the overseer studied the mob before directing the jackeroos to catch specific animals so that he could inspect them. The boys came forward, hoping to push the animal in question tightly within the packed mob or against the wooden fence so he'd be easier to catch, but the rams were wily, sulky creatures. They'd spin and duck or race away at the last moment.

'Why don't you run them up the drafting race?' asked Eleanor as Archie made a grab for a ram and, losing his grip, fell flat on his face in the yard. 'It'd be easier and quicker.'

Mr Goward's arms were folded across a broad chest. His blue-green eyes were clear and bright. 'Patience, Eleanor.' He pointed at one of the jackeroos. 'Wormy, why don't you see if you can do a better job than your mate? Archie's too busy doing nose-plants in the dirt.'

Wormy nodded. Dirt crusted his skin where it mixed with sweat.

'On the fence,' the overseer pointed. The boy made a dive and missed, Archie rushed in, reached for a hind leg and, misjudging, stumbled and nearly fell. 'What are you trying to do? Cripple him?' yelled Mr Goward. 'You never, ever, grab a sheep by its leg. A man would do better with a broomstick and a bucket for staff,' he muttered.

'I gather these two are new,' Eleanor remarked. There was a lot of running, puffing and sliding around in the dirt going on, and not a lot to show for it.

The man by her side gave a brief, almost mischievous grin. 'First year. It's all part of the training, Eleanor. Young men should be quick on their feet. Quick and agile, otherwise they're just being lazy.' Mr Goward took his time rolling a cigarette as the jackeroos leant against the timber railings catching their breath.

'Could I have one please?' she requested. Passing her the freshly made cigarette, he rolled another and then lit both.

'Thank you,' said Eleanor. She was absolutely dying for a hit of nicotine, but one exhalation of the strong tobacco made her cough and wheeze.

'A Webber smoking roll-your-owns,' he smiled, pretending to ignore Eleanor's splutterings. 'I'm impressed. Now, as for your query regarding the drafting race,' he took a puff and gesturing to catch the jackeroos' attention, pointed out another ram, 'I don't believe in letting genetic improvements take precedence over the constitution of an animal.'

Eleanor had no idea what he meant, and said so.

'I'm all for scientific advancement but I like to see an animal moving about, its frame and general condition.' He shook his head as the wrong animal was caught. 'Blocked up in a drafting race should never be the only method of inspection.'

He took another drag of the cigarette and then ground the butt into the dirt with his boot. 'I'm old-fashioned I guess, Eleanor, it's the way I was taught. But I believe that there's a lot more to ram selection than just numbers and it's worth remembering that there'll probably never be a ram bred that won't be helped by a ewe when it comes to progeny.' Mr Goward pointed to a long-nosed ram. 'That's one of them,' he yelled.

The jackeroos were slow to move. Finally, impatience struck and the overseer ran into the mob, caught the animal and was on his knees inspecting it before the jackeroos reached his side. 'Now, this animal,' he explained, barely missing a breath as Eleanor joined him, 'hasn't done as well as the others, granted.'

The ram in question was in poor condition compared to the rest of the mob.

'But look at this.' Mr Goward carefully parted the fleece. 'Beautiful colour, lustrous and soft skin.' He gestured to the jackeroos. 'Pull him out and give him a feed of lucerne hay. And that one as well.' Once again the overseer was in the mob, tackling another ram. Now she understood why the knees of his trousers were always worn.

'He's no oil painting,' Eleanor remarked as the jackeroos shepherded the chosen two away.

'Agreed, but perfect rams rarely improve the gene pool. Look at Uardry 0.1. Superb animal and he earned himself a place on the shilling coin. Produced good, useful ewes but few outstanding sires.'

'I can't imagine the breeders would like to hear that,' remarked Eleanor, as the overseer dusted the dirt from his clothes.

'They'd probably agree, although from a reputation viewpoint they wouldn't say it aloud.'

They walked back towards the gate, where the remaining rams huddled. With the jackeroos having been given new tasks, Wormy went to fetch the lucerne while Archie stomped off. Eleanor was sure he heard the boy swear as he jumped the railings.

The irritated rams packed in close together at their approach and then suddenly a number broke from the mob and rushed forward. One ram caught Eleanor on the left side of her body as he jumped, spinning her off-balance. She landed heavily in the dirt, unable to catch her breath. For a moment there was only the heat of the ground, the pound of hoofs and a need for oxygen that wouldn't come. Then the dusty atmosphere cleared, the air rushed into starved lungs and Eleanor was propped against the railings, supported by the overseer as he probed her body.

'You're alright, nothing broken,' he confirmed. 'Knocked the wind out of you, that's all. It could have been a lot worse.' Mr Goward continued to hold her, the spread of his hot hands on her abdomen and back. His tone was efficient, calming, but his expression was one of concern.

'I'm fine,' she finally replied, her voice a little shaky. 'Really, I'm okay.' Her hair had come loose and she tucked it behind an ear. With the movement, Mr Goward immediately released her. Heat was replaced by coolness where his hands rested and Eleanor gripped the timber fence to steady her balance. A slight headache was beginning to take hold, however, other than that, now she'd regained her equilibrium, Eleanor felt fine – fine except for the awkwardness of having been rescued, literally carried to safety, by River Run's overseer.

He opened a gate and waited for the rams to walk out. Once the yard was empty he retrieved her hat, bashing it back into shape from its recent trampling and brushing the dirt from it.

'Thank you.' Eleanor accepted it, tucking her hair up beneath the crown, embarrassed to have caused such a scene.

'Uncooperative and bad-tempered, rams are.' Mr Goward led the way as they walked back through the yards towards the shed. 'You were lucky.'

'I should have been quicker on my feet,' admitted Eleanor. 'I wouldn't pass muster as a first-year jackeroo.'

The man's look was one of disbelief. 'Sure you would.'

The din of the woolshed rose as they drew closer. 'So why aren't you Stud Master?' The directness of Eleanor's question surprised even her, but it seemed pretty obvious Hugh Goward should have the role. The departure of Mr Sullivan, the last outsider to have held the position, occurred five years after her father's passing. Her stepfather's assumption of the role raised some eyebrows in an industry where major studs always employed a dedicated expert to the position. And after what she'd just witnessed, it appeared that Colin wasn't quite as passionate about sheep as the man beside her.

'You are direct, aren't you?'

Eleanor felt her cheeks redden. 'I'm sorry.'

'Don't be. Actually your mother offered me the position two years ago. I didn't feel I was ready for it. It's one thing to be fully involved in the running of the operation, quite another to be given a title and have your name on the catalogue come sale time.' He hesitated. 'I take the view I'm still learning, will be all my life.'

'No doubt,' she said carefully, 'it helps to have everyone's support,' alluding to her stepfather.

170

'Well, yes,' he admitted, 'there's that too.'

Eleanor persevered, 'And what about now?'

The overseer opened the last gate leading from the yards and she walked on ahead, the red dog rushing to greet them.

'Now,' he admitted, 'if it were offered again, I'd be inclined to accept. It's the right time I think. Don't get me wrong, Eleanor, I didn't show you that selection process to plug my cause.' The dog placed a paw possessively on the toe of his boot and barked.

Eleanor wasn't so sure about that. She figured that's exactly why he'd done it. The last person she wanted to have doubts about was their overseer, but even Rex wasn't too keen on Hugh Goward taking a step up the pastoral ladder.

'It was more a case of sharing knowledge. You seem like a capable woman. I just thought you'd be interested.'

Their conversation was interrupted by a warning shout inside the woolshed, as a yell went up for the first-aid box. They entered the vast woolshed to the refrain of *duck on the pond* as soon as Eleanor was spotted by the men. Subjected to the stares and mutterings of those who didn't take kindly to a woman in their domain, Eleanor did her best to hide her discomfort as a shearer, clutching a filthy rag to a bloodied arm, leant against one of the wool tables. Biting his lip, he grimaced and looked away as Mr Goward probed the jagged wound. A couple of the wool rollers and one of the rouseabouts drifted past to see the injury and then returned to their tasks.

'Nasty one,' the overseer pronounced. 'What do you want to do with it, Johnny? Sew it up here?'

A fleece was thrown, flung some four feet into the air. It settled perfectly on the table. Instantly the wool rollers began trimming the edges of twigs, burrs and dags.

'We might get out of everyone's way.' Mr Goward directed the shearer from the belly of the shed down to the ground level where the men were busy feeding armfuls of fleeces into the wool press.

Johnny leant against a new bale as the presser stencilled River Run on the side.

'It was me own fault. Daydreaming. Lost me grip, I did.'

'Nurse Pappas is at the house,' suggested Eleanor.

The man didn't acknowledge her. 'What cha think?' he asked the overseer. The cut ran the length of his forearm, the skin puckered in places, slicing the figure of a woman tattooed on his arm. 'Look at my beautiful girl, she cheered me up she did, seeing her every morning, now she looks like my wife.'

Mr Goward replied it was up to Johnny to make the decision as to who would do the stitching, however, there was a nurse up at the big house and if he'd not had a recent tetanus shot he'd have to see a doctor sooner rather than later.

'Sooner have Billy stitch me up, I reckon,' the shearer answered. 'Once saw him sew up a ewe's guts, pushed it back inside of her and everything and she survived. And I don't need no tetanus. Had one last year when I cut me finger off chopping the head off an old boiler hen.' Lifting his left hand, he showed the stub of an index finger.

'Fair enough,' the overseer said.

Billy Wright was sent for and a taffy-haired gnome of a man trundled down the board. The man's progress was slow, for although the board was wide, it was an obstacle course of men, tar-boys and animals. Shearers dragged sheep through the swinging doors of the catching-pens opposite their stands and, sitting them upright between bent legs, began to shear. Others, having finished shearing, pushed the sheep out of their chute to the tally pen. The picker-ups gathered fleeces and moved at the trot to the waiting tables, flinging them high in the air to land perfectly.

The taffy-haired wool roller finally reached Billy Wright's stand and waited patiently for the shearer to finish his sheep. Billy pushed the ewe down the chute and straightened slowly, a few words were exchanged and then Billy followed the wool roller back through the bowels of the shed, along the board, past the wool tables and down the three steps to ground level.

'Sew you up good as new, mate,' Billy said confidently to his pale friend when he saw the jagged cut. He stretched his arms out and shook his hands, as if limbering up. When they fell back to his sides, tattoos of naked ladies and anchors twisted and bulged where the muscles bunched.

Water was poured over both the wound and the surgeon's hands and then a liberal dose of disinfectant followed, straight from the bottle. The shearer yelped, his face screwing up in pain. Billy Wright rubbed his palms together and then rifled through the first-aid supplies before settling on thick black cotton and a large needle. 'Tools of a master craftsman,' he said loudly, although it took him four goes to thread the needle before he could begin, his hands were shaking so much. 'That be the worst of a dry shed,' he explained.

'You better have the rest of the day off,' the overseer suggested to the injured shearer.

'What, and let the likes of that bloke from down the Riverina get his numbers up on me? No fear, a bit of a gash never hurt a man.'

Billy bit the cotton and then, in quiet concentration, tied a knot in the end, his tongue poking out between thin, dry lips.

Eleanor wondered if the man from down Riverina way was the troublemaker she'd overheard earlier; the shearer who'd arrived at the village in the battered taxi. 'Think I'll leave you to it,' she said to no-one in particular.

'This'll hurt,' Billy advised his patient with undisguised satisfaction. 'Like I said. Times are when a dry shed's not all it's cracked up to be.' He gave a cackle of a laugh that was quickly drowned by the noise of the shed.

173

≪ Chapter Twenty-one ≫

It wasn't her intention to visit the shearers' quarters but the conversation Eleanor overheard at smoko worried her and the sight of the blue truck parked at the door to the kitchen meant that Rex would be within. The building was of corrugated iron and timber. Two long structures were joined by a covered breezeway and bordered by wide verandas. The five rooms held six men apiece, while Fitzy slept in the sixth, next to the cookhouse, which tagged the end of the building.

The flyscreen door to the mess kitchen was partially open and thick black flies were following myriad scents; smoke from the wood-burning oven, the smell of freshly slaughtered meat, kerosene, something cooking and something burning. The something burning had been tossed out on the flat near the steps she now stood on. An indistinguishable mass that may have once been a cake.

Fitzy and Rex were standing around a large wooden table, in the centre of which was a mound of meat. They appeared to be arguing about the cuts of mutton as the cook gathered up handfuls of chops, throwing them into a cast-iron boiler. In a corner of the room Dawson was chopping meat on a large butcher's block.

The cook pointed to the leg of mutton held in a bear-like grip by Dawson, who quickly dropped the thick meaty end of it on the table, his black skin glistening with sweat.

Eleanor entered the furnace of a kitchen, shutting the gauze door firmly. The men turned towards her.

'How you going, girl?' asked Rex.

'Good, thanks.'

'Pleased you're here I am, Eleanor. Helps having another set of eyes about the place.' Fitzy dragged a rickety chair across the uneven timber floor, his stomach wobbling, and set it down for her at the end of the table. 'Take a load off.'

Boxes and bags of supplies were stacked along a wall-length cabinet yet to be unpacked and stored in the pantry. Through the door leading into the mess where the men ate, a long table lined with bench seats filled the room. Bottles of tomato sauce, black sauce, salt and pepper sat at intervals along the length of the table top.

'Chops and onion gravy for lunch, if you want a change from the old boiler's tucker at the big house, Eleanor.'

'Thanks, Fitzy, but for me it's a bit hot for a cooked lunch.'

One at a time the cook removed two large square cake tins from the twin ovens bordering the fire-box, shutting the cast-iron doors with a boot-kick, and set them on wire racks to cool.

Dawson cleaned the block with vinegar and helped himself to the enamel teapot warming on the stove, poured tea into a chipped mug. He addressed Eleanor. 'I heard Goward was trying to give you a lesson in the finer points of sheep breeding.'

The cook wiped greasy hands across a blue apron. 'Made her follow him into the yards, he did.'

'Actually it was quite interesting,' admitted Eleanor, feeling as if her insides were beginning to cook. She wondered how Fitzy coped with the continual warmth from the oven, especially in this heatwave.

'Diplomacy,' Rex said, his tone almost fatherly. 'The girl gets it from her mother.'

'We ain't seen her,' Fitzy told Eleanor, beginning to butter slices of bread. 'Usually she's down every day, after smoko, has a cuppa with me, half an egg sanger, then she goes and checks the shed, has a yarn to the classer, says g'day to the men. They appreciate it too, knowing she's there but keeping out of things. And the first day. Well it's tradition. She's the boss after all, no offence meant, lass.'

'None taken,' replied Eleanor.

'So it was real good you were there, stepping in for her.'

Dawson was washing knives at the sink. 'She ain't her mother.'

'Routine. People like routine when they're going about their business,' Fitzy said with authority. 'Besides, she's next in line.' He gestured to Eleanor. 'The girl should be stepping in occasionally.'

Eleanor wanted to remind them that she was just visiting, that she had a life of her own. This world was her mother's. 'Mum's got her hands full at the moment.' Eleanor expected everyone to agree. Instead there was a moment's silence.

'And Christ himself wouldn't have thought that young Robbie would do such a thing.' Rex gathered all the meat scraps and set them to one side. 'Dog tucker.'

The cook upended the cooled cakes on the wire racks. 'Bit of custard, tinned fruit. Beautiful.' Opening a bottle of vanilla essence, he swallowed a good slug of the liquid.

'Don't you go getting tipsy on us,' Dawson warned.

The cook scowled.

'You should have seen him, the bloke that young Robbie shot. Laying out there in the dark, a mess of blood, looked dead to me, he did,' said Rex. 'Even Goward thought the poor bloke was buggered. Then wouldn't young Robbie have been in a world of hurt.'

Fitzy, in the process of wrapping the cakes in grease-proof paper and placing them in battered tins with lids, clucked his tongue like an old woman. 'If your father were alive, Eleanor . . .'

Rex completed the sentence. 'Never would have happened.'

'Never,' repeated Dawson. 'Got him locked in his room?'

Eleanor accepted a triangle of half bread and butter from the cook. 'He sure is.'

'Ah, the young fella won't take kindly to having his wings clipped.' Rex stretched his back. 'And the bloke? How's he doing?'

'Still unconscious,' Eleanor answered, licking dripping butter from her fingers.

'And nobody knows nothing about him?' Dawson had positioned himself at the opposite end of the table and was busy peeling and chopping onions. Once a pile had formed, he gathered up the vegetables and dropped them in the boiler with the chops. 'What about the neighbours? They know anything?'

'Uncle Colin rang them all yesterday but they had no idea who he could be. His picture will be in the papers, eventually.'

'Strangest thing,' Rex commented, 'a bloke like that just appearing out of the blue. Like a stray dog looking for a home.'

'We've seen 'em before.' Dawson picked at hairs in a nostril. 'Drifters, plain turkeys, that's what he'd be. Move from shed to shed. Get some decent tucker into them, and then move on. Bit of burr-cutting, nice comfy kapok mattress in a hut. Must have been further out west on another station, heard we were next on the circuit. That's why he's here.'

'So, you reckon he's a scab?' asked Rex. 'Like his hide to try to get work at a Grazco's shed.'

Dawson rubbed at his flattened nose.

'Well, one thing's for sure, I don't think young Robbie needs to worry about the place being invaded by communists.' Eleanor's comment was answered by a wry grin from Rex, while Dawson muttered something about going back to the homestead to wash out the meat-house. The flyscreen door clanged shut with a bang.

'Don't mind him,' Fitzy told her. 'Dawson doesn't hold with any politics, but he's right straight when it comes to people trying to

177

kill another. His own mother was chased down on horseback and hit in the back of the head with a stirrup-iron when she wouldn't lift her skirts for a whitefella up north. It should have been a quick one in the dirt before the gin woke up, but she was laid out cold. Never recovered.' He tapped his head. 'Dawson don't believe in hurting nobody. Not since that day. So politics ain't got much to do with anything, not where Dawson's concerned.'

Eleanor felt awful. 'I'm sorry, I didn't mean anything by it. It's just that Robbie honestly did think that –'

'Damn would-to-Godders.' Rex wrapped some knives in a length of calico, carefully folding the ends of the material inwards. 'I remember getting on the train with your father, Eleanor, when we enlisted in '16 and the local member standing there.' Rex lifted his hands as if he grasped the lapels of a coat, tilted his chin. '"Would-to-God I'd be going with you if I could, boys. Would-to-God."' He dropped his hands which had curled to fists. 'Never was one for politics. Black, white or brindle, you either live a clean life or you don't. Anyway, what the young fella thought and what everyone else thinks doesn't matter. The truth will out. It's a pity it happened though. Especially now at shearing.'

'Unsettling.' The cook wiped the table down with a damp cloth, skirting the pile of buttered bread and flicking bits of meat and vegetable peelings onto the timber floor.

Rex continued, 'But if the man's up to no good, well, he won't get very far laid up down the hall from old Mrs Howell. Locks the bloke in day and night,' he told the other man. 'And the old boiler has the ear of the Boss. Mrs Webber marched up to me straight as you like and said, "Rex, I've been speaking to Mrs Howell and I want you to get something on the window outside the sickroom, something to stop a person from climbing out, just in case."'

'Did she?' asked Fitzy. He lifted the two large baking trays and slid them into the twin ovens, one at a time, kicking the doors shut.

'She did, I tell you. So, I did it. Course I did it. The Boss, well, she didn't come down in the last shower. Can't say I thought it was needed, him being busted up pretty bad and all. Benefit of the doubt, I always say.'

'The depression.' The cook upended a loaf of bread, spread the slices on the damp table and began to butter a second loaf. 'About twenty years ago. Don't you recall, Rex? It got real hot and every man and his dog was down-at-heel.'

'Yeah. Stinking summer it was.' At the sink Rex washed his hands. 'Sheep dead from lack of water. Most of them too weak to shear. Men appearing out of nowhere looking for work, hoping for something to fill their tucker-bags. It was your first year here, Fitz.'

'Got dropped off the back of the truck with ten other men at the boundary gate. The boundary gate.' Sweat dripped from the cook's face onto the table, the bread. He swiped at his skin with a tea towel. 'Miles away. So we took to the road with our swags over our shoulders and bugger me if we didn't come across two blokes trying to thieve ten head. They were struggling to round the sheep up using one mangy dog and a bashed up motorbike. Well, the poor bloody animals just lay down in the dirt and when those young fellas nabbed one, they busted a back leg to stop 'em from running away. As if they'd run.' He dug the flat side of the wooden spoon into the butter and smoothed the dollop down across three slices. 'Real black thing that is, maiming animals, not that I have a thing against the blacks, no, I've had better blacks as friends than whites. But the old-people stuff, the old ways, well, I don't go much on that. Anyway, this blue truck came screaming down the road towards us, throwing dust and dirt and God knows what else across the flat. We all took to the scrub in terror. But the truck, well, it spies the thieves and takes to the bush straight as an arrow, spitting gravel and grime in its wake. And it bashed and whined and got airborne and finally rounded on them as if it were a horse and the man inside were Clancy-of-the-overflow himself. Steered them fellas, your father did, Eleanor, steered 'em both out of the scrub and straight towards us. And we nabbed the thieving buggers.'

'One ended up being Billy Wright.'

'Billy, who's stitching up Johnny?' questioned Eleanor.

'Got cut, did he? Figures. First day. No grog,' said Rex.

'Right you are,' the cook told her. 'It were Billy himself. Your father offered them both a job, taught Billy how to shear. A gun shearer if ever I saw one. The other fella only lasted for a year or so. I heard he died of blood poisoning up near Blackall. Cripes, she's hot in here, Eleanor,' the cook complained. 'You reckon you could spring us a fan?'

Eleanor didn't know if she'd ever be able to get up from the chair. She was stuck to it. 'I'll see what I can do.'

'Good on you. Might just step outside for a breather.' The cook walked outdoors.

'The thing is, Eleanor,' Rex waited until Fitz left, 'you gotta give everyone a chance. Including the fella that's been shot. That's what your father would do. Trust. Trust is important.'

Kindness lay at the heart of her father's personality while trust, in Eleanor's experience, was overrated. 'And the men in the shed, Rex, they're not bothered by what's happened?'

Rex snatched up a piece of bread, chewed thoughtfully, the dough balling in a cheek. 'Some will be.'

'And Mr Goward? He seems like a good person to me.'

Rex lifted a finger. 'A title doesn't make a man respect you, Eleanor. Besides which, he's new compared to the rest of us.'

So there was the heart of the issue. Rex didn't think Hugh Goward had done enough time on the property to be rewarded with such a coveted position. Compared to Rex's tenure on River Run, the overseer would always be the import, the new chum.

'Treat everyone the way you'd like to be treated, Eleanor. Fair, but firm. Like your father did.'

'Benefit of the doubt,' Eleanor replied, although Rex's largesse didn't extend to Hugh Goward.

'Exactly,' the gardener replied.

≈ Chapter Twenty-two ≈

That afternoon, as promised to Nurse Pappas, Eleanor went to the sickroom. On arrival, the room was stuffy and in semi-darkness. Afternoon light highlighted a tiny cobweb on the windowsill and she brushed away the empty nest as the patient emitted a small groan.

The man was cocooned within sheets. The coverings were tucked in so tightly that Eleanor was sure that if she flicked the linen, it would bounce beneath her touch. Loosening the bed-clothes, she rested a hand on the man's brow. Propped up with pillows, his expressionless face was peppered with beads of sweat. 'That's better,' she said softly. The patient was hot to the touch and the scorching temperature leeching its way indoors wasn't helping. Another electric fan replaced the broken one and she turned it on, directing the flow at the stranger.

The washstand held medicines and clean towelling. Taking a face cloth, Eleanor dipped it in the basin of water, listening to the splash of droplets as she wrung it out, before gently dabbing the man's forehead, cheeks and chin. Refolding the cloth, she wavered a little before placing it in the hollow at the base of his throat. It was a deep indentation. Strangely intimate. Her hand lingered, the cloth warming.

She wondered what he was like. How his voice would sound. If he would forgive Robbie for what he'd done. If he would ever wake up. The cloth followed the breastbone fanning out to dampen the muscles across a broad chest. Without thought, Eleanor spread her palm against the warm skin and then just as quickly drew away, dropping the cloth in the basin of water. Still, the man slept.

Eleanor squeezed the drip, noticing the glass phials in a dish on the rickety bedside table. Morphine. How did they even know he was in pain if he was unconscious? She frowned at the sight of them. The ampoules brought back unwelcome memories, long buried.

She may have been a young teenager when her father passed but Eleanor remembered sitting by his bedside as the morphine had been administered, day after day. It was a kind end, a deep, unending sleep of gradually increasing dosages that led to oblivion. Although she was yet to begin her training as a nurse, it was Lesley who'd explained that as well as aiding both sleep and pain, the drug could also provide an assisted end, one preferable to that of prolonged suffering and that under the guise of patient comfort, the medicine didn't go against the church's teachings or the law of the state. It was the right thing to do. All three of them, mother and daughters, had tearfully agreed that their decision on doctor's advice only hastened the inevitable. And yet, and yet, even now it was a hard thing to remember.

The man before her had only fallen from his horse and hit his head. The shoulder wound was minor. If Lesley were here, surely she would agree that their role was to try to ensure that the man recovered quickly, both for his sake and theirs. He needed to wake up, and morphine, no matter how low the dosage, wouldn't help.

She sat and watched the gentle rise and fall of the stranger's chest, but the chair soon grew uncomfortable and her proximity to the patient combined with the cramped, hot room added to

Eleanor's unease. She wasn't sure what caused this sensation as she listened to the sounds drifting through the flyscreen. Dogs barking. Distant, continuous. The whine of the wheelbarrow suggesting Rex roamed somewhere in the garden, while a series of bangs, perhaps cupboards being opened and shut, spoke of Mrs Howell busying herself down the hall in the kitchen.

The main homestead was a foreign land compared to the rest of the station, especially at shearing time. It was as if two unique worlds existed side by side, having suddenly grown overnight into empires in their own right. Nearly every position on River Run was emulated by the invading hierarchy of the shed, down to Fitzy and his helpmates, although there was never as much energy concentrated in one place, at one time, for so many weeks, as there was within the throbbing aged timbers of the hand-hewn shearing shed. If their land was the body, the woolshed was its heart come shearing.

And into this world came this man, Eleanor mused, her thoughts returning to the stranger. She'd brought a book with her from Sydney, Nevil Shute's *A Town Like Alice*. The library at River Run was filled, floor to ceiling, with novels, the majority of which were written by British authors. Her parents' reading tastes rarely included Australian tales, apart from the works of Miles Franklin and Jeannie Gunn. Eleanor glanced at the cover. Red-roofed houses surrounded by bland countryside, blue sky contrasting with white clouds. She read the description on the flyleaf: a novel of war and romance. Instantly she thought of Lesley and Marcus. 'War, everything is about war,' she said aloud. The book remained in her lap as she stared at the man opposite.

Benefit of the doubt, she thought.

'I think you're from a property,' she began, 'and you lost your way. Maybe you're a stockman.' She tilted her head, studying him. 'No, you own land. Somewhere.' She pulled her chair closer. 'You've been to war.' She felt sure of this. 'Fought for us, for your country and survived. The doctor said you carried an old wound on the back of your head. That's how I know that you've returned from the front. It makes sense. My father and uncle both fought and my sister's fiancé, well, he was a casualty too. So we understand. When you do wake up, you don't have to talk about it.' Rising, she rinsed out the cloth, running the material down the length of his arm. 'My mother used to despair of Lesley and I ever marrying,' said Eleanor thoughtfully, lifting his hand to wipe the sweaty palm. 'So many of our young men died in the Great War, but we can't call it that anymore, not now there's been a second one.' She stretched out his fingers on the bed. 'I suppose you're married,' she considered. 'Of course you would be.' Eleanor's cheeks grew red and she fussed with the washcloth, wringing it out repeatedly. 'If it wasn't for the wars I'd probably be married by now as well,' she explained a little more brusquely. 'It's what's expected. You know, women and motherhood being at the heart of society.' She tried to sound flippant. 'That's Menzies' line, anyway.' She washed the other arm. 'I had a friend in Sydney who married and moved to the suburbs. We haven't seen her since.' Eleanor thought of this woman on her wedding day, aglow with love and hope, eventually swallowed by the chores of home-keeping and the simple fact that her husband needed their only car for work and there was no public transport where they lived.

'Anyway, if there hadn't been a war I certainly never would have met Dante and . . . but you don't want to hear about that.' Eleanor put the washcloth aside, brushing away a tear. 'So, here we are,' she said a little more brightly. 'We've just started shearing. It's very busy. Our overseer, Mr Goward, was teaching me a few things about ram selection this morning, which I enjoyed. Actually, I haven't had much to do with him until now, but he's a nice man.' Eleanor drew breath, she knew she was rambling but it was better than sitting in silence. 'I'm sorry about what Robbie did. Truly I am. If I'd known what he was going to do I would have stopped him. But I'm sure you'll be better soon and once you wake up and are able to tell us who you are, well, then you'll be able to go home.'

'Home.'

The sound of his voice startled her. Eleanor moved back from the bed as the patient slowly opened his eyes. His Adam's apple bobbed as he swallowed.

'Water?'

Eleanor reached for a glass and filled it from the jug. Hesitantly, she moved forward holding the glass to his lips. His head lifted ever so slightly from the pillow as he took small sips, his eyes remaining sleepy.

'Have I got one hell of a headache,' he muttered groggily.

The man drank more water and then rested again, his eyes gradually clearing, focusing on her.

'The Greek?' His words were stronger.

'You mean Athena? The nurse?' asked Eleanor. 'She's not here.'

The man nodded. 'She doesn't like me.' He had an accent. 'You're Eleanor?'

'Yes.' Her eyebrows knitted with curiosity. 'How do you know my name?'

'I heard you. You were in the paddock.' The answer was thoughtful, as if he were sharing a dream. 'And then in this room.'

'Yes, yes, I was.' Eleanor sat by his side, leant forward, a hand on the edge of the bed.

'I'm not ready to talk.' His fingers found hers. 'Don't tell the others I can talk. Not yet. They won't understand.'

'But . . . ?' She knew she should tell everyone immediately, although Eleanor also wanted to keep his confidence. He was injured after all and she was partly to blame.

'The nurse will ask questions. Everyone will ask questions. Tired.'

The stranger was awake and a world of people wanted to know who he was, but his fingers were still curled harmlessly around hers.

'Promise me?'

When a voice sounded in the passageway he drew his hand away. Athena entered the sickroom, singing a song in her native language.

'If you keep chattering on like that the poor man may not want to wake up.' Athena stood in the doorway, a brown paper bag in her arms. Sitting the shopping on the end of the bed, the nurse bustled past Eleanor and briefly checked the drip. 'He needs rest and quiet,' she chastised. 'What's the matter? Is everything alright?'

'Fine, everything's fine,' Eleanor replied uncomfortably. Why was she lying for this man?

Athena didn't look convinced.

'Talking to him may help wake him.' Why did he say that Athena didn't like him? Eleanor wondered.

'He has a head wound.' The nurse proceeded to take the patient's pulse.

'I don't think it's a good idea to give him morphine, Athena. That will only stop him from waking and –'

'I didn't know you'd trained.' Satisfied that her patient was comfortable, Athena unpacked the bandages and antiseptic cream.

'I haven't, it's just that –'

'Well then, perhaps you'll leave this man's care to me. Yes?' Athena washed her hands thoroughly.

'I'm only trying to help,' Eleanor persisted, 'and by giving him morphine –'

Athena sighed and began to change the dressing on the shoulder wound. 'He is not being given morphine,' she announced without turning from her task. 'The doctor left it as a precaution.'

'Oh.' How silly she sounded.

'Now please, Eleanor, I do appreciate that your entire family is hanging on tenterhooks waiting for this man to make a full recovery, but let's not try and play doctors, alright? Now come here and help me sit him up so I can change the bandage.'

Athena deftly replaced the dressing on the back of the stranger's head and then applied a clean bandage. Together they lay him back carefully on the pillows. It was the strangest of sensations, holding someone closely, knowing they were awake but pretending to be asleep.

'It's healing nicely,' the nurse told her. 'Although Dr Headley isn't known for his neat stitches, the result will be the same.' She shook out a mercury thermometer, checked the reading and then placed it under his tongue. 'We just need you to wake up.' She looked down at the patient. 'I can see no reason why he isn't awake now.'

Eleanor gave the man the briefest of glances.

'Granted, he has an indentation to the back of his head the size of a chicken egg and there's some messy scarring, which reminds me of some of the injuries I attended to during the war, but all in all he seems healthy. Mind you, I've also seen a soldier live for two months with half his brains missing and another die within a day after falling in the ward. And him with only a few bits of shrapnel to worry about. So it's like Dr Headley says, you never know with head injuries.' Athena checked the thermometer. 'Normal. Well, that's a start.' She washed her hands again, the tar-like scent of the carbolic soap strong in the room. 'I can stay with him now,' Athena told her. Her voice had lost some of its efficiency. 'And I do appreciate you helping out, Eleanor. Really I do.'

But Eleanor wasn't listening, her thoughts were centred firmly on the man pretending to be asleep, and on his request for secrecy. Who was he? Her hand rested on the doorknob as she left. 'Athena, can I ask you, well, do you know any communists?'

The nurse let out a gasp of surprise. 'Out here?' She was rolling a length of clean bandage and it dropped to the floor. 'Damn.' Picking it up, Athena placed it in a bowl with the soiled dressings. 'I'd imagine what with you being in Sydney that you'd have more cause to mix with them, whether you realised you were or not,' the nurse replied, her tone verging on dismissive.

Eleanor thought of the unknown man in the woolshed and the comments she'd overheard.

'Eleanor, who planted the rose garden?'

'My father. Why do you ask?'

'In my country the rose is associated with Aphrodite, the goddess of love. A rose bush grew within the pool of blood spilled from Aphrodite's slain lover. So the rose is the most precious of flowers, it symbolises an immortal love that will never fade. Your father he must have loved your mother very much.'

Eleanor thought of the time her father had spent in the evening tending the roses when she'd been a child. 'Yes, he did.' With a final glance at the stranger who feigned sleep, Eleanor left the room.

❧ Chapter Twenty-three ❧

Robbie patted the balcony door key in his pocket and peered through the newly installed trellis across the pond to the house. He could smell it. Freedom. Opening a sweaty palm, he examined the object briefly before tucking the thing away for safe-keeping. There was movement in the room where the stranger slept, a shadow across the flyscreen. His sister perhaps or the nurse. On the night of the shooting, after he'd been sent to his room, Robbie had lain awake longing to see the man up close again, to shake him awake and make him tell the truth. The closest he'd come to seeing the stranger was last night, however, when after shimmying down the tree he'd glanced through the window; a snaking tube bandaged to a brown arm and the mound of a body under white bedclothes, haunting him until daylight.

Now Robbie was occupied with other matters. Since the shooting two days ago, no-one really bothered to check on him out of school hours, other than at mealtimes. And today the governess had given him an early mark due to the scorching weather. There were three whole hours left before Mrs Howell delivered his dinner tray at 6 pm. Why would things change now? Three hours. Three whole hours before fish fingers and peas, a Monday night favourite.

With a final glance at the house, Robbie ran as fast as he could towards the shearing shed, stopping frequently to hide behind buildings, trees and bushes and reassure himself that nobody was around. The wind struck his face, his heart beat hard. It was good to be outside, to feel the sun and dirt layering his face. To be free. Bluey barked, the pup straining at the chain, muscled shoulders taut. Freeing the animal, they sprinted onwards, Garnet whinnying, racing along the horse paddock fence towards him, but Robbie kept on running, past the machinery sheds and the jackeroos' quarters until the two rectangle buildings where the shearers and shed-hands camped came into view. Here he stopped to catch his breath, the smell of vegetables and roasting meat signalling that Fitzy the cook was hard at work. Ahead the shed rose enticingly, the dull hum of the engine rising and falling on a lifting wind. The cattle-pup lay in the dirt, red tongue hanging.

A row of timber provided excellent cover as Robbie ran from trunk to trunk, avoiding the front of the shearing shed. At each tree his palms touched the comforting protection of knotted bark and as the spaces between timber grew, he took a zigzag route past the plunge dip. The men were engrossed in their work. Murph, Stew and Wormy were keeping an eye on the shorn ewes as they swam along the sunken channel filled with water and Coopers Yellow dip. Sodden, the animals climbed out the other end, cleansed of parasites. Robbie skirted the jackeroos, ducked through the railings of an outer fence and, with a surge of energy, ran the last few yards to the shed flat out, his lungs bursting.

He wiggled between the stumps of the skillion shed that provided additional cover for the sheep if it rained, crawling beneath the slats of the pens across years of sheep droppings. The space was musty and dark. The air was heavy with the scents of manure, wool and urine. The odd thick white cobweb hid small black spiders and Robbie did his best to avoid the sticky nets as he edged his way forward, the pup following. Only a couple of feet above him, sheep waited to be shorn. Hundreds of hoofs clattered nervously. The ground vibrated with the hum of the engines and the movement of men and animals as he wiggled under one of the twin boards and continued on beneath the catching pens that ran down the middle of the shed.

It was hard going. Another year had passed since Robbie had last sneaked into the shed this way. He'd grown, of course, but this area was rarely used to house sheep in wet weather now and the space had dwindled in size with yet another layer of manure having fallen through the slats to the ground below. The warm plop of sheep pooh struck his neck as Robbie wormed his way through the narrowing space. Brushing it away, he slipped down into a depression created by Rex, who shovelled out the manure to fertilise the homestead vegetable garden. At the edge a skillion joined the shearing shed proper and it was here that he crawled out into daylight, blinking at the brightness. The low-hanging branches of a leafy peppercorn tree grazed the tops of wooden railings and through the fern-like leaves, the sheep-yards were a haze of dust where men called to dogs and flying dirt rendered the moving figures ghostly. The cattle-pup growled.

'You just be quiet,' Robbie warned, 'you're lucky to be here. Remember what Mr Goward said.'

The pup sat and stared, one ear erect, the other floppy.

Robbie began digging at the base of the tree until a mound of earth formed on the ground and a glass jar became visible. He pulled it free of the tightly packed soil, twisted the lid open and tipped the container side on. The contents rattled as they slipped into his palm; a tiny piece of shrapnel saved from his father's surgery, a cat's-eye marble, a white feather from a cockatoo and the skeleton of a mouse. He examined these objects slowly, reverently, one by one, as if seeing them for the very first time before placing them carefully in a line at his feet.

Sitting crosslegged at the base of the peppercorn, Robbie removed an object from his pocket. Sunlight slanted through the branches, catching the coin so that the metal glimmered. On one side was the head of a woman wearing a crown, with the words *Liberty* and *In God We Trust* etched on the surface. It was dated 1934. The opposite side depicted a bird holding a branch.

'United States of America. One dollar. Peace,' Robbie whispered, reading the words. A coin he'd spied in the dirt next to the man at the river. 'An American dollar.' Robbie dropped the coin into the jar, replaced the other items and then set about reburying the container. When the glass jar was covered with dirt he thought of the man in their house who wouldn't wake up.

The discovery of the coin worried him. It meant that Eleanor was right and he was wrong. For if the man was a septic-tank, a Yank, then he was on their side. But if he didn't *ever* wake up, and if no-one *ever* knew who he really was, then nobody would ever know for sure that he'd shot a harmless man and eventually he would stop being in trouble. Maybe he'd be lucky, Robbie thought. After all, the stranger was pretty crook.

The problem, of course, was if the man did wake up. If he woke up and he was one of the good guys. On their side. There was nothing Robbie could do if that happened.

With this sobering thought, Robbie bent back a small piece of flapping iron on the side of the woolshed. Within the shadowy building, shearers were walking in and out of the catching pens as they selected sheep, grabbing the animals and tossing them on their backs, before dragging them through swinging gates to be shorn. Two men were standing in one of the pens. They walked through the sheep, climbed over wooden rails and moved down through the enclosures of waiting animals, away from the board and the catching pens. The men were deep in conversation, moving towards the corner of the building. Robbie stood on the other side. Pushing aside massing sheep with their knees, they came to stand near the side of the timber and iron shed, sheep squashing into corners in protest. In the half-light Robbie recognised Mr Lomax. He was talking to the gun shearer, Billy Wright, who'd sharpened Robbie's pocketknife last year. The shearer scratched his crotch vigorously.

'You see what I'm saying, Lomax, don't you? You can't tell me that you wouldn't mind eating something with a bit of fat on its bones. I mean, Fitzy isn't the world's best cook. You and me, well, we're on to him. I had myself a sandwich this afternoon that was covered with dirt. Dirt. All I'm saying is that if the man had some decent meat to work with, well, he'd be happier and I'd be a damn sight happier and the shed would be happier. There's been some talk, you know, more than the usual . . .' He thumbed at the board. 'Grumbling.'

'Ah, the boy shoot the man off the horse.'

'Yes, he did. I mind my own business, I do, and I ain't got nothing against the communists, though I've met some silver-tongued stirrers in my time, yes I have. But that don't mean you go out a-shooting the poor bastards. And something like this, well, it puts the wind up a bloke it does.'

Robbie flattened his shoulders against the shed wall.

'Bad business.' The Chinaman patted a woolly ewe. 'But it was accident.'

Billy didn't answer immediately. He rubbed a stubbly chin. 'That's what the Webber girl said, but she wasn't up the tree at the time, nowhere near the place, she told me.'

'Is that so?'

'There's more. The boy nearly killed that young jackeroo with his shanghai a couple of days ago. 'Course nothing happened to the lad, but young Archie, well, he got put on the wood heap this morning.' His head sunk between his shoulders as he leant forward. ''Course, if the old man had been alive, none of this would ever have happened. The boy would have got the strap two year ago. But that's the problem with life, eventually you gotta die and old Alan, well he was about the best of them. Never came near the shed except on Mondays. Left us to it. And that's the way it should be. The squatters ain't got no business messing about with shearing excepting for a *good day to you, boys* and giving a bit of an encouraging nod to the younger men. That's all that's needed. We've got men like you, Lomax, to keep things shipshape. Now we've got the brother poking his head in every day, keeping an eye on things, when he don't even wear the pants around here. No, the bush ain't been the same since Alan Webber kicked the bucket.'

Around them, the shed rumbled. Robbie inched a little closer. He could almost see the straggly hairs on the back of Billy's neck.

'Some of these men, well, they're true blue union men, workers just looking for a fair go, so you can understand that this business has made some of them very uppity,' the shearer went on. 'Done it hard, they have. Worked real hard to earn a quid. Like you and me.'

'Australia very good place for me and my family.' Mr Lomax moved and a flicker of light showed a round face and flat nose. 'My grandfather, he come here with empty pockets. Now I happy man. I not want any trouble. I not like politics. I not like communists.' His voice rose. 'I hate communists. I spit on communists. I spit on Menzies, on this Country Party, everybody.' He blew air from his mouth. 'I work, I feed my family. I do good job in this shed. Not want any problems.'

Billy winced. 'Jesus, mate, what you been eating, eh? Dead dog or something? Now listen here and steady down. You're one of us now. You're alright. My grandfather had a chink on the goldfields, he did. Said he was the most honest bloke he ever knew. Honest as the day is long.'

Mr Lomax wedged his fists in his trouser pockets.

'You're a good bloke, Lomax. And you're top dog in this here shed. That's why I'm telling you straight. Forget about the commos. If they want to cause trouble up in the big house, that's their caper. I'm here to talk about important things, things that will keep the men happy.'

'Yes?'

'Their stomachs. We could do with some decent tucker. Cheer the fellas up a bit.'

'Tucker?'

'Meat, Mr Lomax, meat. Meat so tender and fat and juicy that it runs down your chin and fills a man up as if he's eating like a king.'

'Ah, yes.'

'Stranglers, culls. That's what we've been eating,' Billy told him, his voice growing confidential. 'Now I don't blame that old gardener, or Dawson, but it wouldn't hurt if we did a bit of choosing ourselves, if you get my meaning.'

The Chinaman grinned. 'Ah,' he lifted a finger, waggling it at the shearer, 'now I understand. But how will we do this?'

'Nice fat ewe, that one,' Billy pointed to a pen of sheep, 'and that one. Pity if the old girls suffocated.'

For a moment Mr Lomax didn't appear to understand, then realisation dawned. 'Ah, you very tricky, Billy.'

'I'll give you a call when one's a-coming. Mum's the word, eh?' The two men pushed their way back through the sheep.

Robbie slid down the shed wall, squatting in the dirt. Billy thought the man he'd shot *was* a communist and the rest of the shearers were angry about what had happened. But then Mr Lomax said he hated communists.

Picking up clods of dirt, he threw the lumps up in the air, catching them as they fell. The pup watched intently, jumping up on his hind legs and snapping at the dirt. Maybe Robbie didn't understand what they really thought about the Reds, but the one thing Robbie did know was that Billy and Mr Lomax were going to kill some of their good sheep instead of the ration sheep already selected. The branches of the peppercorn tree spread across to the shed's guttering. Robbie loaded his pockets with clods of dirt and began to climb.

From the peak of the woolshed roof, Robbie thought the countryside resembled a patchwork quilt on a lumpy bed, many parts flat and open, others rising and falling amidst the afternoon haze as if the land itself were breathing. In the middle of it all, the shearing shed vibrated like a monster from another time. It ate up sheep at one end, spitting them out at the other, smaller, whiter, some showing red welts if they'd struggled under the comb. To the north, a smudge of dust on the horizon marked the progress of a shorn mob being walked to a holding paddock. To the south-west, half hidden by trees, the homestead blinked at him from two windows visible on the second floor. When the shed finally cut out for the day, he'd have to hightail it home.

Bum-crawling his way across the corrugated iron, Robbie inched down the roof to the guttering. From above, the dark bowl of Mr Lomax's head bobbed as he moved from pen to pen, counting out the shorn sheep and writing the numbers in the tally book next to the shearer's name. At the number one stand, the gun-shearer's stand, Billy Wright's stand, Robbie squatted and waited.

A large yard to the east opened out into another holding paddock boarded by a line of low scrub. Movement made Robbie lift his head, supporting his chin with his hands. Someone approached on horseback. A spec at first, growing in size until three distinct figures formed. A dog barrelled in from the stubby bushes towards the riders, the animal padding alongside the horses, every so often darting left or right.

A gate squeaked. Below, Mr Lomax stood back and counted sheep from a pen.

'One for you, Mr Lomax,' a gruff man called out over the noise of the shed.

Robbie peered over the edge of the guttering.

A shed-hand dragged a shorn ewe the length of the emptied yard. 'Busted leg.'

The Chinaman wrote in the tally book and, pocketing it, joined the man. He bent to examine the injury, the bony curve of his spine showing through worn shirt, before the shed-hand continued dragging the sheep clear of the pens. The Chinaman ducked into the shearing shed, reappearing with a couple of splints and a length of bandage. The broken hind leg was quickly straightened and bound and the animal lifted over a fence to limp around a small yard.

Mr Lomax resumed the emptying of the pens. Robbie hunkered back down on the roof.

'Another one for you, Mr Lomax.'

A big woolly was yanked out into the first tally pen by a shed-hand. Mr Lomax gave the sheep the briefest of looks and waited until the last shorn sheep jumped through the gate of the pen he was counting. Then he was dragging the animal away, hefting it over the fence and with the help of a shed-hand, lifting it onto the tray of a truck and quickly slitting its throat. The task was done within minutes and the Chinaman returned to resume the counting out.

'Another one for you, Mr Lomax.' Robbie recognised Billy Wright as he ducked his head out of the chute. He felt for the clods in his pocket. As the Chinaman bent to drag the big woolly away, Robbie called down to the man:

'Another one for you, Mr Lomax!'

The Chinaman looked up to the roof.

Robbie aimed the shanghai at the shed overseer and fired, the clod hitting the Chinaman right between the eyes. The man stumbled and fell.

'Yes!' Robbie's fist punched the air.

'Robbie! What the hell do you think you're doing?' Three horses were tethered to a railing. His father was shaking his cane. 'Get down here, *now*!' he bellowed.

Mr Goward was calling out to the Chinaman, asking if he was alright as he went to his aid. Mr Winslow pushed his hat to the back of his head as the red dog ran around to the carcass on the truck and began to chew on the dead sheep's bloody neck.

From nowhere, the blue cattle-pup appeared, stocky back legs pumping fiercely, as it jumped up repeatedly in an effort to reach the carcass as well.

Very, very slowly, Robbie turned away. Walking along the roof, his father yelling out at every step, he verged towards the centre of the building and scrambled to the peak. His dad was still calling to him as he took a step and began to slide. The tin was burning hot on the north-western side of the structure and he skidded uncomfortably, falling on his bottom and losing control, until a skylight halted his descent. He moved cautiously to the gutter edging the building and then, carefully levering his body over the edge, hung for a few seconds before dropping to the ground.

'You're having a busy week of it, Robbie.' Mr Goward laid a hand on his shoulder and marched him back to his father.

⚞ Chapter Twenty-four ⚟

Margaret Winslow was perfectly at home at River Run. Maybe a little too much at home, Eleanor considered, as the woman mixed gin martinis, glass tinkling as the swizzle stick hit the sides of the jug. Condensation dripped onto the mahogany sideboard as the pitcher's contents splashed into two glasses. Checking her reflection in the mirror, Margaret passed one of the cocktails to Georgia. Having been ensconced in a game of bridge for a good part of the afternoon, it seemed that the unlikely pair had become friendlier.

'Another for you, Eleanor?'

'No thanks, Mrs Winslow,' she replied. Eleanor was yet to develop the tolerance the older set showed towards alcohol, especially in this heat.

'Call me Margaret, dear. I was never one to stand on ceremony. Besides, it makes me feel quite aged continually being addressed by the younger set as Mrs.'

Reluctantly, even Eleanor was beginning to warm a little towards their house guest. The Winslows' visit, having been extended beyond the original weekend with the discovery that their car needed urgent repairs, had unexpectedly assisted in easing the tension created by recent events. Eleanor was grateful for the diversion the Winslows presented, particularly as it meant that her mother and uncle had to at least give the appearance of being the loving, compatible couple that people assumed.

Margaret relaxed into a comfortable sofa, complimenting Georgia on her choice of decor. Her mother answered vaguely. Her thoughts were obviously centred on the afternoon's events and, so far, even the socially adept Margaret Winslow found it difficult to lift Georgia's spirits. It was after six and the women were showered and changed for the evening. Eleanor, not one for pre-dinner drinks, had made an exception this evening with the intent of informing her mother of what she'd overheard in the woolshed. That is, until she'd been told of the details of Robbie's latest escapade.

Eleanor sat curled in a curved-backed armchair, bare feet tucked under the hem of her skirt, a gin fizz in one hand with a desperate craving for a cigarette. Robbie's antics were beyond normal. 'Mum, do you think –'

Georgia waved at her dismissively. 'Please, Eleanor, not now.'

Margaret Winslow poked a manicured fingernail into the contents of the martini she held. The grandfather clock ticked loudly. Maybe it was women's intuition, or maybe it was natural to be imagining the worst after the last few days, yet Eleanor couldn't shake the sense of impending doom that seemed to have settled in her bones. A stranger beneath their roof, shot by her own brother, who didn't want his return to consciousness revealed. There were the words of the disgruntled shearer overheard earlier in the day and now Robbie was in trouble again. A pedestal fan clicked ominously in one corner, barely stirring the hot, thick air.

'Heavens, we need a couple of those little black boys with palm fronds.' Margaret leant back in the sofa and took a sip of her gin concoction. 'Better. Much better.'

'I asked Mrs Howell to fetch another fan but she tells me the storeroom was empty,' Georgia replied. 'I must get her to bring one in from the dining room.'

The last Eleanor had seen of the spare electric fan was it being transported carefully – and at her request – in the back of the truck to the shearers' mess.

'I'm sorry you're here, Margaret, with all this kerfuffle going on.' Georgia hadn't stood still for the last twenty minutes. She was at the record player again and when the needle dropped on the vinyl 45, Nat King Cole began to sing 'Mona Lisa'.

'Don't be ridiculous, Georgia. It's not like Ambrose Park can't manage without Keith for a few days. Anyway, if the car had been easily repairable we would have been out of your hair by now.'

Georgia walked around the oblong perimeter of the room, opening the curtains now the light was dwindling. 'Well, I for one am pleased you've stayed, Margaret. It's helped having someone else to talk to, someone who understands the joys of child-rearing.' The words dripped with sarcasm. 'Honestly, I just can't understand Robbie. And I know you're right when you say that boys get up to the most dreadful of things, but what's happened, well it's just too much. He's my child and I love him, but I don't know if I even understand him anymore, let alone like him.' At the mantelpiece at the opposite end of the room, Georgia adjusted the framed selection of Chinese fans her grandmother had procured in the 1870s from a travelling hawker.

'He's just a kid, Mum.' Eleanor defended her half-brother. It was clear the boy's problems needed to be addressed, however, there was more involved with this latest drama than the antics of an uncontrollable child. 'Robbie thought he was doing the right thing today.'

'The right thing? Robbie shouldn't even have been out of his room,' replied Georgia. Returning to the matching sofa upholstered in flowery reds and greens, she sat at right angles to Margaret, chewing on a toothpick-impaled olive. 'How he managed to get out that balcony door . . . When I think of the subdued look on your brother's face whenever he's been locked in that room for mis-behaviour, and all the time he's been sneaking outside as soon as my back was turned.'

It was best to keep quiet on the subject of the balcony key, Eleanor decided. If she'd not produced the key on Saturday, Robbie would never have gone to the river in the first place.

'It wouldn't be the first time a shearer tried to pull a swiftie.' Margaret fanned herself with a copy of *The Australian Women's Weekly*.

'No it wouldn't.' Colin walked in, accompanied by Keith and the overseer. All three men smelt of sheep, sweat and manure. 'You'll have to excuse us, ladies.'

'Not at all,' answered Georgia.

Colin poured three measures of rum, adding ice and water, and the men congregated near the sideboard, toasting the first day of shearing. Stocky and shorter than his companions, Colin looked his age next to the other men. Keith was rather distinguished with his trim figure and flecks of grey peppering his hair, while Hugh Goward, tall and broad-shouldered, stood out with his blond hair and deeply tanned skin. It was rare to see the overseer without a hat. With or without it, he was a good-looking man. Eleanor thought of his steady hands on her body following the incident in the yards, and looked away.

'I told Robbie that we're sending him to the King's School to board.' Colin barely met his wife's gaze. 'He can leave on Sunday's train.'

Georgia gave a barely perceptible nod. 'I might have another,' she replied, holding out her glass to her husband.

'Here, I'll make myself useful,' offered Margaret, taking the glass and heading to the sideboard. The mirror reflected a beguil-ing smile as she made a point of turning side-on towards Colin, as if the space between the men was narrow and needed to be squeezed through.

'We were lucky there was an opening,' considered Colin as he leant on his stick. There was a troubled tone to his voice as he sipped his drink. 'Robbie's in his room and I've told Miss Hastings that the position of governess is redundant. He can stew upstairs for the next few nights before he leaves.'

'What about clothes, uniforms?' Georgia was concerned.

'I'll send a telegram to my sister in the morning. She can purchase what's required and have a trunk railed to Parramatta, care of the boarding master.'

It was obvious that neither parent wanted Robbie to be sent to boarding school. They stood at opposite ends of the tastefully decorated sitting room, two custodians of a great rural heritage faced with a quandary that neither knew how to handle. Her mother was visibly upset at the thought of her son being packed off to Sydney and Uncle Colin was topping up his glass, the muscle in his jaw tightening. For the first time, Eleanor wondered how much of Georgia's and Colin's marriage depended on their son.

'I've been meaning to ask you, Colin,' Margaret broke the momentary lull in conversation and even Eleanor turned gratefully in the direction of the sideboard and the familiar sound of Mrs Winslow's martini-making. 'About your leg. Last Christmas you were considering having another operation.' Margaret sipped the gin blend through a straw to check the strength of the mix, adding a smidgeon of Noilly Prat.

Colin's eyes clouded. 'An operation? Yes, sorry, Margaret, I was miles away. I can't see the point of another quack digging around for a piece of shrapnel.'

'I can see how being rendered unconscious, cut open and probed yet again would lose its appeal.' Keith patted his wife casually on the bottom as he helped himself to the ice-bucket. 'My father had that arm of his re-broken and reset three times and he still had a bend in it like a banana, with limited use until he died.'

'Anyway,' Colin explained, as Margaret walked past him and handed Georgia her cocktail, 'it's been in there since 1917. And what if the worst-case scenario, as those quacks term it, occurs? No, at sixty-one years of age I think I'll put up with the discomfort. At some stage in the future I may well be wheelchair-bound, but I'm not hastening that sunny day.'

'And I don't want you to go through all that pain again,' Georgia agreed.

The overseer placed his empty glass on the sideboard. 'I should go.'

'No, Hugh,' Colin topped up the overseer's glass, 'you've been caught up in Robbie's antics, as we all have. Just have one more drink, eh?'

Her stepfather's conciliatory attitude emphasised how much Robbie's behaviour was affecting everyone.

'Of course, the lad should get points for catching them out.' Keith lit a cigarette and offered them around. Everyone accepted, including Eleanor. Her mother appeared ready to complain but instead waited patiently as Keith busied himself, moving around the room with his lighter.

Eleanor took a relieving drag of the menthol cigarette.

Mr Goward skolled the rum and water. 'Except that sometimes it's better for the men to play their games. What's a couple of fat ewes, after all, if the shed stays peaceful and the job gets done? Especially with everything else that's going on at the moment.'

'Well, I don't agree with you, Hugh,' Georgia replied, accepting a drink from Margaret. 'We run a good shed, the men are well fed. There's no need to be stealing from us. The men concerned should be fired.'

'That would be Mr Lomax and Billy Wright,' the overseer stated. 'Two top men, Mrs Webber. The Chinaman's been coming here for twenty years and you know Billy.'

Georgia cradled the martini glass. 'I'm sorry to hear Billy was involved.'

'He's a gun shearer,' the overseer reminded her, 'and he has the ear of the men.'

'That's true enough,' Georgia conceded, 'and it's a well-known fact through the New South Wales sheds that if there's an accident, the men would rather have a leg set or be stitched up by Billy Wright than a doctor. But in this case, I have to wonder at Billy's loyalty after all we've done for him. All the steady work provided these many years. He always knows there's a job here for him, shearing or not. You remember me telling you the story, Colin, about how Billy came to work for us?'

Colin nodded. 'Alan took him under his wing, gave him a job, taught him how to shear,' he explained to their guests.

'The boys are a bit strained, what with the shooting,' Mr Goward answered conversationally. 'I suggest we let things rest. Let the dust settle a bit.'

'My father would never have tolerated such behaviour.' Georgia took a puff of her cigarette, too lost in thought to realise that everyone, including her husband, was waiting for her next words. 'They should be let go.'

'Mr Lomax has a cut over his eye, thanks to Robbie's marksmanship,' Hugh explained. 'Billy reckons that the ration sheep were too tough to eat and Rex and Fitzy expressed similar concerns. We all understand the meat has been affected by the dry season, however, I think Billy thought that with the recent happenings, some decent meat might placate the men.'

Georgia appeared unconvinced. 'Are the men grumbling?'

'Why don't you come down to the shed in the morning? Have a chat to the men. Like you usually do,' Mr Goward added politely. 'It might calm things after this latest incident and the men would appreciate it. I'm sure they expected you there today.'

'Mrs Webber's had other things to attend to,' Colin stated.

'Of course. It's just' – he swirled the glass he held as if it would provide answers, gave Colin a sidelong glance – 'you are the Boss. They respect your opinion, Mrs Webber. Respect you, full stop.'

'You're right, of course, Hugh. But I'm sure what with everything that's happened, they understand my absence. Besides, if I can't rely on you and Colin to stand in at times like these, then the business is hamstrung if I'm not around. But I'll make time to visit the shed in the next couple of days.' Georgia moved to the mantelpiece, the green-gold Chinese fans flanking her so that she looked like a foreign queen. Flushed from the continuing heat, she dabbed at her face with a handkerchief. 'Contact Grazco's and tell them we need someone to replace Lomax and Billy as soon as possible. When you have word of their arrival, pay out the other two and let them go.'

The overseer scratched his head. 'Mrs Webber, I have to be honest with you, I don't think that's a real good idea.'

Georgia adjusted the gilt-framed fans, which were hanging at a slight angle.

'I heard something in the shed,' Eleanor shared. 'One of the men was annoyed about *The Worker* being torn into shreds and used as toilet paper.'

'Colin?' Georgia walked to the record-player as the strains of 'Mona Lisa' came to an end. She'd already played it twice.

Her husband shrugged. 'A bit of harmless fun.'

'There's more.' Eleanor took a final drag of the cigarette, reluctantly stubbing it out. 'He sort of implied that we all hated the communists and so naturally we were against people like him, against the workers. He sounded pretty angry.' She met Hugh's gaze.

'Well, of course we hate the communists,' replied Margaret, repeatedly dunking and sucking on the olive in her cocktail. 'It all goes back to the blasted Russian Revolution. And look what they did over there. Shot the Tsar and his family. It's before your time, Eleanor, but in the thirties there were various protests and fights in Sydney between the New Guard and the Old Guard, between fascists and communists and normal-thinking people.'

'I was there,' Keith interrupted his wife, 'when that blasted New Guard man, de Groot, slashed the ribbon at the opening of the Harbour Bridge. Well, we both were,' he quickly corrected, pleasing his wife with a kindly smile.

'God, wasn't that an uproar,' Colin agreed. 'But even before that, the bush was getting caught up in the general political ruckus. Hell, we were shearing in '29 on my father's place when one of the shed-hands started harking back to the troubles of 1891. We were arguing about something that had occurred near-on forty years ago. Anyway, I had a fist-fight with the bloke out on the flat and sent the bugger packing.'

'Colin, you didn't?' Georgia halted her search through a stack of records.

'Yes, I know, my dear, Alan wouldn't have done that, and you're right, he didn't dirty his hands. He handled the bets. Cleaned up pretty well too, I recall.'

A shadow flickered across Georgia's plump face.

Keith burst out laughing. 'The general strike of '91,' he began when he'd finished chuckling, 'my father thought that was bloody marvellous.'

'What happened?' Eleanor queried. After the disagreement between the overseer and Georgia, it appeared everyone was ready to change the subject.

'Well,' Keith moved to the centre of the room, 'the Queensland shearers and bush workers organised themselves into unions and, in response, the local graziers met in Barcaldine and formed the Pastoral Employers Association. They wanted to be able to employ men in sheds free of union rules, except that they pushed it a bit far by announcing wage reductions, refusing to negotiate and effectively challenging the union's right to exist.'

Eleanor was listening intently. 'And then?'

'The squatters were accused of attacking the union and they set up strike camps.' Colin commandeered the story. 'Over 4000 of them there were, camped out on the flat under their so-called Tree of Knowledge, an old Ghost Gum.'

'So the colonial government sent in the army.' Keith took up the yarn again. 'Eventually the whole thing died down and a handful were arrested. Scabs were used to shear the clip at Coreena Station.'

'If you ask me, the trade unions are top-heavy with communist sympathisers,' Georgia declared. 'Well, I mean they have to be when you think of union history. Here it is,' she waved a record, 'Doris Day, "Bewitched".'

'I adore that song,' Margaret said enthusiastically. 'I saw her in *Tea for Two*, you know. She's a wonderful actress as well.'

'There was something else I overheard at the shed.' Eleanor twirled the glass stem between her fingers. 'I heard that the man that Robbie shot *could* be a communist, and if he was, then the shooting hadn't been accidental.'

'It's just talk, Eleanor,' the overseer said as he finished his drink. 'Something happens on a run, something out of the ordinary, and people's minds go into overdrive. You know what it's like out here. Not much happens in the bush most days and you add a bit of boredom and loneliness and grievances are quick to rise up. Dissatisfaction. That's all it is.'

'Exactly, Hugh.' Colin sat tiredly on the sofa, oblivious to his wife's annoyance at the filth of his clothes as he rested the walking stick against the upholstery. 'Dissatisfaction breeds discontent.'

'Which is exactly why I wouldn't go firing anyone, Mrs Webber,' the overseer suggested politely. 'It doesn't take much to rile men, not when there's already talk. And we've only just started shearing.'

'Just do it, Hugh,' responded Georgia.

Mr Goward made his excuses and left for the evening. He was yet to go to the shed and check the numbers yarded for the next day's shearing with Mr Lomax, as well as today's tally.

'Well, he's become quite opinionated.' Colin stared at his wife. 'You've created a monster.'

The front door clicked closed. Eleanor worried that Hugh may have heard her stepfather's comment and said so, as respectfully as possible.

'And?' came his blunt reply, as if Hugh Goward's sensibilities were of any concern.

'Entertaining staff, Colin, is something you introduced if you recall, not me. But that being said, Hugh is a major asset to River Run and I always pay attention to what he has to say, even if I don't agree with him at times,' Georgia stated.

'Those times,' her husband muttered, 'are very few.'

The air in the room grew stuffy with heat and cigarette smoke.

'The ongoing success of the property is dependent on new ideas. What do you think, Keith?' asked Georgia, clearly looking for support. 'You'd have to agree?'

Their house guest raised his hands in mock defence. 'Two things a man never does, Georgia, interfere in another man's business affairs or with his wife.'

'Heaven's, Keith, you're so old-school.' Margaret clasped a telescopic cigarette holder. 'Wife-swapping is quite in vogue in the Eastern suburbs at the moment. It really takes the humdrum out of our housewifely lives.' The holder dangled provocatively over the edge of the armchair. Margaret waited until the ash was just about to fall from the tip of the cigarette onto the silk-weave rug, before tapping the cinders into an ashtray. The action broke the silence and the atmosphere was instantly relieved by Keith's full-throated laugh.

The fact that Eleanor couldn't actually tell if Mrs Winslow was serious or not was, however, both disturbing and intriguing.

'She's right, you know,' Keith replied. 'We've heard stories of dinner parties where they chase each other round the table. Catch 'em if you can.' He winked at Eleanor. 'Why, my father said it was all the rage in the twenties as well.'

It was a fine attempt at lightening the mood but it didn't last long.

'All that aside, something had to be done with Robbie,' Colin admitted sullenly, gazing into the dregs of his glass. 'His behaviour is disappointing. Very disappointing.'

'Well, I feel sorry for Robbie,' Eleanor announced to raised eyebrows. 'He's only a kid and a lonely one at that. One minute we're saying he's done the wrong thing by sneaking from his room and hitting the shed overseer with a lump of dirt, and the next we're calling those two men thieves. Robbie caught those men red-handed.'

'So you think they should be fired too?' Mr Winslow asked.

'No. No, I think they should be given a warning,' replied Eleanor.

The 45 had finished playing but the scratchy noise of the needle on vinyl continued. Finally, Georgia turned the record player off.

'Surely we have to ask how responsible he is for his recent actions. Why Robbie's done what he's done,' Eleanor persevered. Her mother and uncle were staring at her while Keith poured another drink and Margaret continued fanning the magazine, the light wind stirring stray hairs about her face. 'I don't think he should have been given a rifle in the first place. He's too young.'

The glass Colin held landed on the leather-tooled top of the occasional table with a thud. 'That's rich coming from you, Eleanor. You know what I just found in his bedroom? Comics. A whole range of comics. Detective comics, crime comics, the hang 'em high, shoot 'em up Western comics that your mother strictly forbid in this house and which you gave him. If he is bored and as his imagination appears to have been *most definitely* running riot last Saturday, then may I suggest that his actions were probably not helped by that trash. The same trash you have hidden in your bedroom. That pulp fiction rubbish that you try to fob off as literature.'

Eleanor stood. 'You went through my things?'

Georgia's hand reached for the cross around her neck. 'You're still writing that, that –'

'I think I might go and have a shower before dinner,' Keith said amicably, gesturing to his wife to leave the room as well. But Margaret was having none of it. She crossed her legs, settled back in the sofa, smiling sweetly. 'Refill please, Keith.'

'No, you will not leave this room, Eleanor,' Georgia said angrily, waiting until her daughter sat back down. 'You will respect the rules of this house when you are here and that is final.'

'You do understand that you're just being used by these second-tier publishers,' her stepfather lectured. 'Everyone, left and right, the rabble-rousers and church groups, everyone is against these lurid publications.'

'This is the 1950s!' Eleanor replied, outraged.

'Don't speak to your stepfather like that, Eleanor. Those trashy comics and novellas only appeal to the lower classes. Work like that is damaging to the fabric of society. It's immoral. I blame myself for letting you run off to Sydney alone. I should have ensured you always had a chaperone. If I'd done that, you'd be married by now. Married, rearing children and safe.'

'How wonderful, Mother,' Eleanor retaliated. 'And look at the extent of your domestic bliss. With a stranger unconscious in this very house shot by your son and your eldest daughter getting over a breakdown and all this on your second marriage to my uncle only months after Dad died. And you're talking to me about morals? Bloody old Menzies should be the one shot, spouting the virtues of marriage and children as the fabric of society.'

Georgia collapsed onto the sofa. Keith found something engrossing out the window. Even Margaret was agog, lighting another cigarette with a match from a River Run monogrammed matchbox. The flame burnt her fingers and she blew out the offending blaze with a loud ouch.

'That's enough,' said Colin quietly.

Eleanor stalked from the room and, once outside in the hallway, leant against the wall to catch her breath.

Margaret was the first to speak. 'Well,' she drawled, 'feisty little thing, isn't she?'

⫷ Chapter Twenty-five ⫸

Eleanor walked furiously along the entrance hall until reaching the rear of the homestead, then she headed towards the kitchen. Mrs Howell and Nurse Pappas were eating dinner, a concoction of cold meat and hot vegetables that was also to be served up to their guests in the dining room in an hour's time.

'Eleanor, whatever is the matter?' the housekeeper asked, knife and fork poised in the air.

'Nothing.' Eleanor glanced around the room, half inclined to find something breakable to throw.

The seated women exchanged a brief glance as Eleanor moved from one side of the room to the other and back again.

'Eleanor,' the housekeeper reprimanded, placing her cutlery on the dinnerplate, 'please be still. You're reminding me of a dysfunctional cuckoo clock.'

Taking up residence near the sink, Eleanor was considering marching straight back to the sitting room and telling her uncle exactly what she thought about his snooping.

'We heard about Robbie, you mustn't get so upset about –'

'I'm not annoyed about that,' Eleanor snapped at Mrs Howell.

'Well, I suppose I am considering Robbie thought he was doing the right thing. It's Colin. He went through my things. He actually went into my room and searched it,' she told the women. 'And practically blamed me for the shooting! Then, then, he and Mum gave me a dressing down in front of the Winslows. I can't believe it. It's the 1950s and what am I? A child?'

Mrs Howell took a sip of water. 'He found your writings?'

Eleanor looked at Athena. That's all she needed, for the village to start gossiping about her hobby as well.

The nurse raised her hands. 'This is not my business, Eleanor. I have problems enough of my own. Your mother is watching my every move. She dislikes me being here.'

'My hands are tied when it comes to your mother and stepfather, Eleanor.' The housekeeper poured a glass of water and gestured for Eleanor to drink it. 'I can only say that, unfortunately, when you're under this roof you have to abide by their wishes. You know that. Would you like a tray in your room later?'

'I'm not hungry, Mrs Howell,' she replied, refusing the water.

'Perhaps a cup of tea?' Athena offered.

'No, thanks.'

Mrs Howell sighed. 'Well then, perhaps you could go and check on the patient so Nurse Pappas can enjoy a more leisurely meal, and if you're still at loose ends in a couple of hours, you can come back and help with the washing-up. Alice has the night off.'

'Fine.' Leaving the kitchen, Eleanor walked smartly along the corridor. Mrs Howell and Athena were talking softly as she stepped inside the sickroom.

The patient was awake as Eleanor drew a chair to his bedside. He coughed and winced, his breathing laboured.

'Are you alright?' asked Eleanor, feeling her anger subside at the sight of the wounded stranger. 'You look very red in the face.'

It seemed to take time for him to recognise her, which surprised Eleanor considering how alert he'd seemed earlier. 'It's the heat. It's as if the world is burning up, with me in it.' His voice was weak, barely a whisper.

The patient's voice was well-modulated, and Eleanor was sure there was the hint of an accent, but it was difficult to tell when he spoke so softly. 'You're not used to this type of weather then?' Wringing out a cloth in the bowl on the washstand, Eleanor folded the damp material, resting it across the patient's brow. He didn't actually feel that hot and when Nurse Pappas had taken his temperature earlier in the afternoon it was normal. So then, she thought, if he wasn't used to hot weather, he wasn't from around these parts. 'What's your name?'

He looked at her blankly. 'I don't remember.' He lifted his uninjured arm slowly, tentatively touching the bandage on his head.

'You hurt yourself pretty badly when you fell off your horse. Do you remember that?' Eleanor didn't want to be the person to tell him that it was her own brother who was responsible for his injuries.

The man probed the back of his head as if only just realising how badly he was wounded. 'My shoulder?'

'You were shot. My brother,' she said, her tone apologetic, 'he's only eleven, well, he shot you by mistake.'

'By mistake,' he repeated. 'What day is it?'

'Monday. The accident happened on Saturday.' He stared at her as if he were having difficulty comprehending. 'You don't remember anything that happened? You were out riding on our property. Near the river. You said this morning that you remembered my voice from the paddock.'

He shook his head. 'I'm trying to remember, but . . .'

'Don't worry.' Eleanor patted his arm. 'Nurse Pappas said you'd given yourself a bad hit to the head. You've an old injury in the same spot.'

'Nurse Pappas?' he queried.

'Yes, the Greek nurse. This morning you said she didn't like you and that I wasn't to tell anyone you could speak yet.' It took some time for him to digest what Eleanor said and they sat in silence as he stared at the ceiling.

'Where am I?'

'River Run. It's a sheep station. My family owns it. We just started shearing today.'

The man ignored this, tracing instead the tubing that ran from the drip into the arm with the bandaged shoulder. 'I heard shouting earlier,' he said quietly.

'That would be my stepfather. I write, well, scribbling he calls it, comic books and things like that.' Eleanor shrugged. 'He and my mother hate me doing it. Apparently I'm contributing to the downfall of society.'

The patient tried to laugh. Eleanor smiled.

'I used to paint,' he shared. 'My father thought it a waste of time.'

'Used to?' He gestured for water and Eleanor held the glass as he took a sip. Her gaze rested on the indentation of his throat, on the same intimate stretch of skin she'd touched only hours earlier. She felt him watching her and she withdrew the glass, resuming her seat.

'It was a hobby, before the war.'

'I knew it. I knew you'd fought on our side.' Eleanor felt ridiculously vindicated, especially after all the absurd talk of the poor man before her being a communist.

'What other side is there?' he asked.

Eleanor relaxed in the chair. 'What other side indeed. I should let you rest. I'm tiring you.'

He lifted a hand. 'No, please stay. You talk and I will listen.'

'Okay. So, what did you paint?'

'Like Picasso. But very bad. And you, what are you writing?'

Eleanor found herself talking of the novella she'd written and of Dante's deception, doing her best to omit the strength of her feelings for the lover who'd stolen her work. 'I didn't think it was that great, to be honest. But I wrote what I knew. It was a story of a country girl who moves to the city. Anyway, the publisher liked it. He must think Dante has a terrific imagination for an Italian immigrant.'

'Italian?' the patient interrupted with obvious interest.

'Yes, anyway, I was foolish I suppose. My girl-friends said I should have known better.' The man was looking at her intently. 'I guess I don't have much time for Italians anymore.'

'You were in love with him?'

Eleanor felt her cheeks redden.

'Forget him. You will write another work, a great work.' He gave a raspy cough and grimaced.

Eleanor gave him a grateful smile. 'I should let you rest.'

'You'll come back?' he asked, his eyes already sleepy.

'Sure.' It was nice to be needed, Eleanor decided, nice to talk to someone who understood her, who was not judgemental like her parents or perhaps trying to curry favour in hopes of a promotion. And if she were truthful, she had to admit that he was not un-attractive. 'I'll be back,' she promised, 'tomorrow.'

Only later did she wonder at his ability to recall his interest in art, when he was yet to remember his name.

Tuesday

Arrivals and Departures

❈ Chapter Twenty-six ❈

Tightening the girth strap, Eleanor did a couple of leg hops and pulled herself up into the saddle. Hilda whinnied in complaint and, with grudging slowness, walked forward only to stop again. No amount of coaxing would budge the mare until a quick jab in the flanks with the heel of her riding boots stirred the horse to action. Fingers tightening on the reins, Eleanor felt the snap of the horse's head as the mare took the bit firmly in her mouth, stretching out hard and fast. As if to prove a point, Hilda's surge in pace did not last very long and within seconds of the mare's enthusiastic dash, horse and rider were back to a dawdling walk.

They soon caught up with the tail end of the sheep. Slow and plodding, the ewes were in no rush to join up with the main mob, whose leaders were already raising dust on the horizon. The sheep knew where they were headed. Shorn and put through the plunge dip, their paddock beckoned and they were in a hurry to reach it and leave the two-legged creatures behind.

Ahead, a crow hopped across the ground, purple-green flecking the black of the bird's glossy plumage. The red dog scrabbled out from nearby undergrowth to tear after the creature who nonchalantly took to the air with a defiant *caw*. Ahead, the overseer and one of the jackeroos, the white-skinned red-headed Archie, walked their horses silently on either wing of the shorn ewes. The jackeroo, a coastal lad, had barely uttered a word in her presence since discovering she was coming along for the ride.

The need to be free of the homestead and the people within drove Eleanor outdoors at daylight and she'd wandered to the stables. Little convincing was required when Mr Goward arrived, suggesting she join them. Too much had been said in the sitting room the previous evening. Her inclination of returning early to Sydney postponed due to the stranger who'd placed his trust in her. Eleanor no longer felt ill at ease at having kept his return to consciousness a secret. If anything she felt justified, although the choice embraced both the thrill of the stranger's confidence and a strong dose of anger towards her mother and uncle. There was, however, something else that made Eleanor rethink her leaving. She would be running away again. Coming so close on the heels of the Dante debacle, she could now recognise her tendency to flight and was determined to start addressing what could only be classed as a weakness. There was little place in the bush for such a flaw. Being home on River Run was a reminder of that.

Hilda broke into a trot as they moved towards the stragglers. The red dog dropped his head between muscled shoulders and growled at a recalcitrant ewe who'd turned around angrily to paw the dirt. The animals eyed each other. Neither gave ground. Then the dog took a step forward, breaking the impasse. The ewe turned and ran off, rejoining the single line of trailing sheep, who trotted along a track of brittle dirt bordered by inward curving grasses.

Across the grass country the red dog bounded left and right. Something stirred him. Now and then he turned in tight circles, stopping to sniff the air. The hairs rose along the ridge of a narrow back, the tip of his tail pointed towards the sky, and then whatever ailed him was forgotten and he turned back to the sheep and the steady task of keeping the animals moving.

The overseer's dog was a constant pursuer, making Eleanor's role redundant. She guessed Hilda understood the limited task set them, for when she next tried to coax some speed from the shrewd mare, she was totally ignored. While the two stockmen stayed on the opposite wings of the large mob, the dog followed the trampled path as the wind grew stronger. They were riding towards the west and the indecisive breeze, which began in the south before shifting direction, grew steady and strong.

A line of blue-grey cloud made bright by the sun's rays bruised the morning sky. The formation lengthened and thickened until a screen of darkness tipped the trees on the horizon. If this was the beginning of a storm, it would be brief, Eleanor decided. Through the rain clouds streaks of light were visible, as if the sky attempted to pull apart the gathering moisture and step through the misty veil.

Further on, the overseer rode hard on the wing as a couple of hundred ewes bolted for nearby scrub. The red dog sprung after his master, racing low and fast. The animal soon blurred with the landscape, its progress marked by the arcing of the gathered sheep as they were speared back towards the mob. Mr Goward slowed, the job already done. A few minutes later, the animal was back in front of Eleanor, eyeing her briefly with disapproval before resuming his position at the rear of the mob.

The westerly wind grew stronger. It tugged at the grey cloud of dust, which lay coiled above the walking sheep, pulling the mass left and right until it smeared the mid-morning sky. The wind brought tears to Eleanor's eyes, stinging her cheeks. She was sure that for all the red dog's tenacity, he too was hunkering lower to the ground, seeking to escape the blast of air. Eleanor squinted her eyes and the world dwindled to a smudge of beiges and browns, indistinguishable shapes that formed themselves into a prone body that she'd laid her hands upon. Was it possible that the stranger had been awake when she'd moved the damp cloth across the broad chest, when she'd touched the hollow at the base of his neck? The thought caught Eleanor unawares. She drew Hilda to a standstill. The gale-flattened grasses grew silver-white beneath the sun, before clouds shadowed the land and a darkness crept from the west. The wind howled.

'What's the matter? We've been waiting at the gate.'

Eleanor opened one eye a little wider, burrowing chin to chest. The lanky youth was close enough to touch. She guessed she'd held them up by not pushing the sheep along faster, for the boy scowled and galloped off, his yells of *get a move on, yah bastards* carrying back to her on the wind. Her hat blew away with the next gust. The dog was gone. Eleanor tugged lightly on the reins, turning her back to the stinging wind. Even if she'd wanted to keep pace with the jackeroo, Hilda boycotted any thought of it by halting behind the first clump of trees. The wind whistled through the leaves. Smaller twigs began to break off to fall through the branches above. Leaves and dirt spun around them. Eleanor slid from the mare's back, finding protection at the base of a tree. Here she crouched, her arms wrapped about her body, her forehead touching knees. The wind grew stronger, the swaying tree limbs creaking ominously overhead. The rain came. Sharp and cold, plastering her hair to face and neck.

She ran to open ground, already drenched, lying next to a fallen log.

'There you are.'

It was the overseer. He'd found her. Mr Goward jumped from his horse and came to her.

A crackle of electricity bit through the air.

By her side instantly, he wedged his body next to hers, and wrapped an arm around Eleanor's shoulders. Lightning continued to fizz around them. Eleanor cowered against the ground, feeling the length of the overseer's body pressed against her side. The red dog appeared from nowhere to squeeze between Eleanor and the fallen timber. She peered over a flapping shirtsleeve as the world grew wild. Branches flew around them. A loud bang sounded. A wrenching crack. Then it was over. The wind dropped to the barest of zephyrs. The red dog walked a few feet away and shook himself dry. Rolled in the dirt. Lifted his leg and peed. Overhead, the clouds rumbled as the sun reappeared.

'Bloody warrigal wind,' Mr Goward stated, withdrawing his protective arm. 'All show and no wet stuff.'

They sat up awkwardly. Eleanor did not want to move from the safety of the man and yet wondered why the overseer was not already on his feet, extending a hand, brusque and business-like. There was comfort in consistency, she decided, and yet for two days running now he'd literally come to her rescue. The thought barely entered her mind, then he was standing, clasping her hand in his and pulling her upright.

'A warrigal wind,' he repeated. 'Some time since we've had one of those.' He glanced at Eleanor before turning around abruptly. The red dog walked to his master's side as if he'd been called.

Eleanor realised she was soaked through. The white of her bra showed beneath the beige of the long-sleeved shirt. Plucking the material away from her skin did little to help. She would have to wait for the sun to dry the fabric, which wouldn't take very long.

A tree, only a couple of hundred yards away, had been stripped of branches on one side of its trunk. Another was split in half, struck by lightning. The cleaved side lay on the ground, as if carved off by a giant. 'Isn't that your dog's name? Warrigal?'

The dog tilted its head, studying her.

'They say his grandmother was part dingo.' The overseer brushed the brim of his hat free of dirt. 'He has the look of it and the temperament to match, so I named him Warrigal. It means wild animal to some, wild horse or dog. To me it's anything that's got a wild streak in it, that can't be tamed. Like that young brother of yours.' He studied her, waited for a response, an understanding. 'Like that twister that just went through,' he continued. 'That there was a warrigal wind. A narrow storm, I reckon. Probably blew itself out within a mile. My great-uncle never did take to a warrigal wind.'

'Why not?'

'Here one minute, gone the next.' To the east, stringy lines of blue cloud twisted against the sky. 'A warrigal wind never really goes, that's what he'd say. Once it comes to a place, it knows the way. It's a sign of things to come.'

'But we've had windstorms before, Mr Goward.'

The man tapped fingers against a thigh. 'I think you better call me Hugh. We've just shared a patch of dirt and rescued a near-dead man after all.' He looked at her directly, careful to keep his gaze away from her damp clothes.

'And you helped me yesterday,' Eleanor reminded him. The horses were grazing a few yards away. He whistled them up, but Hilda and the mare kept their heads down. 'It seems like I'm always thanking you.'

'Must be near forty years ago when that warrigal storm hit my great-uncle's place,' Hugh began, choosing to ignore her gratitude. 'Watched it for days, he did. A dirty smudge on the horizon. He told me it was like a living thing. Sitting out there, biding its time, waiting and watching. Some days visible, others nowhere to be seen. A storm like that, well it gives a man the willies. But he'd seen it, my great-uncle, so when he wasn't working he set himself up on the veranda in an old camp chair and waited. Waited ten days, give or take. His wife left him. Told him he was a nutter. Walked out and left the old man to fend for himself. Of course it came late one afternoon when he'd nodded off. Came out of nowhere, like something conjured up out of the ground. He'd seen plenty of storms before. The low spiral that spins up into the air, the thick column that sucks and spits as it passes by, and the rain, thick and pounding. But this one carried dirt like a man carries buckets of sand. Like a sheet it was and the wind, well, afterwards he said he'd never seen anything like it. Flattened the district. Blew the house flat. Him in it. But he survived.

'A month later my great-aunt wrote him and said that she was sorry for not believing. That she was coming home. They say he ferreted out every sheet of iron he could find. Dragged half of it by hand across the ground, did his best to untwist it and then used bits of wire and rope to build a lean-to so his wife would return to a home, of sorts. Nearly busted himself with the making of it, he did. Then, after all of that, old Marge never made it. That warrigal storm came back to finish what it had begun. They found her dead, eight miles from the house. Caught fair in its path, thrown from her horse. A couple of years later the Archduke was murdered and then the war began. My great-uncle swore the storm started it all. As I said, it's a sign of things to come.'

The sun was uncluttered by cloud, the land already drying.

'So it's been a long time since I've seen a wind like that. It's nothing like what hit my great-uncle's place, but it tells me something's out there. That something's coming. I'm not a superstitious man, but a warrigal storm . . .'

Eleanor thought of Robbie and the wounded man and figured the *something* had already been and gone. 'Maybe it's the rain, maybe it's finally on its way,' she suggested. 'We could use some.'

'That we could.'

They stood together companionably, Hugh rolling two cigarettes and lighting hers. Eleanor noticed the way he cupped a hand to protect the flame of the match. His nails were oval, and slightly dirty, his fingers long and strong. He smelt slightly of aftershave and soap and something else, he smelt of the earth, after rain. They smoked in silence, watching the twists of blue cloud disintegrating in the east, feeling the dry air against their skin. Ahead, the horses sank their teeth into the stubby grass. When nothing further could be coaxed from the butts they dropped the ends to the ground, grinding them out with the heel of their boots. They set off towards the grazing animals.

Hugh was the first to speak. 'Any word on the patient?'

'Nothing.' The lie was starting to grow out of all proportion and Eleanor discovered that she was uncomfortable not sharing the truth with Hugh. 'But yesterday his temperature was normal and there's signs he's close to waking.'

'The sooner the better, I reckon. It must be pretty unsettling to have a total stranger in your home.' He whistled and this time the horses acknowledged the call. The mare ambled towards them, Hilda reluctantly following. 'Well, you better head home, Eleanor. I'll go back and find young Archie. Put the sheep in their paddock. Get back to the shed.'

'Archie's the one that annoys Robbie.' She tucked a length of matted hair behind an ear.

'They annoy each other. Robbie has everything, although he's too young to know it yet, while Archie comes from nothing. He's got a chip on his shoulder that would have sunk the *Titanic* if the iceberg hadn't got there first. But give him a couple of years and he'll be fine. Takes a bit of doing, you know, to leave your childhood behind, to become a man.'

In the middle of the bush, surrounded by space and light, Eleanor discovered that she wanted to know more about Hugh Goward. This was a good man, a kind-hearted man, and he was integral to the family business, much to her stepfather's annoyance. Which in some ways made being friends with him, which Eleanor knew they now were, even better. At a guess he was in his early forties, a young pup in Rex's view. But he was far older than his age. In his company, at times she felt like a child.

'Off you go,' he said, when the horses finally drew level with them. 'Rex will be back from town in a few hours and I'm sure you'll want to be there when your sister arrives.'

Eleanor frowned, surely she'd misheard. 'My sister? Lesley?'

'She's coming on the train today,' Hugh explained, his words suddenly stilted upon noticing her surprise. When she didn't reply he continued, 'Rex said your mother organised it a few days ago.'

Eleanor knew she must have appeared stunned. She studied the grass, patches of red earth between the clumps.

'You didn't know?' The overseer hooked a thumb in a trouser-pocket, fingers tapping the cloth. 'She's had a bit to deal with, your mother.'

Lesley was coming home. After all these years.

Grasping the reins, Hugh swung up into the saddle. The red dog hunkered down onto his back legs and then sprung onto his master's lap. The mare snorted. 'You be right?' The easy comfort between them broken, the overseer appeared anxious to be gone.

'Yes, of course,' replied Eleanor, grabbing Hilda's reins. The prospect of her sister's return was beginning to release long-buried memories. 'Sorry, you've thrown me a bit, Hugh. I had no idea Lesley was coming home.'

The man didn't reply.

'Has the shed quietened down a bit?' she asked, changing the subject.

'I'll tell you when Billy Wright and Lomax are given their walking orders. I'm yet to hear when the new men are due and who they'll be, but firing a gun shearer is one thing, getting rid of the shed overseer . . .' His mount snorted, shook its head impatiently. 'And it's only the second day of shearing.'

'I always liked Mr Lomax. Billy I didn't know very well.'

'Billy's a man's man. Always has been.' The overseer tugged on his nose. 'Tell me, Eleanor, that conversation you overheard yester-day morning. Who was doing the talking?'

Hilda nibbled at her hair. 'I didn't see them. They were sitting on the other side of the rainwater tank but one of the men was older than the other, and he had a really faint voice.'

'Donaldson from the Riverina. Throat cancer. I'll keep an eye out.'

'Can I ask you, do you think my mother has done the right thing by firing them?'

'Wool is worth a pound a pound, Eleanor. Who knows how long this business in Korea will go on for. High prices like this don't last forever. We should swallow our pride, give the men involved a talking-to and then concentrate on getting the fleeces off and the wool to market.' The overseer flicked the reins.

'And the wounded stranger,' Eleanor persisted. 'He complicates things?'

'Robbie's part in it gives the rabble-rousers an edge to work with.' He waited patiently as if expecting further questions. 'I really have to go.'

But he didn't go, at least not immediately. He sat astride his mount, one wrist resting atop the other, staring down at her so intently that Eleanor became immersed in the blue-green of his stare. Eventually he tipped his hat, gave a lazy smile. Eleanor smiled back. With a feeling bordering on regret, she watched Hugh ride away.

Retrieving a notebook from her shirt-pocket, Eleanor wrote down the story of the warrigal storm. When she'd finished, she thought of Jillian and Henrietta, sitting side-by-side in the typing pool, waiting for their tea-break and a longed-for cigarette. At this very moment, Eleanor wouldn't have changed places with them for all the world.

✎ Chapter Twenty-seven ✎

In the sickroom Athena sat at the end of the bed, lifting her feet from the floor as Mrs Howell swept around her, before proceeding to dust the skirting boards. The air was tense. The nurse glanced briefly towards Eleanor when she appeared in the doorway and then back to the patient.

'He's awake. Not speaking but awake,' Athena told her. 'He woke last night. I've informed your parents.'

The man's eyes were closed. 'Really?' Eleanor wondered if he was asleep and why he'd suddenly changed his mind when he'd been so adamant about keeping his secret yesterday. 'He's said nothing?' she asked, trying not to sound too inquisitive.

'Nothing,' the nurse replied. 'I've rung the doctor, but he's over three hundred miles away and won't be here for a couple of days.' She stood, moving to collect the tray, which held an empty soup bowl and partially eaten bread. 'This is his second meal in seven hours so I think we can safely say that he'll make a full recovery, that is, when he decides to speak.' She stared pointedly at the patient. 'There is no reason why he shouldn't be speaking,' Athena raised her voice, 'unless he's got reason not to.'

'There's no need to shout.' The housekeeper glanced warily at the stranger. 'Did you know? About Lesley, Eleanor? I only heard this morning. *This morning.*'

'Mr Goward told me,' Eleanor answered. She should have sought out her mother on her return but another argument was the last thing any of them needed.

The older woman's frown line was deep, angry. 'Five years she's been away. Five whole years.' Her offence showed in brusque movements as she bustled about the cramped room, which over the past days had grown to resemble an infirmary with its antiseptic scent, dull lighting and pristine surfaces. 'Beds need to be made, rooms tidied, then there's the menu. They'll be seven at table tonight. Seven.'

Athena excused herself, carrying the tray back to the kitchen. Eleanor beckoned to the housekeeper that they should follow and they shut the door on the patient, locking it behind them. The three women met at the kitchen table. The nurse filled the kettle, lit the gas stove to heat the water and began setting out cups and saucers, milk and sugar.

Mrs Howell sat tiredly, mopping her face with a hanky. 'Where have you been? You've been gone half the day.' She noted Eleanor's dusty clothes and messy hair. 'You look like the wreck of the Hesperus.'

Eleanor adjusted the speed of the electric fan. 'I went mustering with Hugh. We got caught in a storm out in the back paddock. A warrigal wind and –'

'Hugh is it now?' the housekeeper said curtly, watching as Athena added two tablespoons of tea to the pot on the sink. 'Storms and boys with rifles and unknown men and Frederick Barnaby Rivers' granddaughter on friendly terms with the overseer.' She drummed knobbly fingers on the table. 'A warrigal wind, was it?'

'Yes, it came from nowhere. Hugh was telling me –'

Mrs Howell lifted a hand. 'I've got enough to worry about, Eleanor, without such stories. My father spoke of a warrigal wind.

Had us children cowering under the bed for nights on end, he did. My mother used to say, don't go talking about it, Michael, you'll only entice bad things.'

'And did it?' asked Eleanor. 'Entice bad things?'

'I'm sure that you and Hugh,' Mrs Howell said the man's name with a certain terseness, 'have talked about it enough for one day.'

From the direction of the gas cook top where Athena stood came a restrained giggle. The housekeeper pursed her lips together. 'I'm getting too old to be at River Run. I've always considered myself to be a member of this family, but this business with Robbie and now the last-minute news that Lesley is coming home . . .'

The kettle on the stove whistled. Athena poured the boiling water into the teapot, sat it on the table and then retreated to lean against the cupboards, as if not wanting to intrude.

'This house will go to pieces if you leave.' Eleanor clearly wasn't the only one offended by hearing of her sister's imminent arrival secondhand. 'Say you won't leave?'

'But you'll go back to Sydney eventually, Eleanor,' the older woman replied.

Eleanor really didn't want to think about Sydney. Her holidays had only just begun.

'Anyway,' continued Mrs Howell, 'it's all becoming a bit too much for me. I'm no spring chicken and I've got a widowed sister on the coast who could do with some company, and I wouldn't mind a bit of cool, damp air.' Swirling the tea in the pot, she poured cups for each of them. The tea was strong and black. 'Every year when the hot winds blow I feel myself dry out a little more. If I don't leave soon, eventually that blasted wind will take me with it.'

'You won't rush the decision? Promise me?' Eleanor pleaded.

Mrs Howell sipped her tea and fidgeted with the beaded doily covering the milk jug. 'What about your sister then? It's exciting news, even if your mother didn't deign to share it with me in advance.'

'Nor me,' Eleanor reminded her.

The housekeeper's look suggested she didn't believe her. 'So you said.'

'When was the last time you saw your sister?' Athena's question broke the unease as she joined the women at the table.

'Six months ago, but only briefly,' Eleanor revealed. 'The convent is quite strict when it comes to visitors and when Lesley does consent to see us, it's invariably brief. The nuns say that she is happiest by herself or working.'

'Five years for me.' Mrs Howell added the scantest drop of milk and blew on the steaming tea. 'Of course, staff don't count in the scheme of things, not where family is concerned, even if you have nursed them as little ones and cared for them as if they were your own.'

'But you never go to Sydney, Mrs Howell,' Eleanor reminded her.

The housekeeper ignored the remark.

'You must be excited to see her then, Eleanor,' said Athena.

'Yes, of course I am.'

'But?' the nurse asked, weighing in on the silence.

Eleanor wet her lips, tasted dirt. 'It's just that I don't think Lesley should be coming home now, not with everything that's going on. It's not that I don't want her back here, but –'

'I know, I know. We all want her home,' Mrs Howell agreed. 'But to expect her to nurse that man down the hallway.'

Eleanor paused while adding sugar to her tea. 'What?'

'I was asked to stay on for a day or so,' Athena took a sip of tea, wrinkling her nose, 'until we're assured your sister is comfortable and capable of nursing the patient, although as your mother advised that your sister is a trained nurse, I'm sure she will be fine.'

'But that's ridiculous,' Eleanor argued.

Athena shrugged. 'Perhaps, Eleanor, your mother feels that by keeping your sister occupied it will make her homecoming easier.'

In a cupboard she found honey, added a good dollop to the hot drink, tasted the tea and nodded her satisfaction.

'Your tone suggests you don't think it will?'

'Death changes people,' replied Athena. 'I know very little about your sister except that she has had difficulty coping with a great loss. The young man is buried here, is he not? On your family's land?'

The wagging tongues in the village had been busy. 'Yes, he is. He was living here at the time of his death. He committed suicide. It was the war, his experiences there. He never fully recovered his health and I think Marcus knew that his future offered limited prospects.'

'The war. Yes,' Athena nodded, 'some things are too hard to bear, even for the strongest. We come back to a life that we no longer feel that we belong to and then of course there is the guilt of surviving.' Athena looked directly at Eleanor. 'And your sister, she too tried to take her life, yes?'

Eleanor could only nod. 'After she recovered, she stopped speaking. Lesley totally withdrew from us, from everyone. It was Mum's decision to try the convent. Gradually she came out of herself. It took time, but within a year of living with the nuns, she was better, talking, eating properly. The problem is she's never wanted to leave the place.'

'And she has not been home since?' Athena queried thoughtfully. 'To the last place her fiancé lived and where he is buried?'

'No, she hasn't,' Mrs Howell answered slowly, topping up her cup with more tea. 'Is that a problem?'

'It will be hard for her.' Athena scratched a nail against something dried on the table. 'It would be hard for anybody. She will be reminded of what could have been. The loss may well hit her anew. Did she make the decision to return home, or your parents?'

Eleanor thought back to Sunday, after the shooting, when the doctor first announced that Athena would be nursing the stranger. Her mother had been against the woman coming to River Run,

233

citing her dubious background. She recalled Georgia leaving the table to make a telephone call, mentioning that there was someone else capable of fulfilling Athena's role. 'My mother made the decision.' Eleanor was sure of it.

'Then one can only hope that it was the right one to make,' Athena concluded. 'It takes much strength to survive tragedy. With such a death, part of you also dies.'

'You nursed during the war,' Mrs Howell stated. 'You'd know about such things.'

'Unfortunately, yes.' She pinched the bridge of her nose, obviously tired. 'I will be leaving here this afternoon, Eleanor. Your mother expressed concern at my personal situation the day of my arrival.' She gave a slight smile. 'I have a child, you see, and the rumours that my little girl was born out of wedlock are quite true. My morals are questionable in her view.'

'I'm sorry,' Eleanor said simply.

'Don't be. I can't comprehend such attitudes, especially when it comes from a woman who is fortunate to live in a country untouched by war. I only stayed because a duty was required of me, otherwise I would have left sooner.'

'But what about him?' Eleanor worried. 'What if Lesley isn't up to caring for him?'

'She has trained and so I trust in her ability. Besides, there is little that has to be done, now that he is recovering. He is no longer on the drip now that he is eating. I will dress the patient's wounds before I leave,' Athena explained. 'Tomorrow when they need changing, join your sister in the task if you are concerned. You have already assisted me so I know you are capable should she require help.'

'Okay.' Eleanor cupped her hands around the cooling teacup. 'I am so sorry if my mother offended you.'

Mrs Howell cleared her throat.

'I am new to this world. I have only been here for six months but I have learnt how quickly rumours begin in a country town and how bigoted people can be. I don't worry for myself, but I do worry for my family, for my child.'

'You're embarrassed to be associated with us,' Eleanor stated.

The younger woman was surprised. 'Not at all. Who am I to judge another? But my continued presence will cause your mother discomfort. They have their beliefs and I must respect them. More importantly, I miss my daughter. A mother should always be near her child.'

'And the patient?' Eleanor recalled the man saying that Athena didn't like him. How would he know such a thing? 'Have you never wondered who he is or where he came from?'

'I am wary by nature, Eleanor. An unknown man, who arrives on another's land unannounced and then pretends to be unable to speak when there is no reason for such a disability, must be cause for concern.' Her hands rose to the tabletop, she interlocked her fingers. 'There is another thing too,' she faltered. 'He looks Italian to me. I'm sorry, but the Italians were on the Germans' side during the war. It was a bad time for my people. It has been difficult for me to tend to him, it is not so long ago, the war. For many of us, not enough time has passed.'

'Maybe he's an American-Italian, maybe he was on our side?' Eleanor knew by the expressions on both women's faces that she should have remained silent. 'Well, it's possible.' She thought of the conversation shared with the patient yesterday, of her comments regarding Italian immigrants. Eleanor hoped the stranger wasn't Italian and if he was, she dearly hoped she'd not offended him.

'War. There will never be enough years between then and now.' Mrs Howell patted the nurse's hand. 'We understand, lass. I'll keep him locked up until he leaves. Rex told me that the local newspapers are running a story about him in today's paper.' The housekeeper was on her feet, running a rag across the pristine stovetop, returning it to the pocket of her apron. 'So it will only be a matter of time before someone claims him. Which is as it should be. The sooner we're rid of him, the better.'

'I think it would be for the best,' the nurse replied. 'I tried questioning him last night after he woke. I've seen that look before.'

'What look?' asked Eleanor.

Athena met the women's inquisitive stares. 'Evasion. He could nod yes or no, write his name on the paper I offered. But no, instead he stares as if dumb.'

'Maybe he can't speak English.' Mrs Howell pursed her lips. 'Maybe he is a foreigner, just as young Robbie said.'

'I speak a little Italian and the German that I picked up during the war, among other languages.' Athena put the lid on the pot of honey. 'He doesn't react to anything I've said.'

Eleanor knew she should share the truth. Tell the women that the man could indeed talk. But he'd placed his trust in her and, besides, he still couldn't even remember his name. Athena rose from the table. 'I have no other information except my instinct. I think I'll change the patient's dressings now. My uncle is coming to pick me up within the hour.' She shook hands with Mrs Howell. 'Thank you for everything. I've taken the linen from my bed and put it in the laundry. And Eleanor,' she said, turning to her, 'if you need anything, telephone me, even if it's just to talk.'

'Thank you,' Eleanor replied gratefully, hugging the woman automatically before Athena left the kitchen.

'She wasn't that bad, I suppose.' Mrs Howell gave a sniff. 'At least she picked up after herself. Although the girl likes the sound of her own voice. Sings every minute of the day she does, in that funny language of hers. I've known worse and better.'

'I like her,' said Eleanor.

'It's easy to admire the strong. It's what drives people that concerns me. Athena isn't worried about how her presence here may affect this family, she's only concerned about herself and her child.'

Eleanor agreed in principle. 'And isn't that as it should be, after everything she's been through?'

Mrs Howell cleared the tea things from the table. 'I'd expect a woman like that to be selfish. You shouldn't be so fast, young lady, to take people on face value, to trust them. Most people in the world have their own agenda. Not everyone, but most.'

Eleanor thought of Dante, of the stranger down the hall.

'Now, before I start making lunch there's something I must tell you. Rex said that the *Sydney Morning Herald* –'

Eleanor let out a puff of air. 'Oh, no. What now?'

Mrs Howell stabbed at a daddy-long-legs spider, squashing the insect on the wall. 'Well, the truth of what happened has to come out if we're ever to discover who this man is.' She gave the kitchen a sweeping glance and, satisfied with her handiwork, turned her attention to Eleanor. 'I may as well be the one to tell you, lass. Pattie Hicks at the telephone exchange overheard the story on the party line and eventually Rex got hold of it.'

'Stickybeaks,' Eleanor decided.

The housekeeper ignored the interruption. 'There are pictures of your mother and Robbie at one of the stud sales in the *Sydney Morning Herald*, as well as the photograph taken by the police of our patient. Better to have it all done and dusted, even if the tone of the write-up wasn't at all favourable.'

'Why? What was in it?'

'I only heard secondhand, but something about a line drawn in the sand between the Country Party and the unions and the desire for capitalists such as this family to keep the toe of their boots on the necks of workers. And apparently your mother and stepfather are the epitome of the tall poppies on the land, too busy partying to keep their young son in check.'

'Heavens. And now Mum is making Hugh sack Mr Lomax and one of the shearers, Billy Wright.'

Mrs Howell's eyebrow arched upwards until it appeared like an inverted V. 'I know. Rex told me. Eleanor, listen to me. It sounds like the reporter was quite adept at ferreting out information. There was reference made to your writing – pulp fiction, they called it – and Rex said something about you frequenting some models ball where they have a parade of homosexuals in fancy dress with Vaseline on their faces and beauty spots.' The housekeeper's tone was condemnatory.

'All my friends go to those balls, Mrs Howell. They're harmless. Just a bit of fun and –'

'You are a River by blood, Eleanor, not some fly-by-night little Sydney piece. You should remember that when you're out gallivanting around with River Run's overseer. It's not seemly, I tell you. Not seemly at all. Now, you best go and get yourself cleaned up. Your sister's coming home.' The brass key ring lay on a kitchen bench and she picked it up. 'I think I'll wait while Athena changes those bandages, then I'll lock the patient's door.'

≈ Chapter Twenty-eight ≈

The entire household were waiting on the front veranda of the homestead as Rex drove down the circular gravel drive and parked outside. Lesley, seated beside him, looked out the open window of the truck at the two-storey building as if seeing it for the first time, before meeting the fixed, smiling faces of her family. The expressions of those waiting – her mother, Colin and Mrs Howell – were at odds with Eleanor's own emotions. While she did her best to emulate a sunny smile, her eager anticipation at Lesley's arrival was mixed with an element of apprehension, an uneasiness compounded by Nurse Pappas's opinion. Behind them, the Winslows waited discreetly in the hallway, for once Margaret's chatty demeanour subdued by the occasion.

'My dear girl.' Georgia ran down the stairs, wrapping Lesley in her arms. Eleanor and Colin followed. 'My dear, dear girl. Home at last.'

Lesley returned the hug. 'Yes, Mum, I'm home.'

Georgia held her daughter at arm's length. 'It looks like you could do with some good home-cooked food. I'm pleased you're home, Lesley. It's been too long, far too long.'

Eleanor noticed that her older sister had changed little in appearance since her brief visit to the convent six months ago. She was still very slight and pale, a paleness accentuated by lacklustre reddish hair.

'Uncle Colin.' Lesley extended a hand and was swiftly subjected to a kiss on the cheek.

'It's good to see you, Lesley, you're looking well,' said Colin.

'Poor as a crow,' Mrs Howell muttered from where she waited on the stairs. 'Just look at her. She's probably living on stale bread and gruel.'

Eleanor walked forward and held her sister tightly in her arms. God, she'd missed her, she'd missed her big sister so much. Eleanor could have hugged Lesley forever, but the frailness beneath the simple beige dress surprised her and she moved away, clasping Lesley's hands. 'You look great, sis,' she said brightly, trying not to cry at the sight of the washed-out woman who used to be her vibrant older sister and confidante. 'It's so good to see you and to have you home, at last.'

Lesley gave a wan smile, her tone flat. 'I forgot how far River Run was from Sydney. Sister Anna had to remind me with a map.' She squeezed Eleanor's hands before turning to Rex, who was waiting by the truck. 'Thanks, Rex. I know I've already said it, but it's good to see you.'

The gardener's eyes grew moist. 'It hasn't been the same without you, Miss Lesley.'

'Don't forget what I said, Rex,' Lesley told him, 'a Bex powder will ease those aches and pains at the end of the day.'

'I'll remember. You let me know if you need anything, won't you?' Rex passed Lesley's suitcase to Colin.

'You'll be the first person I'll ask,' replied Lesley.

Rex's face crinkled up into a grin as he got into the truck and drove away.

'Come on, Lesley,' Georgia interrupted, 'let's get you inside and out of this afternoon heat.'

'We must call Sister Anna and let her know that I've arrived. I promised that I would.'

'Yes, yes,' Georgia agreed, taking her daughter by the hand.

Lesley joined everyone on the veranda. 'Mrs Howell, how are you? How's the lumbago?'

The housekeeper, overcome by emotion, embraced Lesley like a lost child.

'Don't cry, Mrs Howell, you'll make me start,' Lesley complained kindly. 'I'll come down to the kitchen and we'll have a nice cup of tea together once I'm settled.'

'Bless you, Lesley,' Mrs Howell sniffed.

'And you remember Mr and Mrs Winslow, Lesley?' Georgia directed her daughter inside the entrance hall to where their house guests waited.

'It's very nice to see you again, Lesley,' Margaret said politely as she scrutinised the girl from head to toe.

'And you. Hello, Mr Winslow.'

'Hello, dear, a bit of country air will perk you up, although I'm afraid it's a bit warmish.'

'Where's Robbie?' asked Lesley, looking around the hallway.

'Young Robbie is in his room. You'll see him at dinner,' Colin informed his stepdaughter.

'Oh. Rex told me about the shooting and Robbie's involvement. I didn't realise that the patient was here on his account. I was under the impression it was a family friend who'd been injured.' Lesley was clearly unimpressed not to have been told of Robbie's implication. 'Sister Anna said that −'

'There was no need to trouble the Sister with our personal family business, Lesley,' Georgia cut in. 'No need at all. And I certainly didn't see the need to bother you with a long-winded explanation. In short, it was an accident. But the stranger was trespassing. I'll fill you in on the details once we're upstairs.'

'Everyone thinks he's a communist,' Margaret Winslow added.

Lesley appeared only mildly intrigued.

'Regardless,' Georgia continued, 'he needs care. But you'll meet him soon enough. Come now, let's get you settled,' Georgia told Lesley, walking towards the staircase. 'Mrs Howell, a slightly earlier dinner if we could, please. Cocktails in half an hour,' she suggested to the Winslows.

'Fabulous,' Margaret said enthusiastically. 'We'll shower and change for the festivities.'

'I'll get some ice and perhaps we could have some of those tasty savouries of yours, Mrs Howell. Prunes and bacon?' Colin requested.

Mrs Howell's tight smile was noticed by Eleanor. 'Sure, I'll just run to the corner shop.'

'What was that?'

'Nothing, Mr Webber,' the housekeeper answered. 'I'll do my best.'

'Good woman,' Colin replied brusquely, heading towards the stairs with Lesley's suitcase.

Eleanor and the Winslows walked behind Georgia, Colin and Lesley. Once upstairs, the Winslows went to their room to change as Colin deposited Lesley's belongings in her bedroom.

'I'll be down directly, Colin,' Georgia informed her husband. 'I'll get Lesley settled first and then I'll show her the patient before dinner. Off you go, Eleanor. You two girls can catch up later.' Georgia closed the bedroom door, leaving Eleanor standing in the corridor.

'Don't take it personally, Eleanor,' Colin said from the landing.

'I'm learning not to take many things personally, Uncle Colin,' she replied, pointedly.

Her uncle appeared ready for an argument but surprised Eleanor by walking downstairs. She listened to the tap of his wooden stick before heading to her own room, where she shut the door. Lesley may have returned to River Run, but in her heart Eleanor knew that her sister didn't really want to be there.

✴ Chapter Twenty-nine ✴

Robbie's feet dragged as he followed Mrs Howell down the staircase, his finger tracing the wooden banister. It wasn't that he didn't want to see Lesley, although he barely remembered her, and it was true that he expected his parents to yell at him, again. These things, however, were unimportant compared to what lay ahead – boarding school. And with another dinner, another night, the thought of the too few sleeps left before it was time to go frightened him. Hard-faced Howell was urging him to hurry up, to lift his feet and walk properly, to stop his whinging, to stand up straight. The woman walked stiffly, grasping the banister for support, trailing a powdery scent. At the bottom of the stairs she bent low, straightening his shirt, and checked his face for the fourth time. Used spittle to settle his hair. Robbie cringed. Her hands were hard. They scraped his skin like splintery pieces of wood.

'Get those hands out of your pockets, Robbie. Pockets are for keeping things in. Hands are for constructive activities. Idle hands make idle minds, and I'm sure you don't want your parents to think that they've bred an indolent youth.'

Who would check the crow-trap, track the person who'd stolen his cray-bobs, keep an eye on jug-head ugly Archie or the Chinaman and Billy Wright? And what about the communists? Okay, maybe Eleanor was right. After all, there was an American dollar coin hidden at the base of the peppercorn tree down in the yards. So maybe the stranger wasn't a commo, but they still didn't know that for sure and perhaps the communists wouldn't attack River Run, but that didn't mean some of them weren't here, down at the woolshed, waiting and watching.

The long entrance hall stretched out like a tunnel. Laughter sounded from the dining room. Mrs Howell glanced over her shoulder ensuring that he still followed. Robbie's eyes were on the solid timber door at the end of the hall; on the brass knob and stained-glass pane. Outside, lay the garden, the bush. There were plenty of places to hide. He stuck a finger between his neck and the buttoned-down collar of the shirt he wore, trying to increase the gap. When he swallowed, the sweaty skin of his throat stuck on the material. He could run now, he thought. Head to the stables and ride away on Garnet, hide in the tree at the river.

'Lesley's been through a lot so you be nice to her.'

They'd stopped at the door to the dining room.

'No talking back or misbehaving,' Mrs Howell instructed. 'The Winslows are still here, treat the place like their own they do, but that aside, they're important people. Remember that, Robbie. Best behaviour. Don't talk with your mouth full. In fact, don't talk at all, unless someone talks to you first.'

Up close the old woman was all flat grey hair, squiggly lines and puckered skin, but her eyes were clear and hard and Robbie knew from experience that she could move like the wind when she felt inclined. More than once he'd felt the sharp sting of a slap to his backside. He nodded and mouthed okay, scared of talking lest he start to cry. No-one understood. No-one understood anything.

'Chin up, Robbie.' The housekeeper smoothed the neat white

collar of her dress. 'This is an important family occasion, what with your sister being back and all.'

'But they're sending me away,' the words spilt over each other, 'and I don't want to go, Mrs Howell. I don't want to leave Garnet and my cattle-pup. I don't want to share a room with ten other boys, or live in the city. What will I do in the city?' He was holding her arm, squeezing the papery skin.

Very gently she prised his fingers free. 'Calm down, Robbie, you'll just make yourself sick.'

'But what do I want all that learning for? I can read and write already and I promise I won't steal any more of your tinned food.' He could feel his lip quivering.

'Smarten yourself up, young man.'

Robbie buried the knuckles of his hands in his eyes. He felt the housekeeper squeeze his shoulder ever so slightly.

'Not all of this is your fault, Robbie,' Mrs Howell said a little more kindly. 'I know that. You've been left alone a lot and your parents, well, your parents have done their best, but things have happened, bad things, and it's best for everyone now if you go away to school. Besides, it's the duty of every young landed man to make sure he makes the most of his education. Especially if he's going to inherit a fine property like River Run. Now wipe your face, everyone's waiting for you.' She opened the door, shuffling him into the room. Six pairs of eyes turned towards them as Mrs Howell led him to a seat in-between his half-sisters. Everyone spoke to him at once, as if they were pleased to see him.

'Hello, Robbie. You've grown.'

'Hello,' he answered. Lesley was softly spoken, pale with red-gold hair and a narrow face. She wasn't pretty but she wasn't ugly either and when she smiled, he noticed that her bottom teeth looked as if they'd been partially ground away.

'There, here we all are.' His father lifted a glass. 'All together again.'

245

The occupants at the table clinked their glasses and smiled too-bright smiles. Robbie swung his legs back and forth. The horse-faced Winslow woman was staring at him, smoking and staring. He studied the ceiling, the silver knife and fork, the two electric fans at either end of the room blowing hot air across the polished oak table. Mrs Howell cleared away the individual salad entrées eaten before his arrival, as moths outside fluttered against the flyscreens on the wide windows. Everyone looked hot and the room smelt of perfume and sweat and cigarette smoke. Miss Hastings arrived to serve plates of hot corned beef with string beans, potatoes and a mustard sauce. Robbie tried to catch the governess's eye so she'd know he was sorry. He didn't mind her, not really.

'Are you okay?' asked Eleanor, following the direction he gazed. 'Don't expect a smile, Robbie. She's lost her job now you're leaving. She's only helping out tonight as a favour to Mrs Howell.'

'But what if I come back?' he asked. 'Who will school me then?' He twisted the linen napkin Eleanor smoothed across his lap. Mrs Howell was leaving the room and he really didn't want her to go.

'By then you will have finished school,' Eleanor told him, 'and you'll have no need of a governess.'

Robbie digested this news as the adults began to eat. Was he never to come home then until he'd finished, not even for holidays? 'But –'

'Eat your dinner, Robbie,' Lesley's quiet voice soothed. 'There are many people in the world who sit down to empty plates this night.' Her small hand took his, giving it a gentle squeeze. He noticed the large wooden cross hanging from a chain about her neck. 'Sister Anna always reminds me that God will forgive those who are sorry for their crimes.'

'But –'

'Pray to the Virgin Mary and she will help you.'

Somehow he didn't think God or Mary were going to be much help to him at all. Not unless they could pick the padlock so he could open the balcony door. His father was telling a joke, something about a buck-jump rider with a harelip.

'Not in mixed company,' his mother warned, salting her meal.

'Later,' he promised the adults.

'The injured man has woken,' Lesley continued speaking to Robbie. 'Already there is hope, for him and you.'

Robbie tugged his hand from Lesley's sweaty grasp, the back of his throat going dry. He reached for the water glass, spilling a little of the contents as he drank.

'Don't look so worried, Robbie. He can't speak at the moment,' Lesley explained, 'but I'm sure it won't be long.' Her bottom teeth were short and grey. 'Aren't you interested to know who he is?'

Robbie didn't know how he should answer.

'Oh God, yes,' Mrs Winslow spoke up from across the table. 'I, for one, am dying to know who he is. I'm only sorry that I've not been able to even have a peek at him. Restricted visitors, that's what that Greek nurse told me.' She flipped the lid of a cigarette lighter with a vivid pink nail. 'Talk about boringly dictatorial.'

Robbie stared at the great chunks of corn meat and the thick sauce on it.

'Well, she's gone now.' Georgia dabbed at the corners of her mouth with a napkin. 'Took off in a huff after lunch, apparently.'

'I think she was offended, Mum,' Eleanor spoke up.

Robbie could tell by the edge to his sister's voice that she and their mother weren't happy with each other. Everyone at the table concentrated on their meals.

'Athena Pappas was employed in a short-term capacity, Eleanor. If she expected more then she was mistaken. I can't help that.'

'What she expected,' replied Eleanor, 'was not to be judged. Someone's personal life should be just that, personal. And how they choose to live their life is totally up to them. No-one else.'

Robbie sunk a little lower in the chair. His father's forkful of food never made it to his mouth. A long bean fell to the plate, then a splodge of sauce. Robbie guessed this was about the comics that his father found yesterday. He'd been furious to discover them in Robbie's room and when he had, he'd searched Eleanor's bedroom as well.

'Is that right, Eleanor?' Colin said slowly. 'Well then, that would mean that you'd have to keep your opinions to yourself regarding relationships. All relationships.'

It was the smile on his father's face that bothered Robbie. It just didn't look right. Like it was pretend or something.

Eleanor took a sip of water.

'Is this a private conversation or can anyone join in?' Mrs Winslow interrupted. 'Now, let's get back to more fascinating conversation, like the young stranger under your roof, Georgia.'

'He's not some freakshow, Margaret,' her husband chastised.

She waved his remark aside. 'What's he really like? Do tell, Eleanor. Everyone's been very short on description, including you.'

Eleanor placed her knife and fork down. 'Umm, tall. Six foot, I'd imagine. Dark-haired, with a bushman's tan. You know, red neck and brown from the elbows down.'

Mrs Winslow propped her chin on a hand. 'Handsome? Like that overseer of yours?'

'Not bad-looking,' Eleanor hedged.

Margaret laughed. 'A non-committal response if ever I've heard one.' She turned to her hostess. 'He must be handsome, Georgia. Best you keep your wits about you now you have your two young women tending to him.'

'I still say that either he doesn't speak English or he's hiding something.' Mr Winslow tapped out a cigarette and lit it, took a couple of quick puffs. 'If it was me, I'd get him moved as soon as possible.'

'We only need the all-clear from the doctor. He's no longer on a drip.' Georgia rang a small silver bell at her elbow and Miss Hastings appeared. 'More sauce please.' She pointed at the silver sauce boat and the governess carried it back to the kitchen for a refill.

'I hear you're going away to school, Robbie.' Lesley cut a small piece of meat and chewed slowly.

Robbie thought about the American silver dollar hidden in the jar at the woolshed. What if the man he'd shot really was innocent, just like that gunfighter wrongly accused of murder in the comics?

'I loved boarding school, well, we both did, didn't we, Eleanor?' Lesley persevered.

'Once you get used to it.' Eleanor stabbed at the beans on her plate. 'Mind you, we were sent away younger than you, Robbie. You'll find it easier than we did, simply because you're a bit older.'

'I don't want to go, Eleanor,' Robbie whispered.

'I'm sure you don't,' she agreed. 'It will be hard to get used to at first, but I'm sure you'll enjoy it.'

Lesley leant forward and frowned at her sister. 'Robbie wants to hear positives about boarding school, Eleanor.'

'Well, don't count on the food, young man,' Mr Winslow interrupted. 'Worse food I ever ate was at boarding school, and the bugger of it was there was a lot of the stuff. Used to go to the chook pens in the evening, snuck out we did to steal the eggs. We boiled them up out on the flat in the dead of night in a broken pot. When the senior boys discovered what we'd been doing, they stuck our heads down the toilet and flushed them. Not good.' He shook his head. 'Not good at all.'

Robbie looked from his mother to his father. Surely they wouldn't actually send him to such a place.

'Keith,' his wife giggled, 'that is hardly appropriate dinner conversation.' She took a sip of her drink, resting her cigarette in one of the individual ashtrays placed in front of each adult. She proceeded to eat and smoke simultaneously and Robbie noticed that from time to time she stared a lot at his father, who, in turn, made a point of not looking in her direction.

'We thought we'd get an early start in the morning,' Mr Winslow announced. 'Good mechanic you've got in the village, Colin. The man seems to know his way around an engine. And Margaret and I want to thank you and Georgia for having us. I feel we've really out-stayed ourselves.'

'Don't be ridiculous,' Georgia answered, 'we've enjoyed having you both. We're only sorry it's been a little dramatic here over the last few days.'

'To say the least,' Mrs Winslow agreed. 'But on the positive side, to date, we personally haven't had a mention in any of the papers and in comparison to what's been going on here, we really can't complain about you purchasing a portion of your ram requirements from Sinclair. In fact, I'm sure it will be a very good move for your stud.'

To Eleanor, this rather sounded like an attempt by Margaret to distance herself from River Run and recent events.

'Well, I'm not quite as generous as my wife. Obviously I hate seeing a client, especially when that client is a close friend, moving elsewhere.' Her husband blew his nose in a flowery handkerchief. 'But I must say that I like the way that overseer of yours thinks. Hardy, big-framed animals with bright wool, and he's a visual man. There's a lot to be said for classing outside the confines of the drafting race.'

'A few years ago I wondered why he continually had the knees out of his trousers,' Georgia countered. 'Then I saw him down in the yards one day. Hands-on like my father was. Dyed-in-the-wool sheepmen. It's good to see it in the next generation.'

'If it wasn't for us,' Colin retaliated, 'he'd have the arse out of his trousers.'

'I doubt it,' Keith argued. 'You may have given him a position here, but clearly he's had a very solid start. Besides which, ability always outs. The lad was telling me that he left the Territory to pursue his interest in sheep. He's certainly worked on some big runs in Queensland. Surely you'd like to be freed up to do other things, Colin. Have you considered appointing him Stud Master?'

Robbie's father's cutlery clattered.

'It was offered a couple of years ago,' his mother replied. 'Turned it down flat. I was surprised actually, but then he's had other issues to deal with.'

'Such as?' Mr Winslow enquired.

Georgia gave the slightest of hesitations. 'His wife contracted polio in the early forties. She spent the last four years of her life in an iron lung. Vivien died in the winter of '46. Shocking disease.'

There were murmurs about the severity of the last outbreak of polio. Robbie wanted to ask what an iron lung was but his mother was already talking about how pretty Vivien was.

Now Eleanor understood Hugh's maturity. He'd lost a wife and in the doing, lost his world. She knew, in a much more limited form, how that felt. 'You should offer the Stud Master position to Hugh again, Mum,' Eleanor spoke up. 'I think he'd say yes this time around.'

'Interesting, I may just do that. I'd like to see him in the role.'

'Canvassing for votes, is he?' Colin stated, as if it were fact.

'Heavens, Colin darling,' Margaret blew smoke from her mouth and nostrils, 'what is it? A need for control? Not wanting the competition? Younger man syndrome? If Ambrose Park was fortunate enough to have Goward on staff, we'd give the man what he wanted. I may not have the industry acumen that Georgia has, but I can recognise ability as well as the next person. Give him the job, Georgia.'

'Hugh won't let us down, Mum. I'm sure of it.'

'The man is an employee, Eleanor. Best you remember that. This first-name basis is far too familiar for my liking.' Colin pushed back his chair. 'I think I'll check on that sauce. Robbie, eat your dinner.'

Robbie put his head down and did just that.

⋘ Chapter Thirty ⋙

Despite Eleanor's persistence that they catch up in her room immediately after dinner, Lesley pleaded exhaustion. The idea of sharing their news, as if they were schoolgirls again, as if nothing had altered over the past years, had made Lesley feel awkward. Tomorrow would be soon enough. Besides, she doubted her daily regimen at the convent, which consisted of prayers, the hospice, tending the vegetable garden and more prayers, would prove interesting to anyone. It wasn't a stimulating existence compared to Eleanor's life, which was exactly why it suited Lesley. There was something soothing in the monotony of her days and the strict regime that was a part of convent life. Little was demanded of her and it was a world that had, over time, become increasingly important to her. Just how much was evident the moment that she had stepped into the taxi that morning, having finally let go of Sister Anna's hand.

'You can do this, Lesley,' Sister Anna had said with conviction.

'I know,' came her reply. But Lesley wasn't convinced and she wondered whether Sister Anna realised how difficult it was for her to simply step outside the convent walls.

'You need only stay for as long as your services are required, Lesley. We talked about this day, how important it was for you to go beyond our life here and confront the world again. It will be a challenge. I understand that, my dear. We know how you have suffered, but this is your family that you're visiting and they love you. Take strength from that and God will guide you.'

'God will guide me,' Lesley whispered now as she made her way to the sickroom. It had taken all her strength to get through the afternoon and evening, to say the things that everyone expected her to say, to behave like an ordinary girl who had simply come home after a long absence. She had not been untruthful when she'd told Eleanor she was exhausted. She was. But nor could she go to bed. It was far too hot to sleep. Not that she would be capable of sleep. This first night, and each one after, would be a nightmare for her while she remained on River Run.

A telephone call to Sister Anna prior to dinner, assuring the nun of her safe passage to the property, was the anchor Lesley needed to persevere. If not for the nun's comfort and guidance, Lesley doubted her strength to do what was expected of her. Sister Anna reminded her of why she'd made the decision to return, for despite her mother's command, the choice was Lesley's. She'd come home out of a sense of duty, and part of that duty lay in the sickroom.

Unlocking the door, Lesley entered the stranger's domain. The bedside light flickered with the varying charge of electricity produced by the generator as she sat in the chair by the patient. Although all the lights were still on in the house – the Winslows were enjoying night-caps with her mother and uncle – Lesley had a large torch, which she sat on the floor by the chair. When the generator was turned off for the evening, she would not be alone in the dark.

The patient was sleeping quite soundly, his injured arm resting across a bare torso. The man's skin colour appeared nearly normal and Lesley knew that the stranger was indeed on the mend. As she studied the long eyelashes and gentle rise and fall of his chest, the patient woke. They stared at each other, Lesley unflinching under the directness of his gaze. Rising, she lay a hand on his brow, gave a practised smile of comfort, before returning to her seat. His eyelids fluttered and closed again.

She could do this, Lesley decided. If she kept to the house and garden. If she didn't allow herself to dwell on the past. If she kept so busy that she fell into an exhausted sleep, then the dreams wouldn't come and if the dreams didn't come, then she only had to worry about thinking. Controlling her thoughts was a discipline Lesley was yet to master. Sister Anna assured her that with time and practice, prayer and meditation would still the memories that haunted her. Certainly there had been progress. The bouts of shaking which struck her unawares were decreasing in frequency. The night-sweats were all but gone and she could now sit quietly without a single thought entering her mind for nearly ten minutes. Most of all, the overpowering sadness that so often in the past led to crying seemed to have reduced as well. What hadn't altered was the strength of Lesley's anxiety. These attacks arose unbidden, resulting in breathlessness and a tightness across her chest which was frightening.

Don't, Lesley chided herself. Don't think of your problems. Don't think of the past. She sat in the chair opposite the injured stranger and imagined a drawer in her mind. Into this compartment she mentally folded and stacked everything that caused her pain; the sadness, the love, the loss, the loneliness and the guilt. It was the guilt that most shadowed her. A sense of blame for Marcus's death that Lesley couldn't speak about and had, to this day, never shared with anyone.

A knock sounded on the door and Mrs Howell appeared. 'Lesley, you're here. Will you join me for tea? I've just made a pot.'

Glad of the interruption, Lesley nodded. 'That would be lovely, Mrs Howell.' Locking the sickroom, she followed the housekeeper to the kitchen, sitting the torch on the table.

The housekeeper poured tea into two china cups, humming as she set the table with milk, sugar and blue cake plates with matching silver cake forks. She noticed the torch and raised an eyebrow, before placing the housekeeping ledger to one side. 'We're quite out of stores, what with our visitors. Considering the weather, they certainly have healthy appetites. Milk?'

'I drink it black now,' Lesley replied.

'But you'll have some of my teacake?' The older woman cut a slice from the cake she'd sat in the middle of the table and passed it to Lesley. 'I know how much you like cinnamon.'

Lesley smiled her thanks and sipped the steaming drink, using both hands to stem the shaking that had suddenly manifested itself. Not now, she thought, please.

'It's good to have you home, Lesley,' Mrs Howell said with feeling, choosing not to notice the young woman's tremors. 'It's been quite frightful here this past week, what with the shooting, the injured stranger and the Winslows staying.' She leant across the table. 'I don't go much on that Margaret Winslow. We had the police here and everything.' She took a sip of tea, and bit into the moist slice of cake. 'And of course right when shearing is on. A fractious time of the year for everyone, as you well know. And in this heat.'

'It is very hot.' Lesley picked at the cake.

'Would you like a dash of something in your tea, to help steady your nerves? We all know it must be hard on you coming back to River Run, after everything.'

'No, Mrs Howell. I'll be alright.'

'Well, there is a bottle of brandy in the pantry if you need it.' She continued eating the cake and drinking her tea. 'With luck we'll know who the patient is in a day or so. His picture's in the paper.'

'It must be an inconvenience having him here, even if Robbie is responsible.'

'A total stranger is one thing, but with all this talk of communism, let's just say I'll be pleased when he's gone. Of course

Eleanor was with Robbie when the shooting occurred. I must say I was surprised. She used to be so level-headed. I had to give her a talking to about gallivanting around the property with the overseer.' Mrs Howell pointed at Lesley's plate. 'Aren't you hungry?'

'Not really,' she replied apologetically.

Mrs Howell pushed her cup and saucer to one side. 'You will come and talk to me when you're ready, Lesley? You know I'm always here for you.'

'I know, Mrs Howell.' Her being on River Run was awkward for everyone. Even Mrs Howell seemed a little ill at ease in her company although Lesley knew how pleased they both were to see each other again.

'Right, well I best let you go to bed then.' The housekeeper began clearing the table.

'I'm going to sit with the patient for just a little longer,' Lesley told her.

'Not too long,' Mrs Howell fussed, 'you look tired.'

'No, not too long,' Lesley lied.

⚔ Chapter Thirty-one ⚔

It was far too hot for sleep and little better outdoors, however, beyond the confines of walls and ceiling, the air was a little fresher, a touch kinder. Eleanor sat on the balcony, a kerosene lamp by her side, protected from the unknown by the solidness of the homestead, the wrought-iron railings and a wing of stars, which glinted peacefully. In her youth, she and Lesley had dragged mattresses onto the terrace during the claustrophobic summer months, revelling in the sense of freedom their makeshift beds provided. How distant those years seemed now.

Lesley. They'd spoken little since her arrival, although Eleanor intended to rectify that in the morning once her sister was refreshed. With the patient no longer needing fulltime care and Nurse Pappas leaving instructions that the man didn't require a night-time babysitter, she had to agree that Lesley looked like she could do with an early night. With rest, Eleanor hoped her sister would benefit from the return home. Nonetheless, Athena Pappas's words left an element of doubt.

For the moment though, there were other things to think on. Shearing was over for another day and tomorrow the Winslows would

257

depart. Hugh Goward would be appointed Stud Master and things would go on, as best as possible, until Robbie left for boarding-school and she too returned to Sydney. Eleanor decided to make the most of her time while she was on River Run. She was enjoying sketching the property and recording some of the stories and phrases she heard. And, more importantly, she felt stronger and quite confident and capable when she was out and about on the run.

Eleanor curled up on her side, the boards hard against her hip. Everyone slept or at least tried to. She wondered if Hugh slept or if he dreamt of the wife lost to illness. To think of him, caused agitation. It was these whirring thoughts that kept her awake and Eleanor did her best to forget him. He was River Run's overseer after all. It was better to think of the man downstairs. The mystery stranger who'd come into their lives with his memory loss and war wound and attractive appearance. He wasn't like Hugh with his blue-green eyes and calm efficiency. In fact, if Eleanor compared the two men, she'd guess that the stranger was passionate and direct, filled with energy and verve. They didn't know who he was and he was still personally lost within the ether of injury, but that didn't make him any less appealing. A stranger riding across a paddock towards River Run. Intriguing, yes, but the very image was captivating. There was a novella there, she mused.

And so she lay quite still and listened to the bush that never slept. Even now, the middle of the night, a bird twittered. In the garden below there was a rustle in the shrubbery and then the familiar pounding of kangaroos. The animals often invaded the homestead grounds. They nibbled the freshly watered lawn and plants, taking advantage of the green feed. There was comfort in these nocturnal wanderings, a contentment that eased through Eleanor's body bringing the hope of sleep.

The light in the garden shed flicked on. Disturbed, the kangaroos bounded clear of the intrusion. Eleanor moved to the wrought-iron balustrade and, still sitting, clasped the bars, resting her forehead on the metal. She'd not taken Rex to be a night owl, for the man was well known for his seven o'clock bedtime and four am risings. But who could sleep in this weather?

A figure appeared in the doorway of the garden shed. Framed by the brightness of the electric bulb, it took time for Eleanor to become accustomed to the intense glare. Gradually the outline of the individual gained form and features. With a mixture of apprehension and curiosity, Eleanor quickly concluded that the person was not Rex. In fact, it wasn't a man at all.

A woman stood at the entrance to the shed. The slender form, accentuated by a narrow waist and curvaceous hips and thighs, stood as if posing for an invisible audience. Arms were lifted slowly, indolently, until each hand grasped the side of the doorway in a seductive pose.

Eleanor brought a hand to her mouth in shock. The light from the building framed the person. There was no mistaking the obvious. The woman was naked, quite naked. And even were it not for the build and height and that mane of hair, Eleanor still would have recognised Margaret Winslow. What on earth was she doing? Where were her clothes?

Goodness. Eleanor crossed herself from habit, rather than belief. Was she so naive as to not fathom what was so blatantly laid out before her? She was undoubtedly and quite unwittingly party to an assignation of some kind. A tryst in the very grounds of which the woman was a guest. As these thoughts percolated in Eleanor's mind, Mrs Winslow ran languid hands very slowly across her thighs and stomach, before concentrating on her breasts. It was almost as if she were a cat, the way she arched her back, a stretch of indecent proportions and then the display was over. The woman walked back inside the shed and closed the door. A few minutes later the light went out.

Dumbfounded, Eleanor strained to hear footsteps, struggled to decipher a voice, her fingers gripping the balcony railing, but there was nothing. The night was so dark that even if there were another person with the indecent Mrs Winslow, it was impossible to tell who it might be. In frustration, Eleanor crawled back to lean next to the French doors of her bedroom.

Of course, one could make assumptions. While there was no proof that Eleanor's stepfather was Mrs Winslow's companion, there wasn't exactly a potpourri of eligible men on River Run that Margaret Winslow could take her pick from and, most importantly, necessarily depend on for confidentiality. And Eleanor doubted that Keith Winslow was the type of man who'd be interested in sharing an intimate night in the garden shed of one of his closest friends. Nor was it probable that his wife carried a penchant for walking around in the nude in the middle of the night, unless there was an ulterior motive.

Eleanor stayed awake until it was impossible to do so any longer. When sleep finally claimed her, it did so intermittently, leaving her with a heavy heart.

❧ Chapter Thirty-two ❧

'Y̲ou're Lesley.'

Lesley woke with a start. Having fallen asleep in the sickroom chair, she was momentarily disorientated. The room was in darkness and she searched frantically for the torch. She'd not woken when the generator had been turned off and now she was alone, in the dark, with a strange man. 'Where is the torch, where is the torch?'

'Hey, calm down.'

On hands and knees, Lesley swept the floor with her palms. Finally, the bulky torch was found and she clicked the button, shining it first on the floor and then the bed.

The patient smirked. 'There's a lamp under the washstand.'

Lesley didn't answer. Locating the kerosene lantern and matches, she lifted the glass flue and struck a match, her hands shaking. It took three attempts before the room filled with yellow light, so bad were her trembles.

'Better?' He sounded amused. 'Can't say I usually have that effect on women.'

'They said you couldn't speak.' Lesley placed the lamp on the washstand, her heart thumping.

'I couldn't remember anything after the shooting,' he admitted. 'So I decided I would be better off keeping quiet for a while.'

'I see.' Lesley checked the contents of the washstand, and finding a thermometer, shook it out, before placing it under his tongue. The task calmed her and more importantly bought her some time before a more detailed response was required. 'I can understand that. Sometimes the last thing a person needs is to be interrogated.' She knew that from bitter experience. She had been told, however, that the man was still recuperating and most definitely couldn't speak. 'It's now Tuesday night and the accident happened on Saturday.'

'And?' he said laconically.

'Well, I'm wondering how long you've actually been conscious for and when you discovered you were able to speak?'

She watched him, watching her. 'You don't really look like your sister.' The thermometer rattled against his teeth. 'In fact, you're not like her at all, are you?'

'Shush,' she chastised, warning him to be quiet until she removed the thermometer. 'No temperature. Are you in pain?'

'My head and shoulder aches, but it's not too bad. I've had worse.'

In the hospice she met new people on a regular basis. Some needed the nuns' care for months, others weeks only, but all their patients came to the hospice to die and in the time left before their passing, it was quite extraordinary how much of their lives they shared. Lesley had become adept at listening and skilled at giving comfort to those suffering not only from a terminal illness but the concerns of family and loneliness, and it masked the pain of her own misfortunes. She placed the thermometer on the washstand. But this man, he was different. He wasn't dying, he certainly didn't seem grateful for the care shown him and he was being deceitful. 'How did you know my name?'

'Pretending you're asleep has its advantages.'

The comment made Lesley uncomfortable. She looked out

the window to the darkness beyond and shivered. The remark reminded her of something Marcus had told her on his return from the war. He had feigned unconsciousness in the hopes the torture would end. Immediately, Lesley's heart began to race and she braced herself against the washstand. She'd steeled herself to not think about Marcus . . . at least, not the terrible things.

'That young brother of yours shot me,' the patient went on. 'Aimed the rifle directly at me and pulled the trigger. If you were me, laid up as I am, you'd probably be a little cautious about the family of the person who'd deliberately shot you.'

Lesley tried to push the image of a battered Marcus, his body smothered in leeches, from her mind. She'd not had one of these attacks for over twelve months. She had come so far with Sister Anna's help. Lesley gritted her teeth. Had she been anywhere else she would have cried out. 'My mother told me it was an accident. Have you been on morphine? You did tell me a moment ago that you couldn't remember anything.' She resumed her seat.

'He did shoot me, the rest of your family are just covering up for him. Are you alright? You don't look so good.'

Lesley tried to visualise the large wooden cross hanging on the stone wall of the convent. 'I see, and you've decided to place your confidence in me because?' she asked. Lesley had forgotten what it meant to be wary of someone. Apart from dredging up unpleasant memories, which to be fair wasn't his fault, the stranger was not only disconcerting, but also, what was the word? Manipulative. No, that wasn't right, he was simply direct. Stating his case. And he certainly had every right to. She was the one with the problems.

'You're not one of them. I mean you're family, but you don't live here. I thought you'd be unbiased.'

'Yes, of course.'

'Are you sure you're okay?'

'You're the patient.' Lesley knew her voice sounded brittle. 'Your accent sounds American. Is it?'

'So you can understand why I didn't speak,' he continued, disregarding her question. He adjusted a pillow, sitting up a little further in the bed. 'Everyone seems to think I'm this bad person, especially that Greek nurse.'

He was passionate. Young and vibrant, close to Marcus's age had he still been alive. 'Well, she's no longer here.' Lesley felt her eyes begin to water. It was some time since she'd been in the presence of a man who was in his prime. It reawakened all that she had lost. 'Can you recall anything that might help us work out who you are?' Breathe, she willed herself.

The stranger looked up at the ceiling. 'It's all muddled. I remember riding across a paddock and then waking up in this room. My thoughts are all mixed up with other things.'

'What things?' Lesley was grateful for his self-absorption.

'People talking about shearing, dogs barking, boards being nailed over the window, shouting, an Italian lover . . . there's too much.' He lay back on the bed, breathing heavily.

'I think,' Lesley said kindly, 'you were probably given a shot of morphine. It can confuse, you know.' Tea, she needed another cup of tea.

The patient turned his head on the pillow to face her. 'Why are you so sad?'

The question hung between them.

'You must be tired,' Lesley finally replied, 'and I've had a long day. Please go to sleep.' She rested against the chair and sat on her hands, which were shaking uncontrollably. In all the conversations she'd had since Marcus's death, no stranger had ever made such a comment to her. Was her pain so visible that even an outsider could see it?

'Don't you sleep at night?' he asked. 'You don't have to stay with me. Didn't you notice? I can't go anywhere.'

'Can we not talk, please?'

The stranger shrugged. 'Nowhere better to be, eh?' He turned on his side and faced the wall.

Lesley looked at his taut skin, the defined arm muscles stretched along the length of his body, and quietly began to weep.

Wednesday

The Great Escape

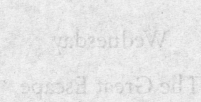

❧ Chapter Thirty-three ❧

The hum of the Lister engine in the woolshed carried on the morning air, punctuated by the sounds of barking dogs. Already the heat of the day was upon them. Eleanor wished she'd woken earlier feeling more refreshed. However, after what she'd witnessed in the garden shed last night, there was too much filling her mind. It felt as though her family was splintering, and the heat certainly wasn't helping anyone's dispositions. It wound about the property like a shroud, so that the land and its inhabitants appeared weighed down by the debilitating ferocity of the sun.

Lesley was standing by the ponds in the garden when Eleanor found her, her sister's attention focused beyond the back gate. The blue truck was parked outside the meat-house, the slim shape of Dawson, his arms moving back and forth, suggesting he was sharpening a knife. Eleanor carried two cups of coffee as she crossed the lawn, having decided not to invade Mrs Howell's space as she cooked bacon and eggs for the rest of the household. How the Winslows could consume so much food and so many alcoholic beverages in this heat amazed Eleanor.

'I still can't understand why Robbie shot that man.' Lesley's first words were not ones of greeting. Thin arms were folded across her chest as she surveyed their surroundings, the pale brown of the ponds, the trellis and two willie wagtails hopping across the lawn.

Eleanor instantly noticed that her sister seemed different to yesterday. She was certainly not the composed young woman who'd arrived with Rex.

'How old is he, eleven? It just doesn't make sense.' She rubbed her arms as if she were cold.

'I'm sure Mum's told you all the details,' Eleanor said in an attempt to pacify her sister. She really didn't feel like re-hashing recent events. Having Lesley home, in spite of her worries regarding her complete recovery, was the one positive thing to come out of Robbie's actions. 'I know I said it yesterday, Lesley, but I am so glad to see you. To have you home.'

'But you were there.' The pitch of Lesley's voice grew thin and tight. 'How could you let it happen?'

Eleanor didn't respond, instead, she handed her sister a mug of coffee. 'White with sugar, just how you like it.' She hadn't expected condemnation from her. The old Lesley would never have reacted that way.

Lesley frowned. 'Coffee? I don't drink it anymore.'

'Oh.' Put off by the dismissive tone, Eleanor tossed the contents of the mug onto the lawn. 'Are you alright? You seem a little on edge.'

'I'm fine.'

Eleanor shrugged. 'I'm sure Mum told you I wasn't actually in the tree with Robbie when the shooting took place.' The answer came slowly as she regained her equilibrium, sipping the milky beverage. When Eleanor had finally awoken this morning, for once her first thoughts were of something pleasant, the ride out in the paddock yesterday and Hugh's story of the warrigal storm. And last night's revelation regarding his dead wife had added a little more to the puzzle that was Hugh Goward. She could fantasise about

270

the man locked in their downstairs room, but Hugh captured her reality.

'But still?'

'Yes, but still,' Eleanor replied abruptly.

'Well, Eleanor, you can understand everyone's point of view. I mean, you're the adult. You were with him.'

Eleanor took another sip of the coffee. She'd not realised that *everyone* had taken a stance that laid the blame for the shooting squarely on her. 'Perhaps I should be the one being packed off to school then?'

'Now you're being ridiculous.'

'And you're being unfair, Lesley. As are Mum and Colin, if they're apportioning blame on me instead of taking responsibility for Robbie's behaviour. I didn't give him the rifle. I didn't let him run wild. He's just a kid.'

'Well, you've been quick to forgive his actions,' Lesley accused.

Eleanor felt a rush of anger for the woman standing opposite, her hands clasped together, nose in the air, as if she were a school marm. 'And you've been even quicker to take sides,' Eleanor retaliated.

'Well, thanks to Robbie we have *him* here.'

'And what were we meant to do with *him*?' replied Eleanor, wondering at the escalation of their conversation into an argument. 'Leave the man out in the paddock to die?'

Lesley rubbed her temples.

'Where the hell have you been for the last five years?' Eleanor couldn't help herself. 'Curled up in a ball in a convent, when you've obviously been quite capable of living a normal life for some time now. If you'd been around for the last few years you may have noticed that things aren't peachy here on the family run. They haven't been for quite a while. You're not the only one with problems.'

Rex rounded the corner of the house with an iron bucket, a creamy mass inside and one long almost translucent streamer, sausage casings, hanging over the edge. He waved at the girls, climbed the garden fence and headed towards the meat-house.

'I didn't come home to argue with you, Elly.' Lesley's reply was barely audible.

'Looks like they're making sausages.' Eleanor flung her own coffee across the lawn, the milky liquid disappearing in the grass.

Lesley cleared her throat, touching the crucifix hanging at her neck. 'Mum said the shearers aren't too happy with everything that's been going on.'

'Well, she should make the effort to get down to the woolshed,' said Eleanor. 'We started two days ago and she hasn't shown her face there. It might ease things if she did what's expected, what she's always done.'

'You still haven't forgiven her for marrying Colin.' It was more a statement than a question. 'Is that what the sniping around the table was about last night?'

'That was just Colin being Colin.' Sitting the cup on the grass, Eleanor wound her hair into a knot, pushing it under her hat. 'Can't we just talk like sisters for a change, Lesley? I've missed having you around.' She touched her sister's arm affectionately.

In the old days, Lesley would have relented, smiled and probably hugged Elly in return. But Eleanor was beginning to realise just how much her older sister had changed since Marcus's death. The flickering smile, once so quick to appear, the playful light in her eyes, the confidence and poise . . . none of it had returned.

'Just remember what you said last night, Eleanor, those things about a person's life being their own. The same applies to Colin and Mum. That's why Uncle Colin looked so pleased with himself. Hypocrisy tends to stand out like the proverbial.'

There it was again, an unkind remark delivered with what could only be called disinterest.

'Don't look like that,' Lesley continued. 'I'm not on their side. I've just had a few things on my mind to worry about other than a marriage formed through mutual need.'

A dog began to whine, low and plaintive, the noise momentarily distracting the sisters and easing the tension between them. Eleanor began to talk of other things, of Athena and the stranger and particularly the nurse's doubts towards River Run's patient. Lesley, however, wasn't particularly interested in the Greek nurse's views and she said as much.

'Why not?' Eleanor asked. 'She and her family may have come from the other side of the world, but they're not much different to us.'

'The hospice is full of people born in Australia. We should be looking after our own kind, not importing more refugees.'

'I see. And the patient,' Eleanor queried, eager to change the subject. Her sister was clutching and unclutching handfuls of her dress. 'How did you find him?'

'He's been shot. He'll recover,' said Lesley bluntly. 'But he can speak. Has been able to for quite a while I'd say. I think it's a good idea he's locked up. Who knows who he is?'

Eleanor turned towards the house and the ground floor sickroom. 'He talked to you?'

'Yes.'

It was a relief not carrying his secret around, but at the same time she felt quite deflated. The only positive was that if Lesley were the one to reveal the man's return to full health, her protection of the stranger need never be known. 'I knew he could too,' Eleanor revealed. 'He asked me to keep it a secret.'

'Well, it's not a secret any longer. He said he was confused initially, lack of memory, which is possible considering he hit his head, but I don't like him. I don't like him at all.'

'Really?' By the tone of Lesley's voice Eleanor was convinced that something had occurred last night, which didn't seem possible. The injured man was . . . well, she liked him. He was simply suffering from amnesia. They'd talked of art and writing and Eleanor felt quite relaxed in his presence. So it seemed at odds with the little she knew of Robbie's victim, that he'd intentionally upset Lesley. And yet something had set her sister on edge. 'Did he upset you?'

'I don't want to talk about him.'

'Well, did you find out what his name is?' Eleanor asked.

'No. He can't remember.'

'What did you talk about?'

'Nothing.'

'What's happened, Lesley? Yesterday you were –'

'Normal?' Lesley challenged.

Eleanor was at a loss to understand the change in her sister. 'Okay, if you don't trust him, let me sit with him this morning. I'll see if I can find out a bit more about our mystery man before we tell Mum. Regardless of who he is, I think he's disturbed our family enough with his presence.' This seemed to placate Lesley and she gave a slight incline of her head in agreement.

'It was so dark last night, and hot.' Lesley looked at the sky, shielding her face against the morning glare. 'I'd forgotten how hot it could get.'

'Nearing the dark of the moon,' said Eleanor.

Lesley gave a tired smile. 'You always were the dramatic one. It's the new moon, Eleanor, call it as it is.'

They could have continued arguing, instead Eleanor lit a cigarette courtesy of Mr Winslow from last night. 'Did you want to come back?' Exhaled smoke tumbled out with her question.

'Mother can be persuasive. Funds are needed for our charitable works and when I was asked . . .'

Eleanor inhaled and exhaled deeply, the smoke streaming from between her lips. 'She bribed the convent?'

'I offered to come back, Elly. The convent saved me. I belong there.'

'But did you want to come home, to River Run? It's a simple question.'

Her older sister turned towards her. 'Mum and Uncle Colin,

clearly they're having problems. But all partnerships require compromise, Elly. You shouldn't be so hard on Uncle Colin. Dad and Mum, well they understood each other. They were partners in every sense, but Colin,' she turned towards the homestead, 'a man like that can't live in the shadow of a woman. He's not like Dad was. Dad had nothing to prove to the world, but Uncle Colin does. As a second son, with limited funds and no land to his name, he really needed to be with someone less dominant. He was never going to be given the opportunity of running things his way. Not here. So don't be so hard on him, Elly. Everyone is fighting their own battle. The only thing I was concerned about was Margaret Winslow and the way she was looking at him last night. Probably just as well they're leaving.'

'Don't you give straight answers anymore?' Eleanor probed.

'Don't you respect a person's right to privacy?' countered Lesley.

'I would have thought you'd have had enough of that, cooped up in a convent all this time.'

'Running away, that's what you mean, isn't it?'

Eleanor ran fingers through stringy hair, wondering if the dust of the bush would ever wash out.

'I'm not like you, Eleanor. I never was. I was only ever good at two things, nursing and loving Marcus. I wasn't made for anything else.'

'Now look who's being dramatic,' Eleanor replied softly.

'I didn't come back to argue.' Lesley walked ahead towards a bench, barely shaded from the morning sun by an old gum tree. 'Actually I didn't want to come back at all. But the work we do at the hospice is important. We're always short of money for food and medicine. Coming home was my way of contributing to the convent's needs.'

So there was the truth of it. Georgia wanted her eldest child home and the stranger provided a reason for her services. The monetary contribution to the convent was further incentive. 'I'm sure Mum thought that bringing you home would help.'

Lesley stretched her legs out in the sun as she sat down, and appeared to think on this. 'It's not the place for me to heal, if that's what everyone hoped. If it had been, I would have come home sooner.'

'Why not?'

'River Run isn't important to me, Eleanor, and quite honestly I can't say if it ever was. As a childhood home, yes, but I've never had the attachment to this place that Mum has, that Robbie probably will have. I can appreciate the land for what it is, for what it's given us, and I am in awe of Mum's family. They were absolute pioneers. But that's where it ends. But you, you look comfortable here.' She gave a shy smile. 'The last time I saw you at the convent you were in your cream twin-set and pearls. Now look at you with your leather boots and long-sleeved shirt. I bet you go out with the men and they probably don't mind having you tag along.'

Eleanor joined her older sister on the bench seat. 'It's more than that, isn't it? Are you well now, Lesley, have you . . . ?'

Lesley patted Eleanor's hand. 'Have I recovered? Have I got over Marcus?' She wore a plain blue house-dress that she began crumpling between her fingers. Her hands began to shake, ever so slightly. 'Have you ever been in love?'

Eleanor thought of Dante, of the young men in her life prior to his arrival. 'I thought I was once, but it didn't work out.'

'Maybe you were lucky. Maybe it's better not to know that one great love. It can make the rest of our life pale into insignificance and then, when you lose it . . .'

'I don't understand that kind of love. A love that hurts.'

'I believe that the great loves always do.' Lesley gave a weak laugh. 'They blind you and annoy you, and by its very nature such a passion constrains and pressurises. Such a love doesn't work for many. Such a love doesn't leave space or time for anything else. But for some, for me, it is everything, *was* everything,' she corrected. 'There was never anyone else. There never could be and I know it was the same for Marcus.' A wind rose, rustling the branches of the trees around them. 'I didn't set out to feel that way and I'm sure Marcus didn't either. It simply was. And it's an extraordinary feeling, Eleanor. It's all-encompassing.'

'Wouldn't Marcus want you to let go, to move on?' Eleanor asked hopefully.

'He's here, you know, Eleanor. From the moment that I arrived yesterday I remembered everything. Everything I'd tried to forget.' Lesley squeezed her sister's fingers, the lightest of touches. 'I still expect him to walk around the corner of the house, up the stairs, into the dining room, across this very lawn. You probably don't remember but we were shearing when he died.'

'I remember,' Eleanor lied. 'Would you like to go down to the shed later?'

'I've spent five years grieving, five years trying to forget him, but I never did.' Beyond the garden, something drew Lesley's attention. She leant forward, almost with anticipation, and then just as quickly relaxed back against the hard planks of the bench. 'I'm tired after last night. I might sleep in your room during the day if that's alright?'

Eleanor assured Lesley that she didn't have to nurse the stranger. That she would stay with the patient if it was required. 'Hang on, why my room?' And then she realised. 'Marcus. He slept in your room, didn't he? Without Mum knowing.'

For the first time Lesley brightened, albeit briefly. 'I couldn't bear it. To lie there in the dark on that same bed. In this heat. I'd imagine him breathing, his arm on mine, his lips on mine. We spoke of so many things, Elly. We'd stare up at the covering of Granny's four-poster bed and talk of our life together. Marcus said he'd paint stars on the canopy for me so that the heavens were always twinkling while I slept. My own Southern Cross. I can still smell him sometimes, he smelt of hope, of goodness. Then afterwards, when he came back, he was already gone. I tried to bring him back. I asked him to come back to me. But he couldn't. They'd already taken him. He was already gone.

'They took him from me in the jungle. I knew it then, and I know it now, but still I can't forget. Can't let go.' She began to sob. 'That morning when I went looking for him, and found him . . . Eleanor, help me. I can't get past it.' Lesley fell to the grass in a heap and began to sob. 'People keep telling me to be brave, to move on, but they don't understand, no-one understands.'

Rex was running towards them, dropping the bucket of freshly made sausages so that they spread out across the grass, pale and limp.

'What don't we understand, Lesley?' Eleanor pleaded. 'Tell me?'

Lesley gasped. 'He left a note, Elly. Marcus left a note.' She reached for Eleanor's hands. 'He knew he wouldn't be able to lead a normal life because of the injuries, because of what they'd done to him. And he didn't want to burden me, Elly.' She sobbed. 'He didn't want to be a millstone, an obligation. Marcus killed himself so that I could be free.'

Stunned, Eleanor sat on the ground beside her sister.

Rex arrived. Ignoring Eleanor's protests, the old man lifted Lesley up as if she were a feather, carrying her across to the shade of a tree and placing her gently on the ground. 'Look at her, Eleanor. What are you doing sitting her out in the sun? She's been locked up with a bunch of nuns for years. She'll be burnt to the bone not wearing a hat.' Rex patted Lesley's face with a filthy handkerchief as she sobbed. 'Let it all out, little Lesley, let it all out.'

Gradually the weeping eased and Lesley leant back against the tree. 'You have to let him go, girl.' Rex patted her arm. 'He wouldn't want you to keep pining for him.' Lesley closed her eyes. 'How about I get Mrs Howell to make you some tea?'

'You always liked her tea,' Eleanor encouraged.

'No, no tea,' she said quietly, wiping her eyes as her breath steadied. 'Don't tell anyone, Eleanor. Don't tell Mum. Please, promise me, Rex. I won't be here for long. I never intended to stay long.' She gave them a weak smile. 'A donation from River Run is not something to be ignored. I'll go for a walk. Clear my thoughts. Alone.' Rex helped her stand and they watched as Lesley moved slowly through the garden and out the back gate.

'Cripes,' Rex scratched his chin, the jowly skin of his neck wiggling, 'she ain't any better at all, is she?'

'Maybe, maybe once she spends a few days here.' But Eleanor knew Rex was right. Lesley should never have come home. Now that Eleanor knew the truth of Marcus's suicide, she could only imagine the guilt and despair Lesley felt, the utter sadness.

Rex walked back to the spilled sausages and, picking them up, dropped the slimy mass back into the bucket. 'Covered in dirt,' he muttered, looking in the direction of the kitchen. 'The old battle-axe will have my guts for garters.'

Behind him, Lesley could be seen near the row of trees where the working dogs were chained. They barked on her approach. 'She must have put on a good show at the convent for them to let her out.' Rex straightened his back, bucket in hand.

'I think she probably felt safe there,' Eleanor answered, 'but being back here reminds her of Marcus. We'll keep it to ourselves just for a day or so, as she asked.'

Rex poked at the sausages. 'If you reckon it's the right thing to do.'

'She needs to know she can rely on us, Rex, don't you think?'

'Maybe you're right, girl, I don't know. On your say so I'll agree to it, but if it happens again, if she collapses like that, I'd have to tell your mother.'

'I understand, and I agree. Thanks, Rex.'

'Well, I'm glad someone does, cause I don't understand nothing. Nothing at all.' He scratched under his arm. 'Goddamn blood month, no moon, the goddamn stranger. It's all no good, no good. I was right sorry when I heard the young fella was being sent away to be schooled, but now I'm not so sure. Probably a good thing

279

I reckon, a real good thing. All of this started with the shooting and ain't no good come of none of it since. No sir, nothing at all. The boy's an albatross, shoots an innocent man, gets Billy and Lomax fired and now your sister's here and she shouldn't be. All cause of him. Because of Robbie. Maybe it would be better if the boy never came back.'

Eleanor knew Rex carried a soft spot for Lesley but she was still surprised by the ferocity of Rex's words. 'Don't say that, Rex. He's just a kid.'

'I'm just a-saying, girl. Family all over the papers. None of you showing up for church last Sunday.'

'But we couldn't go,' Eleanor's eyes were beginning to moisten, 'none of us could. The police came and then the doctor. You know that, Rex.'

'I'm just saying. There's always been River Run family at Mass. Always.' He looked skyward. 'Goddamn it all, we ain't never had such troubles since your father died. 'Bout the same time it was too, now I think on it.'

'No it wasn't, Rex,' argued Eleanor. 'Dad died in the spring.'

'Yes it was, girl. Same time all right. Around the dark of the moon.' He stomped towards the kitchen, his wiry body supported by bowed legs. At the kitchen door he flung the flyscreen open, dropped the bucket on the landing and hollered for Mrs Howell.

The housekeeper appeared, waved to Eleanor, the gesture urgent. On joining the older woman and Rex, Eleanor was smartly rebuked for wandering around outside. The Winslows were leaving and it had been decided that they would give Robbie a lift into the village and put him on the train.

'What, *now*?' asked Eleanor. 'But he's not meant to leave until –'

'Easier for everyone,' the housekeeper shared, 'that's what Mr Webber said. Doesn't want your mother all upset by waving the lad off at the railway station. And Robbie was very sad last night when I took him back to his room, so it's probably for the best.'

The distant whining of a dog's low, mournful sound developed into a howl.

'Mr Webber's sister will put Robbie up for a few days before he goes into school. Now stop talking or you'll miss him, Eleanor. They're about to leave.'

❦ Chapter Thirty-four ❧

'We've been waiting for you,' Colin stated sharply. 'Where's your sister?'

Eleanor took in the scene before her: Keith Winslow sitting inside the gleaming Studebaker, Robbie enveloped in his mother's arms and Margaret Winslow standing nonchalantly to one side, studying Colin. The woman was wearing an expensive fuchsia-coloured Dior travelling outfit, and as Eleanor studied her she recalled the wanton movements of a woman fondling her own body.

On noticing Eleanor, Robbie broke away from his mother's embrace and ran to her. Georgia fumbled with a handkerchief.

'Lesley's gone for a walk,' Eleanor finally answered her step-father, her eyes wet with tears. Robbie, beyond speech, hugged her tightly. 'It'll be fine, fine, I promise,' she told her half-brother. Eleanor looked suspiciously at her uncle while he spoke to the Winslow woman. Leaning forward, his hand touching Margaret's hip, he kissed her on the lips and squeezed the woman's buttocks. Georgia, caught up in the emotion of the moment, didn't notice but Eleanor did. She saw her uncle's hand lingering on Margaret's backside. And Margaret saw Eleanor watching.

'Eleanor,' Margaret drawled, as if only just seeing her, 'I must say goodbye.' She left Colin, meandering across the gravel drive as if there were all the time in the world, high heels crunching the pebbles. 'Now, young Robbie,' she ruffled his hair, 'off you go and give your mother another hug.'

Reluctantly, Robbie let go of Eleanor, as Georgia called to her son.

'Goodbye, my dear.' Margaret took Eleanor by the hand. Her grip was warm, confident. 'It's really been the most interesting of visits. I know both of us have learnt a thing or two, about each other, about how the world works.' Her grasp remained firm. 'And we certainly wouldn't like that fragile Webber veneer to be cracked by an out-of-wedlock relationship with an immigrant or,' she finally released Eleanor's hand, 'a moment mistaken between two old family friends. Would we?'

Blackmail! The woman was actually warning Eleanor, should she choose to cause trouble.

From her handbag Mrs Winslow took a packet of cigarettes, tapped one out and lit it. Exhaling, she picked a shred of tobacco from the tip of her tongue. The cigarette was ringed by red lipstick. 'Here, take these. I think you're going to need them.'

In Eleanor's hand was the packet of Lucky Strike tailor-mades. She smiled, her nerves tingling. 'And did you leave the garden shed tidy last night, Mrs Winslow?'

'Time to go, Robbie.' Colin opened the front passenger door.

For once, Margaret Winslow was speechless. Turning abruptly, she walked to the waiting car, where she kissed her host on both cheeks, twittering something about it being the European way, and then a length of bare leg was slowly drawn within the vehicle's interior.

'What about Lesley?' Georgia asked Colin, her hands on her son's shoulders.

'They have to leave now if they're going to make the train in time, and besides Lesley can see him at school,' he replied. 'Come on, Robbie. Get in the car please.'

The smell of gasoline hung in the air. The fumes coming from the exhaust were a grey-black. Robbie looked to Eleanor, pleaded with his eyes, but Georgia was settling him on the back seat and then the door was closed.

'I'll write,' she mouthed, but it wasn't enough. Eleanor saw it in his eyes as he looked at her through the rear window. She ran to the car, leant inside the window. 'I've been to boarding school too, Robbie. Don't forget that. I know what it feels like.'

'My pup,' he gulped.

'I'll look after him, and Garnet, I promise.'

He spat in his palm and Eleanor did the same. They shook, confirming the solemn promise.

Rex arrived out of breath, in time to take in the last sight of the young boy, a small hand pressed against the rear window. Eleanor watched the departing vehicle with mixed feelings, before noticing that her mother was silently weeping. Colin went to Georgia's side and tried to take her hand. She shook him off and disappeared into the house, leaving him alone on the veranda. Her stepfather lingered only briefly before walking back down the stairs and around the side of the homestead.

'She'll be walking the boundary like a cow that's been weaned of its calf,' Rex stated, referring to Eleanor's mother, 'you'll see.' He kicked at the ground where cigarette butts were scattered across the gravel drive. 'Them Winslows must have slaves, eh?' He began to pick up the cigarette stubs, cupping the butts in the palm of his hand. 'Wanted me to polish his Studebaker, he did. Offered me a fiver for my troubles. I said no.' His eyes were dark as he faced Eleanor. 'I'm just saying. We've got jackeroos for that. Anyway, the weather ain't improved none. Be a real scorcher I reckon. You best go find that sister of yours before she gets herself sunstruck.' But they didn't move, waiting until the noise of the vehicle faded with distance.

From around the corner of the house the cattle-pup ran, short legs pumping, dragging a length of chain. Bluey ran straight and true, past the thorny rose bushes and the trickling fountain, trailing the dust left by the departing vehicle.

Rex coughed and spat on the ground. 'I'll go fetch the young fella's dog.'

Eleanor was sure she heard the word 'albatross' as the old gardener limped away.

⋙ Chapter Thirty-five ⋘

'Your brother's gone?'

'Yes, he's gone.' Eleanor made a fuss of checking the container storing fresh bandages.

The patient was sitting up in bed, reading a copy of *The Pastoral Review and Grazier's Record*. He looked over the top of the magazine with its distinctive map of Australia positioned next to the title, and *Established 1891* displayed prominently on the cover above a large-framed Merino ram. 'Australia's major concern should be the preservation and improvement of its soils,' he read, 'and this should be the watch-word of every man occupying the land.' He placed the magazine on the bedcover. 'The writer's got a point. Half your farm will blow away on the next wind if you don't get rain soon, and this heat. I don't know how any of you live out here.'

'This isn't a farm, it's a sheep station.' He wore a close-fitting white t-shirt that contrasted sharply against the brown of his face and arms. 'Your accent sounds American, but there's something foreign in your voice as well.'

He rested his head against the wall. 'Have you known many Americans?'

'No.'

'Would you like to?' he enticed, patting the white sheet.

Eleanor ignored his lighthearted banter. 'You're obviously much improved, managing to lift your arm to put that on.'

'Hurt like the blazes,' he admitted, patting the bulky dressing beneath the shirt, 'but none of my other clothes seem to be here and with all you young women about, I thought I should cover myself for decency's sake.' His grin revealed a cheeky dimple and white, irregular teeth. Eleanor thought of the feel of his skin beneath the washcloth, how she'd been enamoured with the hollow in the base of her throat. Her attention was instantly drawn to that very spot. It would be churlish to deny the fact that he was good-looking, in a boyish sort of way. 'I'll check on your clothes,' replied Eleanor, shaking a bottle containing painkillers. There was a sweet smell in the room. A bed pan stuck out from beneath the washstand. Having not noticed or even thought about such things, she appreciated Athena's efficiency anew. 'If you can dress yourself, there's no need for you to stay here any longer.' Eleanor thought she heard the slightest of noises, something verging on a grunt.

'And your sister? Where's she?' the man enquired, ignoring the statement.

Eleanor, wondering how to broach the subject of Lesley, seized the opening. 'Resting. You didn't leave a very good impression on her. Did you say something to upset her? And what's with this sudden decision to speak to everyone.'

'Everyone?' he frowned. 'Your sister was upset last night. It seemed the right thing to do. Talk to her. Instead of her sitting in that chair staring into space.'

'Oh.' At her response, the patient appeared almost relieved. But she couldn't quite bring herself to apologise. The man had been so resistant to people knowing he could speak and then that all changed when he met Lesley. On the other hand, Eleanor thought, the slightest of things could cause Lesley's mood to alter. She'd been witness to that this morning. Of course she should have gone out in search of her sister immediately after Robbie left, but the thought of another melancholy meeting coming so soon after her brother's departure didn't appeal. Already a warm wind was circling through the flyscreen. The morning sky was almost white with haze. In an hour or so, Mrs Howell would be closing the curtains to block out the day's heat.

'You're still unsure, aren't you?' The patient studied her, unhurriedly, from head to foot and back again. 'I didn't say anything to upset your sister. Why would I?'

How was she supposed to answer? 'She's been through a lot.'

'And you're just being protective.' When he didn't receive a reply, he continued, 'How'd the kid take the news of being schooled away from home? I gather he was sent away because of me.'

She turned to him. 'You must learn a lot when you pretend to be unconscious.'

'I know you have a kind heart and that there was a guy named Dante.'

'I'm leaving.'

'Hey, whether I'm awake or asleep, you obviously needed to talk to someone.' He reached for Eleanor's wrist, the back of his hand still bandaged from the recent drip. Encircling it, his grasp was strong. 'You can talk to me,' he said quietly, 'I'm a good listener.'

The action shocked Eleanor, and for a second she pulled against the force of his grip. She knew she should have been afraid, or at least wary, and perhaps she was, just a little. But so much had occurred since last Saturday, she doubted anything would ever shock her again. Robbie was gone, Lesley shouldn't have returned and something was clearly going on between her uncle and Margaret Winslow. Then there was this man, young, attractive, offering help, and yet something didn't feel right. 'I don't know who you are. And I don't know if you're still suffering from memory loss or pretending. But you're right, Robbie was sent away because of you, among other things.' Eleanor tried to free herself from his grasp, although she wasn't as forceful as she could have been – he was still injured after all. 'My sister returned to nurse you and, believe me, Lesley never should have come home.' Her words were condemning.

The stranger merely gave a single tilt of his chin, a sign of understanding, then released her, making a show of touching his injured shoulder.

'It was only a flesh wound,' Eleanor said dismissively. Dragging the chair a few feet away from the bed, she sat down.

The man stared at her, a lock of hair falling across a wide, intelligent forehead. 'Are you always so hard on people?' The stranger sounded genuinely let down, as though he'd expected better of Eleanor. She drew back, not knowing how to respond.

'I can imagine how much of an imposition it's been having me in your home. But I can't say I did it deliberately.' Placing the magazine he'd been reading on the washstand, he bashed at the pillows supporting his back and shoulders before resuming a more comfortable position. 'She sat right there,' he pointed to the chair's original position near the bed, 'stared at the bedside lamp all night. Every time I woke she was there, your sister, just staring into the light.'

'Lesley. Her name is Lesley.' Eleanor wanted to be angry at this familiarity but at the same time she regretted her attitude. The stranger had suffered the brunt of her pent-up frustration.

'Your sister, Lesley. She's a beautiful girl,' he told her, 'like you.'

'Where are you from?' asked Eleanor.

He tugged at the pillows, repositioning them again, as if he would never get comfortable. 'Everywhere, nowhere.'

'I'm serious. I'm not lying for you anymore.' She waited for a response too long in coming. 'If you don't tell me everything, right now, I'll walk straight out that door and tell everyone that you can speak. Then your game will be over.'

The stranger poured a glass of water and took a long drink. 'What game? Lesley knows I can talk.'

Eleanor felt like an idiot. Frustrated, she appealed to him, 'Please, what's your name? Where are you from? What are you doing here?'

The man's features darkened. 'What's riled you? You sound like the Greek woman.'

He reminded her of Dante, attractive, charming but quick to anger. Eleanor let out a sigh. 'You've put me in a difficult position, making me lie for you.'

'I didn't make you do anything,' he said gently. 'I simply told you the truth, what I'd prefer, what I was comfortable with, considering the situation. Whether you chose to honour my request was up to you, Eleanor. It was your decision. And it doesn't matter anymore anyway. Does it? Now Lesley knows I can talk.'

She stood abruptly, walked around the cramped room, feeling caught, wanting to leave, but desperate to know the truth. Was this man manipulating her, as Dante had done? 'This is ridiculous. You obviously have something to hide, otherwise you would have said who you were by now.'

'And you obviously trusted me enough to give me the benefit of the doubt, Eleanor.' Flipping back the sheet, he swung long, lean legs over the edge of the bed. Eleanor moved to the far wall, looked towards the door. He pulled at the bandage on the back of his head, the dressing coming away cleanly with only a hint of dried blood. 'Happened in the war it did, fighting the likes of the Greek nurse.' He probed the injury. 'I was knocked out, you know, Eleanor. That wasn't pretend.'

So then, this was a beginning, she decided. 'And your accent? I can't pick it.'

'Italian-American,' he confided. 'But if my mother's around, then I'm all Italian.' He dropped the bandage on the washstand. 'My mother never forgave my father for dying early.' Stretching out his injured arm, he rotated it left then right.

Leaving the far wall, Eleanor approached the bed once again. 'So you're on our side.'

He didn't answer, instead dragging the chair closer to the bed and patting the seat.

Eleanor ignored the gesture. 'You're not a communist?'

He laughed, loud and strong. 'I'm not bloody anything, Eleanor. I'm just a man trying to make a living, who happened to get lost and ended up in the wrong place at the wrong time.' There it was, that dimpled cheek again. 'Boy, was I in the wrong place.'

'You're a scab.' Eleanor decided.

His eyes widened. 'One of those blokes who aren't part of a union? No, I'm not one of those. And I've been here long enough to know that out here, in the bush, that's an insult.'

Eleanor folded her arms. So far he'd divulged very little. 'Depends what side you're on, I guess.'

'Well, I can tell you that I never expected to get shot. But it's not so bad, I've been shot at before, by experts.' He probed the shoulder wound once more. 'Guess I should be used to it by now.'

'Robbie's a good shot. You were lucky.' Eleanor sat on the chair, crossed her legs, one socked foot moving up and down.

His fingers gripped the thin mattress, blue veins ran the length of his arms. 'You're proud of the kid?'

'Not for hurting you.' It was the truth. 'What were you doing out there, in the paddock?'

The stranger had been looking around the room, at the planks outside the window, at the door, as if seeing everything for the first time. 'I told you, I got lost. I was out riding, visiting a neighbouring property. Next thing, I was shot and I fell. I can't remember much else.'

Eleanor tilted her head with interest. 'Who were you visiting?'

'Harris's place.'

'Never heard of him. Where is the property?'

'I'd hardly expect you to know them, Eleanor, I was riding for the good part of two days.'

'Try me,' she interrupted. 'Firstly, you'd have to ride for a good three days at least to get on our land and, secondly, my family's been here for a very long time. We know everyone.'

'Not in this case, it seems,' he replied brashly.

Eleanor couldn't decide what to make of the man opposite her. He appeared genuine enough and she certainly wasn't immune to his easy smile and clean, country looks.

'Anyway, I followed the river. At least I had water and I found some freshwater crayfish in a trap. I didn't want to steal them but I had to eat something.'

Eleanor could have told the man that they'd been Robbie's, but she kept the information to herself, feeling a little more comfortable that the stranger's story was starting to make sense. 'What's your name?'

'Chad. Chad Reynolds.' He smiled. She gave the barest in return.

'You know, Eleanor, I'm a bit wary of people, always have been, I guess. And I really didn't know where I was, or what I was doing here, when I woke up. Everything was confused. I heard people talking. People saying that I was a communist. That I had to be locked in this room. That I had to be watched. And then there was that bloody nurse and the nailing of the boards across the window.' His eyes grew distant, thoughtful. 'I don't mind saying that for a while there I thought I'd lost my marbles.' He tapped his head. 'Or, as you Aussies say, I had a few loose in the top paddock. I was confused. I thought I was in some military hospital. And that Greek nurse, always asking questions. So I said nothing. But then my head cleared and I began to realise that I was in someone's home and I remembered you, your voice, from the paddock. I thought I'd imagined it, then I woke and there you were.' Their eyes met. 'Thank you.'

This time when he smiled, Eleanor found herself responding in kind.

'But that nurse, Athena, what a corker she is. A goddamn, bleeding-heart immigrant trying to start a new life. I'm pretty sure she's a German collaborator.'

'What?' asked Eleanor. 'But how would you know that?'

'I wouldn't have, except for the singing and the questions she asked. If I'd ever been in Athens. What side I was on in the war. If I had been wounded in Greece. I wasn't expecting her.'

'What do you mean, her?' quizzed Eleanor.

Chad studied his glass, filling it with water again. 'You know. I meant meeting someone like that here.' Chad's voice became softer, as if he were remembering something difficult. 'It was the night before she left.' The muscle in his jaw twitched. 'I'd heard the song before, during the war, in Athens. It was in German.'

'German?' Eleanor didn't understand. 'But she's Greek.'

'Yes, Greek. A Greek who became a German collaborator. I'll bet my life on it.' His face grew strained. 'It was in Athens,' he began haltingly, 'in the spring and summer of 1944, that the Security Battalions executed civilians suspected of leftist leanings. People were ordered to leave their homes and stand in the street. If you didn't,' he swallowed, 'you were murdered in your own home. They rounded up entire districts and shot or hung people, Eleanor –' He stopped mid-sentence, as if the memory was still too vivid.

'But I don't understand, Chad, what has this got to do with Athena?'

'The only way a Greek woman would ask the questions she'd asked of me, would be if she'd joined the other side. If she'd turned on her own people to survive. I'd never believe anything the woman said, trust me.'

'She said a similar thing about you, Chad.'

'I'm sure she did. She probably guessed I was Italian.'

'I didn't.' Eleanor didn't understand. 'Why are you so worried about her?'

'Because if she is who I think she is, then she's the enemy.'

He sounded so convinced. Eleanor sighed. 'The war's over Chad,' she said softly.

Shuffling back on the bed, he pulled a sheet awkwardly around his legs. 'Maybe for you. She probably slept with the bloody SS, received food and protection and jewels.' Chad's eyes widened. 'She should be the one locked up, not me. She should be tried for treason. She should be sent back to Greece.' His face paled with the effort of his speech.

'No-one has said anything about locking you up.' For a moment it was as if he hadn't heard her, then he lay down on the bed and closed his eyes. 'I'm sorry. I'm doing my best, Eleanor, really I am . . . sometimes I have moments when I'm back there and –'

'It's alright, Chad.' Eleanor took his hand in hers. 'I understand.' And she did understand. Chad was clearly still suffering from his time at the front, as her father did when he was alive, as Marcus had. There were the effects of war on the body and then there were the invisible scars, the wounds to the mind that in some cases were impossible to heal. Their family knew that all too well.

The knot within her chest loosened. Chad needed care and comfort, not keys and boarded windows. He wasn't a communist, only a man lost in the world after the war. 'Can I get you anything?'

He squeezed her fingers. 'Thank you, Eleanor, thank you.' Chad's words were muffled as he covered his face with an arm.

⊰ Chapter Thirty-six ⊱

The car travelled over a stock grid, rattled loudly, gave a shudder and started to slow. Hunched on the back seat, Robbie sat forward, straining to see what animal had caused Mr Winslow to reduce speed. Far ahead in the distance the red road flickered, weaved and spun, forming patterns as it fused with hot, white air. The optical illusion held his attention until the morning glare forced him to blink and he shut his eyes tightly, feeling the pressure of lid on eyeball. They felt itchy and dry, as if they too were in need of rain.

On either side of the track, scattered timber and low-lying bushes sheltered birds and kangaroos. Overhead, a wedge-tailed eagle circled. There were sheep grazing in the distance, their freshly shorn skins bright against a backdrop of faded green and beige. And behind them a quarter mile, the peeling signpost that pointed to the River Run cemetery. Seven miles down a lonely track lay great-grandparents, stockmen, children and staff. Happily, Robbie realised they were still on the property. He was still home.

Mr Winslow steered the car onto the side of the dirt road, as his wife queried what was wrong, why the vehicle had lost power.

The driver did his best to explain that he had no idea. That it was probably something simple that could be fixed in a jiffy. The Studebaker rolled onwards at a crawl, gave a final shudder as if an animal dying, and stopped. They sat in silence for the merest of seconds, and then Mrs Winslow pointed out that it would have been better if her husband had managed to get the car parked under the shade of a tree rather than leaving them in full sight of the blazing sun, on the side of the road. After all, what would happen if they were stuck here? In fact, they could be here all day before someone appeared, she challenged. Mr Winslow grunted, said that with shearing on they couldn't expect much traffic. His wife lit a cigarette. They didn't have any water or food. She didn't want to have to sleep in the car and, besides, they'd boil to death in this heatwave. I could be so lucky, Mr Winslow replied.

Robbie quickly noted that the closest tree was a good twenty yards away.

Mr Winslow got out of the vehicle, slamming the door closed. He lifted the bonnet, walked around to the boot, popped it and walked back to the front of the vehicle carrying a spanner. The sound of metal being bashed vibrated through the air. Mrs Winslow was instructed to slide across the passenger seat and try starting the engine. The woman obeyed reluctantly, muttering something about the uselessness of bush mechanics, of husbands who had too many staff, and of godforsaken places in the middle of nowhere. The engine made a clicking sound and then died. The bashing continued, punctuated by Mrs Winslow turning the key in the ignition when she was called upon to do so. Outside, Mr Winslow called the car a useless, rotten bastard of a thing.

Robbie waved away the cigarette smoke filling the interior of the vehicle and rested his chin on the windowsill. Tiny brown birds were darting between the branches of a bush, the air growing thick as the sun moved higher. There was a dryness in the atmosphere, a brittle scent of withering plants and gasping soil. There was also the stench of something dead. He moved across the seat to the other window, stuck his head out and looked back in the direction they'd come, and then forward. There it was. The reason the wedge-tailed eagle circled overhead: a dead kangaroo on the side of the road.

Mr Winslow opened the driver's side door, told his wife to move and sat at the steering wheel looking at the instrument panel. She complained about the smell and asked what it was. Her husband merely tapped the windscreen and pointed at the rotting carcass before beginning to recite all the things that may have gone wrong. Out of oil, radiator boiled, a broken belt, a burnt-out spark plug. Margaret Winslow voiced the opinion that in other words her husband had no bloody idea. Robbie said nothing. They would miss the train to Sydney. He took off his jacket and lay it on the seat.

Mr Winslow accused Sweeny Hall in the village of not knowing a bloody thing about cars. Mrs Winslow blamed her husband first and then the Studebaker and the makers of the automobile. Americans, damn unreliable, she decided, besides which, there was little point owning an automobile if bush mechanics didn't know the first thing when it came to fixing them. Then there was the pointlessness of the journey, when they'd lost valuable ram sales. Which, added to the lack of loyalty shown by their fairweather friends, all in all the visit was a complete waste of time.

Robbie didn't think he'd ever heard a woman complain so much.

Mr Winslow sat clenching the steering wheel, his knuckles growing white. Finally he lit a cigarette and in a low voice made a retort about wives behaving themselves. Mrs Winslow replied that she'd take Ambrose Park to the cleaners if she felt so inclined.

Robbie got out of the car. The Winslows followed, complaining about the heat, about how further south, on their property, it never seemed to feel quite as hot. That you had to be made of tougher stuff to survive out here on the plains. Hard country, Mr Winslow announced, staring down the empty road. Cultural desert, his wife stated. From the open boot, Mrs Winslow rifled through a suitcase, found a blouse and carried it to the tree. Here she sat, using the shirt as a blanket between her and the ground, tugging the length of skirt tight around her body, keeping her feet drawn up close. She lit another cigarette. Took two puffs and threw it into the scrub. Robbie found the glowing butt and stomped on it. Mr Winslow reprimanded his wife. Told her that the boy had more sense than her. That a lit cigarette could start a fire. The woman observed disinterestedly that there wasn't much to burn and that using the word 'sense' in the same sentence as Georgia's child was a joke. Mr Winslow apologised to Robbie, said it was the heat. That he was sorry that they'd miss the train.

Robbie walked around the other side of the tree and sat down. He wasn't sorry at all.

The adults talked for a bit. About what they should do. How long they should wait for. The wife wondered if one of them should start to walk to find help. Not in this heat, Robbie warned, twisting his neck around the knobbly trunk of the tree. Mr Winslow agreed. He knew more than his wife. Rex will come along at some stage, said Robbie. His words calmed the adults and they began to talk more quietly about towing the vehicle, leaving the car in the village if they couldn't be assured of getting it properly repaired, and taking the train to Sydney before heading home to their own property.

What Robbie didn't say was whether the blue truck would appear today or tomorrow. They'd already collected the shearing supplies. Unless there was a breakdown, a serious injury or Mrs Howell ran out of something, no-one would be driving down the road to the village or coming in for quite a while. Everyone was too busy. You could drink the water in the radiator, he suggested. Siphon it out if you've got a bit of tube.

Mrs Winslow said the very idea was disgusting.

Someone will come, her husband comforted.

Robbie imagined a pile of white bones, one lot long and angular, the other thickset and round. The smaller bits would probably be picked up by a canny bowerbird, the bigger ones carted away by foxes, wild dogs or pigs, the rest eventually washed away on the crest of the next flood. It was just as the priest said. Everyone came from dust and would return to dust. It was simply a matter of time.

The adult talk slowly dwindled and, with the quiet, the eagle reappeared, circling downwards to land on the edge of the road. It was an old bird. The mid-brown of youth having darkened to a blackish-brown shade and with such maturity the eagle had grown cautious. It pecked at the kangaroo carcass, occasionally lifting its head to check the surrounds. Robbie watched the bird for some time, wishing he too could fly away.

The heat made his eyelids sag, made his limbs tired, his skin itch. Out in the west a pale stream of brown appeared. It rose vertically, dark against a silver sky. A dust storm or a dirty cloud signalling a westerly buster. The willowy pattern lengthened, thickened and then shrunk in height and width as if struck by indecisiveness. Robbie formed a square with his fingers, framing the indistinct shape where it sat on the horizon. It was similar to the haze he'd seen late on Friday afternoon before the shooting, before everything went topsy-turvy, but it neither drew closer nor retreated, and Robbie came to the conclusion that it was a fire. Someone was burning off, miles away. But when he looked again the pale line of colour was gone, engulfed by wispy cloud.

As the morning dragged and the countryside drew dazed with heat, he peered around the trunk of the tree. The Winslows were asleep, the bark providing a pillow, the man and woman's gentle whistling snores sounding like contesting birdcall. Mrs Winslow's silver lighter lay next to a packet of cigarettes. Robbie snatched it up, slipping it into a pocket, then quietly walked to the boot of the car and opened his suitcase. Beneath the neatly folded clothes was his wide-brimmed hat. He'd snuck it in after his mother finished packing. Straightening out the squashed bits, Robbie put it on and then rummaged around until he'd found the shanghai. This he stuck in a back pocket, along with a pocketknife. Then, certain there was nothing else he could make use of, Robbie gave the sleeping Winslows one final check and walked off into the scrub.

◄ Chapter Thirty-seven ►

Leaving Chad to sleep after depositing his laundered clothes on a chair in the room, Eleanor set out to find her sister. A quick search of the house suggested that she'd not returned since the episode in the garden. Eleanor entered the kitchen, where a bustling Mrs Howell was dabbing at the perspiration dribbling down a lined cheek.

'You best find her,' the housekeeper advised when Eleanor explained there was no sign of Lesley. The woman removed a large roasting pan from the oven, sitting the sizzling meat on the sink. 'We don't need her wandering off and getting all maudlin.'

It was a little late for that, Eleanor thought. 'The place reminds her of Marcus,' she shared, moving to stand near the whirring electric fan sitting on a bench top. 'She shouldn't have come home.'

'So, Athena Pappas was right,' Mrs Howell replied, somewhat reluctantly. 'Well, the woman's trained, so I guess it's natural she should know more about these things than the rest of us.'

'It seems so,' said Eleanor, remembering anew Chad's allegations. She hoped Chad's state of mind was making him imagine the very worst of the Greek woman, but it was possible that Athena

had been on the wrong side during the war. He was certainly convinced of her involvement. Such a recrimination made Georgia's
misgivings regarding a child born out of wedlock the least of their
concerns. Eleanor felt sorry for Stavros Pappas. He was a boon
to their district, but once word got out that the family were on
the other side during the war, it was doubtful whether they would
want to stay in the area.

'I put this leg on so we'd have cold meat for lunch, but quite
frankly I don't think our appetites will be quite what they were
yesterday. Except for our patient, of course. The man eats like a
horse.' Spearing the sheep meat with a three-pronged fork, the
older woman lifted the large leg of mutton onto a platter and then
covered the dish with a domed gauze meat-keeper. 'That will keep
the blowies away. What I wouldn't do for a bit of rabbit. Your mother
loved it. Stock, a few carrots, onion, flour and a sprig of thyme. Of
course now with this myxomatosis thing, a person can't go near
it for fear of getting poisoned. Rex told me we're selling rabbits
abroad like it's nobody's business, now that no-one is buying them
here.' She clucked her tongue. 'You wait, Menzies won't hear the
end of it if people start dropping dead at their dinner tables on the
other side of the world.'

'I don't think the disease can actually be transferred to humans,
Mrs Howell,' replied Eleanor.

The housekeeper peered down her long nose. 'That's what
people once thought about mice and the plague. Anyway, enough
of this. What's the matter with you?' Mrs Howell asked Eleanor,
once the oven had been turned off. 'You have that guilty look on
your face you used to get when you were a child.'

'Nothing.'

The older woman regarded her with an air of disbelief. Eleanor
responded with an innocent smile. It was not that she didn't want
to share with the housekeeper what she had so recently discovered
from their patient. Once she did, however, an in-depth discussion

would certainly ensue, one that would lead to endless supposition regarding Chad Reynolds' self-imposed silence and his accusations regarding Athena. Eleanor, concerned about finding Lesley, wasn't prepared to delay any further. Besides, she reasoned, Chad's story seemed totally plausible. He'd clearly been in the wrong place at the wrong time. 'Where's Mum?' she asked.

Georgia, having apparently taken heed of the overseer's suggestion of visiting the woolshed, was changing into work-clothes, following the Winslows' departure. 'And about time too,' Mrs Howell said with an air of reproach. 'One's duty should never be shirked for the sake of entertaining visitors, even if River Run is a client of Ambrose Park. Things will be difficult for a while,' she admitted, alluding to Robbie's departure and Lesley's return, 'but once the stranger is gone, eventually life will get back to normal.' Selecting two lemons from a bowl on the table, she rolled each one to soften them and then grated the rind from one before cutting each in half, the sharp knife slicing the scarred wooden chopping board.

Eleanor wasn't quite as convinced as her old confidante. Firstly, there was her mother and stepfather's relationship. It appeared there were three people in it. Eleanor may have felt a little more disgusted about Colin's behaviour had it not opened up the possibility of his leaving River Run and her mother forever.

Mrs Howell squeezed the lemons into a bowl, stopping to pick the pips from the juice with a teaspoon. 'Lemon tart,' she explained. 'Of course a woman's a fool for cooking desserts in this heat.'

Still, there was something else, something that just didn't feel right, and it had nothing to do with Lesley or Robbie or Chad's ongoing problems following his wartime service overseas. No, there was something unsettling Eleanor. Try as she may, she couldn't understand what it was.

Mrs Howell walked into the pantry, returning with eggs and caster sugar. 'Well, off you go, Eleanor. Go and find that sister of yours and bring her back here. I'll make her a nice cup of tea and then you and I will sit her down and we'll have a little talk. It's time that young lady got her two feet back firmly on the ground.'

Outside, there was little improvement in the weather. Eleanor drew the hat down further over her forehead, hoping Lesley was resting in a shady spot and that the fresh air and open space would provide some much needed perspective. The sun bit through the cloth of the shirt she wore, as Eleanor scanned the garden, circumnavigating the front and rear lawns, shrubberies and roses. Already the backs of her hands showed a line at the cuff of the shirtsleeve between pale skin and a deepening brown, and her cheeks, chin and neck were noticeably tanned.

With no sign of Lesley, the outbuildings beckoned. Eleanor left the house surrounds to follow the rutted track past the school-house and meat-house. The shady trees near two derelict timber structures showed no trace of her older sister and Mr Goward's cottage was quiet. Robbie's cattle dog Bluey was laying in the dirt at the end of a taut chain. He barely moved as she passed by. Pining already, Eleanor decided. Cattle dogs were notoriously loyal. As there were few enticing spots left to investigate, she headed towards the woolshed, hoping that Lesley may have walked in that direction and become caught up in the activity of shearing.

Ahead, the large corrugated iron roof reflected the sun's rays with dazzling brightness. Eleanor continued walking across the rough ground, listening for the familiar sounds that she would forever associate with summer. But something wasn't quite right. Eleanor stopped walking, started again and then slowed. It was the lack of engine noise. The sheep still called to each other, the dogs barked intermittently, however, the hum of the Lister engine was absent. A breakdown. That was the only reason for the machine not to be running. It wouldn't take long for tensions to rise, not in this heat. A few minutes was one thing. The men could spend the time having a smoke, sharpening combs and cutters or resting aching limbs by lying flat on the lanoline-smoothed board. Any longer, an hour, two hours, meant the day's work would be delayed. Every shed always had an agitator among its men. Someone willing and able to stir up trouble. Little was needed to rile tempers at times.

Taking a steadying breath, Eleanor rubbed at her temples. Her brain felt tight, as if it were being pushed and pulled in too many directions. Lesley should really know better than to wander off, she thought angrily, especially with everything else going on. Thoughts of Robbie mixed with the Winslows. Did Keith Winslow know of his wife's philanderings with her stepfather? Did Georgia pull her arm away from Colin earlier this morning because she blamed him for Robbie's leaving, for giving a young boy a rifle? Or because she was aware of Colin and Margaret's relationship?

Rivulets of perspiration ran down her spine and pooled across her stomach. Surely the heat would ease soon. For six days since her arrival home the weather had remained unrelenting. It hung heavy and hard like a blanket, causing Eleanor to drink so much water that she felt like a puffer fish, but her thirst was never satiated. The corrugated iron roof of the shearing shed glistened. She wiped at the sweat trickling from her hairline. In a shirt-pocket was the packet of Lucky Strikes gifted to her by Margaret Winslow. Eleanor cupped her hands to light a cigarette as a wind rose, extinguishing the flame. She lit another match, exhaled deeply and blew out the burning sliver of wood. The smoke curled upwards before it was caught by the breeze and whisked away.

The action of smoking comforted Eleanor. Although standing out in the middle of the flat in the heat didn't make the cigarette particularly enjoyable, it turned her thoughts to more pleasant things. Georgia and Colin would have to sit down with Chad, hear his version of events. Dinner would be the perfect opportunity. Her offer was not without selfish reasons. It was true that everyone needed to hear Chad's story and the truth couldn't have come at a more perfect moment now Robbie and the Winslows were gone. The thought of their four remaining family members happily coming together over pre-dinner drinks was an almost impossible thought, making Chad an ideal diversion, for more than one reason.

There were so many things Eleanor was interested in knowing about him. Where he lived. Why he was visiting the Harrises. What he did for a living. Why he'd decided to immigrate to Australia after the war, for clearly that was the case. She told herself such curiosity was natural. That it had nothing to do with attraction. That it was simply relief at knowing the truth about the wounded stranger who, by tonight, would be a recuperating house guest. Considering Robbie's actions, Chad's recovery and seeming lack of anger towards his attacker, and by extension the Webber family, was most charitable.

As for Athena, that situation was beyond Eleanor and too difficult to fathom considering the friendship shared between them in such a short time. The nurse was in Australia now, hopeful of a new life. Passing judgement on another, for incidents that may have been impossible to avoid, didn't seem right or fair and none of them were equipped to deal with Chad's accusations. Besides which, Eleanor had read enough newspaper reports and heard many stories from within her own circle of family and friends, to know that wartime made people do extraordinary things to survive. She was of little doubt that Athena's primary concern would have been the safety of her child, which didn't make any of her actions right, if what Chad said was correct. Yet, Eleanor's father once spoke of the German soldiers, saying they were ordinary boys, like him, following orders and doing what they could to stay alive. Of course, Eleanor understood Chad's concerns. He'd been fighting for all the right reasons, on their side and the war was still fresh for him, as it was for many. This, however, was Australia. The war was over. While she may not have been at the front, the Webbers were the recipients of their own share of tragedy. Eleanor didn't want Menzies' immigrants bringing their recriminations and anger with them, like so much unwanted baggage. This was meant to be a new world for them. Leave the bad bits of the old ones behind.

A steady line of smoke streamed from the chimney of the shearers' quarters. Clothes flapped on the line outside the jackeroos' bunkhouse. In the distance the squeak of the Southern Cross windmill resembled nails down a blackboard. Suddenly the wind dropped. To the west a line of brownish smoke hung on the horizon. Eleanor stamped out the cigarette and stared at the dirty streak smudging the blue sky, before resuming her path.

The grouping of men outside the woolshed soon became obvious. Eleanor slowed, not wanting to draw attention to herself as she tried to make sense of what was going on. Shearers, rouseabouts and wool rollers stood in a circle, along with the classer, wool presser and other shed-hands. Arms folded across Jackie Howe singlets and cotton shirts, fists plunged deep into pockets, they fidgeted and mumbled, their voices like a gathering wave.

A few yards away, directly opposite, stood Hugh Goward, her stepfather and the jackeroos. These men were quiet and watchful. Clearly outnumbered, they waited for events to unfold. It was only when Eleanor was nearly upon the crowd that she recognised Dawson, Rex and Fitzy. The threesome were gathered at a right angle to the main group and maintained a respectful distance, clearly reluctant to take sides. For just a second Eleanor was sure a wad of cash exchanged hands between the cook and the Aboriginal. She knew she shouldn't have been shocked. Rex, on spotting Eleanor, held his hand up for her to stay where she was.

But she didn't.

In the middle of the circle of men sat Mr Lomax and Billy Wright. The Chinaman was drawing in the dirt with a stick while Billy glared at the opposition, the River Run men. Head tilted to one side, the shearer ran an experienced eye over each of the men, from top to bottom and back again, as if judging who was the better fighter, and who the weaker opponent.

'So, that's our terms. Either you leave Lomax and Billy be and let them finish the job, or we all strike.' It was Donaldson, the faint-voiced shearer from the Riverina. A watermelon-headed man with beefy arms, Eleanor immediately recalled her first sighting of the shearer in the village. The man pushed through the tight grouping of men to stand like a towering prow in front of the agitated crowd. 'The days of you toffy-nosed squatters laying down the law to us men is over. Hear? We don't have to take crap from the likes of you anymore.'

'It's not the forties now,' the overseer said firmly. 'Each of you signed agreements, all except you, Donaldson. There's always one who has to ruin it for everyone else. And you're the new man.'

A slight mumble flickered through the shearers. Mr Goward's carefully chosen words struck a chord.

'We pay the agreed rates,' Colin spoke up, 'house you and feed you according to the pastoral rules.'

In response, a few of the gathered men began to nod in agreement. Eleanor looked to Hugh, tensions were starting to ease.

'But we have to put up with stealing?' said Colin, who appeared to have grown angrier. 'Is that what you're telling me?'

The men fell silent. Eleanor wrinkled her nose. No, no, she thought, don't give them reason to argue.

'Maybe if you gave a man something decent to cook with we wouldn't have to go foraging, on and above like,' Billy Wright countered from where he sat.

Colin took a step forward. 'Eat that well at home, do you?'

Through the diminishing space, Eleanor watched Rex shake his head.

'Come on now,' Hugh said quickly, 'there's a right and a wrong way to do things. This ain't it.'

The wounded shearer, Johnny Daisy, who sported a roughly stitched forearm stained pinkish-brown by mercurochrome, spat in the dirt. 'A man can put up with a lot of things, but once a fella gets personal . . .'

Goward took a step forward.

'I'll handle this,' Colin stated. 'I want all you men to get back to work immediately. If you did what you were paid to do, you'd be too busy to whinge.'

Oh for heaven's sake, Eleanor thought.

'Says who?' Donaldson challenged.

'Who cut up *The Worker* for us to use as dunny paper, eh?' a man yelled out.

'The cook's in it too,' Billy Wright said loudly. 'Dirt sandwiches. That's what I got yesterday.'

'What's this really about?' asked Hugh impatiently. 'It's damn hot. We all know that. If you want to sit down until the weather improves, that's up to you.'

'A bit of hot weather never pulled a man up doing the long-belly blow.' Billy Wright had gone from glaring adversary to interested participant. 'But there ain't no fans. There should be fans in the huts when it's this hot.'

'That can be arranged,' the overseer replied slowly, trying to make eye contact with as many of the shearers as he could.

'He's just trying to soften us up.' Donaldson twisted the heel of his boot in the sand. Flicked it behind him like a bull kicking up dirt. 'Bloody fans when a man's been shot. You lot are soft in the head. Got a skippy-full running around in the top paddock, you lot have. A man nearly died here.'

'What about that boy of yours shooting an innocent man?' someone called, his comment receiving shouts of *that's right* and *can't trust the bastards.*

'You did it cause you thought he was a commo,' Billy Wright spoke loudly. 'A commo that might of had some aff-aff-aff–'

'Affiliation,' Donaldson finished.

Billy nodded. 'That's right. Some affiliation with the union. You lot are trying to keep the heel of your boots on our throats, trying to stop them that are all for a fair go for the worker, from getting a fair go.'

'Pack of bastards.' Donaldson wiped roughly at his nose. 'Here we are doing all the sweating, while you lot couldn't work in an iron lung.'

Eleanor thought immediately of what she'd learnt at dinner the previous evening. Clearly she was not the only person aware of Hugh's loss, for Rex and Fitzy's expressions turned to dislike.

'An iron lung, did you say?' Mr Goward said, almost too quietly.

Donaldson was grinding his knuckles into the palm of his hand, the action flexing tendons, veins and muscles too plentiful for one man. 'This ain't no joking matter. Who will be next, eh, when one of these toffs lifts his rifle? Me? Him? Or him?' He pointed randomly at his colleagues. This time the men's voices grew to a loud rumble.

'If the man was a scab,' Rex interrupted, 'I guess I'm not that fussed.' If the remark was a humorous attempt to defray the situation, it didn't work. There wasn't even a chuckle, although the cook smiled widely at the gardener.

'This need not involve everyone,' Hugh announced. 'If it's a fight you want, Donaldson, well, I can accommodate you.'

Eleanor wasn't sure who moved first, but in a split second Donaldson and Hugh were throwing punches at each other, while a few of the rouseabouts and shed-hands grappled with the jackeroos. Murph fought like a thrashing machine and even Wormy landed a few good hits, while Archie laid into everyone he could with his boot.

'That's not fighting,' the shearer, Johnny Daisy, complained. Walking from the group of bystanders, he landed a punch to Archie's jaw that sent the boy sprawling in the dirt. 'This is the bush. We don't fight like guttersnipes out here.' He casually walked away to sit on the wooden support of the rainwater tank. Archie lay on the ground, out cold.

The spectators, including Colin, Rex, Dawson and the cook, took bets anew and rolled cigarettes while men tumbled around in the dirt. Dogs were barking, men were yelling, the noise combining with the dull thud of jaws, chests and stomachs being walloped. The Chinaman and Billy Wright found themselves in the middle of the scuffle and they moved quickly. Billy caught sight of the cook laughing and charged the bigger man, head down. The two of them rolled around in the dirt. The white, wobbling girth of Fitzy spilt free of his shirt as he wrestled with the wiry shearer. The Chinaman ran in the opposite direction to stand on the rainwater tank-stand beside Daisy, grinning at the chaos below.

In the middle of it all stood Hugh and Donaldson. Squared off opposite each other, throwing punch for punch, it appeared as if the demand for murder was mutual. The Riverina man's nose was bleeding profusely and a cut above Hugh's eye was clearly restricting his sight.

'For heaven's sake, Hugh, stop it!' Eleanor called out, balling her fists. 'Colin, do something.' Her stepfather shrugged. She looked about for something she could strike Donaldson down with and picked up a length of wood.

'Not this time, Miss Eleanor.' Dawson was beside her, grasping the lump of timber and stilling her progress. 'This be man's business,' he said quietly. 'And if it be man's business, how will it look if a woman goes and saves him?'

'But –' Behind them the red dog, Warrigal, barked and growled.

The Aboriginal wrested the timber from her and threw it away. 'And besides, you being a white girl, you supposed to be a lady, aren't you?'

'I suppose, but –'

'You be the Boss's daughter, so best you can do is be ready for the bandaging.' He gestured at the overseer, who stood stoically trading punches with Donaldson as if they were at a prize fight. 'If that whitefella Goward wants to make a point,' Dawson explained, 'then he'll stand there and fight until he can't stand no longer. I seen him like this before, most of us men have. But Donaldson,' he gave a chuckle, his teeth bright and white against dark skin, 'Donaldson, he have no idea that if Goward falls he'll keep on fighting. Bite him on the ankle, if that's all he has left to use.'

'And Donaldson?' Eleanor winced, as the shearer landed an upper-cut to the overseer's jaw.

'Oh, him?' The Aboriginal gave a nod of approval. 'He's real good too, so they say. That's what makes it interesting. Especially for a blackfella, two whitefellas laying into each other.' He grinned. 'But don't worry none, Miss Eleanor,' he told her, seeing the look of concern on her face, 'why I seen the overseer fight two men and him with a busted leg, years back, in Queensland. He won. That's the type of man he is. 'Course he didn't know his leg was broke until afterwards.'

Eleanor thought of the money exchanged. 'So he'll win?' She was unexpectedly pleased by the idea.

Dawson rubbed his chin. 'Probably.'

Hugh staggered under a blow to the stomach.

'That's not particularly positive.'

The blackfella shrugged.

Georgia Webber arrived in a battered farm truck and, slamming the door, walked straight to the overseer's horse where she grabbed the stockwhip. Eleanor and Dawson stepped out of her way as the doyenne of River Run strode towards the fighting men. Unfurling the whip, she cracked it three times in quick succession. The overseer landed one final punch, bringing Donaldson to his knees, Goward swaying but remaining upright. The other men quickly stopped fighting, turning towards the woman who stood furiously among them.

'What the hell do you lot think you're bloody well doing?'

Eleanor had never heard her mother swear, ever, and watched on in amazement.

'This is a goddamn sheep property and, strange as it may seem, I thought we were meant to be bloody well shearing!' Georgia began to wind up the stockwhip. 'Anyone else think that's what should be going on here?' Threading the curled raw-hide whip through an arm, she rested it over a shoulder.

One by one, the men who'd been fighting brushed themselves down and moved back towards their original groupings. Fitzy tried a number of times to clamber to his feet, but he was like a beached whale. Rex and Billy Wright managed to help him up.

Donaldson was staring at Georgia with undisguised contempt.

'Donaldson,' Hugh said loudly for everyone assembled to hear, although his voice sounded dry and ragged, 'this is Mrs Georgia Webber. The Boss,' he said with emphasis.

The shearer nodded. 'Missus, Boss,' he confirmed, his eyes flitting briefly in Colin's direction.

'State your grievance,' Georgia said bluntly, taking a step towards him until they were only a foot apart.

Donaldson was quick to list everything previously mentioned before the fight broke out, from *The Worker* being used as dunny paper, to his mates being fired, to the dirt in yesterday's sandwiches and, finally, Robbie's shooting of the stranger.

Georgia answered each complaint slowly and carefully. 'I'm not sure what goes on down in the Riverina, Mr Donaldson, but here on River Run the days are long and hot, a bit of a harmless joke shouldn't be cause for major offence and I'm sure Fitzy will do his best to ensure the food returns to standard.'

The cook, red-faced from the exertion, agreed.

'As for Mr Lomax and Billy Wright,' she stepped past Donaldson and addressed the shearers and shed-hands, 'those of you who have been coming to this shed,' she walked along the group of men, nodding at each one individually, 'know that I have always done my utmost to ensure that this property is run in accordance with industry standards. No man is underpaid or hard done by, or forced to put up with any inconvenience where humanly possible. And if,' she continued, 'you have made demands of me, they have usually been met, even if those demands have taken advantage of the labour shortages that have ravaged this country since the Great War. A war that eventually claimed my first husband.'

Some of the shearers hung their heads.

Georgia returned to stand in the centre of the two separate groups. 'All that aside, I expect my men to behave. Regardless of whether it's bloody hot or not.'

There was a smirk or two. Not only did the men respect her mother, Eleanor realised, but they liked her, grudging though that admiration may be.

'Now, by my reckoning, this is day three of shearing. Why don't we say it's Monday and we've just begun?' Her tone grew pleasant, conversational. 'Mr Lomax and Billy, you can have your jobs back. But, be aware,' she lifted a finger, pointing at both men, 'I'll be watching. And you.' She turned to Johnny Daisy.

The shearer looked over his shoulder as if Georgia addressed the man behind.

'You,' Georgia repeated, finally getting his attention, 'get that wound cleaned and bandaged and no more mercurochrome. If it gets infected we won't be able to tell before it's too late, the way the antiseptic's stained your skin.'

'Yes, missus. I mean, Boss,' Johnny answered sheepishly.

'What about the shooting?' Donaldson persevered.

'We don't shoot people here for their political leanings, Mr Donaldson,' replied Georgia. 'Although I'm not sure how such things are handled in the Riverina.'

A chuckle rose from the assembled men.

Georgia didn't wait for the mirth to subside. 'My son Robbie has been sent away to boarding school, so he won't be causing any more trouble. As for the patient, he is awake, but yet to speak and expected to make a full recovery.'

Eleanor concentrated on the sun glinting on the woolshed roof.

'Very good, very good,' Mr Lomax answered, as if speaking

on behalf of everyone. 'We go back to work now. I like Australia. Australia has been very good to me and my family.'

'And we like having you here, Mr Lomax.'

Georgia's reply was answered with a grin.

There was a moment's silence and then the men dawdled back towards the woolshed, to disappear inside the cavernous building. Donaldson was among the last to leave, as if by lingering he was making a final, if pointless, gesture of contempt. Georgia matched the man's steely gaze until, almost reluctantly, he too finally turned away to follow the last of the men.

From inside the woolshed came the putt-putt sound of the Lister engine being cranked up. Fitzy, Rex and Dawson were arguing over money as they headed towards the shearers' quarters.

'But he nailed him,' Dawson argued.

'But neither fell,' Rex countered. 'Donaldson only went to his knees. Out for the count. Those were the terms.' The gardener clucked his teeth like an old woman. 'Very disappointing show.'

Eleanor noticed that her stepfather was examining Archie's wounds. The young jackeroo was holding his jaw and whining.

'It's not broken, lad,' Colin advised. 'Fractured maybe, but there's not a lot that can be done for that.'

The boy tried to speak.

'I'd go back to your quarters, Archie. Clean yourself up and then lay down for a bit. You lads,' he addressed the three remaining jackeroos, 'get back to work.'

'You best tidy yourself up as well, Hugh.' Georgia ran a critical eye across the overseer, taking in dirt-covered clothes, missing shirt buttons and the wounds to his face. 'I can't have my Stud Master looking like a common street fighter,' she said with a smile.

'Sorry, Boss.' He wiped blood from his mouth. 'And thank you, Mrs Webber, I won't let you down.'

'You look positively goggle-eyed, Eleanor,' Georgia observed, as they walked back towards the farm truck. 'Come on.'

Eleanor exchanged a brief smile with Hugh. 'What about . . . ? I mean . . .' Quickening her pace to catch up with her mother, Eleanor called after her, 'Shouldn't we check their wounds, get some bandages?'

'Bandages?' her mother repeated, walking on.

Eleanor wanted to speak to Hugh, to make sure he was alright, to congratulate him on his promotion. Instead she dutifully followed Georgia, opened the door of the truck and sat in the passenger seat next to her mother.

'What?' Georgia asked, noticing her daughter's wide-eyed stare.

She wound down the window, the interior of the vehicle was like a furnace. 'I just didn't realise.'

'Realise what?' Georgia turned the key in the ignition. 'What it takes to run a property?'

The old truck vibrated noisily. Eleanor couldn't find the words to express her feelings. 'You were –'

'Loud, bossy and I use bad language,' her mother countered, as if acknowledging her faults. Georgia searched the dashboard, rifling through old Cooper's notebooks, empty Fruit Tingle wrappers and an assortment of nuts, bolts and lengths of twine. 'Your father, God bless him, would never have approved, Eleanor.' She turned to her daughter and winked. 'At least not in public.'

When the squashed packet of cigarettes was finally located and one was lit, only then did Eleanor notice that her mother's hands were trembling.

❧ Chapter Thirty-eight ❧

The truck rattled across the road towards the homestead as the red dog, released from the chain, leapt into his master's arms. Eleanor watched the reunion in the side-view mirror, until distance and dust clouded her vision. She hoped Hugh was alright. He'd certainly taken a pounding.

'I should be able to move on, but every single day I think of your father, Eleanor.' Georgia changed gears as the vehicle navigated a pothole in the road.

Eleanor wished she could think of an appropriate response, however, the suddenness of her mother's admission caught her quite unawares.

'It's wrong, I know,' Georgia admitted. 'In some respects I'm no better than Lesley with my grief, except that I've managed to internalise it.'

'But you have moved on, Mum,' said Eleanor gently.

Georgia gave a sigh. 'Not in my heart,' she answered wistfully. 'Of course Colin gave me Robbie and it's your brother who has been my salve, especially over the last few years.' The vehicle slowed as it passed the working dogs tied up under the trees, the chorus of yelps quickly petering out. 'I indulged Robbie, well, we both did. It was wrong and I blame myself for having to send him away. I should never have allowed him to be given that rifle, but he's such a mature boy for his age and Colin was so adamant at the time.' The green of the back garden appeared like an oasis. Birds swooped low across the chain of ponds. 'People think children bond them together, and I guess they do for a time, but the reality of any partnership is, whether there are children or not, a relationship either works or it doesn't.'

'Do you still love Uncle Colin, Mum?' For a moment Eleanor wished that she'd not asked the question, but a door had been opened and after everything she'd witnessed over the past few days, she felt she had to persevere.

Georgia's silence lasted the length of the garden boundary, extending past the tree where Robbie's cattle-pup should have been sulking in the shade, but Bluey and the chain were gone. By the time the vehicle turned through the side gate and travelled along the gravel at the rear of the house, Eleanor's expectations were fading.

'I was so lost after your father died, Elly. Colin was there when I needed someone. And being with him, well, it was like I still had a part of your father with me. It's hard to explain, but in those early days, when Colin was with me, your father was as well. I don't know how I would have coped without him back then.'

'And now?' Eleanor asked, tentatively.

Georgia worked down through the gears of the truck as they neared the kitchen entrance. 'Robbie was conceived before Colin and I married.'

Eleanor couldn't believe what she was hearing. 'But how can that be?'

'Do you really need the birds and bees talk at this stage, Elly?' Georgia laughed. 'You girls were at boarding school. Only Mrs Howell and Rex knew the truth of things, because they couldn't miss it. Robbie was nearly ten pound when he was born, although there's never been a word breathed about it by anyone. As far as the district and you girls were concerned, Robbie was premature.'

Eleanor digested the truth of her mother's marriage with a mixture of disbelief and shock. 'So you may not have married Colin if –'

'No,' interrupted Georgia, 'I may not have. But I did,' she said firmly.

Was this why Georgia was so outspoken about Athena's illegitimate child? Perhaps, Eleanor decided, her mother felt that Athena should have done the right thing and married, as she did. Or maybe Georgia resented Athena's strength in electing to remain a single mother.

Rubber screeched on gravel as the vehicle came to a stop. For a moment, both women remained in the vehicle, their eyes on the kitchen screen door.

'This is to stay between you and me, Elly.'

Eleanor's mouth was dry. 'Of course, Mum.' She desperately wanted to know whether her mother was aware of Colin's philandering. While she'd not witnessed anything beyond flirtation, the farewell kiss and Margaret's appearance at the garden shed were suggestive of something larger at play.

Georgia got out of the vehicle and slammed the door of the truck. 'What a week.'

'I have to go find Lesley.' Eleanor addressed her mother across the roof of the work truck. 'I haven't seen her since this morning.'

'Lesley, yes, of course,' she sighed. 'With everything else that's happened today, I must admit I'd briefly forgotten about your sister. Really and truly. There's grief and then there's self-pity. Wouldn't you think Lesley would channel her energies into hating the damn Japanese? That's what I'd be doing if I were her. I still get a lot of satisfaction out of despising the Germans.'

At their arrival, the screen door to the kitchen opened and Mrs Howell appeared. 'Glad as a youngster on Christmas Day

I am to see you, Mrs Webber.' The housekeeper held the door open for them to enter, taking the opportunity to glare at Eleanor.

'What's happened now?' asked Georgia. 'Is it Lesley? Elly said she's not been seen. Is she back?'

The housekeeper's hundred-yard stare was directed at Eleanor. 'No, she is not, but –'

'It's about the stranger, Mum.' Eleanor sensed that the truth she'd been harbouring regarding the patient was out. She couldn't delay telling her mother any longer. 'Well, his name is Chad Reynolds. He's an Italian-American.'

'He's regained his speech?' Georgia questioned with surprise, once they were standing in the kitchen. 'When?' Lifting the doily from a jug, she poured water into a glass and drank the contents thirstily.

'He's done more than that,' Mrs Howell said tightly. 'Someone forgot to lock his bedroom door.' She looked directly at Eleanor. 'He's gone.'

Georgia sat the glass on the kitchen table before rushing along the passageway to the empty sickroom. Eleanor followed Mrs Howell, peering over the two women's shoulders as they stood in the doorway. Sure enough, the room was empty, the key still hanging on the hook near the door.

'Eleanor was last in the room,' the housekeeper tittle-tattled.

Mrs Howell and her mother exchanged looks and then, very slowly, turned to where Eleanor stood. She gave a wan smile. The key was exactly where Eleanor had left it after delivering Chad's laundered clothes. She'd never even thought about locking the door. Not after all he'd told her.

'Have you checked the house, Mrs Howell?' enquired Georgia, ignoring her daughter.

'Do I look like a woman who wants to tempt fate?' the house-keeper retaliated. 'Keep him locked up, I said. Board the windows so he couldn't get out, we decided.'

'But he's an immigrant,' Eleanor replied, as she and Mrs Howell trailed Georgia. The mistress of River Run was marching along the passageway at a cracking pace, turning into the airy entrance hall. 'A man shot by accident on our property,' she persisted.

'Every room,' Georgia stated. 'We will search every room in this house.' Her mother took a heavy brass poker from the hearth in the sitting room as they continued their sweep of the building: sunroom, dining room, station office and library.

'Don't you think you're over-reacting, Mum?' Eleanor cautioned.

'Over-reacting,' Georgia intoned, 'would be taking my father's shotgun from above the mantelpiece in the office. One wonders why he didn't come straight to you in the kitchen if he was up and about, Mrs Howell.' Georgia closed the cupboard under the stairs, which was large enough to hold a person. 'You've been there all morning.'

'All morning,' the housekeeper established.

'I don't like this,' Georgia observed, her riding boots loud as she moved through each room. The ground floor, with its stately public rooms, quiet nooks, storage areas and staff sections, were deserted.

'He's probably outside, taking in some sun,' Eleanor told the women. 'He has been bedridden.'

They were at the foot of the substantial staircase. Georgia raised a hand for quiet and then, very slowly, looked towards the floor above.

'He's been in the war and everything.' Eleanor couldn't understand where Chad may have gone to. 'He was with the Americans.' Her explanation was beginning to sound like a plea. 'He fought in Greece. On our side. He's not quite himself, Mum. It's not shellshock or anything like that, but he's got problems from the war. You know, mixed up, a bit like Marcus was.'

The two older women turned as one, their stares equally condemnatory.

'That's quite a conversation you've had with this man, Eleanor,' her mother replied. 'A man we know little about. When exactly did this Chad person regain his speech?'

'But that's what he told me,' Eleanor persisted, ignoring the question. 'He said he'd been in the area visiting the Harris's and that he got lost. He admitted to stealing Robbie's cray-bobs but only because he was starving.'

'What cray-bobs? And who are these Harris's?' asked Georgia, a bewildered expression crossing her features. 'I've never heard of them.' She turned to the housekeeper for confirmation.

'The name's not familiar to me,' Mrs Howell replied.

'And he didn't like Athena Pappas,' Eleanor continued, traipsing up the stairs behind her mother and the housekeeper, although her enthusiasm for the man's cause was beginning to wane. She was trying to justify her trust of the man, but it was rather bizarre that the moment she'd left the door unlocked, the stranger disappeared. Had she really been so mistaken?

'Go on, Eleanor.' Her mother's tone was less than conciliatory.

Actually, Eleanor didn't know if she wanted to. 'He heard Athena singing a German song.'

'And?' Georgia prompted.

'Well, Chad accused her of being a German collaborator. That's why he elected not to speak. He was confused and –' Eleanor froze. 'Oh.'

'Oh, what?' asked her mother as they walked upstairs.

'Athena said the same thing about Chad.' Who was right? Who was being falsely accused?

Georgia made a *tsking* sound with her tongue. 'And you took the word of a trespasser over that of a woman employed in this household? How long exactly has this Chad person been able to speak for, Eleanor?'

Eleanor hung her head. 'A couple of days.'

Mrs Howell gave a harrumph. 'It seems to me, young lady, that you've been caught on a line like a big, fat, yellowbelly. Won your confidence he did, plain as day. Bided his time and then . . .' She rubbed one palm quickly against the other. 'That's one slippery individual we've got prowling around River Run, Mrs Webber.'

'But he did seem out of sorts, Mum. Honest.'

Georgia climbed the stairs quickly, adjusting the poker in her grasp. Once on the second floor, they went from room to room, frightening the young housemaid, Alice, who was cleaning the Winslows' recently vacated bedroom, a pile of linen in the doorway. 'Oh, it's you, Mrs Webber,' Alice said politely and with some relief. 'I heard banging and clanging, but I didn't want to disturb you in your room.'

'Disturb me?' Georgia repeated. She looked the length of the hallway to where the door to her bedroom was ajar.

Mrs Howell snatched up the broom the girl held and then together the three women moved briskly along the carpeted hallway towards the room. Once outside the ornately panelled door, Eleanor and Mrs Howell traded worried glances. They braced for what lay in wait within. Georgia lifted the brass poker aloft, as if weighing its effectiveness as a weapon and then, with a breath, flung open the bedroom door.

Wood jarred wood, the noise loud and sharp. Inside the room, the day encroached through large windows framed by cream silk curtains. Mint-green walls and a moss-green carpet highlighted dark pieces of antique furniture and a four-poster bed complete with brass bed-knobs. The large bed was freshly made, the white coverlet, creaseless, while the dress Georgia had changed from earlier that morning lay across a pale cream and green chair.

'Is everything alright?' Alice asked, from where she stood in the hallway, her arms filled with bedlinen.

Georgia walked directly to the mahogany dresser. A number of the drawers were open, clearly rifled through. Eleanor watched as her mother withdrew a red velvet box, lifting the lid.

'My jewellery.' She looked horrified. 'It's gone. The pieces your father gave me, Elly. They're all gone.'

❧ Chapter Thirty-nine ❧

By mid-afternoon, with the house, grounds and outbuildings scoured for a second time, and neither Lesley nor the mysterious Chad Reynolds located, new search parties were organised. Colin, Hugh, Dawson and two of the jackeroos, Murph and Wormy, were joined by a fiercely unyielding Billy Wright in the search for the missing patient.

'Making amends for being an idiot, I am,' the shearer announced when he appeared at the front of the house where everyone gathered on the veranda to discuss the search plans and eat hastily prepared sandwiches. 'No arguments. I heard what was going on. I'm here to help.'

Eleanor, having been thoroughly questioned and reprimanded by both her mother and stepfather for her part in Chad Reynolds' duplicity, found Hugh Goward's disbelief when told of her involvement particularly uncomfortable. The loss of his good opinion, which Eleanor sincerely hoped she'd held, made her anxious and embarrassed. She waited quietly on the veranda as Billy Wright repeated his offer of assistance. Georgia lifted an enquiring eyebrow in Hugh's direction. It was the slightest of gestures, and

Eleanor doubted if anyone else noticed, except for the intended recipient.

'We appreciate the offer, Billy,' Hugh said, between swollen lips. The morning's altercation was behind them, however, Hugh and the jackeroos carried the scars. 'I think we'll be pretty right. Besides, you don't want any of those younger fellas getting the lead on you in the shed with the tally. It's always hard to catch up.'

The shearer took no notice of the Stud Master. 'No, siree. I'll find that Yankee whippersnapper and then, if little Lesley hasn't been found by the time we bring him in, well I'll search for her too.' He shoved his hands in his pockets.

Eleanor wondered how long it had been since Billy last saw her elder sister. It was years since her childhood.

'Search for her all night, I will,' the shearer continued. 'I remember when she was knee-high to a grasshopper. Came down to the shed, she did, one shearing. Brought a doll she'd been given for Christmas. Done up in a white wedding dress. Well, that little 'un was pleased as punch. Yes, she was. Told me she was going to have a dress exactly the same when she was all grown up. Told her I had one exactly the same, a bride doll, that is. Well, you should have seen the smile on her face.'

Rex cleared his throat. Dawson, who remained standing on the driveway, only feet from Billy, scuffed at the small stones beneath his boots.

'A man barely talks for twenty years and then he can't shut up.' Rex's muttering was heard by everyone, however, Billy appeared not to care.

The shearer adjusted the canvas waterbag hanging on a shoulder. 'So I'm a-coming too.'

'We can expect the police in a couple of hours,' Mrs Howell reminded everyone, as she sat a jug of chilled water on the table. 'The constable did say that he would leave immediately.'

'You'll have to man the fort, Mrs Howell.' Georgia, having downed a stiff shot of whisky earlier, was already on the gravel drive where the yellow truck was parked, eager to search for her daughter. 'And you will also have to let the police know how many of us are out and about. I'm hopeful that my wandering daughter will simply show up.'

'I'll keep an eye out. I'll be surprised if Lesley doesn't appear very shortly,' the housekeeper responded. 'The girl will be needing a drink sooner or later, the way this heat is creeping up.'

'Worse than yesterday.' Colin, who'd barely spoken a word since his return from the fight at the shed, sat a hat firmly on his head. 'I'll leave this property map on the table for when the police arrive. I've marked the areas we'll be heading to first. And lock the doors after we've left, Mrs Howell. We don't know who we're dealing with. At the very least this import we've cared for since Saturday is a crook.' On the table were three boxes of rifle cartridges. Colin handed one a-piece to Hugh and Murph, pocketing the third.

'I'll head to the cemetery,' Georgia told everyone. 'That's the only other place Lesley might be, visiting Marcus's grave.'

Eleanor noted her mother carried the German Luger brought back from the war by her father.

'She's right fragile, missus,' said Rex, following his employer to the battered farm truck. 'I never expected she'd still be in such a state after all these years.'

Colin doubted Lesley would walk that far in such scorching weather.

'You're a blackfella,' Billy said to Dawson, 'you should be able to track little Lesley.'

'Sure,' Dawson's face turned sour, 'I'll just go grab my nulla-nulla and change into my tracking clothes.'

'No need to get wise on me,' replied Billy.

'I might be of the old people,' answered Dawson, 'but I'm a townie and a butcher by trade.'

'Rex,' said Georgia, 'I'd like you and Elly to go back to the woolshed and keep an eye on things until cut-out. We don't want the men getting a fit of the willies.'

'Alright, missus,' answered Rex.

'Watch yourself out there,' Colin said to his wife.

Georgia gave an off-hand wave and the truck headed off in a flurry of flying grit. The men mounted their horses, checked water-bags and rifles and then, after final confirmation as to timings and directions, they began to ride off in pairs. Hugh and Wormy were to head towards the river, Billy and Murph out towards the back paddocks beyond the shearing shed, while Colin and Dawson were to ride in an ever-increasing circle using the homestead as a fulcrum of sorts.

'Do you think you'll find him?' asked Eleanor. The rest of the men were already leaving as Hugh buttoned down the flap on his shirt-pocket, inside which was the outline of a red Cooper's notebook. The cut above his eyebrow was crusted with blood and dirt, his swollen lip purple-red in colour.

'The bush is a big place, but I guess it all depends on how experienced this Chad bloke is. If he's smart he'll head for the closest waterway. Or double-back and try to thieve a horse or vehicle. Did he say anything else, Eleanor? Anything that might help us find him?'

'Nothing.' Eleanor didn't look at Hugh. 'I'm sorry.'

'Hey, it's not your fault that you're the trusting sort.' Hugh gave her a smile. Warmer than Eleanor felt was deserved.

They stood together awkwardly, River Run's newly appointed Stud Master holding the reins readying to mount as Wormy waited, his horse letting out a whinny of discontent.

'I was sorry to hear about your wife.' The words of sympathy were expressed without thought. 'I didn't know,' Eleanor said softly, suddenly embarrassed at having broached the subject.

The man opposite her responded with an unflinching gaze. 'You're a good person, Eleanor, your mother's lucky to have you as a daughter.'

Eleanor found herself remembering the shared warmth of their bodies as they'd sheltered beneath a tree from the warrigal storm. 'Where's your dog?' she asked, conscious of prolonging the conversation.

'Tied up,' Hugh replied. 'Where he belongs. It's too hot for him.'

Hugh seemed hesitant about leaving, although Eleanor guessed she only imagined such a thing for he soon swung up into the saddle, adjusting the .303 rifle in its holster.

'Righto, righto,' complained Rex. 'We best get ourselves down to the shed, Eleanor.'

Hugh touched the brim of his hat and turned his mount after the jackeroo.

'Come on then,' the gardener said impatiently.

Eleanor didn't look back as she and Rex drove away from the homestead. She had the strongest urge to do so, which made her even more determined not to. This is ridiculous, she thought. Not only was Hugh Goward fifteen years her senior and an employee at River Run, he was so unlike the young men she'd previously walked out with, so unlike Dante, the man she'd given herself to.

'Got his way then, eh?' said Rex, as the truck travelled down the bumpy road. 'The young whippersnapper.'

Eleanor was puzzled. 'What do you mean?'

With his eyes on the road ahead, Rex gave a snort. 'The golden-haired boy. Got ourselves a new Stud Master, we have. And your stepfather ain't too pleased.'

Eleanor didn't respond. It wasn't really Rex's place to comment on the managerial ladder although she was quietly pleased that he took her into his confidence.

'You're for him, aren't you?'

She felt her face flush. 'For him?'

'Yes,' said Rex. 'You think he'd be good in the role, better than your stepfather.'

'Oh. Yes, yes I do, but obviously it was Mum's decision.'

'It's a done deal then. I reckon if a man has two River Run women on-side, he can pretty much take on the world. Well, good luck to him, I say. Let's just hope he knows what he's doing.'

It was nearing the hottest part of the day as they pulled up outside the woolshed. The noise of the shed hit them immediately. Perspiration made every inch of clothing stick to Eleanor's body and she wiggled her shoulders and tugged at her shirt, trying to ease the damp fabric away from her skin.

Once out of the vehicle, Rex looked skyward. 'It's been a long time since I saw a blood month like this.'

Eleanor felt as if she was cooking from the inside out, as if the very heart of her was melting. And it would be worse within the confines of the woolshed. As if reading her mind, Rex drew her to the shade of the adjoining shed where freshly pressed bales had been rolled for storage before transportation to market.

'We'll take a breather out here, girl, before entering the furnace.'

Eleanor was happy to oblige. They sat on a bale, staring out at the endless tangle of trees and shrubs that opened and closed across country stretched brown and flat.

'Do you ever wonder what's beyond the horizon?' asked Eleanor, wetting her dry lips.

'To answer a question like that,' Rex replied, 'is to make a man feel too small.'

'But still,' she persisted, 'do you wonder?'

The old gardener scratched at a jowly neck. 'No, the bush makes a man think too much. If he's a loner and a dreamer, well, a man can get messed up in his own thoughts. He thinks on the same thing, again and again. Gets fixated. Loses perspective.' Rex tapped the side of his head. 'It's hard out here. So no, I don't want to be thinking about what's beyond the beyond. I've got enough problems just plain thinking. Your sister's fiancé was a bit like that. Always thinking. That's what killed him in the end. He couldn't forget. Couldn't forget what they did to him over there.'

'Maybe you could tell Lesley that. It might help.' Eleanor observed the muscles in his scraggly face stretching and contracting like a cow chewing on its cud.

'I'll tell her, but it won't help,' he finally answered.

'Do you think Lesley is okay, Rex? I mean with that man, with Chad roaming about?'

'She's a smart girl, your sister,' Rex said.

Eleanor allowed herself to be pacified. 'Lesley didn't trust him.'

'Well then, there you go.'

Eleanor wondered at her own naivety.

'I can hear your brain ticking over,' commented Rex.

She gave a half-hearted smile. Eleanor had been considering Chad's easy charm and Hugh's solid presence. Comparing the two men, who in less than a week had become central fixtures in her life. Attractive men certainly knew how to influence her, understood how to deceive. Chad, Dante and now Hugh? He was Stud Master now after all and she'd helped him attain the position. Was he the right man for the job?

'Rex, about Hugh –'

The gardener stood, stretching out his lower back. 'I'm stiffer than a board,' he commented. 'He's got it all ahead of him, girl,' Rex patted her gruffly on the shoulder, 'and if he doesn't work out,' his old eyes glimmered, 'well, then, we'll give Hugh Goward the boot.' He grinned mischievously.

Immediately Eleanor felt better about Hugh's promotion and her part in it. Nothing was written in stone after all. But she hoped Hugh was good at his new job. River Run needed the best. That's what was most important, she told herself. The fact that she liked him, quite a lot, was irrelevant.

In a nearby tree, a bird fell from a branch, landing dead on the ground.

'Heatstroke,' Rex proclaimed. 'Had a day like this last February. Came out of nowhere the heat did and the birds dropped like flies.

330

Still, it's a damn fine day to be alive even if we've got troubles akin to a tangled roll of barbed wire. But you, girl, I'd imagine you'd be itching to hit the big smoke after everything's sorted. It's just been one calamity after another since you arrived home.'

'It's not so bad,' replied Eleanor.

Rex gave his signature grin. 'You've been making yourself useful. And a person who's useful can eventually become indispensable.' He winked. 'It's worth remembering that, I reckon.'

Indispensable. That was something Eleanor had never considered of herself. Especially with her role at the hardware store. Anyone could do it.

'Come on then,' said Rex. 'Let's front the mob inside and make sure they're shearing these sheep of ours proper-like.'

But Eleanor didn't immediately follow Rex inside the woolshed. Something else caught her attention. Out in the west, hugging the horizon, brownish clouds swirled.

⊰ Chapter Forty ⊱

It was after five o'clock by the time they made it back to the homestead. Kicking off their boots, Rex followed Eleanor indoors to where Mrs Howell waited. A swarm of flies took advantage of the briefly open door.

'Lesley's here.' The housekeeper swished at the insects with a swatter. 'Your mother found her at the cemetery. She's upstairs with her now.'

'Holy trousers.' Rex sunk into a chair, removing his hat. 'I'm glad to hear that.'

Eleanor joined him at the table, pushing sweat-plastered hair from her face and stretching out her legs to relieve the ache in her thighs and backside. Having spent the last few hours helping in the shed, she was exhausted.

'You look like you've both seen enough of the day.' Mrs Howell poured tepid water into two tall glasses. 'No ice, I'm afraid. I used what we had in the bath to cool your sister down. The generator overheated and cut out. I haven't dared touch it or open a fridge since then.'

'And she's alright, Mrs Howell?' asked Eleanor. 'I mean, apart from being hot and tired?' The water was warm in her mouth.

The housekeeper wrung out a clean cloth and gestured for Eleanor to wipe her face and neck. She obeyed as though still a child, noting the grime left on the pale cloth.

'How right can a person be, who's silly enough to be out in this heat without a hat or a waterbag?' Mrs Howell retrieved the dirty washer, dropping it in the sink. 'Gave me the willies when your mother staggered in with her. Half-carried her, she did, up the stairs.' The housekeeper blew her nose. 'I'll never understand how one person can have the strength of an ox, and another be weak and dainty when they're blood kin.'

'So she's not maudlin?' Rex held out his glass for more water, consuming the offering noisily.

'Well, I can't answer that.' Mrs Howell directed the oscillating fan so that the hot air blew directly at the table. Instantly the perspiration dried on Eleanor's skin. 'As far as I know Lesley hasn't said one word. She's been affected right badly by the heat.'

'I should go to her.' Eleanor rose.

Mrs Howell was beside her instantly, placing a restraining hand on her shoulder. 'You'll do no such thing, my girl.' She pushed her back down into the kitchen chair. 'You've been out working in the blazing heat and I don't mind telling you that you look a fright. So you can just keep to that chair for a bit and,' she placed the water jug in front of her, 'you'll be finishing that water before you move.'

'Sipping it though,' Rex decreed, 'no gulping.'

The housekeeper folded her arms. 'That's right. No gulping it down either.'

Eleanor took another sip of the blood-warm water. This was a turn-up for the books, those two actually agreeing on something.

Rex slammed his hand down on a tiny black sugar ant that was making its way in a zigzag path across the surface of the table. The housekeeper immediately began a reconnaissance of the kitchen, finally locating a trail of ants travelling across the windowsill, down the wall and onto the sink.

'Rain?' Mrs Howell asked the gardener.

Rex screwed up his nose. 'Seen ants I have, same as this lot, out west at Mount Hope. Gets a man all tingly with expectation. Three black cockatoos in a Belah tree, invading ants, flowering cacti, red sky in the morning, crowing roosters that keep the rain away. My father's patch of hard-scratched heaven had more dead roosters than I've had cooked breakfasts. The clouds come in, the rain comes down and rain it does. Rains for forty days and forty nights and you only get forty points. I'm just saying that's Mount Hope and they've got the same ants as us.'

'So you're not hopeful,' the housekeeper answered with more than a hint of sarcasm.

Rex shook his head solemnly.

'And no more problems at the shed, Rex?' Mrs Howell refilled Eleanor's glass and watched her drink it.

'Nope, anyone would think we'd employed a bunch of choirboys this afternoon.' The gardener drained his glass. 'There's been no sign of the others then? Mr Webber or Goward?'

'No sign,' Mrs Howell answered.

'Righto.' Rex placed both hands on the kitchen table and levered himself tiredly out of the chair. 'I'll check the generator in the power house. No other news?'

The housekeeper brought the swatter down on a large blowfly, squashing the insect on the table with a thud. 'Haven't seen a soul. And the police haven't shown themselves either.' Scooping up the mangled insect, Mrs Howell flicked the remains from the swatter into the sink and then topped up Eleanor's glass.

'Well, keep the doors locked, Mrs Howell,' advised Rex.

'Right you are, Rex. And no more wandering around for you, young lady,' the housekeeper directed at Eleanor. 'Your mother says you're to stay put in this house as well.'

After Rex had departed, Mrs Howell sat a dish on the kitchen table. The bowl was filled with a brown liquid. 'I made tea.' She dipped a finger into the container. 'It's cooled off enough now, as have you. You've gone from poppy-red to pansy-pink,' she observed. 'Finish that water and then you can take this up to your sister's room with these clean cloths. The tannin will help take the sting out of the sunburn.'

Eleanor stood, surprised at how stiff and spent she felt. 'Will she be alright, do you think?'

The housekeeper handed Eleanor the bowl and towels. 'My dear girl, the sunburn, fatigue and dehydration can be managed, but as for what else ails your sister . . .' She tutted. 'Honestly, I don't know anything anymore.'

The dark bedroom was a touch cooler compared to the rest of the homestead. Wet sheets were strewn across open windows, balcony doors and on large clothes racks that usually sat in the laundry during winter. Two electric fans started up as the generator came back on line; they blew air through the damp linen hanging on wooden frames, the gentle circulation directed towards the large four-poster bed. Beneath a canopy of beige silk and gathered mosquito netting, Lesley lay in her underclothes. Her elder sister, dwarfed by her grandmother's bed, within which Georgia herself had been born, appeared to be sleeping although their mother was at her side, alternatively mopping her daughter's brow and talking softly. She turned at Eleanor's arrival.

'Good, you're here.' Georgia appeared hot and dusty. Her hat and scarf lay on the floor where they'd been discarded, her riding boots flung in a corner.

'Mrs Howell said to bring this up.' Eleanor moved closer to the bed, sitting the bowl on a side table.

'None of the others back yet?' She took in her younger daughter's appearance. 'It's a bad day to be outside.'

'No-one, and no sign of the police either,' Eleanor told her mother. 'Shearing finished up for the day with no other problems.

Rex said they were like a bunch of choirboys. And he's right. The shed was very subdued.'

'Good. I wondered if they'd pull up stumps early with the heat.' With the departure of the Winslows, the society gloss that came so easily to Georgia Webber was also diminished.

'How is she, Mum?' asked Eleanor. Her sister looked terribly vulnerable.

'She's suffering, but Lesley is young. She will survive the exposure, hopefully with minimal scarring.'

Eleanor felt tears well. How had it come to this? If this was what love did, then she would go through life emotionally detached. She would cut her palm and watch her blood drip into the red soil of River Run and swear to the old gods and the new that she would never love again. Eleanor didn't want such passion in her life. Who would, if the loss of it could lead to this?

'Fast asleep,' Georgia soaked the clean rags in the cold tea, 'that's how I found her. Resting against his headstone. Lovely man, Marcus. A lovely, lovely man.'

'Don't, Mum.'

Georgia lay the wet material in strips across Lesley's arms and legs, the brown water trickling down bare skin to stain the white sheets beneath. Her older sister was burnt badly by the sun. Her face was beetroot-red and her lips were already blistering. Eleanor drew a chair to her sister's bedside as Georgia lay another rag across the burning forehead. The blue day-dress Lesley had been wearing barely protected her from the weather. There was only the slightest difference in colour between Lesley's exposed skin and that which had been covered.

'After Marcus died I tried to reason with her,' Georgia began. 'I knew only she could deal with her grief, and the terrible shock of being the one to find him. I was aware that all we could do was offer support, our love, but maybe we could have done more,' she said pensively. 'I never understood the depth of her despair until

I found her in the bath.' Her voice quivered. 'It's not something I could easily understand, Eleanor.'

'What? The extent of her love for Marcus?'

'No. Don't take this the wrong way, but it's a weakness, isn't it, to consider taking your own life instead of picking up the pieces and looking to the future.'

Lesley gave a whimper in her sleep. Reaching across the expanse of white linen, Eleanor gently touched her sister's hand.

'I tell myself, she'll pull through, that she'll recover, but it's been years now, Elly, and nothing and no-one seems to be capable of drawing Lesley out of the melancholia that's engulfed her. The doctors suggested an asylum initially; electric shock therapy, ice-baths, rigorous exercise.' She looked briefly heavenward. 'If only your father were alive at the time.' Georgia gave a little cough as if the action might clear not only her throat, but memory as well. 'Colin thought such treatments should have been pursued. Apparently there have been good results with returned soldiers of known mental fragility. I didn't agree. Another may have. How could a mother send a child to such a place? To endure such indignities, alone. And there was something else . . .' It was as if Georgia spoke to herself, weighing the merits of a decision made long ago. 'To be rendered so low by such treatments, when there is already such despair. I was foolish, I suppose, to consider a more gracious alternative, to look at the world through rose-tinted glasses.' She gave a sad smile. 'That's what my mother would have said. I can hear her voice so plainly. *You're a River, Georgia, and the Rivers are made of sterner stuff.* Let me tell you, Elly, it's a hard road indeed to be an only child.'

'You made the only decision you believed right at the time,' Eleanor placated.

'Love caused Lesley's grief and so I hoped that love would save her.'

'But you sent her to a convent,' Eleanor interrupted, not comprehending.

Georgia swirled the pieces of rag in the brown water. '*Our* love, the love of her family, wasn't enough, Elly. You know that. If there was any chance, any chance at all that Lesley was to be saved from the terrible anguish that's eating her, I thought perhaps the convent would help.' Lifting the bowl of cold tea, she placed it closer to Lesley. 'The convent offered love, prayer and reflection within a cosseted environment. My own mother depended on the Virgin for guidance, swore to me in my youth that with faith, with deep belief, came understanding and understanding allowed one to withstand anything in life.' Georgia met Eleanor's gaze. 'But I was wrong. Religion has not saved your sister.'

'Maybe it did for a time, Mum.'

'Until I made the mistake of bringing her back here, you mean? I expected your sister to be of stronger stock,' she answered defensively.

'You didn't expect it, Mum, you hoped that was the case,' replied Eleanor carefully.

'Ah, yes. You see, Elly, there's that word again, hope. It is starting to be empty of meaning for me. If it isn't already.'

Georgia looked at Eleanor as if maybe she could provide an answer, but it appeared that there were no solutions to Lesley's grief. Maybe her older sister should have undergone some of the therapies mentioned, for it occurred to Eleanor that Lesley needed to be jolted out of the overly sentimental thoughts that were destroying her young life. This was an illness for which there was no medication, and although Eleanor had read about such things in romantic novels, the kind of stories where women actually did pine away from a broken heart, she would forever be astonished to have witnessed so heart-rending an example in real life. Fiction had become fact, and yet this wasn't the Middle Ages, this wasn't even the nineteen hundreds. It was 1951. 'Religion can't save anyone, Mum.'

'No, you're right, it can't. Religion is supposed to give us hope, and it is hope that has the ability to save. But I look at Lesley and I know that despair has replaced faith.'

Lesley emitted the softest of moans.

'Hush, Lesley,' comforted Eleanor, 'you'll get better. I promise you will.'

'When Lesley is sufficiently recovered, I will take her back to Sydney myself,' Georgia stated pragmatically. 'I'll return her to the care of the nuns.'

With Georgia's ministrations finally completed, Lesley was swathed in tea-damp material, the only parts of her skin visible were her eyes and mouth. Opening the distinctive gold pot of Rawleigh's Salve, Georgia gently dabbed a little of the antiseptic cream on her daughter's blistered lips. 'Well, we can do no more. The cold bath brought her temperature down and she was able to swallow a Bex powder before sleeping. There is little else we can do for her at the moment.'

'You should rest, Mum,' suggested Eleanor. 'I can sit with Lesley for a while. At least until the cloths need to be dampened with tea again.'

'Yes, you're right of course,' her mother said tiredly. 'I guess there's nothing that can be done until one of the men return or the police arrive. Actually, I thought they would have been here already.' Georgia patted Eleanor's arm. 'Thank you, Elly. Thank you for coming home.' It was some time since they'd hugged, but they did so now, Eleanor feeling a surge of ferocious protection.

With her mother's departure, Eleanor sat quietly by her sister as the light through the sheets screening the French door began to fade. She noticed how quiet it was. Apart from the generator, there were no twittering birds or yelping dogs, or the distant call of sheep or men. Even the windmill with its clunky mechanism and screeching whirr was silent. It was easy to be contemplative within such an environment. Eleanor found herself replaying her mother's words in her mind as the fans whirled and the sheets rustled. Rex was right, she decided, a person could think too much out here.

When the material swathing Lesley finally dried, Eleanor carefully peeled off each of the strips and moistened them in the tea, before repositioning them on her sister's damaged skin. The last piece, the one across her forehead, needed to be removed and Eleanor leant over Lesley, dabbing at the strip with a wet cloth before carefully prising the rag free. She could feel the heat emanating from her sister's body, Lesley's breath coming in little puffs.

'Elly?' Her voice was a whisper.

'Yes, I'm here.'

'Robbie.' Lesley reached out, clasping her wrist. 'You have to find Robbie.'

'Shush now,' Eleanor replied soothingly, laying her sister's arm on the bedclothes. 'Robbie's gone to school. He left this morning. But we can go visit him when you're feeling better.' Dunking the cloth in the tea, she wrung it out and then lay the dripping material across Lesley's brow.

'No, no, you don't understand.' The patient tugged at the newly placed rag, so that it fell onto the pillow. 'I saw him. I saw him walking in the bush.'

'Don't upset yourself, Lesley. Please lie back and let me place the cloth on you. It will make you feel better.'

'I tried to call out, but my throat . . .' Lesley swallowed noisily.

There was water by the bed. Eleanor brought the glass to her sister's lips. Lesley barely moistened her tongue before brushing the drink aside. 'He's out there, Elly,' she pleaded. 'He's out there, in the dark, without a moon. You know what happens to our family when there isn't a moon.'

The last time Lesley voiced the same fear that haunted Eleanor, was after Marcus's death. It was, as if in trying to make sense of the loss of their father and then Marcus, they had fixated on the night of their deaths, on the new moon and in doing so had called up their childhood phobia of the night. Out there, in the dark, lay the unknown and the unknowable. And into this void had been taken those they loved.

Trying to comfort her sister, Eleanor lay a gentle hand on a shoulder, while replacing the damp cloth. 'Remember when we were young, Lesley, we always had our little night lights. Scaredy-cats, weren't we, you and I? There really isn't anything to be afraid about when it's dark, you know.' Did she sound convincing?

'But Robbie –'

'Hush, you're upsetting yourself for no reason,' Eleanor said firmly. 'He'll be in Sydney by now. He's to stay with Uncle Colin's sister until he starts at the King's School next week.'

'No, he's not, I tell you.' Rising on an arm, Lesley wobbled and then fell back onto the bedclothes, exhausted. 'He's not. He's here. Find him.' Her eyes were wide and dark with fear. 'We can't lose anyone else, Elly. We can't lose Robbie.'

Eleanor couldn't remember ever having seen her sister so convinced, so desperate.

'Find him.'

'Rest now, Lesley, I'll be back to check on you in a little while.' Outside the bedroom, in the darkening hallway, Eleanor stopped. It was all too much. Her sister, her beloved older sister, was delusional.

341

≪ Chapter Forty-one ≫

A deep red smeared the sky, spreading across the treetops. The multicoloured birdlife drinking and bathing in the dying light took flight at his approach, as did the sheep and kangaroos on the opposite bank, only to return moments later. Stripping off his clothes, Robbie walked straight into the water, collapsing beneath the surface like a stone. He lay on the sandy bottom, feeling the delight of cooling skin and the gentle lifting of dirt from the whorls of eyes, nose and ears. Through the brown tinge, light filtered downwards. He lifted a hand, as if he could touch the fracturing rays, before rising from the depths, spluttering and coughing, pushing dripping hair from his face.

In the shallows, water lapped at Robbie's chest in gentle waves. Leaves and twigs and tiny pieces of floating gunk gradually formed a high tide mark around his body, as insects gathered on the green-brown surface. Gradually the shadows began to stretch out across the scrub. By the time he crawled from the river, his fingers and toes were wrinkly, his limbs were stiff with cold, but he was cool again. Robbie could breathe.

He lay on the sandy edge, studying the dappled light patterning the riverbank, the heels of his feet resting in the water. The walk from the road and the Winslows' broken-down car had been long and hot. It was rough going, travelling across country, following his line of sight, and after the day's walk Robbie experienced a grudging respect for his old nag and even more for the stubborn cattle-pup, who would drop dead from exhaustion rather than be left behind.

The distance from road to river was probably only seven miles, however, on setting out that morning Robbie knew he would have to have frequent stops if he were ever going to make it to water by dark. Walking, resting, walking, resting, surely this was the longest day ever. Every time he thought he was nearing the destination, the scrub would open up and he would drop his chin and grimace. Even the distant sight of the station cemetery hadn't cheered him, for there were still a further three miles to tramp. It was only when a flock of birds flew overhead that he knew his objective was close. But he was here now. He was safe. He'd survive.

Robbie wasn't so sure about the Winslows. He didn't mind the mister so much, actually he didn't mind him at all. But the missus, well, if she died, he was beginning to think that it wouldn't be much of a loss. He'd never heard someone grumble so much. They didn't even carry a waterbag with them and he doubted that the lady would drink from the radiator as he'd suggested. No, she was too toffy-nosed for that.

Dressing, he dipped his hat in the river, waiting as the fluid soaked into the felt crown so that he could suck the filtered liquid from it. It wasn't much of a drink. And Robbie couldn't be sure that there wasn't some dead animal contaminating the water, but he didn't slurp up much and it was better than nothing.

'Right,' he said loudly. His voice echoed along the waterway, startling the animals dipping thirsty mouths in the river water and causing the birds to take flight. 'Sorry about that,' he stated, bending to select some river pebbles and putting them in his pocket. He began to trudge along the riverbank. Now that he'd cooled down a little and it was nearly dark, his objective hadn't altered.

Soon he was passing the cray-bob traps and navigating the lumpy roots and sprawling, fallen branches that lined the river's banks. Robbie dug his toes in the dirt when the verge grew steep, and moved to where the ground evened out and made for easier walking. The tree – his tree – when it finally appeared, stood tall and safe, just as he'd imagined.

Clambering up the knobbly trunk, Robbie swung between the sturdy branches, grunting as he hefted his weight over another limb, frowning with concentration as he reached for the next bough, puffing when his fingers grasped the wooden plank and he could finally roll onto the board and laugh at success.

The bush settled for the night. Robbie drank from the waterbag hidden within the woody confines of the tree and then savoured one of the tins of baked beans, sucking out the remnants of juicy goodness from the rim of the container, careful not to cut his tongue. Once finished, he tossed the tin as far away as possible so the ants would not find him, and stretched out on the narrow platform. Through the leafy canopy, the sky steadily turned from a pale reddish light to a purplish-blue velvet. The stars appeared slowly, growing in number and brightness, twisting across the darkness in clusters and ribbons, twirling and dancing as the wind lifted and Robbie's eyes closed.

≪ Chapter Forty-two ≫

The sound of horses on the gravel drive drew Eleanor downstairs. Mrs Howell was already on the front veranda, rubbing her hands anxiously as she hovered near the table.

'How's your sister?'

'Resting,' replied Eleanor. 'The police still haven't arrived?'

'Not a sign of them.'

Hugh Goward, trailed by the other searchers, Dawson, Billy, Archie and Murph, rode straight up to the homestead and dismounted while Colin spoke to the four remaining men.

At the sight of Hugh, Eleanor's anxiety eased a little. 'Did you find Chad?' she asked, moving forward to meet him as he walked up the front steps to the house.

Removing his wide-brimmed hat in greeting, Hugh shook his head. 'No. Not yet.' Gratefully accepting the glass of water the housekeeper offered, he asked, 'And Lesley?'

'Mrs Webber found her at the cemetery,' Mrs Howell explained. 'Badly sunstruck.'

'I'm not surprised. It wasn't a good afternoon to be outside. But I'm pleased to hear that she's safe.' Hugh registered Eleanor's expression of concern. 'What is it? What's the matter, Eleanor?'

'She's not herself,' was all she could reply.

'Well of course she's not herself,' Mrs Howell said with a condemnatory huff. 'She's been out on the flat baking in the sun for half the day.'

Colin limped up the stairs, collecting his walking stick from where he'd left it on the veranda earlier. The butcher, shearer and jackeroos trotted their horses around the corner of the building. 'Any news?' he asked gruffly. He was leaning heavily on the stick, clearly his leg was giving him pain.

'Lesley's been found, the police are yet to arrive and Georgia's freshening up,' answered Mrs Howell.

'And Lesley's alright?'

The housekeeper gave a perfunctory nod.

'Good.' Colin sat in one of the chairs and looked disinterestedly at the water jug. 'We might invest in something a little more medicinal, Mrs Howell.'

'Of course, Mr Webber.' The housekeeper returned inside the house.

'Hugh said you didn't find anything,' Eleanor commented to her uncle.

'Nothing. Lesley?'

Eleanor decided not to go into details with her stepfather. 'Badly sunburnt.'

'Silly girl.' Colin nodded his approval as the housekeeper returned to sit a large silver salver on the table. Selecting the whisky decanter from among the rum and gin, he poured a good nip and drank it down. 'I don't want to upset your mother but it is nearly dark, Eleanor. It's possible that we might never find her jewellery or the culprit who thieved it.'

'That's ridiculous.' Georgia appeared on the veranda in a clean shirt and jeans. 'I mean, the man is on foot.'

Colin poured another shot. 'I'm sorry, Georgia, but so far we've found nothing. At least Lesley's home.'

'Yes, she's home. I found her at the cemetery.' Georgia joined her husband at the table. 'Lesley isn't very well, Colin. She's rambling on about Marcus and Robbie. She's going to need medical attention if she's not better in the morning.'

'I told you not to bring her back out here,' he accused.

Husband and wife stared at each other.

'If the stranger is still recovering from his wounds,' Hugh contributed from where he stood, some feet away, 'I can't imagine he'd get too far.'

'Maybe.' Colin didn't sound convinced. 'I sent the men back to have a break, something to eat. A drink, Hugh?' he offered.

'I'd be grateful for a small rum.'

'Righto.' Colin poured out a neat measure of the sugary spirit, handing it to the Stud Master.

'I've made some sandwiches and coffee,' the housekeeper said to no-one in particular, retreating to her domain.

Hugh joined Eleanor where she sat apart from her mother and stepfather. 'How did shearing go?'

'No problems,' she replied. 'Actually, the lot of them were on their best behaviour.'

He took a sip of the rum. 'Good. And you? How are you holding up?'

Eleanor watched the birds in the stone fountain, their wings outstretched as the last of the day's glow dissipated. 'Considering I'm to blame for this mess, pretty average, but at least Lesley is safe. It's just –'

'What?' Hugh questioned, clearly concerned.

Eleanor studied his fight-damaged face. 'She's pretty mixed up. Lesley thinks she saw Robbie when she was at the cemetery.'

'Well, Robbie's one problem we don't have to worry about.'

'For once.' Eleanor gave a weak smile. 'I'm worried about her, Hugh. Lesley honestly believes that she saw Robbie out in the bush this afternoon. She was quite upset about it, especially with it being dark soon.'

They both looked out at the quietening garden.

'It was a mirage, a hallucination,' Hugh told her. 'Robbie would be in Sydney by now.'

'But she was so convinced.'

'Trust me, Eleanor. I know you worry about Lesley. Your whole family does. But look at the weather she's been out in. The heat can scramble a person's head if you're subjected to it for long enough. And at the very least Lesley would be suffering from dehydration. Give her time to rest and recover.'

'That's just the problem, Hugh. What if she can't?' How could Eleanor possibly explain to someone as level-headed as Hugh Goward that Lesley's ailments went beyond the physical kind? 'Can I get some ointment for you to put on those cuts?' she offered.

'Thanks, but you have enough on your plate without worrying about me. I'll be alright.'

Headlights shone from the direction of the road that passed through the bougainvillea hedge. As the black car drew up in front of the house, Rex appeared. Climbing the steps, he thumbed unenthusiastically towards the policemen alighting from the vehicle. 'The cavalry's here,' he said dryly.

Georgia and Colin rose to meet the officers.

Constable Graham, a peppy fellow with a narrow chin, introduced the two younger members of his team, Rogers and Atwill.

'My apologies,' the constable said with barely a hint of regret or the offer of an excuse. 'Mrs Howell says you've had a robbery. It's the patient, eh?'

'Yes, we believe so,' Colin admitted. 'Eleanor left the door unlocked to his room this morning and he hightailed it out of here.'

The police officer glanced conspicuously in Eleanor's direction. The two younger officers were absorbed by the arrival of the housekeeper carrying a platter of sandwiches.

'But not before taking my jewels with him,' Georgia added.

Constable Graham wrote the details down in a notebook as

Georgia described the rifled drawers in her bedroom. 'And no-one else has been in the house?'

Georgia shook her head. 'Not this morning. Look, the men have been out searching for the thief all afternoon.'

'We didn't find a single track,' Colin conceded, 'nothing.' Choosing a sandwich from Mrs Howell's selection, he gestured for her to offer the food to everyone.

'I can't imagine he could have got very far in this heat,' added Hugh. 'I mean, the man is still recovering from his injuries.'

'That's assuming he hasn't got an accomplice,' the constable told them.

'Out here?' Colin spoke with his mouth full. 'You're telling me that he was laid up here for,' he counted his fingers, 'four nights and he has someone waiting out in the scrub?' He snorted. 'Highly unlikely.'

'Is it?' Now it was the officer's turn to sound disdainful.

'You've had four days to discover who this person is,' Colin challenged. 'I gather you have no leads. Nothing.'

'Actually, we are following a lead, Mr Webber. Over the past couple of years there have been a series of stock thefts out here in the western division. Nothing big. Usually twenty to fifty head. On the bigger places, take yours for example, it can be six months or more before the loss is noticed. And when you're talking big mobs on large acreage, well, quite often the owners put the loss down to a dry spell or fly-strike. But on a smaller holding, a grower soon notices if fifty head go astray.'

'Well, that's not our man,' Georgia stated. 'He rode to the river in broad daylight. And he stole the jewellery my late husband gave me, not sheep.'

'Granted, the patient doesn't quite fit the bill. But whether our man is a burglar or a stock thief, the two types do have something in common. They're opportunists. Anyway, our mystery man is but one of your concerns, is he not?' He picked through the sandwiches before selecting a curried egg. His companions were far less fussy. 'I'll be needing property maps.'

Georgia took a step towards Constable Graham. 'What other concern are you referring to?'

The policeman glanced at his wristwatch. 'I thought you would have received a telephone call by now.'

Rex, choosing a sandwich, shared a look of bewilderment with the housekeeper.

'About what?' asked Georgia.

'About your son, Mrs Webber.'

Colin frowned. 'What about our son?'

The constable considered taking a bite of the bread and egg. 'Your house guests, the Winslows. Their car broke down and it seems your boy took off.'

'What the hell do you mean "took off"?' Colin was on his feet.

The constable's expression never changed. 'Exactly that. The Winslows fell asleep and when they woke up your son was gone. I can only assume that your young Robbie walked off into the scrub.' Taking a large bite of the sandwich, he chewed hungrily. 'We found them broken down on the side of the road on our way out here. That's why we were delayed. We drove them back to the village, to the hotel. They were meant to contact you.'

Georgia paled. 'Robbie ran away?'

'How long ago did they break down?' Eleanor asked.

'Early this morning, Miss,' Officer Atwill replied.

≈ Chapter Forty-three ≈

'That Sweeny Hall needs a good –'

'Colin!' corrected Georgia sharply. Cheeks reddened by the stifling heat, she'd refused a fortifying beverage more than once. 'If you could stop complaining for one minute we might actually be able to think.'

'I always said that Sweeny was about as useful as a frog in a sock.' Rex, leaning on a wooden pillar, chewed the inside of his cheek. 'The mother was no good either. Set herself up as a laundry woman but couldn't even get the copper hot enough to wash things proper-like.'

Next to him, Constable Graham suggested that arguing wasn't assisting the situation. No-one heeded him.

'No good bloody –'

'Colin,' Georgia said loudly, for the fourth time, 'would you please mind your manners?'

Colin halted in his relentless pacing of the long veranda.

A makeshift centre of sorts had been set up on the porch. Insects fluttered about the lights, swam in coffee cups and floated in water jugs. Eleanor picked a drowned moth from a glass and took a sip of the warm liquid. The previous hub-bub of police and maps, search groups and assumptions was lessened only marginally by the earlier exodus of those determined to begin searching. Some of the shearers were happy to assist in the hunt for the stranger and Robbie, and two groups of men with an officer in charge of each were already rescouring the many station outbuildings before fanning out to check the countryside. No-one said the obvious. That with darkness upon them and endless acres of land stretching out like eternity, there was little chance of finding anyone until morning.

Eleanor waited as her stepfather, once again, attempted to control his raging temper. The anger emanating from Colin was quite palpable, causing her to consider if there was some deeper issue at the root of his fury. His eyes were as round as brass door-knobs, his face puffy and greyer than usual. And, most tellingly, he was now the only one drinking. Whisky, straight up. Every time he ventured towards the silver salver with its crystal decanters of various spirits, the nips grew larger.

Constable Graham, having arrived with the superior air expected of the constabulary, clearly understood that, for the moment, he was relegated to the position of bystander. Eleanor guessed at the officer's thoughts. Perhaps he considered them superior, decorated as the family was with a long land tenure, power and wealth, an enviable heritage. Or maybe he merely saw the Webbers of River Run as pretentious or, worse, removed from everyday life. The many years of supporting the district over the generations through employment, of family members being active politically for the benefit of society, their war service, of contributing to the nation's gross domestic product; all accounted for nothing when it came down to bush hierarchy. People were grouped accordingly. The haves and the have-nots, the great landowners and the townies, shearers, the workers and the bosses. The extraordinary thing in Eleanor's mind was that the only detail that really made people different was money, and with that came envy. As her father once stated, *the green eye of the little yellow god.*

Constable Graham dragged Eleanor's mother's flamboyant peacock chair away from the head of the table and closer to a flyscreen window, savvy to the weak draft of air drifting through the gauze. A platter balancing precariously on a dense thigh, he began to munch his way through mutton and Keen's mustard sandwiches, the lower portion of his jaw jutting enthusiastically from side to side. 'You just let me know how you'd like to handle this,' he spoke between bites. 'You people will know best. He's your boy after all.'

In response Georgia looked to her husband, who in turn briskly tapped the glass in his hand. Rex took a drag of the cigarette he smoked. Somewhere nearby a horse whinnied.

Eleanor thought briefly of the Winslows, safely ensconced in the hotel in the village, their broken-down vehicle yet to be towed from the side of the road. Nobody seemed willing to show compassion for the visiting couple, especially Margaret, who, from the accounts of the constable in-charge, was dreadfully weakened by the terrible ordeal, a quite understandable outcome, the policeman emphasised, considering the woman's delicate constitution.

'I can't believe that Robbie would be walking around at night,' Georgie said doubtfully.

'Well, he probably isn't by this stage.' Colin gave a snort of disagreement. 'Who knows when the boy took off? Keith and Margaret clearly have no idea.' He turned to the policeman for confirmation.

'None, unfortunately.' Constable Graham flicked crumbs from the leg of his uniform. 'Mr Winslow believed they dozed on and off for a couple of hours. Your son was sitting on the opposite side of the tree so they assumed he was still there.'

Eleanor glanced shyly at Hugh sitting in a cane chair, the expanse of table between them. He appeared to be dozing, but she knew better. As she studied the man, he met her eyes.

Georgia and Colin were arguing again about Robbie's disappearance, about the Winslows not keeping an eye on their son.

Twice in the last twenty minutes Eleanor had tried to mention what Lesley had confided and twice she'd been talked down. On each occasion Hugh lifted his hand as if patting the air. But what if Lesley really had seen Robbie? Eleanor articulated her thoughts.

'Do you really think Lesley saw him? I mean, Rex told me that your sister isn't quite with us, and I mean no offence when I say that,' Hugh cautioned. 'Think about it, Eleanor. She arrives home after five years and Robbie leaves the next day and Lesley doesn't even get to say goodbye to him. Then she goes walkabout in the heat, feeling sad and sorry for herself and believes she's seen your brother.' He grimaced. 'All I'm saying is that I wouldn't like to create a goose chase for the men. We need to think logically about this.'

Eleanor, torn between wanting to find her brother and the offchance of proving that Lesley wasn't mad, bided her time as their collective group, bolstered occasionally by the appearance of the housekeeper, made suggestions and presumptions when the two duelling heads of the household paused for breath.

'We should never have considered boarding school,' Georgia accused.

Colin stalked to the opposite end of the veranda.

When it came to Robbie, Hugh was unconcerned. 'He'll have hunkered down for the night by now,' he told Eleanor.

'I know, but I still worry about him,' Eleanor quietly replied.

'Don't. He's a tough nut, your brother. He might still think a bit like a kid, but in other ways he's older than his years. That makes things a touch confusing for him.' He leant forward. 'Consider the shooting. Why did he do it? Because he got it into his head that the property, his property, was going to be invaded. Then with Lomax and Billy Wright, he knew they were doing wrong, so he tried to stop them. At the heart of both incidents is a boy doing his best to protect what he loves.' He gave a quirky smile. 'Admittedly, the training wheel fell off the bicycle in both instances, but his heart was in the right place.'

'But he bashes crows to death with a stick,' argued Eleanor.

'So did I once, but it's kinder and easier if you poison the bait.'

The image he conjured was not a pleasant one. 'So he's normal?' Eleanor asked, aware of the surprise in her voice.

'Depends on your definition of normal, I suppose. Right little bastard, I'd call him.'

Eleanor giggled.

'We need a pack of cards, Elly,' Hugh said softly. 'Can I call you Elly?' His tone was hopeful.

'Of course.'

'Do you play cards?'

'Not really. Well, I dabbled in Gin Rummy once, and lost badly,' she added.

Hugh rubbed his hands together. 'There's a dollar to be made here,' he joked.

How pleased she was that Hugh was with her. There was something so solid about him, so normal, so reassuring. This was a man who was relaxed in his own skin, who had direction. The off-shoot of that meant he was comfortable with her, his position on River Run and her family. He held no qualms when it came to reporting to a woman. Maybe people's attitudes in general, towards everything, had less to do with money and more to do with finding their own place in the world.

'She'll be alright you know,' said Hugh, referring to Lesley.

'I hope so.' The more Eleanor thought of Lesley's admission, of having seen Robbie near the station cemetery, the more she believed that it was too much of a coincidence considering the Winslows' broken-down car and Robbie's escape. Her brother was on foot, fleeing boarding school. He would head to one place and one place only. His treehouse by the riverbank. There was food and water there. Safety.

She pictured Robbie waiting until the Winslows were asleep and then heading bush, towards shelter, towards his special place. As long as he stayed in the branches, above the ground, she guessed he'd be quite safe even on a moonless night. Eleanor tried not to revisit Lesley's words, did her best not to dwell on childhood phobias that sanity told her didn't exist, but it was difficult, very difficult.

'I think Lesley is right,' announced Eleanor. 'Now that we know Robbie has run away, well, hallucination or not, he's out there. At the river.'

'Really?' Hugh didn't look persuaded.

'He has a treehouse. You know that. It's the spot where he shot Chad. He's got supplies stashed away there.'

Hugh weighed up the facts. 'It's a long way for the boy to walk in the heat. And Lesley still could have been imagining things.'

'Well, where the hell could he be?' asked Colin, pacing the veranda.

Hugh uncrossed long legs. The skin on his face was red with dirt and still swollen in places from the morning's fight. 'Eleanor suggested that hidey-hole of Robbie's, the tree by the river.'

Georgia blew a puff of air through her lips. 'Absurd. It's much too far to walk. Why, the Winslows were nearly at the boundary. They were past the fourth stock grid near the turn-off to the cemetery.'

'The cemetery,' repeated Eleanor, noting the affirmation on Hugh's face. 'Mum, Lesley saw Robbie walking through the scrub when she was at the cemetery.'

Her mother was caught off guard. 'Yes, yes she did say something along those lines, Elly. But I didn't take her seriously.'

'Neither did I.' Eleanor grew excited. 'The road to the graveyard cuts diagonally cross-country in the direction of the river.'

Georgia's sun-cracked lips formed a small 0.

'Makes sense.' Rex, who'd been quiet, peeled his lanky body from the wooden pillar. 'Well, I mean the boy may well be a right young rascal but he knows a thing or two about the scrub.' He scratched his jowly neck. 'Followed the birds when the sun dropped, he would have. Gone straight to the river and cooled himself down. After that . . .' He hunched bony shoulders. 'I say we all set off after the lad. It's past eight o'clock already.'

'Good idea,' Colin concurred.

Constable Graham rose enthusiastically. 'We'll take my car.'

'We'll be on horseback,' Hugh told his employers. 'And you,' he said to the police officer, 'well, your vehicle won't handle the paddock, Constable. There's no road. Only a sheep trail and once we reach the river the trees make it hard going, they're that thick.'

'Constable Graham, Rex and I will stay here at the house,' Georgia directed. 'In case Robbie turns up.'

'Can I suggest that only Eleanor and I head out?' asked Hugh. 'Robbie may well take off otherwise. He does have the advantage, and he'll have it in his mind that he'll be packed off to school again once he's found.'

Georgia nodded slowly, hesitant. 'You're right of course, Hugh.' She turned to Eleanor. 'Robbie does think the world of you.'

A deep line creased Colin's forehead. 'He is my son.' When this statement brought no response, he lifted saddle-greasy hands in mock surrender. 'Fine. Go then.' He turned away, walked a few paces across the timber floor and then headed back to the table where he poured a measure of whisky, as well as one for the police officer. Constable Graham reluctantly accepted the offering, cradling the tumbler in the palm of his hand.

'Do you think you could find that tree in the dark, Elly? Help me find Robbie?' asked Hugh.

'I . . .' It was so very black beyond the homestead. 'If you follow the sheep trail that leads past the crow trap, Hugh, and head straight to the river, you'll find him. It's a big tree in a clearing and the branches extend across the water. It's directly opposite to where Chad was shot.'

Hugh digested this information. 'I might be able to find the spot, *might*,' he emphasised, 'but it would be easier if you came with me.'

357

Eleanor looked out at the dense blackness, void of shadows, of depth. Rex and Georgia were staring at Eleanor. Hugh had moved quickly and was waiting for her on the veranda steps.

'I just don't –' Eleanor swallowed. What on earth was she going to say? *I'm terribly sorry but I can't help you find Robbie because I'm afraid of the dark?*

'I don't blame you, girl.' Rex finished rolling a cigarette, sticking it above his ear. 'Black as pitch and twice as dark it is. It's not the night to be going walkabout. You live in the scrub the length of time I have and you know when they're out there. The old people roamed this land, still do some say.' Digging a hand in a pocket, matches were retrieved. He placed a splinter of wood between his teeth and began to chew and talk simultaneously. 'Crossed from west to east for better hunting, for foraging and such-like. Been doing it since Adam and Eve. Twice a year and back again in the old days, before the whitefella came and then for a bit afterwards. 'Course back then they made fair use of a full moon, but now' – he ran a finger along the wiry tendons of his neck – 'now, they're out there when it suits and they don't need no moon to guide them. Been in the wrong place at the wrong time, I have. Winter it was and they held me up at the boundary gate. Couldn't see a thing, but I knew they were there. I ain't proud. I turned away right quick and went back the way I came. No point a man messing with things like that.' Rex turned to Eleanor. 'If you feel them, girl, you turn around and come straight home. We might have the run of the place during the day, but at night,' he spat the match into the dark, 'at night, the land belongs to them.'

'Rex!' Georgia exclaimed.

The gardener shook his head innocently. 'I'm just saying, missus, I'm just saying. I'm just telling the girl how it is. Fair's fair. And besides, dark of the moon tonight it is, a blood month, and a goddamn albatross to boot.'

Colin, propped on the edge of the table, scowled. 'Get a grip, Rex.'

'What albatross?' asked Georgia. 'What on earth are you talking about?'

'I'm just saying.' Rex brushed past Hugh, his boots crunching gravel. 'I'll fetch the horses.'

Hugh beckoned Eleanor. 'Come on. Let's go.'

Reluctantly, Eleanor walked out into the night.

⪻ Chapter Forty-four ⪼

They rode with the hot, earthy scents of a land under siege, the countryside gasping for water, for relief as they travelled side by side through wafts of tainted air. Eleanor concentrated on the circle of light formed by Hugh's torch. He knew their land well, for although it was indeed as black as pitch, as Rex warned, his path rarely strayed and before long they were in the middle of the paddock following the depression made by the trampling of sheep. Their steady progress marked by the occasional squeak of leather and snorting of their mounts.

Ahead, a structure loomed. Hugh flashed the beam of light in the direction of the crow trap. The octagonal chicken-wire glinting metallically. 'At least we know where the stink was coming from.' He passed the torch across the battered bodies of the birds within, the light shining briefly on the black-feathered carcasses as they rode by. 'How are you doing, Elly?'

Cocooned by night, they'd barely spoken since leaving the homestead. 'Alright,' she answered quietly. The thumping in her chest suggested otherwise. The reins were slippery beneath the tightness of her grip, Hilda fidgety.

'You mustn't let Rex put the wind up you.' Hugh's voice was steady, calming. 'Old codgers like that have particular thoughts, that's all.'

'So you don't believe what he said? You don't believe it's possible?' Did she sound breathy? Unsure? Eleanor hoped not. 'You don't believe in spirits?' The torch went out. She gave an involuntary shudder before realising that the click heard was the sound of Hugh turning it off.

'I think,' said Hugh slowly, 'that anything is possible. When my wife, Vivien, died,' his voice grew gritty, 'I could have sworn she was in our house for weeks afterwards. Sometimes I was sure it was the scent of her perfume I could smell. It's strange, and I've never told another living soul this, Elly, however, I felt I had to let her go. So I said goodbye and a couple of days later the house felt empty.'

He was momentarily silent. Eleanor imagined him swallowing, closing his throat to stem the sadness within.

'I like to think,' Hugh finally continued, 'that she came back to say goodbye.'

In the darkness, Hugh was the slightest of outlines. Eleanor wanted to ask how long he'd been married for, what Vivien was like. 'Maybe she did,' was her simple reply.

A thudding noise signalled the movement of kangaroos across their path. The horses shied slightly at the disturbance.

'And you?' asked Hugh, his voice lightening. 'You don't seem to come home much?'

The question caught her off guard. She thought of her step-father. It just wasn't the same with Colin at River Run. Eleanor had never quite come to terms with Georgia's second marriage. But more recently, Dante was the reason for her absence from the property. In comparison to what Hugh suffered, Eleanor's crisis was pathetic; the stolen novella was only a book and Dante was merely a man without a conscience who'd betrayed her. 'Well, considering what's happened this past week, it's probably just as well I don't visit much.'

'It's not your fault, Elly.'

She gave a weak laugh, thinking of the balcony key, her presence at the shooting and her naivety regarding Chad Reynolds. Coming on the back of the spurious Dante, there was no doubt that she was starting to chalk up an impressive list of disasters.

'I'm serious,' he said.

'I trust people too easily,' Eleanor answered flippantly, as if it were no great issue. 'But I've learnt my lesson.'

'The world will be a lesser place if you stop believing in people, Elly.'

'Maybe.' But it will be safer, she decided, and far less trouble-some for everyone. Eleanor thought of Lesley lying in their grandmother's four-poster bed, suffering both physically and emotionally. There was enough pain in the world without creating more through poor choices.

'What do you do in Sydney?'

'I'm in nuts and bolts.' It was Eleanor's standard cocktail party answer. 'Hardware,' she clarified when Hugh remained silent. 'I'm a secretary.'

'So it's just something to make ends meet, keep you occupied?'

Hugh made it sound as if she were just filling in time. 'Pretty much.'

'I couldn't do that. I've always needed to feel passionate about what I do. I can't see how you can get any job satisfaction otherwise.'

He was right, of course, but it wasn't something Eleanor felt comfortable admitting. 'I like writing best,' she shared. 'Short stories, novellas, that sort of thing.'

'Well then, that's what you should be doing. If you're passionate about it, you'll be unstoppable.'

Eleanor smiled.

'I have a confession to make. I did show you my ram selec-tion process so you'd put in a good word for me. I've been coming up against a few barriers recently, problems that I thought would affect the breeding program.'

'I figured as much,' Eleanor responded, assuming the problem was her stepfather, 'but my mother wouldn't have offered you the position unless she knew you were capable.'

'Thanks, I appreciate the vote of confidence.'

Eleanor understood that prior to Hugh accepting the role of overseer at River Run, he'd held the same position on a large sheep stud in western Queensland. On reading his references, Georgia ruled he was the man she wanted for the job. Eleanor could only agree with her mother's judgement, but she also reluctantly acknowledged that her own opinion regarding River Run's newly promoted Stud Master had little to do with credentials. Don't go there, Eleanor warned herself, more than aware of the proximity of the man riding next to her and her recent track record with the opposite sex.

'Getting back to what Rex said earlier, Elly, about the bush at night, well, you really shouldn't let him scare you. What he's suggesting should make a man curious, not scared. Wary, but not afraid. I only mention it again because you acted a little apprehensive about coming out with me this evening.'

'Did I?'

'Yes. And I understand that. This is an old country. With an old people. I'm not a smart man, Eleanor, but I do know that just because we can't see something doesn't mean that it doesn't exist.' He switched on the torch, illuminating the narrow trail, quail fluttering from the grass. With their direction confirmed, he flicked the beam off again so as not to exhaust the battery. 'But that doesn't mean we should be afraid of our own shadows. Okay?'

'Okay.' Eleanor could hardly admit her paranoia to Hugh.

'Respect. That's all this land wants, for everything and everyone in it, seen or unseen. She's a woman for sure,' he stated.

'The bush is a woman?' Eleanor quite liked the sound of that.

363

Hugh gave a low whistle. 'Changes her mind on the flip of a three-penny piece, good to bad and back again. Wilful and lavish all at once.' His voice was deep, resonant.

They rode on. The horses plodding carefully across the rough ground, the swish of their tails mingling with the breath of air weaving through the grasses.

⤞ Chapter Forty-five ⤝

The air was dark and still. Only the whisper of leaves and the spiral of stars served to remind Robbie of where he was. There it was again. A scratching noise. A grating sound. It was not coming from a branch above, nor from those around him. He sat up, listening. Disorientated, he waited for his mind to clear and for the sleep that crusted his eyelids to crumble beneath his touch. Robbie guessed it could be any number of animals, a foraging kangaroo or wallaby, a pig digging in the sandy soil, a bird perhaps. Whatever the creature that disturbed him, it was gone, leaving only silence.

Now he was awake, Robbie wondered what to do next. Returning home was not an option. He would only be packed off to school on the next train and probably given another belting as well for his troubles. No, if he returned to the house, it would be to collect a swag, his rifle and some extra supplies. A few clothes perhaps, the pup and old Garnet. He'd go inland to where no-one knew him. To a property where good men were needed. A cattle station. Yes. He could take Bluey then. He'd earn his keep. What station owner would turn down a man with a horse and dog, who owned his own rifle and who knew the ways of the bush?

Okay, Robbie reasoned, he was short for his age and yet to grow a beard of any kind, although the soft hairs on his chin showed great promise. And it was true he was young, but he could easily explain he was simply young-looking, but he was schooled enough to read and write and, if push came to shove, he could fight. He'd be sorry to leave River Run, but he knew he'd be sorrier still if he went to that fancy school in Sydney.

As he planned the next couple of days, a light flickered. He ducked automatically, chastising himself on realising that no-one could see him in the dark. Except that Eleanor knew where the tree was. He'd brought her here. To this very spot.

The light shone steadily. Someone must have found the Winslows and sent out a search party. Robbie wondered frantically what to do next. He figured that his only option was to leave the tree and hide out elsewhere, until whoever was looking for him moved on. He thought of the swim at dusk, at the footprints he'd probably left in the sand. Jiminy Cricket, he mumbled, annoyed.

Like a crab, he shifted his backside across the wobbly planks and, lifting a branch, peered in the direction of the searchlight. There it was. Flickering among the trees. It wasn't a torch. A kerosene lantern, maybe. Rex was partial to using those lamps, as was Mrs Howell when the generator broke down. Robbie watched and waited. If the light headed directly towards the tree he would climb down, backtrack along the river to confuse the pursuers, cut into the scrub and then double-back to the tree, once whoever trailed him moved on. Yes, he decided, that was a good plan.

But the light remained distant. An unsteady shine that glimmered brightly before fading to a pinprick and then brightening once again. Something wasn't right. Not only was the light changing in shape and size, it also appeared to be stationary. Robbie swivelled on the wooden planks, checking directions. The light was further along the river. In the opposite direction to the homestead.

Why would they come that way? he wondered, thinking of

his father and Eleanor. They wouldn't, he was sure of that. The queasy sensation growing in his gut had little to do with the beans and water consumed earlier. No, this was a feeling of things not being right.

Someone else was out here, with him, in the scrub.

Robbie scrambled down from the tree, missed a foothold and fell heavily the last few feet, to land awkwardly on his back. He lay quite still, stunned by the fall and then, momentarily entranced by the heavens, observed the stars as they appeared to dance amidst wind-blown leaves, the Southern Cross angled across the heavens, and near it, the potty in the sky. He rose carefully, gingerly checking each limb and, without further thought, commenced walking towards the unknown light.

❧ Chapter Forty-six ❧

Eleanor trailed Hugh through the mesh of trees hugging the river, the torch revealing living walls of knotty bark and a narrow animal track, kangaroo made. The marsupial's imprint marked the sandy ground, paws and tail tracking towards the waterway. The riders ducked beneath thick, sticky webs spun between saplings. They brushed away large scuttling spiders and frightened wallabies and rabbits from hidey-holes. At every step, Hugh guided Eleanor, calling out to warn of a fallen bough, a web, or the need to veer left or right. She followed him blindly, focusing on the dismal light that emanated from his hand, wondering at every step how he'd actually got her to come with him out into the night.

'Are you sure the water is ahead of us, Hugh?'

He tugged on the reins, bringing their journey to a standstill. 'Smell the air.'

The previous dryness that seemed to crackle around them in the paddock was now replaced with something slightly different.

'There's a tonne of water in the river.' Taking a drink from a waterbag, he passed it to Eleanor. 'That's what you can smell. It's still as hot as blazes, but the slight breeze coming off the river makes a difference.'

She accepted the water gratefully, their fingers touching for the briefest of moments. Eleanor thought of that slight contact as the horses wound through the trees, the gradual slope of the country eventually leading them to the riverbank. Hugh shone the torch across the shadowy expanse of water, the narrow beam highlighting a barely rippling surface.

'Left or right?' asked Hugh.

'Right,' replied Eleanor.

'I do like a confident woman.' He shone the beam on the ground. Boot marks were visible in the sand.

'Are they small enough to be Robbie's?' Eleanor followed Hugh's line of sight as he turned his horse and began to follow the river's edge.

'They sure are.'

A few minutes later, and after a number of false searches, they finally located Robbie's tree. Hugh picked up the empty tin of beans and shined the torch through the branches. They both called his name.

'He's not here.' Eleanor was crestfallen. 'How can he not be here?'

Only the rising wind answered.

'He's moving again.' Hugh, squatting on the ground, checked the direction of the footprints. 'Come on.'

≪ Chapter Forty-seven ≫

Robbie kept on crawling until he was close enough to see the men sitting around the campfire. Edging his way to a fallen log, he stretched out lengthwise so that his body was concealed by the timber and there was a clear view between the hoary roots. They were roasting something gamey, roo perhaps. And he guessed they'd been rough with the butchering, for it was the stink of fur on the air that had helped lead him here. Robbie reckoned he'd walked nearly two miles in search of the unknown light. Certainly his feet were in agreement. And had exhaustion not tempered his enthusiasm, he'd been of half a mind on arrival to confront the men and ask what on earth they were doing on River Run. But he'd squatted behind a tree to catch his breath, finally remembering, with some annoyance, that he had no horse, or rifle for that matter.

While the strangers did. Two firearms.

There were three of them. The two that faced him were rangy looking men with beards. Bear-eaters from the stony mountains to the east, he surmised, remembering comments he'd overheard his father make. The man with his back towards Robbie was slighter in build and yet to speak, engrossed as he was with a length of stick, a chunk of meat speared on the end. With the meat extended over the flames and his companions chewing on their own portions, they talked intermittently. The conversation revolved around a lack of decent tucker, the sour taste of river water and the searing heat.

Roo shooters, he decided. Two rifles rested on unfurled swags.

'What I wouldn't give for a decent feed,' one of the men said, his mouth bunched with meat. 'We've been sitting here for the good part of a week waiting for you to show up.'

A second man with a droopy moustache belched. 'Steady on, McCormack. The boy's explained himself and more. Besides, we'll be leaving with more than we arrived with.'

'No doubt about that,' replied the first man, albeit grudgingly. 'We'd best hightail it out of here afore first light.'

They weren't a talkative mob, thought Robbie. Not like his home where everyone spoke at once and a person had to put their hand up to be heard. He'd given up on that. No, he'd rather be outdoors where no-one could tell him what to do and if he did want to say something, well, the whole of River Run listened. He lay on his back and stared at the stars as one of the men played a soulful tune on a harmonica. There it was again. The same song the jackeroo sang only a couple of days ago. Even his father hummed it occasionally.

Oh, give me land, lots of land under starry skies above . . .

Well, you aren't getting mine, Robbie whispered.

The men settled down for the night, unrolling swags and savouring a last smoke as the yellow flames of the fire wrapped around a burning log. Robbie, mesmerised by the curls of fire licking and stroking the wood, felt his eyelids grow heavy. He drifted in and out of sleep, desperate to stay awake but cursed by tiredness. His plan was to keep an eye on the men until they slept, steal one of the rifles and then wait till morning before surprising them and walking the intruders back to the homestead. No-one would send him to boarding school then.

Near midnight came the barest drop in temperature and a rising wind. A willy-willy gathered dirt and leaves, spinning the earthy debris across Robbie as he slept. He awoke with a start, digging a finger into his eyes and ears in search of the grit that layered his body like a blanket. From somewhere in the darkness came the howl of a dog, matched by a deep, chortling screech of a noise. One of the men was snoring.

From between the chunky timber roots, Robbie could see the sleeping forms of the strangers. The fire was reduced to glowing embers but there was enough light to show the occupants in the clearing and the rifles, carelessly left to one side. Satisfied the outsiders slept and with a confidence provided by the moonless sky, very carefully Robbie began to crawl out from undercover of the tree stump. Inch by inch, he crept slowly across the ground, flattening his body on the dirt, his fingers splayed over the earth until he imagined himself a lizard, in pursuit of prey.

The men's breathing was rhythmic. The snoring continued. Digging the toes of his boots in the ground, Robbie moved closer to where the rifles lay on hessian sacks. Holding his breath, he reached out and clasped the barrel of one of the weapons. The metal was cold as he dragged the firearm slowly across the dirt until it rested safely by his side. Reaching for the second firearm, something in the fire popped and fizzed. Disturbed, one of the strangers stirred, rolling onto his side. Robbie planted his face in the dirt, staying perfectly still for long minutes, hoping for the best.

Dirt edged its way up into his nose. He wriggled his nostrils uncomfortably. It wasn't worth being discovered, he decided, electing to leave the second firearm behind. Instead he reached out tentatively, searching the dismal pile of stores stacked nearby. He located a box of cartridges among a scant supply of flour and sugar. No saddlebags, he realised, no saddles. The men were on foot as well. Relieved by this knowledge, he edged back from the rim of the fire into the safety of the night. The odds were looking a lot better.

Perched against the stump, Robbie ran a hand across the barrel and stock of the rifle. 'Jiminy Cricket,' he exclaimed excitedly, before lowering his voice. 'A Winchester.' Robbie did his best Jimmy Stewart impersonation, repeating his favourite line from the movie: *'That's too much gun for a man to have just for . . . shootin' rabbits.'* He flicked the lever action back and forth and, without thinking, pulled the trigger. The gun went off, flinging Robbie hard against the stump and winding him. 'Holy cow,' he said painfully, grasping his shoulder, which took the brunt of the recoil.

Around the campfire the men were on their feet instantly, searching for boots, yelling at each other, calling into the dark. Dazed, Robbie shook his head and then he too was moving, running through the trees, rifle in hand. He tripped and stumbled, collided into branches and felt spiky leaves scratch his face, as he did his best to place as much distance between himself and the strangers. Suddenly, something large loomed before him in the dark. Robbie drew up hard in the dirt, halting mid-stride. A lorry was parked amongst the timber and his arrival disturbed the animals in the crate on the back. Frightened, they called to each other, their hoofs clattering on the timber tray.

'Sheep,' Robbie muttered, his voice barely audible. They were stealing River Run's sheep!

Sliding under the truck, he hid behind one of the tyres, listening for the crunch of boots on dry twigs, for the low voices of the searchers. One thing he knew for sure was that with a load of sheep on the back of a truck, they certainly weren't kangaroo shooters. Finding his pocketknife, Robbie flicked open the blade and, without hesitating, jammed the point into the tyre. Escaping air made a whooshing sound, as scrambling to the opposite tyre he lay on his stomach and punctured it as well. Then he held his breath while the rear body of the truck dropped towards the ground as the rubber deflated.

The men could be heard walking through the scrub towards the vehicle. Robbie stuck his head out from under the lorry and looked up into a changed sky. The stars appeared wind-blown and blurry, as if dirt and whisper-thin cloud were leeching the heavens. He didn't like the look of it. The distinctive dry tang of the bush was being eroded by a gathering wind and with it came the thick, cloddy scent of dust. Reaching for the Winchester, he opened the box of cartridges, dismayed that only two remained in the carton. Well, he thought dryly, he'd have to make them count. Quietly he loaded the rifle.

'Ouch!' Something grabbed his lower leg. Robbie kicked out in fright, but the heavy weight crawled onto the middle of his back, plying the length of his spine, a wet tongue licking at his neck. 'What the . . . Bluey?' The cattle-pup whined with delight. 'Bluey? Bluey, is that you?'

The cattle-pup barked in response, his yelp unmistakable.

'Shush up.' Robbie grabbed the animal, tucking the cattle dog under a protective arm as a wet tongue coated his cheek with saliva. 'I'm pleased to see you too, little mate,' he whispered. The chain was still attached to the pup's collar and Robbie quickly unfastened it. 'You could have got that caught in a log,' he chastised. 'You could have died.'

'Well, well, well.' Somebody grabbed an ankle and proceeded to drag Robbie out from under the vehicle. He was flipped onto his back in the process, losing his grip on the rifle. Robbie groped and clawed at loose dirt but within seconds he was looking up at fuzzy stars. Free of Robbie's grasp, the pup growled and barked before launching his squat body into the air, latching onto Robbie's assailant.

'Get this bloody mutt off me!' the thief cried. He threw the dog from him, the cattle-pup landing in the dirt with a series of yelps.

Robbie, hearing Bluey whimpering, felt the blood boil in his veins. Yanking the shanghai from a back pocket, he loaded it with a shiny river pebble, aimed at the attacker and fired. The missile hit the stock-rustler in the face. The man fell heavily to the ground, uttering a string of unmentionable swearwords.

In the brief silence that ensued, the voices of the other two men carried on the night air. The sounds growing in volume as they called to their companion, querying where he was, if he were hurt, directed by their injured friend who was yelling for help.

Robbie felt for the rifle, pulled it free from under the truck, and fired a warning shot into the air. 'One more move,' Robbie warned, running to the far side of the vehicle. His hands were shaking terribly.

The increasing noise, made by the pursuing thieves as they ran and then walked through the bush, ceased.

'Drop your rifle,' Robbie commanded. Eyes accustomed to the dark, he made out the shapes of the two approaching men. 'I said drop it. This is my land and you're trespassing. I can shoot the backside out of a duck at two hundred yards.' He swallowed nervously. 'This close, well, it would be between the eyes.'

'It's the goddamn kid.'

The accent sounded American. Cripes, Robbie thought. His eyes bulged, justification surging through him. 'My father and uncle were both snipers during the war,' he told them. 'Don't think I can't hit one of you.'

'What kid?' the man who'd been felled with the shanghai asked, once he was standing again.

'The kid that shot me,' the American revealed. 'Throw that rifle away, I don't need another bullet in me.'

'But he's only a kid.'

Jiminy Cricket, Robbie's trigger finger quivered, now he understood what the western comic-book heroes meant when they said they had an itchy finger. 'Get back.' About them the wind gained in strength and with it came dust, great billowing waves of it. The blast of gritty air shoved him backwards.

'The kid that shot you?' one of the strangers yelled above the blustery weather. 'But what the hell is he doing here? You told us he was packed off to some fancy school.'

'And it wasn't an accident,' Robbie said loudly, interrupting further discussion. The cattle-pup made his presence known by sitting on his foot. Robbie wondered what he should do next. If he tried to get the men back to the campfire, they would try to run and probably succeed. 'Get in the lorry. Go on, you heard me,' he ordered, his eyes tearing from the flying grit.

They approached reluctantly, three silhouettes rendered almost insubstantial by the strengthening dust storm.

'Open the crate,' Robbie directed, his voice rising above the growing storm. 'Do it. Quick-smart, or I'll sool my dog onto you.' Bluey might only be six months old but he could bite.

The sliding door on the crate squeaked open noisily. Robbie could see the men dillydallying at the rear of the vehicle. It wouldn't take much for them to disarm him. 'Get in,' he shouted. He let off another shot, just so they knew he meant business. That was it then. The last of the ammunition.

'I reckon the kid's all out of bullets,' one of the men said.

In the gloom, the campfire glowed an angry red. Spurred by the wind, it crept along the ground, growing in size as it consumed the dry grass in its path.

The intensifying breeze rattled the truck. Two of the men grabbed at the wooden crate, clinging to it in the onslaught of the angry wind. The third made a lunge towards Robbie, knocking the rifle from his grip and clutching at the boy's shirt.

As Robbie yelled for help, a strong gust of wind struck, blowing him off his feet and out of reach of his attacker.

⊰ Chapter Forty-eight ⊱

The noise echoed along the river, reverberating through scrubby bush and timber, carrying loudly the length of the waterway. Hugh and Eleanor drew their horses to a standstill near the steep side of the riverbank. Here, protected from the gathering wind, Eleanor looked to Hugh for guidance. Someone had fired a shot. The sound was unmistakable.

'Sound carries across water,' Hugh remarked. 'I wish to hell we knew what was going on out there.' He patted his mount's neck. 'Robbie wouldn't have a rifle, would he?'

'I doubt it.' If she'd hoped for reassurance, it was not forthcoming from her companion. Hugh appeared distinctly ill-at-ease.

He met her concern with a brief nod. 'Well someone does, and they're not afraid to use it.' The beam of the torch showed Robbie's prints in the sand. 'Come on.'

Eleanor hoped it was one of River Run's search parties. Maybe they'd already found Robbie. Maybe, very soon they would meet up with the men and her young brother and then they could all head safely home.

They kept their horses at a trot, keeping to the water's edge. Eleanor gritted her teeth, clinging to the reins, grateful for

Hilda's cautiousness as they continued on in the direction of the gunshot.

'I don't like the look of this storm,' Hugh commented, when they slowed to side-track a fallen tree.

The stars were beginning to disappear, vanishing one by one, consumed by a dark mass that edged menacingly across the sky. Eleanor thought of the warrigal storm, of what Hugh told her in the paddock that day. 'Is it the same storm, Hugh? Has it come back again?' The scent of dust was strong in the air.

'Keep up, Elly,' was his only reply.

The splash of hoofs in water was quickly drowned by the wind. Eleanor felt a shiver travel the length of her spine. How she wished she'd not allowed Hugh to talk her into coming out with him. Why had she? Because she'd believed in the man. Foolish, foolish woman. What would it have mattered if Colin rode out instead of her? Robbie couldn't keep running from home forever.

Someone was out here with them, firing a rifle and a storm was about to hit, a storm during the dark of the moon. Were Eleanor not so afraid of falling behind, of losing Hugh, of being stranded in the bush alone in the night, with a lost boy and a thief on the run, she would have stopped to spit out the bile fouling her mouth. Instead she leant forward, crouching low along the mare's neck as her hat blew away and the binding holding her hair came loose. At any moment Eleanor expected to be lifted clean out of the saddle by the ferocity of the dust storm.

'Keep up,' Hugh hollered. 'Look!'

Ahead, a red blaze of light stretched through the trees, smoke mingling with the dirty storm. Slowing their horses, they edged through the timber, keeping the river close.

The rushing of wind through the bush grew louder, the water rippling in the glow of Hugh's torch.

The fire was racing in the opposite direction. Curtailed by the waterway and directed by an indecisive wind, it hugged the banks of the river.

'Come on!' yelled Hugh. They rode hard and fast. Water splashed up across their thighs in great arcs as they raced towards the blaze.

'Robbie!' Eleanor called, the words lost in the dust storm. 'Robbie?'

By the time Hugh reined in his horse and dismounted, he was bent low into the airstream. 'Get off!' he yelled above the howling wind. Eleanor did so immediately, sliding from Hilda, who whinnied and took off into the trees.

'Forget the horse, Elly. Come here,' he beckoned, a hand outstretched.

Eleanor struggled to reach him, as the wind buffeted her every move, but he met her halfway, clasping a wrist and leading her to a thick tree trunk. She could barely stand, but Hugh held her safe, pressing his body close to hers, the tree trunk solid next to her back. Eleanor closed her eyes against the storm, grateful for Hugh's protection. She clung to him desperately as branches fell around them and the gale roared.

'What are you doing?' she cried, as Hugh stepped back and began to rope her to the trunk, leaving her arms free. Eleanor reached for his determined hands, fighting the constriction of the rope.

'Stop it, Elly.' Hugh fought her off, as he tied a knot. 'I'm doing this for your own good.'

The stiff twine cut into her waist as she grabbed a muscled forearm. 'Hugh?' she pleaded. She'd never been so scared.

'Hell, Elly, I wouldn't leave you if I didn't have to, but you'll be blown away in this wind.' He checked the rope, making sure it was good and tight.

'But what about you?' she yelled in return.

'Don't worry about me, Elly. I have to check the fire, make sure Robbie isn't caught near it. Either someone's campfire has got away or it's been caused by a lightning strike.'

'Oh my God, you think –'

'I don't know anything,' he yelled. 'It could be that Chad bloke's camp but Robbie's a smart kid. Your arms are still free, Elly, you can release yourself once the wind dies down. This tree's stood for ages. It's not going anywhere.'

'Hugh?'

'I don't know how bad this is going to get. But I do know you'll be safer here. Where I can find you. The wind is blowing that fire in the opposite direction, but just in case.' He slipped a pocketknife into her hand, closed her fingers over it. 'If the wind changes direction, get in the river. If the lightning gets bad, cut the rope, move away and drop to the ground. Don't hug the tree. Promise me?'

The buffeting force grew worse. The wind whipped their faces.

'Don't leave me, Hugh!' Elly screamed.

He gripped her shoulders. 'I can't watch over you and find Robbie.'

'Hugh?'

His hands cupped her face. 'You'll be fine, Elly.'

But she wouldn't be. Not without Robbie and not without . . .

'Trust me,' Hugh commanded, shaking her roughly by the shoulders.

Lightning struck the ground in the distance and in the momentary flash they caught sight of a truck rolling over and over.

'I'll be back,' he told her. 'Don't cut the rope unless you have to. If this weather gets any worse, half the country will be blown away.'

'But –'

'Elly, trust me.'

Eleanor placed her hands on the width of his chest. 'Okay,' she swallowed nervously, 'go and find him, Hugh. Find Robbie.' What choice did she have?

Cupping her face, Hugh's thumb traced the curve of a cheek. He kissed her hard on the lips. Eleanor closed her eyes tightly, feeling his mouth on hers, the hardness of his chest, the strength of his embrace. The wind roared. The trees surrounding them creaked and groaned. Don't go, she whispered, don't leave me. What if he didn't come back? He said he would, but what if he didn't?

Then Hugh was gone, the closeness of his body replaced by the chill of desolation, the fear of being abandoned. Eleanor's chest tightened as she turned her face away from the wind and flying grit. Pressing her shoulders hard against the bark, hands shielding her face, the great tree seemed to groan. All around, the country-side swayed and cracked, woody plants toppling to the ground. And from every direction she was surrounded by the night.

Chapter Forty-nine

Eleanor kept her face turned from the rushing wind, her cheek pressed hard against the bark of the tree. The dust was incredibly thick. It coated her skin, clogged her eyes and made breathing difficult. It was as if the countryside really was blowing away. Soil was being lifted from distant miles to be carried across River Run on a raging wind. Fragile earth, grown loose and powdery through lack of moisture.

God, why doesn't it rain, Eleanor pleaded as the air grew dense with flying grit. The wind continued to lash her body and the very thought of where she was scared Eleanor witless.

Where was Hugh? Why wasn't he back? Why didn't he take her with him?

Think of something else, anything, her brain screamed.

An image of the rolling vehicle entered her mind. Eleanor shrank back further, making her body as small as possible. Who owned the truck? What were they doing out here?

If she were out in the open. If there was a moon. If she could see further than the glow of fire and the blackness surrounding her. But she couldn't. Eleanor could barely see anything at all.

In the past she recalled summer storms often being dry. On the front veranda of the homestead, she and Lesley often waited and watched with their father as a blustery wind and the flare of lightning appeared on the horizon.

'No rain today,' their dad would mutter, 'let's hope we don't get a bushfire out of this.'

Dad, Eleanor cried out, why did you leave us?

The crackle of burning scrub competed with the wind.

Briefly opening her eyes to gritty air and the smear of distant red flames, Eleanor noted that the gale was yet to change direction. There was constancy in that at least. While the wind continued to push the fire away, Eleanor was reasonably safe where she was, although the lightning still fizzed and popped in the distance.

A loud crack sounded and something large hit the ground with a deadening thud.

A branch.

Tears filled Eleanor's eyes. She was beyond scared. All she could think about was running away. Getting as far away from danger as possible. But there was nowhere to go to. Nowhere safe to run. Eleanor's heart was beating so quickly she thought it might explode. You can do this, she willed, trying to stem the negative thoughts engulfing her. You can survive this. So what if it's night-time, she tried to reason. Robbie and Hugh are out in this as well.

Tiredness tugged at Eleanor's limbs even as the air pushed and pulled about her. She would cover her face with her hands, for all the good such protection would do, but every time she released her grip from the tree trunk the wind buffeted her body. It was best to keep pressing backwards, feeling the solidness of the woody plant which so far kept her safe.

After a time Eleanor began to realise that she wanted to fight back. She was desperate to do so. That if she'd been able to pummel the storm with her fists she would have done so. She would have fought the night if given the opportunity, bashed it down into a padlocked box so that the thought of it could no longer scare her. She would have battered the cancer that took her beloved father, and shaken her gullibility into submission when it came to men.

'I'm not afraid,' Eleanor yelled into the storm. 'You can bash and howl and dump all the soil on me that you like, but you won't win. That goes for you too, Dante. You may have stolen my work, but I'll write better stories. You'll see.'

Overhead, a bright chain of rolling lightning spiralled across the sky. Eleanor watched the spectacle with a lump in her throat. How long had Hugh been away? Two hours? Three?

'This is Webber land,' she shouted. 'River Run belongs to us. So do your worst, we're not going anywhere.'

Something struck her in the face.

And body.

Eleanor cried out in shock. When she touched her cheek it was wet.

Exhausted, she wished she could sleep. Prayed that the night would end. That Robbie and Hugh would come back to her.

But there was no-one. Eleanor was completely alone.

She needed water.

Eleanor closed her eyes tightly and began to pray.

When the wind finally dropped and heavy rain came in the hour before dawn, Eleanor cut the rope binding her and sank to the base of the tree.

Thursday
Towards the Light

❖ Chapter Fifty ❖

Hugh woke before dawn, his first thoughts of Eleanor. Beside him, Robbie stirred. 'The worst of it's over, Robbie. We'll soon be home.'

The boy groaned as Hugh propped him against the side of the overturned truck. Overhead, a pale sky began to appear.

'There you go.' Hugh positioned Robbie's leg, splintered between two lengths of timber.

'Is it bad?' asked Robbie between gulps of air.

'It's broken and your collarbone doesn't look too great either.'

Robbie grimaced. 'Everything hurts.'

'I reckon it would, especially when you add on the miles you walked yesterday.'

Bluey crawled out from around the side of the truck and sat beside his master. Robbie petted the animal, feeling the dog's front leg, which he favoured.

'We'll check him out when we get back to the homestead,' Hugh offered.

'He's my attack dog now,' the boy shared. 'Guess what, Bluey, looks like I won't be going to school for a while now.'

Hugh laughed.

Robbie grew serious. 'And the men?'

'I did a circuit earlier in the dark but I couldn't see much.' And what Hugh had seen had been quite unexpected. 'I'm worried about your sister. I promised Eleanor that I'd come back and I've left her alone the entire night. She'll think I deserted her.' He would have tried to find her sooner, however, he was uncertain as to how badly Robbie was injured. It was a hard decision, leaving Elly to fend for herself.

'It was a bad storm,' Robbie said slowly, 'but Elly can look after herself.'

Hugh dearly hoped so. 'Made worse by those idiots with their out-of-control fire. If not for the rain, who knows how much of the property would have been burnt out.' The ground was charred black and littered with dead sheep. 'I'm just going for a bit of a walk and then I'll be back, Robbie. Alright?'

The boy nodded.

Half a mile from where Robbie lay, Hugh found Rex where he'd left him earlier. He guessed the old man had spotted the fire in the distance during the night and ridden out to investigate. It was while Hugh was out searching for signs of the men Robbie confronted during the night, that he came across Rex lying on the ground. Whether he'd been thrown from his horse or suffered a heart attack, Hugh couldn't tell.

'I'm sorry I had to leave you, Rex.' Hugh squatted by the dead man's side. 'I had to get back to Robbie and I've still got Eleanor out here somewhere as well.' He rested a palm on the gardener's cold forehead. 'You should have stayed at the house, old man . . . You'll be missed.' He had no blanket or covering. Hugh hated to leave Rex out in the bush but he reckoned River Run's oldest member of staff wouldn't mind.

As dawn approached, Hugh walked back to Robbie. He wished he hadn't asked Elly to come with him last night. He was so damn worried about her that it made his guts churn. Why had he pressured her into joining him? Because it was an opportunity to spend time with her, alone. That was the truth of it. And when he wanted something he tended to go after it. His recent promotion was proof of that.

Hugh had convinced himself that Elly would be safe. That they'd find her young brother and return safely to the homestead. Sure, he could pretend that her knowledge of the location of Robbie's treehouse was vital, but he roughly knew of the spot and would have eventually found it alone. Hugh also knew that Elly wasn't comfortable in the dark, and she shouldn't have felt compelled to ride out at night. But he'd made a logical argument at the time and her family were in eventual agreement with the plan.

The reality was that he was now filled with guilt for having subjected Elly to such grave danger. Was she injured? Would she be angry with him for not coming back to her as he'd promised? It was not what he'd intended. Hugh hadn't felt this way about a woman since Vivien, and the intensity of his feelings for Eleanor had taken him quite unawares.

'See anything?' the boy queried weakly on his return.

'Rex,' Hugh answered thoughtlessly, his mind still on Eleanor. He sat by the boy's side, then not wanting to upset the kid, he added, 'He'll be fine.'

'It hurts,' Robbie admitted.

'I know, mate. How do you feel about being carried for a while? We could head towards the area where I left your sister.'

'In a little while maybe,' was Robbie's reply.

❋ Chapter Fifty-one ❋

Eleanor awoke curled at the base of the tree. A weak light suffused the bush as she sat up slowly, wiping dirt from her cheek, to stare at the surrounding wrecked land. Branches, leaves and twigs were scattered among larger saplings toppled by the brunt of the storm. The heavy scent of burnt ground clogged the blue air. Stretching out stiff legs, she kicked away leafy branches and rose unsteadily. A heavy pall hung over the area, the silence only broken by the arrival of a kangaroo, tracking its way through the debris in the early morning light.

Eleanor looked heavenward and, for the first time in many years, crossed herself. She'd survived. Not only the storm, but she'd also faced her fear of the night and endured that as well. The kangaroo headed in the direction of the river and Eleanor followed, wary of tripping over, although the ground was sodden from the heavy rain that had arrived before dawn.

At the river, Eleanor splashed water on her face and neck, her fingers tracing the uneven crust across one cheek that pain told her was a cut. The feeling of revival was instantaneous. She was drained of energy but Eleanor also felt strengthened. She thought back through the long hours of the storm and her fierce desire to not only withstand the ordeal but to also overcome some of her own demons. It was as if the whole experience had afforded her a fresh perspective on life.

In clearing her thoughts, the enormity of what had transpired was reinforced. Eleanor gazed at the damaged land. Where on earth was Robbie? And what had happened to Hugh? The bush woke slowly. Birds twittered, swooping low across the ground to search for insects. Eleanor took in the scale of the storm, quickly comprehending that there would be no chance of tracking Hugh. Any footprints had been obliterated by the rain. The most logical decision was to head back to the homestead so that a search party could be sent out for Robbie and now Hugh.

Hugh. He'd said he'd come back for her. Eleanor had trusted in that during the long hours tied to the tree, the wind bashing and howling about her. She believed that he would return for her and he'd sealed his intent with a kiss.

But he hadn't come back. Why? What if Hugh hadn't returned as promised because he couldn't?

The ramifications of such thoughts worried Eleanor more than she cared to admit and she set off in the direction of the homestead. A weak sun straggled into being in the east, light stretching through the damaged bush as she clambered over the fallen limbs of trees, the stench of doused flames growing stronger with the day's heat. With each step, Eleanor increased her pace. Her waist ached from the taut rope, her head pounded and as the fear grew within, all she could think about was Robbie and Hugh lying injured somewhere in the scrub. She had to get back to the house and raise the alarm. It was impossible to take a direct route, so Eleanor veered to the left, stepping over and ducking under branches. It was an effort to forge a path in a direct line of sight towards the house. There was no choice but to cut back towards the river in the hope of easier going. Ten minutes later, Eleanor lifted a low-hanging bough and walked through the rain-slicked leaves to a clearing.

Ahead, the ragged blackness of charred earth spread out towards the east. Logs smouldered, trees were bereft of leaves. The land stretched burnt and barren into the distance where sheep could be heard, as if crying out in pain. The river paddock was a moonscape, and on the edge of this new world was the truck Eleanor witnessed rolling in that lightning flash during the night. The vehicle lay by its side near the river, the water glistening brilliantly in the sunlight.

From this desolation, a figure rose.

It was a man, a man she would know anywhere. Eleanor was so grateful, so overjoyed to see him again, uninjured, that she began to run to Hugh immediately. But he carried Robbie in his arms and the boy was clearly hurt. Behind them, the cattle-pup limped. She met Hugh midway across the fired earth, her earlier concern replaced with joy, tempered by this, their first meeting, after the kiss they'd shared.

'I was coming for you,' Hugh said flatly, the strain of the night obvious in the way he moved. Reaching grass untouched by the fire, Hugh carefully lay Robbie on the ground.

Eleanor touched her young brother's forehead. 'You found him'.

'It's broken.' Hugh gestured to Robbie's leg, the cattle-pup coming to sit by the boy's side. 'And I think his collarbone is as well.'

Eleanor noted the makeshift leg splint constructed with branches. Robbie was pale, but awake, groggy with pain. She knelt by his side and took his hand in hers. Bluey licked her arm, then gave his master a nudge in the ribs. The boy moaned.

'You're alright?' asked Hugh, surveying her briefly, before studying Robbie. 'You've got a few cuts and bruises.'

It was almost an aside, a token comment, as if he was barely interested. 'I hadn't noticed,' Eleanor answered carefully, tracing her own face, feeling the swell of skin and tender areas crusty with dirt or maybe blood. She thought of their kiss. Eleanor was confused.

'The fire did a lot of damage, Elly. It looks like it burnt out a good portion of the eastern corner. I heard sheep –'

She interrupted him. 'I was worried when you didn't come back.'

The briefest expression crossed his face. 'I know. I'm sorry.' Hugh checked the splint on Robbie's leg, asked the boy if he were comfortable. Robbie said he was.

Eleanor wondered if Hugh felt guilty about deserting her. Was that why he was behaving this way. She'd prayed for him to return to her last night, but Eleanor also knew how impossible that was considering the ferocity of the wind and the lack of moon. 'It was a bad storm,' she persevered. 'I was –'

'Scared?' Hugh completed her sentence, nodding in agreement. 'It wasn't a good night to be out, that's for sure.'

'No,' agreed Eleanor, 'it wasn't.' Somehow their conversation didn't seem to match the event they'd all lived through. It was stilted and Hugh seemed strangely formal. 'I never guessed you two were only a ten minutes' walk away.'

'Neither did I,' Hugh replied.

'And Rex?' Robbie said softly. 'Is Rex alright?'

'He's fine,' Hugh assured him. 'Got caught up in the storm,' he explained to Eleanor. 'Rex must have decided to check things out himself. Either that or he saw the bushfire and came to investigate.'

'Where is he?' asked Eleanor.

Hugh answered vacantly, 'Not far. Look, I'll have to leave Robbie here with you, Elly, and head back to the house. We need a vehicle.' Hugh rested a hand on the boy's forehead. 'I'll be back.'

Robbie gave a weak smile. 'I stopped them, Mr Goward.'

'You sure did, Robbie.' Hugh smoothed Robbie's matted hair. 'You sure did.' To Eleanor he simply gestured towards the home-stead, a nod that took in the tangled bush. 'I'll be back soon.'

Eleanor sat crosslegged in the dirt beside her half-brother. This time she didn't watch River Run's Stud Master walk away.

'He saved me, Elly,' Robbie grimaced. 'Did he save you too?'

Eleanor thought of the kiss they'd shared, and how the sensation of Hugh's lips on hers made her feel. It was that kiss that made her keep her word. She'd stayed tied to the tree, endured the thrashing of the storm, cowered as the lightning bit the earth nearby, striking trees only feet away. Eleanor should have run for cover, hidden deeper in the timber. A change in the wind direction and she too may have very well been engulfed in flames.

'Did he save you, Elly?' Robbie asked weakly.

Eleanor looked to the now empty fringe of scrub. If she'd ever wanted to be saved by a man, Hugh Goward should have been the one to do it. He may have tied her to a tree, but Hugh didn't save her. In fact, he'd abandoned her to the elements, knowing how bad the storm was, aware a thief could be nearby, conscious she was uncomfortable alone in the dark. 'No, he didn't save me, Robbie. I saved myself.'

'That's what he said to me, Elly. That's what Mr Goward said that you'd do.'

Tuesday

Beginnings and Endings

⫷ Chapter Fifty-two ⫸

Georgia levered herself up from the roll-top desk, closing the cover on the rows of figures written in the ledger. Having taken refuge from the mourners at the wake by escaping to the station office, she joined Eleanor at the bay window. Rainwater still lay in pools around the homestead, while across the endless acres, the countryside heralded the faintest tinge of green. The thirsty land was drying out. Indeed, in some places the deluge was barely noticeable. Mother and daughter observed twittering birds as they dashed from shrub to waterhole and back, hovering above the place where the toppled bird-bath once stood.

On the gravel drive, locals from the district gathered to say their last goodbyes. Sympathies and fond memories and a store-house of tall tales mixed with discussions regarding damage. River Run was not the only property affected by the wild storm, although it fared worse than most.

'Should we see them off?' asked Eleanor, referring to their departing guests. Pattie Hicks was speaking to Mrs Howell, while a dozen or so other friends and acquaintances were staring at the famed rose garden, or what was left of it.

Georgia pinched the bridge of her nose. 'I've spoken to everyone at least twice, Elly. And I've said my goodbyes. To be honest my brain is numb. I couldn't possibly subject myself to another round of condolences and platitudes. Besides, I think our guests are exhausted as well. It's been a long afternoon.'

Mrs Howell kissed Pattie on the cheek and retreated towards the house. Of everyone associated with River Run, the house-keeper was the most visibly affected by the recent events. Even her grey hair appeared whiter, her footsteps noticeably slower.

'We're lucky to have the support of such loyal workers and friends,' Georgia said with pride. With shearing due to recommence in the morning, the team elected to hold a cut-out party, usually reserved to mark the end of shearing, to honour Rex March, the man they'd buried today.

Eleanor brushed away a tear. It was still difficult to comprehend the magnitude of incidents that had befallen the family in the space of only one week, culminating in a bushfire and the worst storm in decades and, most tragically, the loss of a beloved member of the property.

The damaging storm's path of destruction included a portion of the shearers' quarters, a large section of the woolshed's roof, the schoolhouse and the windmill, which simply vanished, while a trail of decapitated trees marked the wind's route. Mother and daughter surveyed the decimation to the rose garden as cars drove slowly along the driveway. There were few plants left and those that were there were ruined.

'We were lucky in some respects.' Georgia straightened the collar of the plain black dress she wore. 'It could have been worse.'

Eleanor pondered how much worse. The ferocious dust storm and dangerous winds ripped across their lands with such intensity that even now, five days on, Eleanor remained haunted by what she'd witnessed, roped to the tree by the river. The world was turned inside out that night. The land had shrieked and groaned, as if being cut down by some super-human force. And the wind, the wind was a steam engine and she the tethered victim tied to the tracks. Her survival was due more to luck than anything else, but she had survived and come out stronger for the experience.

As if reading her thoughts, Georgia prodded the cuts and grazes on her daughter's face, a result of the flying debris that had struck her body during the height of the storm. 'I don't know what I was thinking, allowing you to accompany Hugh that night.'

'Well, if Robbie had stayed put in his tree we probably would have been there and back before the dust storm hit. Anyway, no-one knew the storm was approaching, Mum. And I wasn't exactly dragged away kicking and screaming.'

'You didn't jump at the suggestion either if I recall. I still can't fathom why Hugh was so adamant that you go with him. I must admit I was furious with him initially, but as it turned out Hugh Goward certainly proved himself to be a good man in a crisis.' Her mother tucked a length of curly hair behind Eleanor's ear. 'You'd just as likely have been blown away as well, were it not for Hugh's quick thinking.'

At the mere mention of the Stud Master's name, a surge of anxiety flooded through her. 'So you keep saying, Mum.'

'And I'll keep saying it. You shouldn't have been out there, but you undoubtedly owe him your life, Elly. Your brother certainly does.' In a corner of the station office, Robbie dozed. Georgia gave her son a fond smile. 'Did you speak to Hugh today?'

'Sort of, no, not really.' Avoidance seemed more appropriate considering Hugh's own evasion. They'd not talked beyond necessity since his return to the spot where he'd left her and Robbie. By then, three hours later, an army of men – shearers, shed-hands and jackeroos – were on hand to tend to Robbie, resume the search for the stock-thieves and begin accessing the damage to livestock. What Eleanor didn't know at the time was that Hugh had already found Rex, the old man dead from a heart attack. There was little wonder Hugh behaved so distantly that morning. He'd been protecting both Eleanor and Robbie. But Eleanor hadn't known about Rex, all she knew was that she'd gone through the most frightening experience of her life, and when she'd finally found Robbie and Hugh, it was as if the man she'd ridden out with the night before had been replaced with a stranger.

Eleanor hoped things would change between them. Revert back to the way it was before Rex's death, but as the days passed she felt an idiot for believing that Hugh may have had feelings for her. Worse, Eleanor guessed he was keeping clear of her because of the kiss they'd shared.

'I'm not avoiding Hugh, Mum,' continued Eleanor. 'He was mustering this morning, bringing the next mob into the yards.' Georgia didn't look convinced. 'Anyway, it's been pretty hands-on here since the warrigal storm hit us.'

'The warrigal? Heavens, I haven't heard that saying for years. But you're right, it has been busy.'

It was thought approximately four thousand head of sheep were burnt to death in the blaze that was started by the campfire in the river paddock. Many more had to be destroyed. Hugh and the rest of the station men, including some of the shearers, were a dismal lot at the end of each day as they returned from the gruesome task of putting down badly burnt animals. Everyone knew the bushfire could have been far worse, were it not for the rain extinguishing the blaze and alleviating the run of dry weather.

With Rex's passing, an era had vanished. Rex had served with Eleanor's father. He'd been on the property forever, and now he was gone.

'You're still intending to return to Sydney?' Georgia asked her daughter.

'I think,' Eleanor breathed, 'I think it's the best thing.'

'Mrs Howell said Jillian rang to see when you were heading back.'

'Yes, the girls are planning a party for Saturday week.' Eleanor and Jillian had talked at length about the troubles that had beset River Run since her arrival. She wasn't surprised by the concern shown by one of her oldest friends, but when Henrietta telephoned later, having been apprised of the situation, she'd firmly suggested that Eleanor should remain at home for an extended period. 'Who cares about your job,' she'd said. 'We can always get you a spot in the typing pool.'

'Well, you won't want to miss that,' answered Georgia.

'No, probably not,' she replied flatly.

Through the window, the two women noticed Colin as he strode among the visitors, shaking hands and chatting animatedly. Athena Pappas and her father, Stavros, were also among the guests, although they'd kept a respectful distance from the family at all times. Eleanor was yet to speak to the nurse.

'You could stay, well, at least until the end of shearing.' Georgia turned her back on the milling guests and her husband. 'It would be lovely to have you here for longer, and I know Lesley would be thrilled by the thought.'

'What about my job?'

'Are you really fulfilled with what you're doing with your life?' her mother countered.

Eleanor thought back over the days since her coming home to River Run. She'd been tested both physically and mentally, and she was defiantly not the same person who'd arrived unannounced that late Friday afternoon.

Georgia touched her chin thoughtfully. 'I could commission you to write and you'd live here of course.' She lifted a hand. 'Now don't go getting excited, my girl. I don't mean that drivel that's been supplementing your *I don't need hand-outs, I'd rather starve* income. I'm thinking something a little more solid, something important. Historical. Perhaps something on River Run.'

'I'm not an historian, Mum.'

'No, but you're a writer and this is your heritage. Mrs Howell told me that you've been carrying around a notebook or sketchpad since you arrived home. Think on it before you make one of your spur-of-the-moment decisions. And while we're talking spur-of-the-moment, you never did tell me why you came home, Elly.' She moved to a green upholstered squatter's chair, sitting tiredly.

'It was nothing important,' Eleanor replied, leaning on the edge of the desk. The pain across her waist from the rope was only just starting to diminish.

Georgia lifted an enquiring eyebrow. 'Affairs of the heart are never not important.'

Eleanor knew she shouldn't have been surprised at a mother's intuition, but she'd barely been in her company when Hugh was around. Nonetheless, the conversation was uncomfortable, especially with Georgia waiting as if Eleanor had more to share.

'Margaret Winslow insinuated you came home to mend a broken heart. Is that true?'

'Margaret Winslow?' Her mother wasn't talking about Hugh at all. 'Margaret Winslow is a bitch.'

'Well, that just about covers that subject,' replied Georgia wryly, offering her younger daughter a cigarette and lighting it. Both of them laughed half-heartedly.

'I shouldn't have said that about her, I apologise.' Eleanor recognised her annoyance lay more with her stepfather than with the manipulations of Ambrose Park's mistress, tacky though the woman was.

'Nonsense. My own opinion of Keith's wife was never overflowing with graciousness.' Cigarette smoke curled out from between her mother's pink-stained lips, 'and it certainly hasn't improved this past week. Anyway, if you ever do need to talk, Elly, I am a good listener.'

Was there more to talk about? No, Eleanor reflected, there was nothing to talk about, nothing at all.

'There's a place for you here, Elly. There always was, and things will be different from now on.'

Yes, things would be different, that was true enough. Rex's death would change River Run forever.

'Mum?'

Mother and daughter turned to where Robbie sat in a wheel-chair, a plastered leg extended out before him and one arm in a sling. He'd been asleep on and off for most of the day. Bluey, elevated to hero status, was lying on his back in the middle of a silk rug, four legs pointed to the ceiling. No-one was yet to tire of the youngest Webber's enthusiastic retelling of Bluey's flying attack on the outsider. The family doubted they ever would.

'Yes, Robbie?' answered Georgia.

'Is it right what Fitzy said earlier, Mum? That Mr Lomax and Billy Wright were out looking for me as well?'

'Yes, Robbie, you know that,' his mother confirmed. 'But it was Hugh who found you.'

Robbie's low whistle brought the cattle-pup to his side. Bluey jumped up on the boy's lap. The fabled antics of the animal earnt him the right to stay at River Run, much to Robbie's father's annoy-ance. 'I don't remember.'

'You should be in bed resting,' Eleanor admonished, picturing Hugh carrying her brother in his arms through the mangled scrub.

'But not before Archie wheels you around the homestead for some fresh air,' Georgia said, trying not to smile.

'But, Mum,' whined her son.

'No buts, young man. There's many a fence to be mended on River Run and if you're to stay here for another year before starting boarding school, you will do as I say. You have to learn to get on with everybody.'

Robbie petted Bluey sitting on his lap, giving a surly nod of his head in reply.

There was a knock on the door and Mrs Howell entered. 'Sorry to interrupt, Mrs Webber, however, the police have found the last of those men.'

Outside, Constable Graham waited on the front porch. Eleanor really didn't want to hear any more about Chad Reynolds and his luckless companions. During the storm one of the thieves was thrown from the rolling truck and killed, while Chad, now in jail, was dragged from the riverbank where he'd been hiding. The third man had, to date, avoided capture.

'Well, we best get this over and done with.' Georgia walked out into the entrance hall, running a finger across a dusty hall table.

'And Archie's here too, Mrs Webber.' The housekeeper gestured to Robbie, a look of doubt crossing her face. 'I'll lead the way, shall I?'

Eleanor wheeled a reluctant Robbie out onto the veranda, where a bruised and clearly uncomfortable Archie lingered. The jackeroo, still suffering the effects of a fractured jaw and bloodied nose following the altercation at the woolshed, was none too impressed with his new role. He waited awkwardly on the veranda, a hat pushed back off his forehead, his hands stuffed in his pockets.

'Take your hat off immediately, young man,' Mrs Howell stated sternly. 'And get those hands out of your pockets. Pockets are for keeping things in. Hands are for constructive activities. Idle hands make idle minds, and River Run doesn't employ indolent youths.'

Archie whipped off the hat, to stand almost to attention, dropping his gaze to the timber beneath his boots.

Robbie, confined to the wheelchair, looked on with a satisfied smile.

'Good afternoon, Archibald,' said Georgia, pleasantly. 'Now, you know what's expected of you, young man. Twice a day, Archie,' she advised. 'That's all I ask. Robbie needs fresh air and exercise and as young gentlemen I expect both of you to behave in a dignified, courteous manner.'

Archie, mumbling a barely audible reply, glumly took hold of the wheelchair. Carefully pushing the patient across the veranda, he eased the chair down the two planks of wood erected to one side of the stairs.

'Well,' Georgia observed as the cattle dog trotted along behind the unlikely pair, 'they'll either kill each other or become the best of friends.'

'Don't go over there, it's too rough,' Robbie complained, as Archie jolted the wheelchair across uneven ground. 'Go that way, it's a lot smoother.'

'Who's driving?' Archie retaliated, giving the chair a shove. 'You or me? How'd you like to be left out in the middle of the paddock somewhere?'

The cattle-pup growled.

'How'd you like to have a sore lip to match that nose?'

'How'd you like me to get up a bit of speed and then poke a stick in those shiny spokes of yours?' Archie wheeled Robbie around the side of the homestead.

'Mrs Webber?'

'Constable.'

Georgia led the officer to the table and they sat, Eleanor and Colin joining them.

'You have news?' Georgia settled in the peacock chair at the head of the table.

'Yes.' Constable Graham and his men were currently perma-nent additions at the homestead while the search for the thieves continued. Notebook in hand, he flipped through a number of pages before reading out the appropriate details. The third man, he announced, had been found that morning, further down the river. By his enthusiasm on sighting the police, he was apparently quite keen to be rescued. 'It seems he was a drifter, has been for some time, as was his dead companion.'

'And Chad Reynolds?' Eleanor was eager to know the truth about this man, even though she was annoyed to have been so gullible where the stranger was concerned.

'Antony James is his real name,' the constable clarified. 'He arrived in Australia with fake papers a couple of years ago after the war. As far as we can tell he served in the army, but that's only based on Dr Headley's initial examination of an old wound, which he presumed was caused by shrapnel.'

Colin patted his injured leg. 'Tends to stand out, wounds of that nature.'

'Was he on our side?' Eleanor asked hopefully, eager for some measure of redemption when it came to her judgement.

'It'll be some time before we know the truth of things,' the policeman admitted. 'We've the odd Yank that went AWOL after the war, but those boys stuck out with their accents and they were shipped home relatively quickly. Few came over here later and if they did, it's my understanding that their papers were usually in order. On the other hand, we did have a bit of an exodus of Australian women following their sweethearts abroad. As for his allegiances,' he caught Eleanor's attention, with another flick of a page, 'there's an element of doubt, him being Italian-American, however, I'm sure the powers that be in Sydney will soon get to the heart of the matter.'

Colin, having done his best to be sociable considering the occasion, appeared quite clear-headed. 'So he'll be interrogated?'

'I'd imagine so, yes, Mr Webber. Well, that's about it, other than to say that our preliminary questioning suggests that the men are the same lot who have been thieving sheep here and there for at least a year. Antony James' role appears to have been one of reconnaissance.' The officer closed the notebook. 'Didn't work so well, wrong place, wrong time, as they say. And your jewellery, Mrs Webber. I'm afraid it's yet to be recovered.'

'And that's it?' Georgia was incredulous at the simplicity of explanation after everything that had transpired.

'Pretty much. Right little man you have in that son of yours. Of course, I can't condone the shooting,' the officer said emphatically, 'however, in the end, the boy redeemed himself. Yes, he certainly did that.'

If there was a heaven, Eleanor dearly hoped Rex was listening.

'If you'll excuse us, my men and I will be out of your hair within the hour. And do pass on my thanks to Mrs Howell, Mrs Webber, a wonderful cook, wonderful.'

'Well, Mrs Howell certainly made a fan,' Colin noted, after they'd farewelled the constabulary.

Georgia pushed the cane chair away from the table and, with a proprietorial survey of the ravaged rose garden, commented on the need to find a new gardener. 'In the meantime, I think I'll commandeer that young jackeroo, Archie. It won't hurt him to do one afternoon a week within the back gate. In fact, I think that will work very well indeed.'

Eleanor remarked on the state of the garden, the work required, if the area was ever going to be returned to its beautiful, manicured simplicity.

'I don't intend to replant, Elly,' said Georgia wistfully. 'When your father selected the first rose, our young men were yet to land at Gallipoli. It was the year Rex arrived on our doorstep by bicycle, one afternoon, seeking work. We'd scarcely learnt his name and there he was, stalking around the pegged-out area, making suggestions on what varieties to plant. Rex was such a good-looking man. Tall and lean, with a swagger to match his feisty personality. He and your father became friends instantly. They were exactly the same. Fearless, sensitive, and as for their work ethic, well, I'm sure those two waged a private competition as to who would be most exhausted by the end of the day.' She laughed at the memory. 'But that time is over now.' Georgia folded her arms. 'I'm going to plant one rose bush only, in memory of your father, and I'll install a swimming pool with a gazebo, and we'll plant some date palms. Yes, I'm sure they'd do very well out here.'

'A pool,' repeated Eleanor, 'how wonderful. But do you really want to remove the rose garden? Dad planted it for you, Mum.'

'And we struggled with it for years, Elly, always replanting, always trying to resurrect frost-bitten bushes or ones that died during the dry spells. Your father would understand. It's a time for new beginnings.' Georgia looked directly at her husband. 'For everyone.' With that rather cryptic statement, Georgia went indoors.

'And what are you doing, Eleanor?' enquired Colin pleasantly, when the two of them were left alone. 'Heading off, or staying for a bit longer?'

Eleanor thought of the response that should be made, something polite, respectful, instead the words from her mouth echoed exactly what she was thinking. 'I could ask you the exact same thing,' she replied.

❧ Chapter Fifty-three ❧

Lesley was awake when Eleanor entered the room. Her older sister was sitting up in bed reading a magazine and scratching her arm in the darkened bedroom. Eleanor dreaded to think how much peeling skin was scattered among the bedclothes. It seemed that her elder sister was shedding a little more of her hide every day.

'I just read that Jean Lee, the woman who helped murder that seventy-three-year-old man is to be executed in Melbourne in February.' Lesley folded the newspaper.

'Not exactly happy reading, sis,' responded Eleanor, side-stepping the pile of recently discarded magazines on the carpet and sitting on the edge of the bed. 'I could find you a novel in the library.'

Lesley patted the Bible next to her. 'It would be better if I had a wireless in my room,' she replied. 'That would be a real novelty.'

'You're looking much healthier.'

'I feel much better.' Lesley shuffled the magazines on the bed. 'I guess being forced to stay inside has made me want to get out and about, Elly. Even at the convent I was nearly always outdoors, pottering around in the garden.'

'Well, you're to be released this evening, if you're up to it,' Eleanor shared.

'Really? I can't wait to see Robbie.' With Lesley under strict orders to stay in bed until recovered and Robbie relegated to the recently vacated room in the servants' area where the ground floor made wheelchair manoeuvrability easier, she'd been removed from the goings-on of the household. Lesley picked at a piece of flaking skin, Eleanor reached out, playfully slapping her hand away. 'Ouch,' Lesley complained. 'If Mother puts any more Rawleigh's salve on me I'll be stuck to the sheets for life. How's Robbie?'

'Improving every day. There'll be plenty of time to see him, Lesley, he isn't going anywhere for a while.'

'And the funeral, was it a decent send-off? Dad wouldn't have wanted anything but the best for Rex.'

Eleanor knew Rex would have been very proud of his internment in the River Run cemetery. 'Yes, it was very sad, but the priest gave a lovely eulogy and we had over one hundred people at the house for the wake., The last of them have only just left. Athena and Stavros Pappas were here as well. Mum even asked Athena to come to the party the shearers are holding for Rex at the shed.'

'I heard them. Actually I was pleased to be relegated to the second floor. I really couldn't have contended with everyone's questioning.' Thin red patches scarred Lesley's arms and face. The doctor hoped that with time the burns would fade.

'You did save Robbie you know, Lesley. If you hadn't been at the cemetery that afternoon, we never would have known that he'd travelled in that direction.'

'You would have guessed, Elly. You were at the tree, you knew it was Robbie's special spot. Anyway, that tree by the river is the stuff of legend now. We'll have to protect it with a picket fence and water it during the dry spells.'

The French doors leading out onto the balcony were wide open, showing a streaky red sky. Lesley left the bed and together the two sisters stood on the terrace as dusk settled across the property. 'Thanks for mounting an argument with Mum for me to stay here, Elly. At one stage she wanted me on the next train to Sydney.'

'I didn't think we could send you back so soon with your skin still falling off. You'd scare the passengers on the train.'

'Do you know, every morning and night I've looked out across the treetops as the sky lightens or darkens. I've seen the richest sunsets and pearly dawns that would take your breath away, and I've described each and every flicker of colour, every divine moment of nature, to Marcus.'

Eleanor didn't know how to respond. Lesley was certainly better physically, however, she'd hoped for a full recovery, unlikely though it was.

'Don't look like that, Elly. I'd have rather been here at River Run, gradually regaining my strength, than in hospital with some stranger in a white uniform trying to rehydrate me. I've seen the most beautiful skies and it's made me long for life. You know, the nuns would never consider my joining their order if I told them that it was nature that saved me, that it was the beauty of River Run that healed me and not God.' She lifted a hand, pre-empting Eleanor's queries. 'I have a long way to go, I know that, but I'm prepared for the journey.' Her smile grew wistful. 'I choose life, knowing that's what Marcus would expect.'

Eleanor was finding it difficult to comprehend Lesley's changed demeanour. 'I don't understand. It's not that I don't want you to be better, Lesley, but it was only a few days ago that –'

Lesley bobbed her head. 'I was a lost cause? But that was before I realised that life does go on, and everyone in our family has moved on, while I've been left behind.'

'And?'

'I made myself physically ill through stupidity and then little Robbie got lost and Rex died. It made me think about life, I guess, and second chances, especially after I saw Margaret Winslow and

Colin walk into the garden shed last Tuesday night and turn out the light.'

'You saw that? I saw her too, Lesley! She was totally nude, not a stitch, and she was standing in the doorway of the shed.' Eleanor stretched her arms wide, emulating Margaret Winslow's provocative stance. 'What I didn't know until now was that it was Colin with her, although I guessed as much.'

Lesley giggled. 'I was with our thief in the sickroom, about to leave when I heard them outside. Will you tell Mum or shall I?'

'Let me think about that,' Eleanor answered. 'I really don't know how much she knows or doesn't know.'

'I know enough.' Georgia walked out onto the balcony, draping her arms about the shoulders of her two daughters. 'The garden shed I wasn't aware of, however, the signs were there, the little flirtations, the private jokes.'

'I'm sorry, Mum.' Lesley hugged her mother.

'Don't be,' replied Georgia. 'Some relationships aren't meant to last forever and besides, to be fair to Colin, he could never replace your father.'

Lesley stood with an arm around her mother's waist. 'I understand.'

'I know you do.' Georgia touched the tip of her daughter's nose lovingly.

'What will you do?' asked Eleanor.

Georgia curled her hands over the banister of the balcony. 'End it. No doubt it will be messy, but I'll offer him the house in Sydney and if he grumbles, I hope to cajole him with hard cash.' She shrugged. 'Endings shouldn't be messy, but where money is concerned they usually are. And Colin was as poor as a church mouse when we married.'

'And you're not worried about what the gossips will say?' Eleanor tested. 'I mean, after everything with Robbie.'

'Colin will feel duty-bound to put his own version of events out in the arena for public consumption. He'll be more concerned about how he's perceived in the district and beyond, and ensuring there's a healthy settlement at the end of the day, than protecting any shred of our relationship. That's the test of honour in a man when it comes to relationships, whether he can let go without animosity or stupidity.'

'He'll be the wounded party,' Lesley said thoughtfully.

'May he get much enjoyment from his martyrdom,' exclaimed Eleanor. 'And Margaret Winslow?'

'Knowing Margaret, she'll live to flirt another day, but I think I can safely say that the woman will never set foot on River Run again.'

Eleanor couldn't resist. 'What about Keith?'

'Ah, now, Keith is quite another matter,' replied Georgia inscrutably. 'What about you, Lesley? Are you really feeling better?'

'Yes, I think so,' she replied. 'I know it will still be hard at times, however, in the last couple of days, I've started to think a little more clearly. Being here, waking every morning in my old room and, most importantly, having time and space . . .' The three women hugged, wiped the tears from each other's faces.

'Wait, you said something earlier about joining the convent. You wouldn't really do that, would you?' asked Eleanor.

'Yes, I think I probably will. I have some serious thinking to do before I commit, but for me the hardest thing,' Lesley squeezed her younger sister's arm, 'will be whether I'll ever be able to love God more than Marcus. But I know I'll never find another man to replace him, at least not on this earth.'

Georgia took her older daughter by the shoulders. 'If it's what you want?'

'It is, Mum.'

Eleanor imagined her sister, with hair clipped short, dressed in white and lying prostrate before an altar. 'I'll never understand that kind of love.'

Lesley briefly touched the curve of Eleanor's cheek. 'You will one day, Elly. It's all about finding the right man and letting go.'

413

Chapter Fifty-four

The party at the woolshed was subdued. A generator was running the electric lights and the machine's rumble competed easily with those inside. Eleanor lingered near the wool press, before walking up the short flight of stairs. Groups of men turned and said hello as she navigated wool tables, large cane wool baskets and continued on until reaching the golden-hued board. Some of the younger men were laughing at the opposite end. They, too, turned on her approach, a couple of them waving irreverently, their giggles halting Eleanor's progress. Amid the chuckles, she heard voices, a man and a woman's. Peering into the semi-darkness of the catching-pens, she noted that Hugh and her mother were sharing a drink together and discussing the next day's shearing. Eleanor backed away.

'Miss Eleanor.' A black-haired, blue-eyed boy approached from the far end of the board. Fresh-faced and smelling overpoweringly of Old Spice aftershave, he held a punch-glass in his hand for her. 'I'm Geoff Ferguson, we met –'

'Trying to catch yourself a keeper, are you, lad?' called Billy Wright from one of the wool tables where he, Dawson and Lomax sat on folding chairs, a deck of cards at the ready.

Eleanor accepted the drink. 'I remember. How are you, Geoff?'

He blushed, doing his best to ignore the ribald remarks being shouted. His blue eyes grew hopeful. 'I was wondering –'

Billy Wright gave a drawn-out cough. 'For the love of a cold one on a hot day, Geoff. Give it a rest.'

Geoff blanched. 'I, I –'

He stuffed large hands in his pockets, pulled them free again. Eleanor could only imagine how much courage he'd summoned up to single her out in front of the team. 'Maybe we can have a chat tomorrow, at smoko,' she proposed.

The young shearer sighed, his shoulders drooping. 'I guess.'

Overhead, stars shone visibly where part of the roof had been ripped free by the storm. Eleanor excused herself and left the board as some of the men set up empty long-necks of beer at the far end and readied to play bowls with a tennis ball.

'Part-time gardener and wheelchair mechanic,' Wormy said cheekily as Eleanor passed. He munched on a corn meat sandwich, as he and the other boys tried to prise the truth of the afternoon's latest story from Archie. Freshly showered, with ironed shirts and clean boots, they crowded around a wool bale, doing their best not to stare at Athena Pappas, who was examining Johnny Daisy's forearm, a beatific expression on the man's face.

'So,' Murph persuaded Archie, 'is it right that within a half-hour of being coerced into taking on the role of nursemaid for the youngest of the Webbers, you pushed the boy's wheelchair over a sandalwood stump?'

'And then you had to carry Robbie?' Stew said.

'I saw him,' Wormy obliged the boys. 'Archie had to carry the little fella half a mile back to the homestead, before returning to mend the punctured tyre.'

'Why can't they just put him on a horse, side-saddle like, you know, the way they did for girls in the olden days?' Archie said dismally. 'Then he could get around himself.'

Murph took a sip of the punch Mrs Howell forced upon him. 'But there wouldn't be any fun in that for us then, Arch. Or should we be calling you The Gardener?'

Eleanor sipped her drink, wincing at the strength of it. Mrs Howell, installed at a long sandwich-laden trestle table, appeared deep in argument with Fitzy. The older woman caught Eleanor's attention, pointing to the supper. Selecting some cheese, Eleanor gathered that the two cooks were arguing about punch recipes. The housekeeper was trying to add mint to the concoction of orange juice, ginger ale and lemonade, while the shearers' cook was intent on increasing the amount of rum in the mix. Next to the glass punch bowl was a large squat ceramic bottle with a short, narrow neck covered in wicker. The demi-john of rum, transported from the homestead under the care of Mrs Howell, was yet to leave her sight, though that didn't stop the cook from wrestling the bottle from her and adding a splash more.

'You are a rude, rude man,' Mrs Howell said angrily, turning her back on the man.

Fitzy ladled the beverage into a glass, tapped Mrs Howell on her shoulder. 'Just try it, will you, Mrs Howell? You really should have one, for Rex's sake. He thought the world of you, he did.'

The housekeeper turned slowly. 'He never said any such thing to me.'

'Nonsense,' Fitzy calmed, 'you know it to be true, Mrs Howell.' He held out the glass enticingly.

Eleanor moved away to stand discreetly within distance of the discussion.

River Run's caretaker of all things domestic accepted the glass tentatively, gingerly sniffing the warm drink. 'For Rex, on account he was quite bearable at times, and in anticipation of my leaving.'

Fitzy, about to raise his glass in mutual salutations, looked aghast. 'Leave? But you can't leave, Mrs Howell I mean, what will they do at the big house? How will they survive? You and

I both know that they certainly can't cook, nor always attend in a timely manner to those things that we, who are used to running big kitchens, know must be attended to.'

Mrs Howell tried, unsuccessfully, to interrupt.

'They say, you know, that many a man sets up in advance certain things for the benefit of his family and you and I both know, Mrs Howell, that you are the most highly regarded, most highly respected of those of us fortunate enough to be employed on this mighty property. Mr Alan relied on you – no, he *depended* on you – to take care of his wife and children, and now you would leave, at this very moment when they need the support of those nearest and dearest around them?' Fitzy skolled the rum punch and dabbed emotionally at his pudgy face with a filthy piece of rag.

Mrs Howell, momentarily lost for words, took a sip of the drink. 'I, I don't know what to say, Mr Fitzgerald. I really didn't think that –'

'That you wouldn't be missed? That the big house wouldn't fall down around their ears in your absence?' He made a *tsking* sound with his tongue and ladled more of the punch into his glass.

'I don't really imbibe,' Mrs Howell told him.

Fitzy winked, patting her delicately on the shoulder. 'Neither do I.'

Eleanor observed the exchange between the two cooks, hopefully. The task of ensuring the formidable Mrs Howell's continued presence on River Run was now in the hands of fate.

'Elly, can I freshen that up for you?' Hugh strode to the trestle table, returning with drinks for them both.

'Thanks.' Eleanor glanced around the woolshed. 'Mum's left?'

'Yes. We were trying to work out the logistics of where to hold some of the shorn ewes with the river paddock burnt out. It'll be all hands on deck walking sheep back to their paddocks. Your mother nominated you for mustering duty tomorrow. Are you up to it? No more warrigal storms or surly rams involved, I promise.' He smiled.

'It's been a long week,' Eleanor hedged, taking two big sips of the punch. The pale blue shirt Hugh wore complemented the dark of his tan. And his eyes . . . Eleanor swirled the glass in her hand. The beverage was obviously more rum than anything else, and it most definitely did have a kick to it.

On the other side of the wool tables, Athena lifted her glass in acknowledgment at Eleanor as, one by one, each of the men appeared to ask her advice regarding some particular ailment. Dawson lifted a leg up, rested a foot on the table and pointed to an ankle.

'About the storm, Elly. I hope you weren't too upset with me leaving you alone the way I did. All I can say is that I'm sorry. It wasn't done on purpose.'

'I had to admit I was pretty scared.'

Hugh looked quite uncomfortable. 'I never should have made you come with me. I was wrong to put you in danger like that.'

It wasn't part of his job description to keep an eye on her. They'd shared a kiss in a moment of stress. That was it. Eleanor knew she was stupid to think anything further could have come from it. 'I'm a big girl, Hugh. It's okay. I can look after myself.'

'But still, I feel terrible. If anything had happened to you . . .' He broke off awkwardly. 'I had to try and save Robbie.' Hugh's usual even-tempered disposition became defensive. 'And I couldn't have left him alone. Apart from that, I wasn't confident I'd be able to find you in the dark. If I'd got lost as well, the three of us would have been in a bit of a mess.'

They stood shoulder to shoulder, surveying the groupings of men, as the combination of beer and rum-punch made voices rise. Geoff Ferguson spun the tennis ball along the board, knocking the beer-bottles down in one go as Mr Lomax argued with Billy Wright about changing the bet placed midway through a game of cards.

'Of course, I understand.' Eleanor passed the empty glass to Hugh. 'I should be going.'

418

'No, I'll go,' Hugh stated, and with that he walked away.

Even if there were something between them, Eleanor mused, watching him leave, which there clearly wasn't, such a relationship would be impossible.

Athena extricated herself from the line of men and walked over to Eleanor. 'It is good to see you.' She kissed Eleanor on both cheeks. 'Your friend is gone?'

'Yes. That's our overseer. Actually, he's our Stud Master now. I keep forgetting.'

Athena's orange-hued dress was cut to perfection, accentuating every curve. 'I think for you such a man is hard to forget.'

'I love your dress. Did you make it?'

The Greek girl waggled a finger at her. 'You're changing the subject, why? It is normal for women to talk about men.' She paused as Billy Wright strolled by, giving the women a low appreciative whistle. 'And for men to talk about us. This is what makes the world such a wonderful place. So, tell me, the man you were talking to, is he your special friend?'

Eleanor was quite taken aback. 'Why on earth would you make a comment like that, Athena? Hugh Goward is staff.'

'Hugh Goward is a man, an attractive man.' Athena leant towards her. 'And there are not so many attractive men in the district, and those that are,' she shrugged her shoulders, 'are either married or they are a little,' she tapped her head, 'a little crazy. But then, all men are crazy. It just depends.'

'On what?' asked Eleanor.

'On whether they are crazy good, or crazy bad. Sometimes crazy bad is good.' She grinned mischievously. 'Other times they need tending, like your mother's rose garden. A little pruning can make all the difference. It is all in the handling.'

Geoff Ferguson did his best to avoid the two women, taking a wide circuit en route to the table where Mrs Howell still sat on the wool bale, swinging her legs back and forth like a child.

'That one,' Athena pointed at the young man, 'that one, I would like to tend.'

'I can't believe you said that!' Eleanor whispered. 'What if somebody heard?'

Athena threw her head back and laughed, her long dark hair flowing over her shoulders. 'Okay, okay. I'll be serious, Eleanor. This man, this Hugh, he likes you. And you,' she said knowingly, 'you like him.'

'That's ridiculous,' Eleanor retorted.

'Your cheeks are reddening. Why is it ridiculous for a man and a woman to like each other? Why would you think such a silly thing?'

'Because, because –'

'Because you are afraid he does not feel the same way. Because you worry that you will make a fool of yourself.' She leaned closer. 'Because you are afraid. You should be. Love can lift you up, but it can also throw you away if you don't make the right choice.'

'Did you make the right choice, Athena?'

A steely expression crossed Athena's face. 'If you have something to say, Eleanor, something to accuse me of, then it is best that you ask now, here, in this place. Instead of – how do you Australians put it? – beating around the bush.'

'Did you ally yourself with the Germans during the war to protect your child?' The words spilt forth, they'd not meant to sound so condemnatory.

Athena laughed briefly and then her features soured. 'Because you know nothing of me, I forgive you. Because you have not been in war, I forgive you.' She took a breath, smoothing her hands across shapely hips. 'My fiancé was shot by the Germans.' Athena waited for this brutal reality to be absorbed. 'Dragged by his hair out into the street and shot. No, we were not married. Yes, I carried his child. And I will never regret loving him. I have nothing to be ashamed of, while you, Eleanor Webber, what do you have to be ashamed of? I will tell you. You live in a free country, a country untouched by war and this man you say you do not care about. This man that you looked for on arrival in this place. That you stared at through the corner of your eye, hoping no-one would notice. Yes, I noticed. This man,' Athena's speech grew faster and more difficult to understand, 'he cares about you and he has left you. He has walked out of this building into the darkness, because you dismissed him like he was nothing. That's what you should be ashamed of.'

They were in the middle of the shearing shed and Athena's passionate outburst had attracted the attention of nearly everyone. Mortified, Eleanor would have run. Anywhere. Immediately. Anywhere to escape the intrigued faces on the men around them.

'Athena, I'm sorry, I really am so terribly sorry. I didn't mean –'

'Forget me. What is the problem?'

Eleanor thought of the kiss she'd shared with Hugh during the storm, of Dante. 'I don't want to make the same mistake twice.' She shook her head. 'Besides, look at Lesley. Look at what she's been through for love.'

'If you don't go to him,' Athena's tone grew low, 'you will never know if it is love.' She left Eleanor alone, returning to the wool table and the men clustered there. Reluctantly, the shearers went back to their drinking and stories.

Confused and feeling more than conspicuous, Eleanor walked down the steps, her fingers trailing the wool bins on either side.

Hugh was waiting at the entrance to the woolshed. Flicking away the cigarette he smoked, he ground it out with his riding boot and then walked back inside towards Eleanor.

'Hugh, I thought you'd gone.'

'I came back to talk to you. I was just in time to hear Athena.'

Eleanor was dumbstruck. 'You heard what she said? Oh, Hugh, I'm sorry. Athena says what she thinks, not that she has any idea what she's talking about.'

'Actually, I thought the woman appeared to be pretty intuitive.'

He leant nonchalantly against the timber wall. From the little she knew of this man, Eleanor guessed he wasn't going to make this easy for her. 'Hugh, I –'

'Eleanor, can you please be quiet for just a moment? Every time I've tried to speak with you since the storm, you either walk away or pre-empt our conversations. I just heard that Greek woman's opinion and she's clearly picked up on something between us.' He moved towards her. 'Why do you have such a hard time admitting there's something there?' Hugh's confidence faltered. 'I mean, there *is* something between us, isn't there?'

'I guess.'

Hugh frowned. 'You guess?'

'Hugh, do you honestly think it would work for us? I mean, you being who you are, and me being me? And you're older,' she added, although in truth that meant nothing.

In not denying their mutual attraction, Hugh was emboldened. He took another step forward, Eleanor one back, as if subconsciously retreating. 'Don't forget the two different-coloured eyes. That could be a real deal-breaker.'

He was now so close to her that they were mere inches apart.

'I'm not offering marriage straight off, Elly,' he told her lightly. 'Let's start with dinner sometime. Take things slowly, see how it goes.'

'And,' dare she even ask the question, 'how do you think it will go?'

Hugh drew her into his arms. 'Damn fine, Eleanor. Damn fine.'

Eleanor relaxed into his embrace. Maybe this was what Lesley meant about finding the right man and letting go.

❧ Author's Note ❧

In the early 1940s my father, Ian, not averse to adventure, decided to run away from home. With his saddlebag packed with tinned food from the pantry, taken while the cook wasn't looking, he jumped on his trusty horse Garnet and rode the mile and a bit to the Whalan Creek. Here he climbed his favourite tree, the one he often used as a lookout in case of a suspected Indonesian invasion. Armed with a .22 rifle, he intended to wait out the night before deciding on his next move.

And so I had the kernel of an idea that would become *River Run*.

Setting *River Run* in 1951 during the heady days of the booming wool industry – wool was worth a pound a pound – reminded me of my childhood. Escaping from the homestead, I would wander down to the shearing shed to peer through the timber slats at the action inside. On one such occasion I boldly strolled into the shed and down the board, clutching a much-loved doll dressed in bridal attire. Interrupting my favourite shearer, I showed him my dolly with pride. Dripping with sweat, his hand-piece poised above a struggling sheep, he grinned. 'Why, Miss Nicole,' he said, 'I have one just like yours too.'

As always, I have had great fun digging through the family archives while researching this work. Thank you to my family and friends for their support in the writing of this novel and to Mr C. Munro, General Manager of Egelabra Merino Stud (HE Kater & Son Pastoral Co Pty) for allowing me access to the historic Egelabra woolshed. To Random House – my publisher, Beverley Cousins, and managing editor, Brandon VanOver – and my agent, Tara Wynne. Thank you for your professionalism and guidance. Lastly, to the many booksellers, libraries and readers: thank you.

I am indebted to the following texts and recommend them for further reading:

Concessions, Conflicts and Collusion: Graziers and Shearing Workers, 1946–1956 by K. Tsokhas; *Afternoon Light* by Sir Robert Menzies; *Pulp Confidential*, State Library of NSW; *The Communist Movement and Australia* by W. J. Brown; *The Reds* by Stuart Macintyre; *The 1950s* by Stella Lees and J. Senyard; *A Home of My Own* compiled by Mary Murray; *Back on the Wool Track* by Michelle Grattan; *Mateship and Moneymaking* by Rory O'Malley; *Wool* by G. S. Le Couteur; *Governing Prosperity* by Nicholas Brown; *Australian Woolsheds* by Harry Sowden and *The Australian Merino* by Charles Massy.